THE HOMESTEAD

THE HOMESTEAD

QUINTUS H. GOULD

Ancile Press

First published in Great Britain in 2022 by Ancile Press.

Copyright © Quintus H. Gould 2022

The right of Quintus H. Gould to be identified as the Author of the Work has been asserted by him in accordance with the Copyright, Designs and Patents Act 1988.

All rights reserved. Except for that which is permitted under UK copyright law, no part of this book may be reproduced, stored in a retrieval system, or transmitted, in any form or by any means without the prior written permission of the publisher, nor be otherwise circulated in any form of binding or cover other than that in which it is published and without a similar condition being imposed on the subsequent purchaser.

This book is a work of fiction. Any resemblance between these fictional characters and actual persons, living or dead, is purely coincidental.

A CIP catalogue record for this title is available from the British Library.

ISBN 9781739217204
eBook ISBN 9781739217211

Ancile Press
71 - 75 Shelton Street
Covent Garden
London WC2H 9JQ

ancilepress.co.uk

*For those who have no voice
with which to speak —
they suffer in silence,
casualties of human nature.*

ACT I

One

Samantha had never been this hungover before in her life. Despite having been conscious for at least ten minutes, she dared not open her eyes for fear of the inevitable scorching of her retinas that would happen as soon as daylight reached them. Her head throbbed — not a little, but a lot — like a jackhammer had been pounding at her skull for the past twelve hours. *Or longer*, she thought, whispering even inside her own brain so as not to wince. She desperately needed a drink of water, but that would mean opening her eyes, and she was still not ready for that.

The pillow on which her cheek rested was soft and cool and smelled like hotel linen. She pressed her nose into the fabric, indulging in the sensation of freshness that was so contrary to her current state of being. She shuddered to think what she looked like, hair matted in clogged drain clumps and last night's mascara staining both her face and the soft, cool, hotel-scented linen... *Wait! Where the fuck am I?*

Samantha had moved back in with her dad three months

ago and had not changed the old, cartoon character bedding once in that time. The last time she spent the night in a hotel she had vomited all over the carpet and had not dared return to one since out of shame.

This wasn't home.

She was relieved to discover the room was dark, or at least dim, when she finally convinced her eyelids to lift. Even in the dim light she could tell she was not anywhere she knew. *Even if I had gone home with that prick Ryan, his place is a shithole.* And certainly, the room in which Samantha found herself was not a shithole.

It was from under the door that the light came in. It was pure white and somehow managed to interrupt the darkness and cast the room in a dark blue glow. As far as she could tell, there were no windows.

Directly across from the bed where she lay were a toilet and small basin. They both looked clean, as did the floor, which was covered in generic white tiles. The walls were likewise decorated, tiles extending all the way to the ceiling. Parallel to the floor as she was, she could perceive a slight slope which led down to a drain in the centre of the room. It was all rather practical and made Samantha think of prisons and school bathrooms. *Same thing*, she thought, not that she had any experience with the former other than through the lens of a television screen.

The blue glow mundanity of the room was disrupted by a red light in the top, far corner. Perched just above the door, which Samantha now saw was metal, was a small camera. It seemed to wink at her as she looked up at it. Self-conscious, she reached down to pull on her top, a thin camisole, which had risen up to expose her stomach. *Fucking pervs*.

Aside from the camera, the bed, toilet and basin, there was nothing else to see. She still had no idea where she was.

A scream outside the room was the first realisation that she wasn't alone in the building — or wherever she was. She heard footsteps rush past the door and onwards to some unknown destination. The floor outside was hard and the sound echoed, as did the voices, mumbling, concerned, hushed tones of men and women. With her hand to her forehead, placed there as if to stop her brains falling out, Samantha raised herself off the bed and shuffled across the tiles to the door.

'How far along is she?' She heard a man ask outside the room. It must have been a corridor from the way his voice travelled. Another voice, *a woman*, she thought, said something inaudible in response. She heard the scream again.

Samantha yet again wondered where she was, this time unable to squash the creepy-crawly tingle of panic that raced down her spine. She wanted to confront whoever was outside, find out where she was and demand to know how she had got there. First she had to confront the door. There was, however, one small problem, or rather, quite a large problem: the door had no handle. She tried pushing it, but there was no movement. Next, she ran her hand down the frame, the coolness of the metal nibbling her thumb as it brushed against the door, searching for a button, a lever, something, anything. As far as

Samantha could tell, there was no way to open it. *At least not from this side.*

Another creepy-crawly tingle down the spine.

'Hello,' she said, slow and uncertain and not anywhere near loud enough to be heard from outside. No one responded.

Interrogating the door had fatigued her. She still felt groggy and her sandpaper throat was miserable. She remembered there was a sink in the room and guzzled some water, her mouth angled awkwardly underneath the tap, before returning to the bed to sit.

Her dad always told her she was a 'smart girl who had simply lost her way' and she tried to tell herself that as she dug her fingernails into the edge of the mattress. Tears threatened to pierce the barricade. She didn't know if she was angry or scared, so she decided she was both as she heard yet another scream reverberate down the corridor outside the room. The sound cleaved her brain in two.

How did I get here?

The events of last night were a blur, and piecing them together was painful, physically and emotionally. Her head groaned as she recalled getting a taxi into town from Martha's house. Her heart flinched as she remembered meeting Ryan at the bar. *How many times?* She would have told herself 'never again', but this time she feared the option to break her own oath had been terribly, dramatically, stolen from her.

Any attempt at remembering what had happened next was like wading through tar. She had met Ryan and then what? Samantha was twenty-two years old and her memory was usually sharp. *Even when hungover.* She had never experienced such a malfunction of cognition. The black canyon of missing time terrified her. Another scream.

She was quite certain the noise was coming from a woman — a woman who was in tremendous pain. The last scream had softened into a low, protracted wail. Outside the room, the footsteps had stopped. The only other sound was that of her own breathing, and even that had become secondary to the screams of the suffering woman. Samantha wanted to go and punch her in the throat. Every sound she made was like a knife being jammed through her forehead.

Breathe, she reminded herself. *Just fucking breathe.*

She wasn't sure how long it was before the door opened. The woman had not stopped screaming the entire time, that much she knew. The constant sound had incarcerated her on the bed, shoulders hunched, head bent over as her eyes looked, unfocused, at the chipped lavender nail varnish on her exposed toenails.

When it did open, it did so without a sound. For all its apparent weight, the metal door glided, opening, just enough, for a person to step inside. Samantha was momentarily blinded by the light coming from the corridor outside the room. Then, as quickly as it had appeared, it was gone. The door was closed and the room was dim again.

'Some food for you, dear.'

The woman didn't sound ominous, but she certainly looked it, standing in the half-blocked light by the door. Samantha couldn't see her face until she approached the bed, a tray of food held in front of her in both hands. She looked to be in her forties. Her face, porcelain white and blemish free, was framed by neat, shoulder-length blonde hair. A strand of pearls hung from her neck and rested on the collar of a delicate blue cardigan. She looked like somebody's mother and smelled like one too. Freshly baked bread and floral soap. She had walked straight out of a Christmas movie.

'Some food, dear,' the woman repeated, gently pushing the tray through the air in Samantha's direction. She took it wordlessly. As she cast her eyes down to inspect the contents of the tray, the woman stood over her watching, smiling. A bowl of what looked to be some sort of porridge and a glass of — *what the fuck?* The liquid inside the glass was a hideous, unnatural shade of green.

'A vitamin drink,' the woman said, as if she had read Samantha's mind. 'To help with hydration and recovery.'

'Recovery?' Samantha had to clear her throat before she was able to force the word out.

'Yes, dear. You've been through a lot,' the blonde woman chuckled. She would have come across as charming if it had not been for the scream which cut short her feminine giggle. Her smile flattened. 'You've arrived at a busy time, I'm afraid.'

Samantha said nothing. She was contemplating whether or not to tackle the woman to the floor. She didn't look like a threat. She didn't sound like one either. Before she had a chance to decide either way, the woman stepped back towards the door.

'Unfortunately, you'll have to wait a little longer before the doctor can see you,' she said as she knocked twice on the door. Samantha heard a metallic click come from the other side.

'Wait — doctor? What happened?' Samantha managed to ask, her eyes straining to examine the woman's face. Half in shadow, half in light, she looked ominous again.

'Don't worry.' Her tone was pleasant and soothing despite the shadows. 'Everything is alright. Just focus on recovery.'

The door opened, the light once again dazzlingly bright compared to the darkness of the room. 'Do eat the food, dear,' the woman said as she stepped outside. 'And don't forget the drink.'

She smiled and then she was gone. After the door closed Samantha thought that if she squeezed her eyes half-shut she would still be able to see that smile, floating disembodied in the air where the woman had stood.

'No chance,' Samantha whispered to herself, looking at the peculiar green liquid in the glass. Her voice was coarse, her throat still painfully dry. Even so, the drink was not remotely appealing. She drew the glass to her nose and sniffed. Samantha decided it smelled like wet hay and dog urine. The blonde woman had mentioned a doctor. Perhaps she was in hospital. Perhaps it *was* a vitamin drink. *Still not drinking it.*

The last time Samantha had been inside a hospital was the day she was born. When her dad fell from a ladder at work and broke his leg — *or arm or back or whatever he broke* — she had been living three hundred miles away pretending to study for a degree. Despite her lack of experience, she still felt quite certain hospitals had windows. *And lights.*

Ultimately, it was her stomach that betrayed her. She told herself that she wouldn't eat it, *no matter what*, but she was simply too hungry. Even porridge mush was better than nothing, and besides, it really didn't taste *that* bad. It wasn't like any porridge she had ever eaten before. Oaty, watery and cold by the time she ate it, the bowl the blonde woman had given Samantha also contained flecks of something else. They crunched against her teeth as she chewed. The colour was off — so was the taste. *Definitely not porridge*. Still, she devoured the whole bowl and felt better for it.

It wasn't until she struggled to stand after relieving herself on the toilet twenty minutes later that she knew something was wrong. Time felt slower and there was a blurriness to her vision that hadn't been there before.

She reached to steady herself on the basin and watched in slow motion as her hand missed the edge of the porcelain. Before she had time to react, she was face down on the floor, her underwear tangled around her knees.

She cursed under her breath, or at least tried to. The singular syllable came out bloated and disfigured. Her tongue felt too big for her mouth and her arms seemed to stretch all the way to the other side of the room. Her top had risen up again, only now the camera could see her exposed backside as well. If she could organise her thoughts properly, Samantha would have reprimanded herself for having eaten the food. Instead, all she could think about was how her undignified captivity was most likely being live-streamed on the dark web.

Contrary to what she assumed a lot of people in her

life thought, Samantha had never tried drugs. She had been offered them — *weed, coke, acid, even knew a guy who sniffed glue during his breaks while working at an old folks' home* — but had never luxuriated in anything stronger than vodka. How she felt as she lay, limbs outstretched, on the cold tiles was a novel experience.

Inexplicably, the world started to collapse, like a piece of paper crumpled inside a fist. Unable to lift as much as a finger, all Samantha could do was watch as the walls turned in on her. A gargle drooled from her mouth onto the floor — an attempt at a scream. She didn't want to die, *not like this*, crumpled inside a paper room. She imagined her dad having to identify her body, rump to the heavens, ensnarled in day old underwear.

Then, pulled back to their usual position, the walls stopped. Blood pounded in her ears. She shifted her legs and tried to move but they were still held in place. Invisible hands. The hands of a translucent apparition that throbbed and pulsated as it manifested above her. 'Sam,' it snarled, pushing her into the tiles. She tried to swat it away with her mind and realised she didn't feel anything, could not feel anything. The tiles melted away from underneath her and she felt her body fall. It fell deep into a well of unconsciousness.

When she eventually woke, she thought the whole thing had been a dream. Then she realised she was still on the floor of that strange room. The screaming outside had long since stopped and, for the first time in a long time, Samantha felt at peace. Her mind was unusually silent.

Pulling herself upright, she wiggled her underwear back

up to where it should have been. Her jeans were likewise reinstated.

There was no way for her to know how long the man had been watching her. When she realised he was there, sitting across the room on the bed, he stood up. The bedframe creaked as he did.

'Hello, Samantha,' the man said from the darkness.

She didn't respond. There was nothing she wanted to say.

He walked over to her and crouched beside her on the floor. The rubber soles of his shoes squeaked on the tile.

'May I help you up?'

He had a nice smile. She knew she could trust him. Nodding, she gave him her hands.

Two

Sixty-one kilograms. A perfectly healthy weight for her height.

'You can step off the scales now, Samantha.'

She did as he instructed and returned to the examination couch.

After helping her from the floor, the man had introduced himself as Robert. He looked to be middle-aged, wore a white coat and appeared immeasurably professional, from his smart, black shoes to the neat comb lines in his hair. When he spoke, he did so with an air of authority that was tempered by gentleness.

He had taken Samantha to a different room. She had bumbled down the corridor, wincing at the light after being in the dark for so long. He had held her by the crook of her elbow, his grip strong, but not too tight, to make sure she didn't fall, she supposed.

The tiles had continued outside into the corridor, colder against her feet than the ones in the room. Subdued and graceless, her head lolled back as she walked. She had noticed the ceiling was made of those hideous fibre board tiles that were a universal feature of hospitals, schools and government offices. *Hospital*, she had thought, eyeing the man called Robert's white coat.

It was a short walk. They had stopped at a closed door, *metal*, like the one in the room. As Robert had fiddled with a set of keys that were attached to his belt by a retractable chain, Samantha had looked about the corridor. Opposite, a short way up from where they stood, was another doorway. This one was open, and inside she had seen a woman propped up in a bed, red-faced and senseless, her hair dishevelled against a mountain of pillows. At the foot of the bed was a transparent plastic baby crib trolley. The infant contained within slept peacefully as the woman, presumably its mother, gazed ahead at nothing. She had met Samantha's eyes, or at least she thought she had, only for a second, before drifting back to her nothingness. Before Samantha had time to dwell on it, the door was opened and Robert had ushered her inside.

Now he was taking her temperature.

Thus far he had worked with basic efficiency, speaking to her only when necessary, returning to a small, leather-bound journal that sat open on a desk every few minutes to write a word or two. Her height, her weight, her temperature. *Doctor stuff*.

Something must have happened after she met Ryan at the bar the day before. She wasn't in pain, and, as far as she knew, had no visible injuries. Her head was the only thing that hurt. She wondered if Ryan was alright, but the thought was transient.

'I need to examine you some more, Samantha,' the man in the white coat said. 'Could you please remove your clothes.'

No question mark. Not a question.

The request sounded harmless enough coming from a doctor, but, even in her disoriented state, Samantha felt a twitch of resistance.

'It's quite alright,' the man called Robert said, sensing her discomfort. 'I've seen it all before!'

That smile again.

He was handsome, of that there was no doubt. His eyes, like his tone of voice, suggested gentleness. They were dark brown — a common colour with an uncommon aura. He vaguely reminded her of a character from a movie she had seen, a character she could not altogether remember, an impotence that bothered her momentarily but was soon forgotten, her mind already sliding to other things.

She took off her jeans first, pulling them down her thighs, over her knees and feet, kicking them away across the floor. Her top was next, then her bra, *double D cups*, and finally her briefs.

'Thank you, Samantha.'

Pulling a tailor's tape measure from an inner pocket of his coat, he proceeded to measure her, his hands warm as they brushed against her naked skin. He began with her neck and then her shoulders, slowly moving down her body, pausing to record each measurement in the journal on the desk. Samantha simply stood, remarkably focused as she tried to stand straight. So close to the man in the white coat, and so very exposed, she was incredibly self-aware. She had never been so thoroughly naked in front of a stranger before.

'Beautifully balanced,' Robert said, seemingly more for his own ears than for hers, as he read the measurement for her underbust. Her breath wobbled in her throat and he was close enough to perceive the irregularity. He turned his face towards hers and smiled. 'Have you ever been fitted for a dress before, Samantha?'

'No.'

'Well, I would say that a tailor and I have much in common.' He turned his back to her as he walked to the desk. She could hear the nib of the pen scratch against the paper as he wrote. 'We both seek to understand the requirements of the individual and make sure they are,' he paused to search for the right words, 'well cared for.'

Every conceivable measurement was taken and recorded in the journal. When the tape measure was returned to his inner pocket, he began his tactile examination, inspecting for inconsistencies, feeling the tone of her muscles, and palpating her bare skin for abnormalities. He worked without speaking. She had goosebumps despite the warmth of the room.

Finally, he asked her to sit. From the examination couch he took her pulse, two warm fingers over her wrist, before returning, as was his habit, to the journal on the desk. He sat close to her, their noses very almost touching, as he inspected her eyes using a tool about the size of a small torch. His face was expressionless as he listened to the heavy lub-dubbing of her heart through a stethoscope.

She had not had a pelvic examination before. His was her first.

Neither said a word as he inserted a metal instrument that looked like a duck's beak into her vagina. There was brief discomfort, but no pain. He slid two fingers inside, made his assessments, and then it was over.

Standing at the desk, three strokes of the pen and the journal was closed.

With his inspection of her body complete, he announced she was 'structurally sound and correct' and told her she could redress.

She reached down to pick up her clothes from the floor.

'No,' he said, interrupting her movement. 'I have something fresh for you to wear.' He patted a folded piece of fabric next to him on the desk. Samantha walked over and took it from him.

It was a simple white dress. Gathered at the chest, it fell to just below her knees and had telltale cotton creases. Her dad would have called it a smock, or something equally archaic, and she felt like a Victorian girl caught out of bed in her night clothes after she put it on. Robert didn't offer her a change of underwear, and her shoes had been missing ever since she first woke in that room. By the time she was dressed, her old clothes had already been cleared away.

He was sitting at the desk now. He smiled and drew her attention to a door in the corner of the room. She hadn't noticed it before. 'I'm sure you need a moment or two to use the facilities,' he said.

She did not, but his tone told her declining wasn't an option. As she moved towards the door, passing close to the desk, he held something out to her. It was a small, clear container.

'I will need a sample, please.'

She simply nodded her head. *Doctor stuff.*

She could hear Robert humming on the other side of the door as she forced herself to urinate. Burnt orange. She was dehydrated. She dabbed herself dry and flushed the tissue away.

'You must feel terrible,' he said when she handed him the container. 'You really should have had the drink my wife gave you.'

Blonde hair, blue cardigan.

'Your wife works here too?'

The words were like golf balls in her mouth. She returned to the examination couch to sit, her legs dangling over the edge, feet contacting the couch's cool metal frame as they swung to and fro.

'Yes,' he answered, looking up from what he was doing to smile at her. 'I'm almost done here.'

She had to suppress a giggle as she watched him fiddle with her urine. He was poking the rancid liquid with something and all of a sudden everything seemed funny to Samantha. The man with the smile that matched his wife's fiddling with another woman's urine. She remembered how he had fingered her and wondered what his wife thought about it.

Robert hadn't said what he was doing. It was, however,

clear to her that he was pleased with the results. His demeanour changed and he suddenly became urgent. Striding to the door, he apologised to Samantha, told her to wait in the room and excused himself, mumbling about there being a 'window of opportunity' as he locked the door behind him.

A window of opportunity?

She still had a terrible headache, but was starting to feel more herself.

The room she now found herself alone in had very little in the way of furniture. Asides from the desk and examination couch, there was a tall chest of office drawers and an uncomfortable swivel stool. After trying the drawers, *all locked*, Samantha glided across the floor on the stool back towards the desk.

The leather-bound journal was gone, Robert seemingly having taken it with him without her realising. There was nothing on the desk, its basic pine-effect laminate surface as bare as she had been only moments before. No framed family photographs. No personal knick-knacks of any variety. *Boring bastard.*

Samantha immediately felt bad. Robert seemed nice enough, if somewhat serious, but seriousness was surely a trait of all doctors.

A quick tilt of the ear told Samantha there was no sound coming from outside the door. She smoothed her hand down the front of the desk and selected a drawer. *Second from bottom.* This time there was no lock.

There wasn't much to see inside. A small plastic tray held

three pens, a pencil sharpener and no pencils. Paper clips jangled against the back panel as she slid the drawer back in place.

The next drawer was equally uninteresting. A box of latex gloves and two rolls of toilet paper.

A niggling sensation and Samantha felt like she was doing something she shouldn't be. She didn't normally bother with such concerns, but on this occasion she felt compelled to look over her shoulder. The door was still closed and — *shit*.

A familiar red light just above the door.

She cursed again, this time aloud. But, then again, she was hardly doing anything wrong. She hadn't found anything interesting enough to warrant a crime having been committed. And besides, what kind of doctor has a camera to record his patients?

The unpleasant taste of bile saturated the back of her throat as she recalled, with terrible abruptness, the camera that had watched her as she lay, half-naked and deranged, on the floor of the other room.

If anyone's breaking the law it's him.

Samantha didn't believe in secrets, or at least not ones other people kept from her. This distaste for hidden knowledge had in the past led her to believe, with a certainty that bordered on delusion, that she had an above average sensitivity to other people's deceit. In reality, Samantha was rather slow to catch on to falsehood, having been cheated on by two different men with no less than seven other women. Mercifully, not all at the same time.

Still no noise from outside.

She quickly devoured the contents of the remaining two drawers — quite literally in the case of the chocolate bar she found in the top one. It was, however, a box of cards in the second drawer from the top that interested her most.

The box was made of an opaque, brown plastic and inside, arranged horizontally, were at least, if she had to guess, one hundred record cards. They looked to be patient cards, the sort that doctors might have used before such information was computerised. All were handwritten in a scrawling variety of scripts stereotypically associated with doctors and mathematicians.

Courtney Anderson. Tabitha Beeston. Alice Furlong. Each card bore a name.

Realising they were arranged alphabetically, and for no reason other than self-absorption, Samantha flicked through the cards searching for her own name.

Samantha Lawrence.

Her address and date of birth were written at the top of the card, although she couldn't remember having told Robert that information. Lower down, in the 'past prescriptions' section of the card, it had been written that she had stopped taking the contraceptive pill three years ago due to side effects. Below that, the words mifepristone and misoprostol had been scribbled, with the dates beside them barely legible. She certainly had not told him any of that. There was no mention of her local doctor's surgery, but she could only assume that it was from there that Robert had got the information.

She heard a key turn in the lock and shoved the box and the cards back into the drawer. She was sitting on the stool in the centre of the room by the time Robert opened the door. He wasn't alone and introduced the young woman who was with him as Mary. Luxurious red curls wreathed her face and she had the most aristocratic cheekbones Samantha had ever seen. Straight-postured and sangfroid, she stood at Robert's side like an equal, despite appearing to be no more than twenty years old. The two women nodded at each other by way of greeting.

'Mary's going to take you to where you'll be staying,' Robert said.

Staying?

'She's going to make sure you're looked after properly.' He smiled and gestured from one woman to the other. Mary did not smile and neither did Samantha. After seeing the camera and reading her name on that card, the fog in her brain was beginning to dissipate.

Still, she was uncertain. Uncertain as to where she was and uncertain as to who these people were. Part of her thought that Robert *was* a doctor and that this *was* a hospital, but another part of her — a part that was growing as the fog retracted — suspected him and everything he did and said.

She had never been in a situation like this before, a situation that asked her to make a judgement call that went against everything everyone around her was doing and saying. Sure, she had rebelled, but she had always been led by someone else. Led by her dad, led by her friends, led by the television. Hell, she had even been led by *that prick Ryan*.

And now she was being led again.

Before she could think any further, Samantha was on her feet and following Mary out of the room.

Three

Samantha had never particularly liked being outdoors. Threadbare sofas that had belonged to too many people, television sets with lost remotes, and sticky, imitation leather bar stools held much more appeal. The Sun made her squint and she still had nothing on her feet.

The path was well-maintained and there was lawn on either side. Bespeckled with red clover, the grass ran into trees and the trees into more trees beyond. From every direction, birds sang about the dark berries that were ripening on the brambles, about the bees that buzzed over the flowers, and about other lovely things. Before very long Samantha had to stop to dislodge several small stones that had gathered in the creases between her toes.

Mary had walked ahead. There was an unspoken expectation that Samantha would follow, but now she stopped to wait for her, scowling.

Samantha flicked the grit away and kept moving.

'Thanks for waiting.'

Mary was not one for conversation.

Behind them was the building from which they had come. It lacked windows and the only opening Samantha could perceive was the thick metal door through which they had exited. The exterior wall, clad in some sort of plastic grey weatherboard, ran perpendicular to the path and away to the edge of Samantha's vision. A high, chain-link fence could be seen jutting from its far corner. She still had no idea where she was.

Four steps forward with another four between her and Mary. Samantha hesitated then spoke. 'The doctor said I'm staying here.'

The red-headed woman kept walking.

'The man I was with last night—' Samantha's voice broke, which surprised her more than it did her silent companion. 'Is my friend okay?'

Mary stopped and turned to look back at her. Sunlight kissed her cheeks and enhanced her freckles. 'Everything is alright,' she said without a trace of compassion.

Samantha couldn't help but think of the blonde woman and the porridge. *That's exactly what she said.*

'I want to call my dad. Let him know I'm okay.'

Mary paused before responding. 'Once we're inside.'

Samantha looked ahead and saw a second building, smaller than where they had come from but equally dull and grey.

'You'd better mean that,' Samantha said, ready for a fight and disliking her companion more and more by the second. Mary merely turned on her heel and continued walking.

She'd better mean it.

As she approached the smaller building, Samantha's whereabouts became no clearer. Mary flashed a keycard at a reader on the door. A metallic click and they were inside.

The first thing which struck Samantha was the heat. Even in the thin dress, the air clung to her. It was a temperature that advocated lanquidity. Inactivity, however, wasn't an option.

Mary ushered Samantha deeper into the building, past closed doors and windowless walls. A stifling labyrinth of beige.

'We're here,' she eventually announced, tapping her keycard against another reader.

It was like an airlock, a transitional space flanked by two metal doors. *More beige.* Mary indicated Samantha should enter first. She was surprised when the door closed behind her, Mary on the other side, visible through the small, wired glass window in the door.

'Hey!'

Mary said nothing. Their eyes met through the window but there wasn't anything there. Her expression was corpselike.

She stepped away and all Samantha could see was the fear in her own reflection.

The other door, the one behind her, had no window. It clicked, as if an electric lock had been released, and she knew she was supposed to go through it. It was still closed, if now unlocked, and so Samantha placed the palm of her hand against it and pushed.

A man and a woman sat on a bed in the centre of the room. They had been talking when she entered. Cross-legged with their heads leaning together, the pair stopped and looked up at Samantha. The woman was wearing the same white cotton dress as her and the man had loose fitting, white trousers. His chest was bare and Samanatha felt like she was interrupting a peculiar, grown-up slumber party. A second woman, also wearing the same cotton smock, was sitting on the floor, her back against the corner of the room.

The woman on the bed was the first to speak. 'Hi,' she said, slow and soft, half-smiling as she looked Samantha up and down. 'You must be new.'

Samantha didn't know what to say, and no one else said anything so the woman on the bed continued.

'I'm Jade,' the woman said. She had curly brown hair that grazed her shoulders.

'Samantha.'

'Nice to meet you, Samantha.'

No one had moved. Jade was no longer smiling and the man beside her had barely breathed since Samantha had opened the door. On the floor, the other woman was staring at the carpet, its deep red fibres as enchanting as mud.

Samantha's gut felt lumpy and she had the distinct feeling everyone else in the room knew something she didn't.

Where am I? She had lost track of how many times she had asked herself that question.

'Why don't you come over and sit with us?' Jade patted the space on the bed between her and the man.

'I'm okay,' Samantha said. 'I'll just sit over there whilst I wait for the doctor.' She nodded towards a wide, red velvet armchair positioned just a few short steps from the door. As she went to sit on it, she saw the fabric was stained in places.

Laughter erupted from the bed. Jade's palms were planted into the sheets, holding herself upright as she tipped her head to the ceiling and howled. Mrs. Doherty, the batty old woman who lived next door to Samantha's dad, owned a parrot whose laughter sounded exactly the same. The man smirked as his companion flicked tears from her eyes. Still, the woman on the floor stared at the carpet.

'No,' Jade eventually said, 'it would be better if you sat with us.' Under the residual giggles there was a forcefulness to her voice that hadn't been there before.

'I'm fi—'

'No,' Jade interrupted. 'No, you're not.'

With those few simple words, the light in the room transformed from a comfortable orange glow to one that was too dark and invited malevolence. The clouds rolled in and before Samantha had time to respond the man stood up and crossed the room to where she sat. She didn't know his name, but his most intimate parts were there for her to see, his masculinity engorged and threatening to pierce his trousers. Then, his hands were on her, ripping her from the armchair, shoving her, pulling her, thrusting her towards the bed.

She couldn't resist. How could she? She was sixty-one kilograms and he must have weighed double. Pure angry muscle. Her hands bounced off him as though his flesh were armour-plated.

When her face hit the bed she screamed, but not the way

damsels in distress scream in movies and fairy stories. She screamed from the bottom of her lungs, from the base of her spine, and it poured from her throat in hot spikes of fire.

She wasn't wearing any underwear and that made it even easier for him.

Is this actually happening?

'I'm sorry,' the woman called Jade whispered into her ear as the man constricted Samantha's wrists inside his fist. 'It really is better if you let him do it.' She was still on the bed, her face so close to Samantha's that she could taste the staleness of her breath.

Twice she tried to buck him off. Twice he pushed her down and tightened his grip.

Sharp, red, easy.

Soft, light fingers sought out her neck and kneaded the skin. Above, over, inside her, he heaved, without sound and without feeling.

'Relax.' Jade's fingers were caressing her hair now. 'So you don't get hurt.'

Samantha could feel the sharpness of her own eyelashes as they bent back on themselves, pressed into her half-closed eyelids under the weight of the man on top of her. Against her face, the bedding was damp, saturated with tears. Salt mixed with a small cut on her lip, the flesh having been sliced open by a rogue incisor that had become trapped between the bed and her bottom lip.

She tried to leave her body, tried to retreat to her head.

Sharp, red, easy.

She tried to go somewhere else, forced herself to dive inward and began frantically ransacking those mental filing cabinets which housed her most precious thoughts and memories. Flames licked the edges of the photographs, smoke smothered the good feelings, the smells and sounds of home. Everything turned to ash in her hands and all that was left was a single thought.

This is not a hospital.

She screamed inside herself.

This is not a hospital.

Deep, woeful sobs — those of a wounded animal in the throes of death.

Twisted in the sheets, she was unable to move her head. Samantha was paralysed. Her eyes, hollow, soulless windows that they were, could see nothing but the woman in the corner, rocking herself like a babe in a cradle on the floor. If Samantha were dying, this woman was already dead.

Her thoughts were in rhythm with the thumping of her own head against the headboard.

This is not a hospital. This is not a hospital. This is not a hospital.

Four

Guinevere first played the piano when she was four years old. Her music teacher, a considerate grey-bearded man called Mr. Swailes, told her she had perfect pianist wrists. Her mummy once remarked that even at her tender age of thirteen she was a more remarkable player than she had ever been. Her daddy liked to listen to her play Debussy's *Clair de Lune* in the evenings when he came in from work.

Today she was playing Beethoven's *Für Elise*.

Her fingers raced across the keys, dexterous and light, exactly as she had practised time and time again. Jumping between A minor and E major arpeggios with her left hand, her body swayed with the continuous motion of the rapturous melody. She felt her soul surge as she drove the sound onward, through the heightened emotions of the composition, faster, then slower, and finally back to the arpeggios.

Under the music, she heard the door to the sitting room creak open.

'Daddy!'

The notes fell flat as Guinevere abandoned the instrument. In the doorway, Robert braced as his daughter catapulted herself into his arms. He lifted her off the ground and kissed both her cheeks.

'Sweet Guinevere,' he beamed. 'How well you play!'

'Thank you, Daddy.'

Robert carried his daughter across the room back to the piano. Placing her on the stool, he guided her small hands to the keys and knelt on the carpet beside her.

'Show me.'

The girl's fingers flowed over the instrument and the room was once again filled with music. It wasn't until she reached the end of the composition that Robert noticed the music book on the stand was closed.

'You learnt it all?'

Guinevere's cheeks were flushed. She laughed and nodded. 'Mummy said Alex is coming home today.'

'Well, I'm sure he'll be very impressed.' Robert reached to tuck a strand of his daughter's sun-coloured hair, which had been shaken loose by the excited motions of her playing, behind her ear. 'Where's Mummy?'

'Making food.' Her fingers had already returned to the keys, her consciousness drifting back into the music. Robert left his daughter to practise.

He found his wife in the kitchen with an apron tied around her waist. It was secured by a neat bow which nestled into the hollow at the bottom of her back, the ties gathering her clothes to her, revealing the feminine shape of her body underneath. Sophie had birthed him three children and it was in the familial setting of their home that he loved her most.

Robert drew close to her, holding her from behind as she cut carrots into rounds.

'How did it go?'

'Okay,' he replied, his arms still around her. 'Better than expected.'

'Really?'

'You made a good choice, my darling.' He kissed her just below her ear, burrowing his nose into her fair skin, savouring her sweet aroma. 'I had to move her sooner than I would have liked.'

Sophie put down the knife and scooped the carrots into her hands. A roasting tin was already prepared beside the chopping board. 'Already?'

'I know. A couple of days to settle would have been preferable, but the timing was perfect.'

'I suppose it's the right decision.' She arranged the vegetables in the tin. 'I never like it when he only has two to cover. You know how enthusiastic he can be. Three's a better number for him. Can you pass me the salt and pepper, dear?'

Robert handed his wife the salt and pepper mills that were on the table behind them. From the other room, *Für Elise* reached its climax for the fourth time since he had entered the house. 'How long has she been playing?'

Sophie tutted and chuckled. 'I'll hear it in my sleep tonight!'

He laughed and then turned on his heel, dancing in time to their daughter's frantic playing. He beckoned for Sophie to join him. *I am blessed*, Robert thought as he spiralled around the kitchen holding his wife. They wove between the table and the range cooker, waltzed past the fridge and spun towards the doorway. Sophie slid out of his arms and slipped away through the door. 'Aurélie,' she said to her husband. 'I left her with your father.'

He laughed as he wafted her away playfully. 'You'd better go save her, then.'

Aurélie was their youngest. An unexpected, but nonetheless cherished child who they had named after Sophie's mother. Both, the child and her namesake, were buoyant, golden rays of sunlight, the older Aurélie having tragically died only two months before the birth of her granddaughter. It was five-year-old Aurélie's lightness of spirit that caused her to need saving from Robert's father.

Robert steadied himself on the kitchen worktop, dizzied by his and Sophie's twirling, and thought of his father.

What sort of a man names his son after himself?

Robert Senior was an autocratic old widower who had passed the family homestead over to Robert some years ago after he begrudgingly realised he was no longer physically able to manage its day-to-day running. The old man had opinions on everything, from how the homestead should be run to the colour of his son's shirts. As irritating as he could be — *an itch that's never quite scratched away* — Robert loved his father and had great respect for him. Even if they sometimes, or rather quite often, disagreed, the elder Robert possessed a sharp mind that brimmed with a wealth of practical experience and theoretical knowledge. Also, he was a loving grandfather, at least to two of his children.

'What time's the lad due, anyhow?'

His wife's footsteps and Robert heard the back door swing shut. A dull, wooden thump sounded down the hallway, his father's walking cane catching against the frame.

'He phoned to say he'd be late,' he heard Sophie reply to his father.

'A lot of unnecessary fuss, I'd say.'

A clean-shaven old man hobbled into the kitchen. Smartly dressed in a green tweed jacket, red tie and brown leather loafers, he was visibly fatigued despite the aid of his cane. Robert would have offered to help his father to a chair, but he knew better than to do such a thing.

The two men looked at each other, the same in many ways, united by genetics, even by name, but separated by so much more.

Robert Senior prodded his son with his cane. 'How goes it, my boy?'

'Aurélie needs a change of clothes,' Sophie called from the stairs in the hallway. 'Keep an eye on the roast for me, please, Robert.'

'Well, Father,' said Robert.

'Sophie told me we've got a new heifer.'

'Yes, she arrived late last night.'

Increasing his grip on his cane, the old man shuffled his weight from one leg to the other. Robert nodded to his father's knee. 'It's still bothering you?'

'Blasted thing kept me up for most of the night,' Robert Senior's grey eyes bulged as he swallowed a wince. An attempt to conceal his discomfort.

'You should see a doctor, Father.'

The old man snorted. 'I am a doctor. And once your boy arrives home, I'll be living in a house stacked full of doctors!'

'I offered to look at it—' Robert began.

'Pish!' His father swatted at him with his cane. 'Your hands are needed for other work.'

The room fell to silence, the only sound being the piano in the other room. Father and son both looked across the kitchen to the window. Outside, the Sun was starting to set. Its orange-red limbs stretched through the branches of the trees, caressing their foliage on the way to the ground. The grass had transformed from green to gold.

He never trusts me.

It was the younger Robert's misfortunate to have a father who, for all of his aspirations of having a son who would someday succeed him, had never been able to acknowledge his once thin-legged boy was now a grown-up man, and a rather capable one at that. In his mind, Robert Senior was the only one qualified enough to inspect Robert Senior. His son was accustomed to biting his tongue.

Quite early on in life he had learned to appreciate peace and quiet, and now, at the age of forty-eight, he lived his life according to the tenets of tranquil living, a personal philosophy which necessitated the conscious avoidance of potentially stressful experiences. In practical terms, this meant an awful lot of tongue biting when in the presence of his father. As such, what might have been an awkward moment of silence for others, was for Robert a chance to breathe and enjoy the stillness.

The egg timer rang and Robert moved to check the roast. When Sophie reentered the kitchen, he was lifting it from the oven. Sophie reset the timer, then drizzled the carrots she had left with a ladle of juice from the meat.

'He phoned again,' she explained as she worked. 'He said the traffic's less now. He should be here within the hour.'

'That's good,' Robert said as Sophie moved around him to retrieve the oven gloves he had placed on the worktop. 'It would be a shame for him to miss all the wonderful food you've prepared.' He watched her and then asked, 'Is there anything you want me to do?'

Without lifting her eyes from what she was doing she suggested he set the table. 'I have the plates picked out already.' She pointed to a stack of porcelain on the old oak sideboard by the door. It was their best tableware.

Robert left his father in the kitchen with Sophie as he arranged the plates in the next room. A simple, white tablecloth had already been spread over the dining table's lacquered surface and handsome, leather upholstered chairs marked seven places. Through the wall, he could hear his father's muffled intonations as he spoke with Sophie. In the sitting room, Guinevere had finally closed the fallboard over the piano's keys and was now giggling with her younger sister.

It had been close to nine months since Robert had last seen

his son Alexander, the start of the year being the last time they were in each other's company. Despite having several weeks off at Easter, he hadn't returned home, informing his father — *by text message of all things* — that he was to stay at university and study. Sophie had been distraught, separation from her child being an even more painful experience than either parent had anticipated, and whilst Robert also missed his only son, he couldn't help but be proud of his diligence. A few months later, as the end of the academic year approached, Alexander did it again, this time phoning to say he wasn't coming home. Rather than immediately return to them at the end of term, as he had done the previous year, he wanted to stay at university for a portion of the long summer vacation. Upon telling her, Sophie's heart had very nearly broken and Robert began to wonder if his son was purposefully choosing to avoid them.

He remembered how, as a small boy, Alexander had demonstrated a great capacity for quiet contemplation. *Unlike the girls,* Robert grinned as shrieks of laughter travelled across the house. A miniature librarian, he had dutifully organised every book in the household by the age of ten and would spend hours, tucked away in secret nooks across the homestead, consuming the contents of each and every one. Introverted and sensitive, Alexander was, in many ways, more his mother's son than his father's.

Although Alexander had never expressed an interest in the practical side of running the family homestead, much preferring his books and musings to the labour of daily chores, he had followed the path expected of him by studying medicine.

An instinctive sense of duty, combined with regular, hectoring lectures from his grandfather, had convinced him of his medical calling — much the same as how Robert had discovered his passion for the field.

Robert straightened the final fork and flattened a napkin on the plate.

A precious namby. Not his words, but those of his father when they had found Alexander playing with some of the livestock one time as a young boy. Robert Senior could be cruel in defence of his family, their homestead and his beliefs.

With the table set and food underway, there was little more to do than await the arrival of their son. Sophie sat close to her husband in the sitting room, talking to him about small, inconsequential things as they watched Guinevere and Aurélie play together on the rug. The past week, their grandfather had been teaching them to play chess and Guinevere was about to be checkmated by a five-year-old. From the armchair in the corner, Robert Senior slapped his hands together and whooped. The older girl pouted as her sister jumped up from the rug and began to giggle, cheered on by her grandfather.

Fortunately, before Guinevere was able to elevate the situation to melodrama, the light of car headlights poured in through the front window.

'He's here!' Sophie leapt from the sofa and flew to the door. Robert followed, as did the girls and, with careful, halting steps, the old man.

The girls rushed down the front steps ahead of Robert to join their mother on the gravel. An old, red car sat in a cloud of its own exhaust fumes on the driveway, its engine idling and headlights still on. With two shudders and a crank, the car was shut off.

'My boy!' Sophie squealed as the driver's door opened. Robert walked to her side, his father looking on from the doorstep.

A young man with hair and eyes the same dark shades as Robert's stepped out of the car. He wore a jumper that was too big for him, and his chin and cheeks were furred with stubble that crinkled as he opened his mouth and smiled. Sophie would have floated across the driveway to her child — indeed, her legs were prepared to propel her — if it had not been for the clunking sound of the car's passenger door. She caught herself, her eyes dragging her face to look at the other side of the car.

From the car stepped a pale-skinned young woman. She was slender, had long brown hair and wore thick-rimmed glasses. She offered a hesitant smile to the crowd that greeted her.

Sophie looked from the woman to her son and then to her husband. He raised his eyebrows slightly, lips parted but making no sound. Behind them, in the doorway of the house, Robert heard his father laugh — a singular, sharp sound.

'Mother,' Alexander said, his voice soft and low, 'this is Tammy.'

Tammy extended a meek hello.

Robert reached for his wife's side and took hold of her hand.

Five

Robert needed coffee. He had chased sleep all night but, like long Sundays and white Christmases, it had evaded him.

At one a.m. — so said the clock on his bedside table — he had watched Sophie resting beside him, the soft strands of her hair ruffled against the pillow, her chest rising and falling with the rhythm of her breathing. Twice she had spoken in her sleep. Her eyelids had fluttered both times, and he had reached to touch her cheek, lightly stroking her skin until she fell back to peaceful slumber. She hadn't said anything in particular. Her words were minced by the fleeting twists and tumbles of unconsciousness, but Robert had sympathised with his wife all the same.

They were emotionally exhausted. The return of their son after so many months had been one thing, but his unexpected companion had been something else altogether. Rarely, if ever, did they open their home to others. And that's precisely what Tammy was — an other, an unexpected, unknown, and therefore potentially dangerous, other. *An outsider.*

Now, standing in the kitchen waiting for the coffee to brew, Robert wished his son had at least provided them with some warning.

'Did he ever mention her to you?' Sophie asked as she opened the drawer next to him and pulled out a spoon.

'No,' he replied. 'Not once. I would have said.'

'I always thought that—'

'Yes, I did too.'

In his mind, Robert couldn't escape the events of the previous evening. In particular, his memory returned to the moment Tammy had told his father she was a vegetarian. The old man had been unfamiliar with the term. When she had explained to him that it meant she didn't eat animals, Robert Senior had barked 'good!' and proclaimed he didn't eat them either, stuffing a forkful of roasted meat into his mouth as he did.

'What must she think of us?' Sophie sighed, shaking her head as she spooned honey into two coffee cups.

Robert plunged the cafetière. 'What we think of her is what I'm more concerned about.'

He would have said more but it was no longer just the two of them in the kitchen.

'Good morning.' Alexander pulled a box of cereals from the cupboard. He was wearing a grey dressing gown that hung about his trousered legs in loose folds. Sophie came to his side and began arranging the tangles in his hair.

'Good morning, my strawberry,' she said as he poured his breakfast into a bowl. Robert watched his wife balance on the tips of her toes so as to reach the top of their son's head.

'Sleep well?' Robert asked his son from the other side of the kitchen. Without looking up, Alexander said that he had and returned the question. 'Yes, thank you,' Robert lied. Sophie continued to fuss her grown-up boy. 'And Tammy? Did she sleep well?'

'I think so,' Alexander said. 'I'll take something up for her in a minute.' He looked up and nodded to the bowl of cereal. Yesterday evening once again came back to Robert. *A good idea*, he thought, knowing his father was sitting at the dining table reading a newspaper dating from last Tuesday. The affairs of the outside world did not so much involve or affect Robert Senior as they did provide him with a source of sardonic entertainment. *The bleaker the better.* In such a spirit, he was best avoided.

'I'd love having you around today,' Robert said in between sips of coffee. 'I've got a dry fresher to examine and I'd appreciate your opinion.'

Alexander looked up at him and considered. 'Sure,' he replied before moving to the fridge.

Sophie offered her husband a refill. He thanked her as the steam from his coffee cup transported the familiar earthy aroma to his nose. 'Come and find me when you're ready,' Robert said.

His son had already left the room.

By the time Alexander sought him out, Robert was sitting at his desk in one of the buildings down the hill from the house. All of the farm buggies were in use and so Alexander rode an old bicycle he found in the garage along the dirt road and through the trees to find him. The chain jammed twice and he wondered why he had bothered, certain that making the short journey on foot would have been quicker as he stopped yet again to fix it. A cool breeze tickled the back of his neck as he knelt in the dust dirtying his fingers. Either side of the road, thinly coppiced trees melted into old growth until all that could be seen was a fusion of forest greens, reds and browns. Not much had changed since Alexander had roamed the woods as a boy.

He nudged the rusty kickstand and settled back onto the worn saddle. Gratuitous excess must have been the intention when the bicycle was designed all those years before — the amount of metal on its aged frame would have made pedalling uphill hellish. Thankfully, the ride was downhill all the way.

Alexander abandoned the bicycle in a bush before entering the old red sandstone building. Inside, the door to his father's office was open. He knew Robert had been waiting for him.

'Alex,' he smiled when he saw him enter. Robert was seated behind a desk that was littered with Manila folders. 'You're just in time to help.'

'What's the problem?'

Robert stood and walked to close the door of the room. Alexander washed his hands at the sink in the corner, then pulled a chair from the opposite wall and shuffled it close to the desk.

'A rare condition,' Robert said when he was seated back in his chair. 'A fresher — experienced, her fifth delivery with us — unable to lactate. I'm looking through some of our older records for any similar cases before I see her again.'

Alexander glanced down at the folders that lay between him and his father on the desk. Each bore a name and a date. Some he recognised as having been written in his father's hand, others in his grandfather's, but for many he couldn't identify the authors.

'What about Grandpa?' the younger man asked as he was handed a wad of folders.

Robert shook his head. 'It's nothing he's experienced, but perhaps something from his uncle.'

Maisie B. 1951. Alexander's first folder had a tea stain on its front fold. The brown ring had smudged the ink, causing the edges of the five and one — the numbers of the date which the carelessly placed cup had once overlapped — to furr and bleed into the stiff fibrous paper.

'He said he remembers his uncle having a particularly troublesome female who always had problems freshening,' Robert continued, looking through his own folder as his son scanned the history of Maisie B. 'Nothing more than that, unfortunately. He couldn't have been any older than ten. Something about,' Robert's voice changed as he delivered the last few words, 'the uselessness of boyish memory.'

Alexander couldn't help but grin at his father's mimicry of the deep and scornful tone of Robert Senior. Looking up from their folders, their eyes met across the desk and father and son both started laughing. It had been a very long time since they had last laughed together.

After they had collected themselves, Alexander asked, 'How long's it been since delivery?'

'Over a week now.'

Dry for over 168 hours. Alexander knew from experience and his studies that thirty-six to seventy-two hours after birth, *ninety-six at the most*, was the usual timeframe for milk to come in. Over a week was not only irregular but exceptionally rare. Maisie B. presented nothing useful. The last page in the folder simply read *per. Winter 1956*, 'per.' being shorthand for the Latin 'peractio', meaning completion. Alexander picked up the next folder from the pile his father had given him and started to read.

'We've had to move the infant on to another fresher,' his father said, eyes scanning a page as he spoke. 'Fortunately, the colostrum came in, so there shouldn't be any developmental issues.'

Alexander nodded and continued to scan the contents of the second folder. This one, *Rose. M. 1953.*, was thinner than the last. *Retained placental fragments*, he read on a page that described the birth of a seven pound seven ounce female on 29th June 1954, *may have provoked the delayed onset of lactation.* He interrupted his father's reading and slid the page across the desk.

'No,' Robert sighed, passing the page back after studying it. 'The delay appears to have been less than seventy-two hours. Besides, in our case the placenta and foetal membranes were intact and expelled cleanly.'

Cleanly. Alexander thought it an odd choice of word

to use for such a bloody moment, but he understood his father's meaning nonetheless. As someone who would have been present at hundreds of births, and felt most comfortable wrapped in a mantle of technical jargon and medical mannerisms, Robert might have been accused of having become desensitised to the whole process.

In the end, Rose M. turned out to be just as unhelpful as Maisie B. Both were put to one side. Alexander went to pick up the next folder but was stopped by his father.

'How about your opinion?' Robert signalled for his son to follow him as he stood and walked to the door. 'That's what we said this morning, wasn't it?'

Alexander abandoned the folders on the desk. 'You want me to examine her?' His words were coloured by reluctance.

'Of course,' Robert smiled. He took the white coat that was hanging on a peg beside the door and put it on over his shirt. 'It'll give you a chance to show me what my money's been buying!'

Alexander laughed. His university tuition was paid for in part by an old family trust fund that had been established by one of their affluent ancestors for all children of the family to receive a full and proper education. In more recent years, the fund had been bolstered by their lucrative wine business. Dionysus, a variety of grape created by the family, was grown in several vineyards spread over the homestead, before being harvested and taken away to be processed into one of the country's premium sparkling wines. It was traditional for all firstborn sons to study medicine at the same prestigious college, and the irony of a medical career being funded by inebriated livers was not lost on Alexander.

'I've already had her separated from the others,' Robert said as he adjusted his collar. 'I thought that maybe there was a bonding issue, so we moved her and the infant to a smaller room a couple of days ago. It's just her now. We bring the infant in twice a day.'

'Do you have another?' Alexander nodded at his father's white coat. Robert pointed to the top drawer beside the sink. 'Thanks.' He put it on, then asked, 'Has there been any improvement?'

'Unfortunately not. It may just be that she's no longer productive.'

Alexander followed his father out the room and down the corridor. 'How long are you going to give her?'

'Grandpa — as you would expect — is pushing for a decision,' Robert smiled grimly. 'But, I wanted to try all options first.'

And I'm one of those options? Alexander knew his father was quite capable of making decisions without the consultation of his son. Robert wanted him to be involved in the process, not because of any value he could provide, but because he wanted Alexander to *want* to be involved.

Alexander cast his eyes to the floor and kept walking. His father stopped and laid a hand on his shoulder. Both now still, Robert looked at his son. His face bore a curious expression, a mixture of pride and scrutiny.

'When you were born, Alex, I always knew you'd be better

than me.' Alexander went to speak but his father carried on. 'Watching your son grow into a man is,' Robert squeezed his shoulder, 'an experience like no other.'

Hope. Expectation. Legacy. Robert's words were heavier than they sounded.

A moment of silence and Robert smiled at his son. His eyes, warm and paternal, radiated encouragement and seemed to say, 'I admire you. I trust you. I love you.' Self-conscious, Alexander offered him a weak smile in return. It wasn't that he was indifferent to his father's affection, he just found the pressure of his expectations distressing. It was the background radiation of their relationship: not intrinsically harmful, but ever present.

They had stopped at the right door. Robert reached into his pocket and removed a plastic keycard. Raising it to the reader beside the door, he asked, 'Ready?'

The woman inside was naked from the waist up. Her light brown hair hung messily over her chest and partially concealed her breasts, which were robust and creamy. She was sitting on the end of a small single bed, her hands wrung in her lap, and looked as if she had been crying. Robert walked to her and sat on a chair that was positioned close by.

'Katie, how are you feeling today?'

The woman sniffed and repositioned herself. 'How is he?'

'He's fine,' Robert soothed, moving his hand to place it over hers. 'I'm interested in how you're feeling.'

Alexander closed the door behind him, being careful not

to make the metal clunk against the frame. The woman on the bed seemed not to have noticed him.

'I want my boy, Dr. Robert. I want to feed him.'

'I know, Katie. I know you do.' Robert soothed her again. 'We're trying all we can to help you.'

The woman's chest heaved as she swallowed a sob. Sorrowful and beautiful, bare-breasted on the bed, her tears glistening in the sunlight that poured in through the window, she looked like a classical painting.

'I've brought my son with me today, Katie.' She looked across the room to Alexander. 'He's a doctor, too, and he wants to help you.'

Alexander offered a hesitant hello, introduced himself and moved to the bed. The springs in the mattress creaked as Katie turned to face him, her legs now folded beneath her.

'What a handsome man your son is, Dr. Robert,' she smiled through her tears. 'Just like my boys will be.'

Neither man said anything. Robert let go of Katie's hand and stood up.

'Alexander,' he urged him lightly, 'if you could help Katie, please.'

Alexander straightened his posture and adjusted the cuffs of his sleeves. His arms were too long for the coat, the fabric not quite reaching his wrists. Katie sat waiting for him to say something. He sucked in a lungful of air. Much of his university schooling thus far had been theoretical, limited to lectures, reading and the occasional dissection, with clinical training being reserved for later into his studies. Even so, growing up he had watched and assisted his father many times. *Remember your education*, he told himself, but for some reason all he could think about was the old bicycle he had dumped in the bush. Worn down and barely serving a purpose, it reminded him of the woman on the bed.

'Tell me about your baby, Katie,' Alexander began.

The woman's face lit up as she described her new child to the young doctor. 'As blue as the sky,' she said as she recalled the infant's eyes.

'And you fed him at first?' Alexander asked, trying to copy the soothing tone that his father had used only moments before.

'Yes. First milk. Thicker and yellow, the same as all the other times.'

Colostrum, Alexander thought, remembering what his father had told him.

'And after that?'

'And after that nothing, Dr. Alexander. My nipples just don't want to give.'

He asked for her permission to touch her. She consented and pushed her hair back over her shoulders. He apologised if his hands were cold and began cupping her mammaries. They were more than ample, and should have easily been able to provide for a newborn. For some reason, however, they were completely dry.

There was no visible discharge. He palpated the pigmented area around her nipples. Katie didn't flinch or react in any way. So soon after birth, they should have been tender. Alexander cupped her left breast and softly bounced it in his palm. It felt surprisingly perky, and not at all heavy or sagging. Her breasts appeared to contain no milk whatsoever and — if he had to draw a conclusion — would most likely never produce milk again.

Alexander's hands still on her breasts, Katie turned to Robert who was now standing over by the window.

'Are you still going to bring me the medicine, Dr. Robert?'

His back was to her, his eyes fixed on something intangible outside in the distance. 'Yes, Katie,' he said, his voice barely above a whisper. 'Mary will bring it to you after we're gone.'

'Thank you, doctor,' her posture softened as she sighed in relief. 'It'll help,' she said with false confidence. 'I've just got to keep taking it. For my baby.'

Robert continued to gaze out the window as his mind plunged toward dark and inevitable things. The truth was, he could examine this woman twice daily, prescribe domperidone, stuff her with ginger root, nettle extract and fenugreek, even compress her breasts with his own hands to encourage lactation, the conclusion would be the same. She was defective. He had brought Alexander here, not to witness him perform a miracle — Katie was beyond saving — but to have him understand the difficult choices he, his father, and one day Alexander himself, would have to make.

This is just how it is, Robert told himself as he watched a blackbird land on the branch of a tree outside. It was important for his son to see this. Sometimes he thought he had been too soft on him. The appearance of Tammy, he feared, had in some way proved this.

'Thank you, Alex,' he eventually said.

His son's hands returned to his side and the woman on the bed moved her hair back over her breasts. Robert left the window and walked to Katie. He summoned a smile and touched her hands again.

'Don't worry,' he said, patting her fingers. 'I'll ask Mary to bring the boy when she brings your food.'

The woman was full of gratitude and very nearly cried with joy. She continued to praise the doctor and his handsome son as they left the room, locking the door behind them.

Six

Although no one in their circle would have suspected it, Alexander and Tammy's relationship had been deteriorating for months.

Their first meeting had been accidental, a confusion in the seating plan at a university dinner. He had never been meant to sit next to her, but it had happened all the same. As he and the others around him dined on lamb in a white wine sauce, she had picked at the edges of a mushroom quiche. He had thought it strange that she had never tasted meat before, but then, looking at the thinness of her arms, to his mind it was obvious she was undernourished. She had laughed when he had asked her why and teased him by saying, 'Surely you've met a vegetarian before?' His serious expression had made her laugh all the more and then the conversation had turned to other things, like what they thought of their new rooms and the schools to which they had been. She was fascinated to hear him talk about what it was like to have been homeschooled.

Their second meeting had been intentional, as had all the

others which followed. She liked it when he took her to the little art gallery hidden at the end of the road behind old Saint Mary's church. It was never full and often they would find it was just the two of them, nestled against each other on their usual bench in the corner by the window, heads turned up so as to admire the canvas on the wall.

Alexander had never had a girlfriend before. Tammy was his first. For weeks he had fretted over the formal series of events that should or were supposed to have happened in order for her to be classified as *his* girlfriend. In the end, none of it had mattered — he had sort of acquired her, and she him, until they ended up spending all of their free time in each other's company.

They shared the same friends and so at social events they would arrive and leave together. Late at night, having spent the whole day making love instead of studying, they would find themselves sitting together in bed, her spectacled eyes turned to a book on the history of mediaeval England and his on the pages of a medical journal. Invariably, his hand would wander across her naked thigh, and their bedtime would be pushed later still, often into the small hours of the morning.

Then, one day, everything fell flat. She needed — *no, really needed* — to study, and the light giggles which had once accompanied his surreptitious touches changed to disapproving half-smiles. That was not to say that the disintegration had been one sided, only that she put more energy into expressing the disintegration through her words and actions. Alexander, on the other hand, simply couldn't be bothered to make the effort.

Visiting his home had been her suggestion. *To try to save it*, she had told him. *It* being the best word she could find to describe their relationship, their love, their hopes, their dreams. After more than a year and a half together, she should have been able to manage something better than that. Still, unable to come up with a good reason for saying no, Alexander had agreed.

Now, on the bed, breathing in her soft murmurings as he held her naked body to him, her face to his shoulder, his hand cupping the back of her head, it was easy for him to acknowledge their relationship was essentially over. Their conjoined bodies, far from representing an alliance of mind or of heart, was merely a way for them to sate their separate, if shared, lust.

He quickly finished after he felt her orgasm. In that instant, she seemed to revel in his ejactualtion, her grip on his smooth back momentarily increasing, but then, over all too soon. She lost interest and removed herself from underneath him. Pulling his dressing gown from the back of the door, she robed herself on the way to the bathroom.

Alexander rolled over onto his back as he heard the shower turn on. Words, once so freely given and generously shared between them, were now few and far between. Silence and sex — *silent sex* — had come to define their private moments.

Lying on his childhood bed, brown eyes fixed on the ceiling, Alexander wondered if his attraction to Tammy had ever been anything more than a way for him to validate his life. Such was a forbidden thought, one he often denied himself the exploration of, but returned to nonetheless.

It was true that he had been captivated by her novelty. In her short life, she had already trod a path that was so very different from his own. Or rather, she had trod *a* path, whereas he seemed to have spent all his time hopping in and out of his father's footsteps, going round and round, roving the same old circles he had in the same old mud.

She had lived in four different houses and even spent a year abroad all before her thirteenth birthday. Her mother was a banker and her father baked cakes on the weekend. She had been to schools, schools that other children went to — *children who are not your sisters, your cousins, or children of your parents' friends.* Tammy represented a world that Alexander had never been a part of.

And now I've outgrown her, and she me. He sat up and retrieved his underwear from where it had fallen onto the floor.

He no longer needed the sense of validation she had once given him. He knew he was alive — the numb ache he felt in his stomach when he dared to think about what they might have been told him that much. Now, when he looked at her, whenever he ran his hand across her hair, he just felt tired. He had wanted her — *the idea of her* — so much, and now that he had her, he realised it wasn't what he wanted after all. When he touched her, he felt her recoil, just slightly, as if only underneath the skin, and he knew she felt the same.

They were irreconcilable.

The water stopped and he heard the door to the shower open. He hadn't remembered her taking any clothes into the bathroom, but when she came out she was already dressed. Alexander pulled a jumper over his head and rearranged the bed. As he straightened the quilt, he could smell her — her natural, intimate scent — lift from the sheets and carry on the air to his nose.

'I was wrong,' Tammy eventually said.

Alexander looked across the room to her. 'I'm sorry, I—'

'Coming here,' she interrupted, raising her arms up, crooked at the elbows, gesticulating to the room around them. 'I thought it would help but I was wrong.'

Her hair was wet and hung in long, heavy clumps down her back. He didn't say anything but out of habit moved to try to comfort her. Lips pursed, she pushed his hand away. To think, only ten minutes before he had been inside of her. *Silence and sex.*

Rejected, his hand moved to his mouth and ran across his stubble, all possible words lacklustre and fatigued.

'I—'

'You never even told them, Alex.'

Wild-haired gunslingers and silver bullets. It was a quick-draw conversation and she had fired the first shot. Rarely did Tammy raise her voice, but in that moment her vocal cords strained under the pressure of moderating her rage. She kept composure and continued.

'Your parents. They didn't know I was coming, did they?'

Alexander's eyes dropped to the floor. 'No.'

'And— and this is just an educated guess, Alex—' her voice quivered when she said his name, as if the word itself had caught in her throat, a malignant lump that tasted of rock and hatred, 'they hadn't even heard of me before, had they?'

'Tammy,' he started, 'you don't understand—'

'Yes, Alex, that is something which is now painfully obvious. I don't understand. I don't understand how the man I loved, and who I thought loved me—'

'Loved?' As soon as he had said it he wished he hadn't, but there it was all the same. *The truth.*

Whatever Tammy had been about to say died in her mouth. She took a step away from him, her back now pressed against the door to the bathroom. Tears gathered in the corners of her eyes. This time Alexander didn't move to comfort her. He wanted to feel anger and pain and misery. He wanted his heart to be broken into a million tiny pieces, destroyed by the woman he had once adored, to be ripped, still beating from his chest, and torn into shreds. He wanted to feel something. Instead, all he felt was relief. Finally, one of them — albeit perhaps unintentionally — had found the courage to say what needed to be said. *Loved.*

It was over.

'I should leave,' Tammy said, her back still to the bathroom door.

'You don't have to.'

'No. I want to.'

The tears had not yet fallen and he wondered if his eyes looked the same as hers. She forced a smile and reached to touch his hand. 'It's okay, Alex,' she said softly. 'I think it's for the best.'

Silent and with his back to her, he sat on the bed. He listened to her open drawers and heard the zip on her suitcase slide along its metal track. He didn't have to wait long — she hadn't unpacked all that much. Full and largely untouched, her suitcase had sat in the corner of his bedroom, an omen of their impending dissolution. There had been no point in unpacking. *She was leaving before we even arrived.*

He said he would drive her to the train station and she thanked him for the offer. He carried her suitcase down the stairs and she held the front door open.

Alexander's old car coughed and juddered as it crunched along the gravel. From the kitchen, Sophie watched it leave. It was early evening and she was yet to serve dinner. Conscious of her son's guest, she had prepared extra vegetables and had even made a soup from Black Russians, her favourite variety of tomato, carefully cut from the plants she had nursed all season in the polytunnel behind the house. Whatever crisis Tammy's appearance had caused, both inside her own mind and in the hard words exchanged between Robert and his father, she wanted her son to be happy.

Sophie was still in the kitchen when Alexander returned just over an hour later. The driver's door did not immediately open. Headlights off, he sat in the car on the driveway. After five minutes, Sophie worried there might be something wrong. Untying her apron and abandoning it on the sideboard by the door, she hurried down the front steps to the car. The tyres were wet and there was mud on the rims. Seeing her son inside, alone, she tapped on the window. He was surprised to see her and rolled down the glass.

'Are you alright, my strawberry?'

Alexander smiled, but his mother could see his heart wasn't in it. Without getting out of the car, he passed his hand to her through the open window. She took it and began caressing his fingers.

'Are you coming inside?'

'In a moment,' he replied, quiet and uncertain, his other hand gripping the steering wheel. Sophie stood outside the car in silence, still holding onto Alexander's hand, waiting for him. Finally, he took back his hand, closed the window, and got out of the car.

He was sheepish and shell-shocked, half-stumbling, as if blind, as he walked towards the house. Sophie wrapped an arm around her child and rested her face against his chest. Walking together, she asked him again if he was alright. He nodded and made a noise as if to say he was. As mother and son walked up the steps and through the front door, the smell of homemade tomato soup sweetened the air. Sophie asked him about Tammy.

'Is she coming back?'

'Probably not,' he replied without looking at her. He kicked off his shoes and went upstairs.

The soup sat on the stove until morning.

Seven

Mary couldn't remember the last time she had completed a crossword. When she had started it at nine o'clock that evening, 'deep chasm (5)' had taken her fifteen minutes to solve. It couldn't have been 'gorge', for the 'o' invalidated 'abdicate (6)', which she knew for certain to be 'abjure'. Finally, she had deduced it must have been 'abyss' and after that it had all been rather simple.

Word games had been her mother's passtime. As a child Mary had been repulsed by the pain of agonising over suffixes and synonyms, letters and lexical fields. Scrabble was by far the worst. But, now her mother was dead, she found herself drawn to the puzzle section of the newspaper more often than she would care to admit. When she was done with them, she would leave the newspapers at the house, on the coffee table in the sitting room, for the old man to read. Invariably, in the course of his consumption, he would complete her half-finished crosswords. *Not this one*, she thought with solemn satisfaction. Today she had made her mother proud.

Mary swivelled her chair and checked the cameras for B Building. Eight bodies tucked into eight beds. The occupant of bed five, a dark-skinned springer who often had trouble sleeping the night through, rolled over onto her side. Asleep, her right arm wandered until it found her enlarged abdomen. She cupped it and settled back to stillness.

A Building was almost as quiet. Camera two showed movement in the main room. The past two nights, Mary had watched the new heifer investigate the door. Tonight she was there again. In the dark, as the others slept on the bed nearby, she ran her fingers over every atom, pinching at the hinges, trying to force her fingernails under the metal, presumably searching for a weak point. This amused Mary. She leant forward on her chair and increased camera two's zoom. She watched the screen as the heifer continued to fiddle with the door. There was nothing to worry about: the room was entirely secure. On a panel on the wall beside Mary, there were override switches for every electronic lock on the homestead.

A crackle on the intercom made Mary jump.

'Hey, Mary, let me in.'

A red light came on when she pushed the receiver button. 'Christ, Frank,' she said. 'You scared me.' The voice on the intercom laughed. She clicked another button and the door to the room buzzed open.

Frank walked in and took the chair next to Mary's. His knees clicked as he sat. 'It's cold out,' he said, rubbing his hands. His skin was so dry that Mary could hear it grind together like fine sandpaper. Just slightly, so as to be imperceptible, she shifted her chair away from his.

'I thought you were giving up,' she said, nodding to the packet of cigarettes that had seemingly materialised in his hands. He took one and slipped the box into a pocket hidden by the oversized lapel of his coat.

'A night like this,' he said, the cigarette now bobbing up and down against the corner of his wrinkled mouth, 'a man needs a smoke.'

Mary tutted and turned back to the monitors. *Infant.* 'I'd rather you didn't do it in here.'

Frank grunted and lit it anyway. *Vile man,* Mary sneered as she tried to focus on the cameras rather than the smell of his tobacco and filth. In her peripheral vision, she saw him snuff the match out with his fingers.

'Robert down yet?' he asked as she continued to avoid looking at him.

'He said midnight,' she replied, her tone short and belittling. 'Is it midnight yet, Frank?'

Frank looked up at the digital clock on the wall. 11:49 p.m. He shook his head. Working with Mary was like holding acid with your bare hands — you'd never be able to neutralise it and you'd burn your skin off trying.

'Well, it's all set up for when he's ready.'

She ignored him and looked back at the cameras for A Building. The new heifer was still at the door. Mary's initial amusement was wearing off, the scene on the screen having become too pathetic for her taste.

Frank smoked his cigarette in silence waiting for the clock to change. At one minute past midnight, the intercom came to life. The light told Mary it had been activated from E Building.

'I'm here,' Robert said through the speaker.

Mary pressed the receiver. 'Is Alexander with you?'

'No—' static '—he's not feeling very well.'

She pressed the receiver again. 'Okay. Frank's with me. I'll send him over.'

Without turning to look at him, she shooed him away with her hand. The door clicked shut and he was gone. The intercom lit up again.

'Just bring her to us, Mary,' Robert continued. 'And try to keep her calm.'

Mary said she would and signed off. She wrapped a chunky red scarf, the same rusty shade as her hair, around her long neck and fastened the buttons of her coat. Taking care to secure the room as she left, she checked the main lock twice before tucking the key, which she wore as a pendant on a chain, in between the layers of her clothes.

Frank was right — it was cold outside. She had been in the homestead's central office — the Seat, as they called it — for hours. Sophie had brought her food and she had eaten it in front of the screens waiting for evening to change to night. It was imperative there were no disturbances that night. Seldom did they deviate from schedule. When they did, there was always a risk that something could go wrong.

Thick clouds suppressed the Moon as Mary cut across the lawn. The grass was wet and it soaked her socks. She scurried onto the path and brought her scarf up to cover her mouth. C Building's red sandstone facade was illuminated by a wall light which had been left on. She wafted her keycard in front of the reader by the door and slipped inside.

All of the habitation buildings on the homestead were warm. Mary loosened her scarf and coat. Her ancestors, in particular her great, great, great, *great* grandfather, had spent countless hours hypothesising, theorising and then eventually implementing various systems which were intended to optimise production and manage livestock in the most efficient way. Climate control was just one of these systems. Warmth engenders lethargy. *A sweaty swine is a stupid swine.* Increased temperature was also found to encourage intimacy — which is why some buildings on the homestead were warmer than others.

It was the third door on the left. The lights came on, her movement triggering the occupancy sensors in the corridor. Everything was white and clinical. *Calming.* Another product of her ancestor's genius.

She raised a clenched fist to the door and tapped twice, the first knock soft, the second a little stronger. 'Katie,' she said through the door, as gently as she was able. 'Are you awake? I'm coming in.' Without waiting, she turned the handle and entered.

Katie was asleep on the bed inside the room. Mary crouched beside where the woman's head lay against the pillow and placed a hand on her exposed shoulder. In a low voice, she called her name again. The woman began to stir. Her eyelids quivered, dislodging the stale crust of mucus that had formed in the corner of her eyes. Drowsy and slow, she at first looked at Mary without seeing, then, as her pupils constricted in the light that came into the room from the corridor, she started to panic, wondering why she was being woken and what Mary was doing beside her bed.

Katie twisted herself away from Mary's hand, which had until that moment still been on her shoulder. Creases convulsed across her forehead and around her eyes and mouth. The covers fell off the bed and onto the floor.

'Shhh — everything is alright. It's only me,' Mary placed her finger to her lips, steadying herself on the bed with her other hand. Katie relaxed.

'Mary?'

Mary nodded, girlish strands of red hair, escapees from the bun fixed against the crown of her head, curling against her cheeks. Katie was just about able to discern her familiar features in the half light.

'What are you—' Mary hushed and Katie lowered her voice. 'What are you doing here?'

Standing up, Mary replied in a whisper. 'I'm here to take you to your baby—'

'My baby!'

Mary hushed her again, this time more severely. Bolting upright on the bed, Katie clamped her hand over her mouth.

'I'm sorry,' she whispered, her eyes bulging with excitement.

Mary shook her head. 'It's okay — just keep quiet.'

She tiptoed to the open door and peered around the frame.

Looking up and down the corridor, she could feel Katie's eyes on her back and remembered to exaggerate her movements. *Head to the left, head to the right. Double check the left and turn around ever so carefully.* It was all a game to Mary. Feigning trepidation, she instructed Katie to follow her.

'To my boy?' Katie asked, her voice wavering above a whisper.

'Yes,' the other woman answered plainly. 'Just follow me and try to be quiet.'

Light-footed and brimming with childish ecstasy, Katie slipped off the bed and rushed to Mary's side. Leaving the door to the room open, the two women edged hand in hand down the corridor and outside into the night.

The pair stole along the path away from C Building. By the light of the veiled Moon, Mary led Katie onward, tugging at her hand, encouraging her into the trees that grazed the back wall of the building. Browns, oranges and reds bejewelled the ground, the woods having recently started its annual purge. These new leaves, not yet dry and brittle, fused with the humus of the previous year to create a spongy surface for the women to walk on. Katie wasn't wearing anything on her feet. Slimy brown leaves and wet chunks of half-decayed twigs stuck to her skin. The thought of her child, however, kept her warm and stabilised her as she almost lost her balance on a tree root that protruded unexpectedly from the soil. Mary tightened the grip on her hand and pulled her forward.

They could, of course, have simply followed the path. There would have been no cold feet or risk of falling. *But what's the fun in that?* Robert had instructed Mary to keep Katie calm. Instead, fuelled by the expectation of being reunited with her baby, Mary was giving her the time of her life.

If it was at all possible, given that it was already very dark, it got even darker the further into the trees the women walked. At her side, Mary could hear Katie panting. Her breath was ragged and laced with adrenaline. In the distance, a branch snapped. Mary yanked Katie close to her and commanded her to stop with a hiss.

Katie's head twisted about on her neck, uncertain as to whether to look left or right. Mary felt laughter bubbling in her belly.

'Wait,' Mary whispered, saturating the word with false apprehension. Katie stopped moving and held Mary's hand more tightly. When Mary announced it was safe to carry on, they continued moving through the trees.

Eventually, they emerged. In the distance, set slightly back where a natural depression had formed in the land, sat a wooden building. E Building. It looked like a barn and had a metal lean-to on its front side. Inside, the lights were on.

Robert had made sure his silhouette could not be seen through the window. Hearing footsteps outside, he shrank further back into his corner. Across the room, Frank was likewise concealed. He had complained the cold was affecting his joints, so had flipped an old tin bath they had once used for sticking upside down to sit on whilst they waited.

Mary's voice cut through the night air. They were close to the door. Robert silently shuffled his gait.

'In there,' he heard Mary say outside. He steadied his breathing. 'Your baby's in there.'

A single pair of feet on the concrete plinth in front of the door.

'Go on — everything's alright. He's waiting for you inside.'

Katie never did discover if her baby was waiting for her inside the strange wooden building to which Mary had taken her. As soon as she stepped through the door, a metal bolt the length of a toothbrush penetrated her skull. Her cerebrum was catastrophically damaged, the vital centres of her brain destroyed. Although still technically alive, nothing remained of Katie save for the mechanical movements of her organs.

Her occipital lobe — the part of her brain that was responsible for visual processing — having been thoroughly lanced by the bolt, meant she was unable to see the bolt gun in Robert's hand as he stood over her, checking her for signs of consciousness. Neither was she able to witness Mary, the young woman who she thought she could trust, enter the room and cast a disdainful eye down at her destroyed body. Her heart, although it continued to pump blood around her body, did not beat any faster when Frank clamped cold metal shackles around her ankles. The sensory receptors in her skin reported no pain as her arms impacted the floor, her body being hoisted up towards the ceiling.

Now upside down, Katie's white cotton smock turned inside out and fell across her face. Frank cut it off her with a knife. Kicking it to one side, he turned and flicked a switch on the wall next to him. Katie's naked body moved along the conveyor belt from which she hung. He flicked the switch again and the motor stopped. She swung back and forth on the chain for a moment, her body still absorbing the residual motion of the conveyor. When she was still, Frank checked she was in the right place and then stuck her. A sharp knife across the neck and the major blood vessels were severed.

Fortunately, Katie did not feel any of this. Her blood simply gushed out from her throat — a humane dispatch — some of it clotting in her hair on the way to the floor, the rest collecting in the large ceramic trough beneath her.

Eight

Food made everything better. For one, an adequately full belly cultivated a warm and soothing sensation unlike any other. Second — and perhaps most important — was the generous dose of sedative concealed within.

Samantha licked the back of the spoon and placed it and the empty bowl to one side. It had now been eight days since she had been brought to this place.

In the immediate aftermath she had wanted to smash the world and burn its leftover parts. That feeling had soon receded and was replaced by shame and self-hatred. She didn't deserve this, by God she didn't deserve this, but then again, she couldn't help but think that perhaps she did.

Maybe this is all my fault.

Her sins, however, regardless of how she added, subtracted and multiplied them, never seemed to quite match the weight of the ones that had been committed against her. Now, after experiencing them — *experiencing him* — over and over, on a daily, sometimes twice daily, occasion, all that remained was numbness.

Stupid and belittled people do not grumble. They do not defend themselves when they are invaded and they certainly do not complain about their shame to similarly violated people. They were all ants to be stepped on without consequence.

And so, the horror had become normal.

It was so normal, in fact, that it could be embraced. In the other room, Jade and Lee — which Samantha had come to learn was the name of her rapist — had been fornicating for hours.

Fucking. Consensual fucking.

Jade had been stretched out on the bed, groaning noisily, her legs held above her by Lee as he pounded into her, when the food had been delivered through the metal hatch in the wall, as it customarily was. Samantha had moved Jade's meal to the table for her to find after she was finished. When the steam above the bowl started to dissipate and Jade was still having her insides clobbered in the other room, Samantha had taken it and eaten it herself.

All that considered, Samantha couldn't say that Jade didn't suffer, only that in a room made up of fragments, each was held together in her own way.

Behind her, the toilet flushed. The door to the bathroom opened and out walked Evelyn. Without saying anything, she lightly touched Samantha's bare foot, encouraging her to move it off the sofa so she could sit beside her.

It had been three days before Evelyn had spoken to

Samantha. Understandably, their first meeting had been far from customary. Yet, the intimate act of one watching the other being raped — and before too long, vice versa — had certainly been a way to accelerate the growth of their friendship. Theirs was a camaraderie of the damned.

That first day, after Lee had finished with her, Jade had helped Samantha from the bed to the bathroom. Although there was no lock on the door to bar him, there seemed to be an unspoken understanding that the bathroom was the women's space. Naturally, Lee had regular cause to use the facilities, but asides from those short visits he left the room to the women, and so it was there that they had made some sort of refuge.

Samantha's body hadn't been her own. It had felt tainted, poisoned even. Evelyn — quietly summoned from the floor to the bathroom sanctuary by Jade — had washed Samantha, carefully drawing the sponge across her shivering skin as she lay crumpled in the bathtub. The dead-eyed woman had not said anything. Jade, by contrast, hands covered in suds as she washed Samantha's hair, had talked the entire time. She had told her about the way the leaves were changing colour and how she hadn't seen a butterfly fly past the window for many days. Childish things. Things that meant nothing and served no purpose other than an attempt at distraction.

The next morning, after Lee had serviced Evelyn, brutally dragging her off the sofa and onto the floor as she was sleeping, Samantha had returned the favour. Still, the dead-eyed woman had not said anything to her. Even her tears had fallen silently.

Jade had been the one to tell Samantha Evelyn's name.

'She hasn't adjusted,' she told Samantha as they ate together later that second day. 'Not everyone does.'

Samantha hadn't known what to say. Was she expected to *adjust*? And if so, what was it that she was supposed to adjust to? *What is this Hell?*

Eventually, she had asked, 'How long?'

At first Jade had been puzzled by the question. Her eyes moved to the right as she thought. 'Well, I think this will be her third.'

'Third?' Samantha had replied.

'Yes,' Jade had said. 'For a while our schedules were out of sync because her first was early. But we had our second — well, my third — within a week of each other.' Sensing Samantha was confused, Jade had stopped and asked, 'Will this be your first?'

'First?' Samantha had shaken her head. 'First what?'

Jade had laughed, not cruelly but in disbelief. 'Your first baby, of course!'

Once again, Samantha hadn't known what to say. The way Jade spoke made it all seem like a joke. *This isn't real*, she had told herself, but the pain she felt in between her legs every time Lee forced himself inside of her convinced her that it was.

On the sofa, Evelyn pointed to the empty bowls on the table in front of them. Samantha shrugged and arranged her legs underneath her so her smock covered most of them. 'It was getting cold.'

'She'll be hungry,' Evelyn said. Her features were mouse-like and her nose twitched when she spoke.

The groaning from the other room was steadily increasing in volume.

Samantha pulled her hair back behind her head and combed it through with her fingers. She wished she had a hair band — *or clip or hairbrush or pair of scissors* — to get her hair off her face. It was tangled and had started to hurt her scalp. By contrast, Evelyn looked relatively presentable, her black hair parted down the middle and drawn into two equal segments over her shoulders and down her front.

'Have you ever tried to, you know,' Samantha leant closer to the other woman before lowering her voice, 'get out?'

The two women's eyes locked for a second before Evelyn pulled away. This wasn't the first time Samantha had spoken of leaving.

On the wall behind her head was a print of a classical painting. The walls of both rooms, the main room with the bed and the smaller side room in which they now sat, were covered with erotic pictures and prints. Evelyn nodded to the artwork and asked Samantha if she knew what it was called. Samantha twisted her head and looked at the image. Imprisoned inside a thin wooden frame was a red-haired woman, naked except for the shackles that bound her wrists to a rock. Her breasts were round and sensual and her nipples erect, her other intimate area cleverly concealed by the angle of her stance. Waves lashed at her feet and some sort of sea monster lurked in the water below.

Samantha turned back to Evelyn and shook her head.

'Andromeda,' said Evelyn, her tone strangely serious. 'Have you ever heard the story?'

Samantha hadn't and so Evelyn explained.

'In Greek mythology Andromeda was made to suffer for her mother's vanity. She — the mother, the queen — thought she was more beautiful than Poseidon's sea nymphs. This was an insult to the gods, and so when he heard of the queen's arrogance he sent a sea monster to destroy—' Evelyn was interrupted by an especially loud and high-pitched squeal, 'to destroy the kingdom. The only way to stop it was for the king and queen to give their daughter to the beast, and so Andromeda was chained to a rock by the sea and left to die.'

'That's dark,' Samantha said.

'Yes,' Evelyn continued, 'but Andromeda was lucky. Perseus — surely you've heard of him?' Samantha had started fidgeting with her hair again and shrugged. 'Well, Perseus — the son of the king of the gods, Zeus — killed the monster and saved her.'

'So she survived?'

'Yes, she survived—'

'Wait, how do you know all this?' Samantha asked, her blue eyes bright and genuine.

Evelyn looked down at the floor. 'I used to do this,' she said. 'I used to work at an art gallery — nothing special, just a small, local place. I'd wanted to teach one day. I'd just started an online course when—' She trailed off. Her nose twitched and Samantha worried she might start crying. Through the wall, Jade and Lee's carnal panting was reaching a climax.

Now there's just eating, sleeping and fucking.

Samantha shuffled closer to Evelyn and placed a supportive hand on her knee. She looked up and swallowed her sorrow.

'Anyway, my point is, that's us. We're Andromeda,' Evelyn said. Samantha turned again to look at the painting. 'That's why it's on the wall — so we know. We're a sacrifice. Chained to a rock. And *he's* the monster. Lee.' Samantha turned back. Evelyn's eyes were wild now. 'And the doctor, Samantha, the doctor, he is Poseidon. Only, there's no saving us. Andromeda had Perseus. We're on our own.'

'So we're fucked,' Samantha whispered.

A long shriek of pleasure and Jade orgasmed in the other room.

'Yes,' Evelyn said solemnly, 'we're fucked.'

Nine

Today was different. Jade and Evelyn were unusually quiet and she hadn't seen *him* since yesterday evening.

She had fallen asleep on the bathroom floor, her arm cradling her skull, a barrier between her innermost thoughts and the sticky, presumably urine-encrusted, linoleum. When she woke her neck was bent and knotted in at least three different places. Moving to the main room, she realised it was just the three of them. Jade was napping on the crusty red armchair and Evelyn was on the bed, half-reading a book from the room's limited library of erotic fiction. The room, always too warm, was perfumed with sweat and desperation.

For breakfast the women were each given a plate of toast and runny-yolked fried eggs. This too was unusual, but Samantha had enjoyed the food all the same. They had eaten separately, Jade only speaking to offer Samantha her leftovers.

The tension in the air was undeniable and, after what must have been at least two weeks of captivity, Samantha couldn't quite believe that Lee would so easily be out of her life. Even so, he was gone and that meant ceasefire. For now, everyone's bodies were their own. She stood in front of the mirror picking food out from the gaps between her teeth.

She wanted to pretend everything was normal. At least once a day she stood in the bathroom and searched her reflection to see if she still recognised the person who looked back.

Increasingly, she felt more and more self-conscious, as if looking at herself in the mirror proved that she was conceited and thus deserving of her fate. *My fate.* She wondered if that were so, if she had somehow been destined to end up here — *destined to end up in this Hell.*

Her eyes looked a little less blue and her hair a little less blonde. Her roots had needed redying before she had been taken and she hated herself for noticing them now. She rubbed the circles under her eyes and worried she was fading away. *If there's anything fucking left to fade away*, she cursed at herself, thinking of all the time and money she had wasted trying to change who she was. Alterations and adjustments, attempts at transformations and transmutations, a life of Fresh Starts and News Years' Resolutions all meant nothing now.

In the mirror, Samantha saw Evelyn enter the bathroom. She perched on the edge of the bathtub and watched her. Samantha splashed cold water on her face, washing away bits of egg and the salt of last night's tears.

'They'll come in today,' Evelyn eventually said.

Samantha turned to face her. 'What'd you mean?'

'They'll come in here. The doctor. Most likely that sanctimonious redhead as well.'

'Mary?' Samantha hadn't seen or heard her since the first day.

'Yes,' Evelyn said, short and plain. 'Her.'

After ending up in this place, Samantha had actively nurtured a hatred of Mary, chewing the memories over and over in her mind, keeping the embers alive so that, when the opportunity presented itself, her revenge would be served hot and blistering. She hadn't forgotten how Mary had tricked her with the promise of being able to phone her dad. At night, she dreamt of her expressionless face when she *knew* what had been waiting for her beyond the door. *She didn't actually promise, you know. You shouldn't have been so fucking dumb to follow her.* Samantha cursed herself and then cursed Mary. Perhaps today was the day.

'I hope they're going to change the bed,' Samantha said. 'This place is rank.'

'Not until we're gone.' Evelyn replied. 'Which is why they'll be here. To see if we can go.' Samantha's face grew animated. Evelyn shook her head and the smile retreated. 'Not like that. They'll never let us go, Samantha, just onwards to the next circle of Hell.'

Samantha leant against the sink and sneered. 'As fantastic as that sounds, I'd rather not.'

'I doubt they're going to give you a choice.'

'Yeah, we'll see about that.' Samantha's eyes grew dark. Jade called them from the other room.

Samantha followed Evelyn out the bathroom. Jade was standing by the sofa holding three unlabelled foil sachets.

'These just came through the hatch.' She nodded to the small metal door in the wall through which their meals appeared.

'What are they?' Samantha asked, her voice hateful, her thoughts still on Mary. 'Packets of tomato ketchup or something?'

Neither of her companions laughed.

'They're our tickets out of here,' Jade replied. Her eyes, usually vivacious, were solemn. She handed one of the sachets to Evelyn. Once in her hand, she rushed back to the bathroom.

Samantha watched her go. 'Is she okay?' she asked Jade.

Jade simply held another of the sachets out to Samantha. 'It's a pregnancy test,' she said. 'You pass, you get out.'

When Samantha didn't immediately take it from her, Jade tossed the sachet on the sofa. 'Suit yourself,' she said as she followed Evelyn to the bathroom.

Samantha picked up the sachet and sat on the sofa. There was no writing on the outside, nothing to suggest it was a pregnancy test or otherwise. Pinching the top of the foil, she tore the sachet open and tipped the contents out into her lap. She discarded the little pouch of 'DO NOT EAT' silica and turned the other two items over in her palm. The test was smaller than she expected — a thin white plastic cassette with two windows, one for the urine sample and the other to show the result. There was also a small pipette, just about big enough to hold two or three drops of urine. *A few drops of piss and I'm out.*

A glass of the rancid vitamin drink they gave the women

had been left unfinished by the bed. She took it, the cassette and the pipette with her to the bathroom.

Asides from the sink and the bathtub, the bathroom had two toilet stalls. Whoever had designed their torture chamber had, at least, considered their dignity in regards to defecation if nothing else. The stall closest to the door was occupied, the other empty. Evelyn was already finished. Her test was lying on the floor. One knee on the linoleum, her dark hair tucked into the back of her smock, Evelyn genuflected before it and waited for it to develop.

Samantha tipped the remaining contents of the glass down the sink and entered the second cubicle. *It'll have to do*, she thought as she lowered the glass into the bowl of the toilet. Positioning herself above it, she remembered the first time she had forced herself to urinate for these people. *A fateful piss.* She wondered if this occasion would be so momentous.

Samantha hadn't considered what being pregnant might mean beyond leaving the rooms and Lee behind. The word — pregnant — had detached itself from its original meaning and, in her mind, had started to sound a lot like 'freedom' and 'it'll be over'. In reality, however, as she pipetted her urine from the glass onto the test, she knew not what waited for her on the other side. And, she certainly had no comprehension of what being pregnant actually meant. Although she hadn't been on the contraceptive pill for years, she demanded all her sexual partners wear condoms. When the occasional mistake did happen, she had always been able to erase it.

But this wasn't a mistake.

Beside her — for Samantha was now also on the bathroom floor — Evelyn was crying.

'Two lines,' she sobbed. 'It's two lines.'

Samantha looked from her test — the result window still blank — to Evelyn's. She was pregnant.

'I'm out of here,' Evelyn muttered between the tears. It was a sacred moment.

Within a couple of minutes, Samantha's test also showed two lines.

'Keep hold of it,' Evelyn instructed — her first words to Samantha after the result had appeared. 'You'll need to show it to them.' Samantha nodded and clasped the plastic cassette in her hands. *My ticket out of here*. Everything else was extraneous.

Jade, meanwhile, hadn't emerged from the cubicle. Realising this, the two women stood and edged towards the stall.

Evelyn knocked on the door and spoke softly. 'Are you alright, Jade?'

There was no response.

Evelyn asked again. After a moment, the toilet flushed and the handle on the door moved. When Jade came out, her face was streaked with tears. Unlike Evelyn, however, her expression was pained. There was no relief.

Evelyn reached out a hand in an attempt to offer some comfort. 'I'm so sorry, Jade,' she whispered. Jade pushed her away and moved to the sink. Samantha stepped out of her way.

'How many fucking times,' Jade snarled under her breath, just loud enough for the other two to hear. Her knuckles turned white as she gripped the rim of the sink. 'How many times did I let that animal fuck me?' The question was rhetorical. Neither Samantha nor Evelyn said anything.

Jade raked a hand through her hair, her breath quickening in the back of her throat. Suddenly, she pushed off from the sink and charged out of the bathroom. Evelyn stepped on Samantha's toes as she moved to avoid a collision. Cautious, side by side the two women followed.

Open palm to the metal, Jade banged on the food hatch. Her curly hair bounced about her shoulders in rhythm with each impact.

'I want another one,' she yelled at the hatch. 'There's something wrong with the test you gave me!'

Enraged, she rushed into the main room and started hitting the door there. Samantha and Evelyn followed her yet again.

'Hello! Can you hear me? I said there's something wrong with my test!'

She was attacking the door with both hands now. The dark skin of her palms had turned red. Next, she grabbed a book from the shelf and launched it at the camera above the door. Samantha went to calm her but Evelyn stopped her.

'Wait,' she whispered, her hand on Samantha's wrist.

Jade threw another book at the camera. It missed and ricocheted off the top of the door frame onto the floor.

'I want another test!' Beads of sweat were starting to form on her brow. She gnashed her teeth and screamed at the door. She was feral.

Samantha looked at Evelyn. 'Do you think they're watching?'

'Yes,' she nodded. 'They're always watching.'

Another book at the camera and the red light was emasculated. Samantha cheered. There were no words coming from Jade now, only rage. Evelyn watched silently, eyes sharp and expectant.

All three of them heard the door to the outside click. Someone stepped into the hallway that separated their rooms from the rest of the building. Shoulders hunched and muscles braced for conflict, Jade backed away from the door. Samantha mirrored her movements. *This is it*, she thought, *I've got to get out of here.*

The door to the room didn't open. Instead a voice called to them from the other side. It was Robert.

'Jade,' he said, his voice mellow and slow. 'I want to help you, Jade, but first you need to calm down.'

Samantha saw Jade's eyes flash. She laughed. *No chance.*

'You should have eaten your breakfast, Jade,' Robert continued. 'You wouldn't be feeling like this if you had. It's all for your benefit.'

Even Evelyn had to laugh now.

Samantha heard Robert sigh on the other side of the door. She wondered if he was secretly enjoying this — the drama of it all — or if it was an annoyance. An inconvenient and mildly irritating side effect of his depraved occupation. *Is this what this is to you, doctor? Is this your job?*

'Give me another test, Robert,' Jade said through clenched teeth. She and Samantha were standing shoulder to shoulder now. Evelyn had moved to sit on the bed.

On the other side of the door, Robert considered and then said, 'Yes. We can do that.'

They heard the external door click again. Minutes later, the hatch in the other room opened. Jade rushed to it and snatched the foil sachet that had been pushed through. She closed the door to the bathroom behind her.

Silence dominated the rooms as Samantha and Evelyn sat on the bed waiting for Jade to squeeze some urine from her empty bladder. Samantha stared at the blind camera above the door, aware that a second one was watching her from the opposite corner of the room. She knew Mary's eyes were on her — looking at her through the camera's lens. She could *feel* her. Heart racing in her chest, Samantha imagined removing the red-headed woman's eyes with a piece of rusty metal.

Jade's second outburst was even more impressive than the first. Samantha's forgotten glass of urine was the first thing to be thrown at the wall. The seat of the toilet was next.

From the bed, Samantha marvelled at Jade's strength, having previously never questioned whether or not she was able to rip something — so deftly — off its hinges. It would be inaccurate to describe her slender arms as muscular, but, there she was, tearing objects from the floors and walls of the room and lifting them above her head. *She hasn't adjusted*, Samantha remembered Jade saying of Evelyn. *Not everyone does.*

Robert was as calm and soft spoken as usual. No doubt wary of coming into the room, he once again stood in the hallway and spoke through the door.

'I'm disappointed, Jade,' he said. Evelyn raised her eyebrows at Samantha. 'This sort of behaviour is beneath you.'

Jade cracked a picture frame across her knee, splintering it clean in two. Shards of glass littered the red carpet. Samantha realised for the first time that it was the colour of blood.

'Since you won't calm down,' he continued, firm yet gentle, 'you leave me with no choice.'

Evelyn jumped up from the bed. 'Wait, doctor!' She hurried to the door. 'Robert, what about us?'

'I'm sorry, Evelyn,' he sighed from the other side.

Now she was hammering on the door, eyes as crazed as Jade's. It was too late — he was already gone. Samantha hurried to Evelyn and prised her hands off the door. 'What's wrong?' she demanded, holding her by the wrists, 'What's he sorry for, Evelyn?'

'This has happened before,' she stuttered, nose twitching and eyes wide. 'He's done this before.'

Jade was screaming at the ceiling.

'Lie down,' Evelyn commanded Samantha. 'Back to the bed.'

'What—'

'Now!'

Underneath Jade's screaming, Samantha realised there was another sound in the room. A new sound. *Flat tyres and inflatable paddling pools.* A faint hissing was coming from the air vents.

Evelyn was standing in front of Jade, trying to grab hold of her. She wriggled and screamed, tears cascading down her cheeks. 'Jade,' Evelyn shouted, 'you need to lie down!' It was no use — she was indomitable.

The gas continued to pour into the room. On the bed, Samantha was also crying. *What is happening, what is happening?*

Evelyn's arms were clamped around Jade's body now. They looked like quarrelling lovers, locked in an embrace to the death. Struggling, screeching, the one tried to drag the other to the bed. A burst of strength and Jade threw Evelyn off and onto the floor. Acknowledging a lost cause, she crawled up onto the bed.

Samantha's brain felt like cotton wool and the room tasted of candyfloss. Even lying on the bed, she felt dizzy. Next to her, Evelyn was squeezing a pillow to her chest, giggling. Samantha saw her and started to laugh too. She felt light and tingly and sleepy.

Jade's back was to the window when she collapsed. Her head thumped against the end of the bed on her way to the floor. Crumpled on the carpet, she never saw the butterfly that went past the window. Solitary and free, it flew into the Sun.

Ten

The wind collapsed and with it the girls' kite. Aurélie squealed down the hill after it as it tumbled from the sky. Above her on the grassy verge, Guinevere began winding in its line.

Alexander sat on a wall and watched his sisters play. Earlier, Guinevere had asked him to join them. He had helped them launch the kite — throwing the red diamond-shaped sail into a gust of wind as it ripped across the crest of the hill — but after its first crash his heart hadn't been in it anymore.

He hadn't spoken to Tammy since he had left her at the train station two weeks ago. *Two weeks and one day.* He had anticipated some sort of contact — a phone call, an email, a text message — and found himself unexpectedly hurt that she had cut him off so thoroughly. Late at night, when he slumped against his bedroom wall, half leaning out the open window, puffing smoke into the stars, he wondered if he should have made more of an effort to fix things. Then the cannabis took over and the thought was disarmed.

Now, sitting on the wall, his brain hurt.

Watching his sisters run and laugh and skip, it was easy to forget that they were not a normal family. Families in the books he had read as a child didn't keep the sorts of secrets his kept. They didn't segment themselves off from the outside world like incontrovertible hermits, only making the climb down from their Mount Olympus to reap and rob, returning richer and yet somehow ever more encumbered than before. Nobler, laughing, self-satisfied, supping on ambrosia.

Is that what I am? Am I one of them?

Alexander thought of how his father looked at him since he had come back from university. Not his open looks, but his hidden ones. Those sideways glances he sometimes glimpsed when Robert thought his son wasn't looking. *He worries I'm not like him — not one of them.* Maybe he should have made the effort. Maybe he should have got on the train with her.

He needed a hit.

The Sun sat high in the sky as Alexander walked the path down the hill and into the trees.

Autumn was undoing the success of summer, change all the rage and death cheap, branches casting off leaves like they were useless, troublesome things. A step and a snail's shell crunched underfoot. He felt a pang of guilt.

The back wall of the Seat bled into the woods that snaked across much of the homestead. Alexander leant against the damp, moss-covered stones of its wall and pulled his phone from his pocket. He quickly sent a text message then slumped down the wall and onto the wet ground.

He had taken the tobacco pipe from his grandfather's house. Robert Senior lived in a small cottage behind the main house on the homestead. The red stone building had once been a pigsty — back when the family used to keep pigs all those years before — and Alexander found it amusing that his boorish old grandpa lived amongst the ghosts of swine. *He won't miss it*, Alexander rationalised as he stuffed the old pipe with cannabis. It had an amber stem and a silver band hallmarked to 1872. If anyone were to have asked, Alexander would have said he acquired it from a friend of a friend — the same as the drugs.

When Mary found him he was high. She had read his text almost as soon as he had sent it, but had ignored his request for fifteen minutes on principle. As much as she desired Alexander, she refused to be anyone's chattel.

His breath smelled sickly sweet as he glided over her skin. She hated the stench of his habit but allowed it for fear that it was the only thing that bound him to her. Despite having grown up together, constantly in each other's sight, Alexander had never looked at her twice. For many years, he had had trouble even considering her a friend, let alone a potential mate. That had all changed two weeks ago. The first time he had made love to her she had cried tears of joy.

It had happened in her bed. A quiet knock on her bedroom door followed by an unexpected conversation. She had been in her pyjamas, her hair loose about her shoulders. Sitting on the bed across the room from where he stood, she had felt somewhere between uncomfortable and thrilled. He had never seen her like that before, and, after a few softly spoken minutes, he made it clear he would very much like to see more. Of course, he had been surprised when he spotted the blood on the bed sheets afterwards. He hadn't stopped to realise until it was too late. For her, it didn't matter — if he had asked, she would have given herself to him years ago.

Now, she let him take out his frustration on her. Mary hoped that by being a vessel for his crisis she would eventually transcend to something else, until he found himself unable to exist without her by his side. It was, after all, what everyone had hoped for them from the start. *We are meant to be*, she thought as he pushed himself deeper inside of her. Lying on a bed of leaves, tears glistening in her eyes, she stroked his stubbled cheek as he poured himself into her.

She stayed on the ground with him after he had finished with her. They lay apart, their outstretched arms bridging the void between them. She hoped that by him holding her hand afterwards, it signalled that his feelings for her extended beyond simple lust. *Such emotions are for the animals*, and she and Alexander had been born better than that.

His eyes were closed when he eventually spoke. 'Do you ever think you'll leave?' His voice was soft and slow.

'I'm going to stay with my father after my birthday,' she replied as she watched the leaves swirling in the air above them.

'No, not like that,' Alexander said. '*Leave*. As in for good.'

Mary rolled onto her side to look at him. She wondered what he was asking her — *does he want me to leave*? After a moment's consideration, she said, 'This place is as much my home as it is yours. Where else would I go?'

Alexander was silent, his eyes still closed. A yellow leaf landed on his chest. Without moving, he said, 'I want to be free.' Then, he started giggling. His chest shook as he rolled about on the ground, his eyes squeezed shut, his mouth capturing lungfuls of air to feed the laughter. Mary started to laugh as well, first out of awkwardness and then because she was happy. Even though he was with her like this, he was still with her.

'Have you ever seen the trees, Mary,' Alexander said through the laughter. 'Have you ever looked at them — really *looked* at them?' Laughing, she shook her head. Still holding her hand, he pulled her closer to him and, with his other hand, gently tilted her chin up. They were now cheek to cheek.

'They're like us,' he whispered into her ear, pausing to nibble her ear lobe, 'rooted into the place they were born.' Another leaf fell onto them, this time settling on Mary's hair. 'They would die if they were moved,' Alexander continued, still holding her chin. 'Do you think if we moved we'd die just the same?'

Mary didn't know what to say and was about to murmur some sort of reply when her phone rang. Alexander released her and she pulled it from her coat, which lay, where it had been thrown, on the ground next to them.

'It's your father,' she stated, looking at the screen. 'I've been missed.'

Alexander playfully reached for her ankle as she stood up. Flicking the leaves out of her hair and off her clothes, Mary pulled up her tights. 'You should probably—' she looked down at him, his eyes wide and hair a mess, 'clean yourself up a bit, too.'

She left him where she had found him, lying on the ground amongst the leaves and the trees. He seemed to have no intention of moving and so she covered him with her coat before walking away. 'You can give it back to me later,' she whispered as she tucked it around his shoulders. Alexander didn't say anything, his eyes already too busy as he raced through time and space, the Devil loose inside his head.

Eleven

Sweat had built up between the leather strap and her forehead. She would have reached up to try to wipe it away, but her wrists were likewise strapped, which, along with her ankles, bound her so very completely to the examination couch she found herself on.

Samantha had no recollection of being moved. She could only assume that someone had relocated her whilst she was unconscious. Tied to the couch, watching Robert move about the room he had first examined her in, she hated him and every other godforsaken soul who perpetuated the place she had come to regard as Hell. If given the chance, she would kill them all.

Robert had surprised her when he had apologised.

'No one really likes the covering period,' he had said as he had drawn blood from a vein in her arm. 'But, you can rest assured that it'll be a good little while before you have to see Lee again—' Robert had caught himself and sighed. 'Ah, what am I saying, I shouldn't imagine you'll ever have to see him again.'

Samantha had said nothing. Her usually sharp tongue had been blunted, this time not by the drugs they tricked her into consuming but by the strength of her hatred for the man who pranced around in a white coat playing doctor. *It's what he wants*, she had thought, biting her lip as the leather strap bit into the skin of her forehead. *Why give him another thing to jerk off to?*

He had taken her blood and left her alone to stare at the ceiling tiles.

Samantha had no way of knowing what had happened to Evelyn and Jade. All she could do was hope they were safe. Her friend Martha — *will I ever see her again?* — had half-heartedly believed in the power of manifestation. The ability to shape reality simply by believing something is true. Stolen, imprisoned, raped and impregnated by people she had never met before, the power of her own consciousness was the only tool Samantha had left.

When Robert had returned he had been humming. Samantha had instinctively wondered what there was to be happy about, but then realised that, for Robert, there was every reason. He was living a life unrestrained by the rules everyone else was expected to follow; he could do whatever he wanted and take whatever he pleased. *He is Poseidon.* She remembered Evelyn — sweet, mouse-eyed, damaged, *unadjusted* Evelyn — and wanted to cry. *Just another thing*, she gulped down a sob, *just another thing for him to jerk off to.*

Of course, life was not so simple for Robert. The sight of an outsider, especially one as imperceptive as Samantha, was rarely ever so clear. As much as Robert considered himself to be blessed — blessed to have Sophie for a wife, blessed to have three beautiful children, and blessed to be in good health — he was troubled.

'It's happy news,' he smiled at Samantha. 'You are indeed with child.' She didn't smile back and he had no expectation that she would. *They are always so ungrateful,* he thought, still smiling outwardly.

'I will need to examine you further,' he continued, moving to the desk, 'to check you're healthy and ready to carry this baby.' From one of the drawers he pulled out a pair of latex gloves.

Robert thought about how Alexander was slipping away from him. *Slipping into a man very different from the one I had expected he would become.* After so many months of separation, he was saddened to see Alexander withdraw from his company, apathetic to his work and all too eager to hurry off and spend time alone. Robert had hoped that his son would return with a fervour, enthusiastic and ready to learn more about the position he would one day inherit. *And now I am slipping into my father!* He shook his head as he lifted Samantha's smock to above her knees. She tried to wriggle away from him, but the straps around her ankles, which creaked as she squirmed, held her legs in place.

'Please hold still,' he said, assertive yet gentle. 'I don't want to hurt you.'

A laugh. 'Yeah, because you wouldn't want to do *that.*'

Looking up the length of her body, Robert could see that

Samantha was snarling. Self-control, it seemed, was only able to withstand so much. Flaming and acidic, her eyes looked hot despite their cool colour. It was an expression Robert had seen many times — too many times — before. He stood up straight and moved away.

Why do they never accept their fate? Accept what they were born to be.

Robert sat on the stool in front of the desk and swivelled round to face her. 'Samantha,' he drew out the syllables of her name and softened the sounds to make them more pleasing, 'I want you to live a life with no pressures — no anything.' He paused to see if she would respond before continuing. 'Your food, your shelter, your health, all taken care of.'

'You call this being taken care of?' Samantha spat from the examination couch. She was angry and believed she had every right to be, *but she is wrong.*

Robert wheeled the stool closer to her, his breath warm on the side of her face. Strapped in place as she was, she was unable to turn her head to meet his gaze.

'What else could you want?' he asked softly.

Samantha scoffed, the spittle that gathered in the corners of her mouth a visible sign of her contempt and disbelief. 'How about my freedom!'

Now it was his turn to laugh. 'You believe that you were free before?' The stool squeaked as Robert leant back. 'Tell me, Samantha, how do you define freedom?'

Surprisingly, there was not a hint of condescension in his tone. Rather, he was genuinely curious. Robert, like his son, was a man of contemplation. Whereas his father was a blunt instrument, only ever concerned with the end and never the means, he and Alexander were more refined in their processes. *Only through learning*, he told himself, *can we achieve betterment.* It was something that his ancestors had believed so thoroughly that they had designed their whole lives — and in turn the lives of their descendants — to be one great experiment. *Learning in motion. Application and not supposition.*

'Not this,' Samantha hissed. 'It's to make your own choices. Not be kidnapped by some perv and his fucking family, tricked and drugged by his wife and daughter, taken to —'

'Daughter?' Robert interrupted, concerned as to how she knew of Guinevere or Aurélie.

Samantha's face turned red as she strained against the head strap. 'That ginger bitch,' she snarled.

'Ah, Mary,' he said, relieved. 'A good point, actually, Samantha. Where is she?'

Robert crossed the room, leaving Samantha on the couch fuming and gnashing her teeth, her rant smitten from existence. He went to a tall chest of office drawers and unlocked the top drawer. Inside, there was a small black box, a wire running from it to the back of the drawer, then out and away to some unseen connection. He pushed a button on the box and a red light illuminated.

'Mary,' Robert said into the intercom. 'Are you there?'

The crackle of static was the only reply. He buzzed the Seat again and waited, but nothing.

'I'll try her phone,' he said to himself as he pulled an

old, silver flip phone from the drawer. He dialled but no one answered. Behind him, Samantha had gone quiet. 'I shan't be a moment,' he said, glancing over his shoulder. She continued to stare at the ceiling tiles.

Running his fingers through his hair, he waited a few seconds before calling again. This time, she picked up.

'I know, I'm sorry,' Mary said, the sound of birds in the background. 'I'm on my way.'

Robert didn't say anything and hung up. Closing the phone and slipping it into his pocket, he moved back to the examination couch. 'Now,' he said, beaming, 'where were we?'

Her cervix, the lowest part of her uterus, was already softer than it had been when he last examined her. *Speedy work*, he mused, ever impressed by Lee's virility. In many ways he had been the most valuable asset on the homestead when Robert had inherited it from his father twelve years earlier.

'Everything looks and feels as it should,' Robert concluded, gently removing his fingers from Samantha's vagina. 'And you haven't had any spotting?'

'No.'

'And how do you feel? Any nausea?'

'No.

'That's good,' he said as he removed his gloves. 'Although it may still be too early. Any breast tenderness?'

'No.'

'Problems urinating?'

'No.'

'Well then,' Robert stood and stretched his legs, 'you're on track to have a perfectly healthy pregnancy. I will, of course, check on you throughout, and you must let me know if you experience any problems.'

Robert deposited the gloves in the bin by the desk and then went to the bathroom to wash his hands. When he returned, he saw Samantha had tears in her eyes. He moved to stand over her. Softly, he placed a hand on her cheek and hushed her. 'A great, easy life,' he whispered as his thumb stroked her skin. 'No responsibilities. No consequences. Everything taken care of.' A single tear rolled down her cheek and dropped from her chin onto her chest. Tenderly, he hushed her again and said, 'How is that such a great price?' *There is no use in fighting.*

A knock on the door and Mary entered the room.

'I'm sorry, Robert,' she apologised, visibly flustered as she smoothed her skirt. He removed his hand from Samantha's cheek and waved her off.

'It's of no consequence,' he said. 'Samantha here is finished and impatient to meet the others. I'm sure she can manage by herself,' he looked down at her and smiled, 'but perhaps you would like to take her there all the same?'

Cheeks still flushed from the outside, Mary nodded. She walked to the examination couch, the key to the Seat swinging on the chain around her neck, and nudged the brakes off the wheels with her shoe.

'Oh no,' Robert said, 'I think Samantha would like to walk by herself.' Effortlessly, the action having been much practised, he loosened the strap that bound her forehead. 'That won't be a problem — will it, Samantha?'

She shook her head, the flames in her eyes extinguished.

'Samantha understands that we are going to look after her,' Robert continued, moving to undo the other straps. 'And that you are going to take her to the best place for her.'

'Of course,' Mary said, looking at the other woman and attempting to imitate Robert's buoyancy.

Now free, Samantha sat up and swung her legs over the edge of the couch. She rubbed her wrists where the straps had been. The chains may have been slackened, but she knew she was still bound.

'I think you will like it, no—' Robert chuckled. 'I *know* you will like it. We even have television.'

Samantha didn't say anything. It was simply of no use.

'Go on, Mary will take you there.'

Hands on hips, Robert watched them leave the room. Samantha first, Mary just behind. As she turned the corner, he called to her, 'You have something in your hair, Mary.' With a finger he signalled and she reached behind her head. A single yellow leaf.

'Thank you,' she blushed, before exiting with Samantha.

Twelve

Samantha's aunt had been a cruel woman. Although now dead for five years, the influence that she had exerted over her brother's daughter's early years had been unrivalled. She had, after all, been one of the few female figures of Samantha's childhood, a position that she had embraced so absolutely that her hug had transformed into a stranglehold. With no children of her own, and no husband or boyfriend to command, she had dominated her useless brother and his motherless child.

As a girl, Samantha had always wondered where her grandparents had got the name Corinthia from. It was unusual for anyone in her family to have such a name, especially considering these were the same people who had named her dad Brian, but that was her aunt's name all the same. As such, Corinthia wore her name as a badge of honour, a badge that explicitly stated she knew better than everyone else, and was allowed — no, *obligated* — to inform them of their inadequacies.

Lazy was a word invented solely to describe Samantha's intolerable predisposition — or so aunt Corinthia used to tell her. Storming through the front door every Saturday, arms laden with shopping bags, she would rail at her niece as she lay stretched out on the sofa in her pyjamas. *It's two o'clock, for heaven's sake*, Corinthia would scream, slamming the bags on the kitchen floor beside the fridge. *How can you be so lazy, Samantha!* She had always been like that — angry about something and everything.

Of course, she had been correct. Samantha *was* lazy. Just perhaps not as lazy as her aunt accused her of being. Takeaway pizzas and back-to-back episodes of reality television shows were staples of Samantha's teenage years. Rarely did she spend time outdoors other than to travel the distance between the house, the passenger door of the car, school, then back to the car. Exercise was anathema. It was a thing that other people did. Something to maintain or even improve your health. Something you did if you cared about looking after yourself. And Samantha rarely felt the need to do that. It was easier to eat crisps and watch television. And besides, the more Corinthia screamed at her, the more her mind and ears closed off to other possibilities.

All of this was not to say that Samantha was overweight. She wasn't. In fact, Samantha had — to her aunt's persistent irritation — a remarkable ability to remain slender, despite all her neglect and laziness. Her dad always pulled out the deep fat fryer on Saturdays, even though that *simply isn't a fair or responsible thing to do as a father.*

I can still take her though, Samantha thought as Mary passed her in the corridor. *She's about my age. She's only a bit taller than me. She doesn't look any stronger.* Mary reminded Samantha of her aunt. *She thinks she's better than me*, and Samantha felt certain that the slight, smug, red-headed woman who she blamed for all that had been done to her wasn't.

Even so, she knew she had to wait for the right moment. They were still inside the building and there was simply no way she was getting out on a whim. If she was going to run, she had to have at least a vague idea as to where she was running. Leaving Robert's office, she knew that the room she had first woken up in all those weeks before was somewhere to the left. They had drugged her that day, but she still recognised the basic white floor tiles, charmless white walls and hateful lighting. All this meant that, somewhere close by, there was a door to the outside.

When she saw it, she hesitated. She had dreamt of escaping for weeks. At night, as Jade and Lee had slept together on the bed, and Evelyn lay passed out on the sofa in the other room, Samantha had poked and picked at every crack she came across. If she could have found a hole, she would have made it bigger. If a screw had been loose, she would have loosened it some more. But there had never been an opportunity. The chains had always been so tight — until now. *He undid the straps,* she thought, *why would he do that?* And now she could see that thick, metal door — a door she knew led to the outside.

It took a lot of courage to elbow Mary to the side and run to that door, courage which, until that very moment, Samantha had doubted she was capable of mustering. *I am not lazy*, she screamed inside as her bare feet slapped against the tiles.

I can do things for myself. Her hair, thick and tangled, billowed behind her like a cape. She was a superhero. First, she would free herself and then come back for the others. She imagined going to the police, crying at the station as she told them about all the abuse she had suffered. She imagined Robert being led away in handcuffs and Mary being stuffed into a police car. *Watch your head, miss,* the kindly officer would say as he guided her, hands bound, into the back of his car.

As she locked her fingers around the door's cold, metal handle, she thought of her dad, of all the worrying he must have done, of all the horrible, dark thoughts he must have suffered in the weeks since his only child's sudden disappearance. *Does he think I'm dead?* If she could take back all the things she had said to him in the past, she would have. Thinking of the pain he must have been feeling was almost worse than the pain she had herself endured.

She was certain she felt the handle give under her weight. But then she felt something else, a tightness around her waist whose suddenness winded her. Coughing to catch her breath, Samantha felt the door slip from her grasp.

She lost her balance as she was yanked backwards. Flailing, Samantha tried to steady herself on the walls of the corridor as she was twisted through the air. Mary's elbow struck her cheek and sent her to the floor. It was more the shock than the pain which stunned her. Before she was able to react, Mary kicked Samantha onto her side, moving her back away from the wall with her shoe as though she were a scrap of rubbish on the floor. Mary said nothing, her eyes empty and expressionless.

Samantha tried to fight as Mary grabbed her from behind and locked her arms around her chest, but the other woman's strength was incredible, her grip so constricting that Samantha winced as she was dragged upright, Mary's clenched fists digging into her collar bone. On her back, she felt a sharpness as the key that Mary wore ragged the gaps between her ribs. Their heads were pressed together, Mary breathing down her neck and into her ear. Her curly hair merged with Samantha's, and it smelt like apples and cinnamon as it tickled her nose.

Mary dragged Samantha down the corridor. Wriggling and writhing, screaming and shouting, her bottom slid on the tiles all the way back to where she had instigated her futile attempt at escape. Robert had left his office and was now standing with his arms folded across his chest in the middle of the corridor. He watched on as Mary retrieved his patient, not saying anything until Samantha was crumpled at his feet.

'I gave you the chance to cooperate, Samantha,' he said, almost too quiet to hear. 'I gave you freedom — the ability to make your own choice. And you made yours.'

Samantha tried to lunge for his leg, but Mary yanked her back, crushing her chest even more and pulling the collar of her smock up against her throat.

'The sting on your cheek,' Robert continued unfazed, 'is a consequence of your freedom. Surely it is better to live a life without consequence? A life without freedom?'

'You're a monster!' Samantha screamed at him, her blue eyes bulging.

Robert simply shook his head. 'No, Samantha — you are.

It is you who is threatening the wellbeing of an unborn child. Upsetting yourself and trying to fight. I only want what's best for you — best for you both.' He paused then looked from Samantha to Mary. 'Do you need help?'

Mary shook her head. 'No, I'm okay.'

Mary tensed her muscles and began dragging her captive once again. She didn't say anything, but Samantha screamed and kicked all the way to their destination. This door was new and behind it was a new life for Samantha. A life without consequence. A life without freedom.

Thirteen

Savory, marjoram, rosemary, thyme and oregano. These were the smells of Sophie's childhood.

In a small bowl, she mixed the herbs with flour and wholegrain Dijon mustard. A roasting tray of melted lard, pulled by Sophie's gloved hand from the top oven of the range, completed the mix. She placed the joint in the hot tray then brushed the herb and mustard mixture onto it. A whistle and it was in the oven. The heat immediately began blistering the joint, melding the herbs and mustard grains to its thick rind of white fat. In an hour and a half, it would be roasted to perfection.

It had been her mother, Aurélie, who had taught Sophie how to cook. Or rather, how to cook well. *Anyone can cook*, Sophie smiled, thinking of her fair-haired mother as she fastened the lid on the jar of mustard, *but not everyone can cook well.*

Sophie's mother had grown up in France. Under the tutelage of her elderly Provençal *mémé*, Aurélie had learned how to pick wild summer savory — *wait for the morning dew to dry, mon chou* — and how best to slice aubergines for ratatouille. *Les herbes de Provence* were not pre-prepared mixtures sold by supermarkets in little glass bottles, but were picked by hand, used individually and with discernment, or blended together, selected for flavour and purpose. All of this Aurélie taught her daughter and hoped one day, like her own *mémé* had, to teach her granddaughters.

A minor chest infection that went badly wrong had been all it took to separate Sophie from her mother. Eleven dreadful days and it had been over. In the third trimester of her third pregnancy, swollen-ankled and uncomfortable being more than a short walk away from a bathroom, Sophie had returned to her parents' homestead to attend her mother's funeral. The weeping ash trees that lined the driveway had quivered and wailed in the wind as they had driven up to the house. They too, it had seemed, were in mourning. The night before the burial, she had sobbed on her childhood bed, fidgeting and unable to rest under the weight of her ballooning womb. Robert had held her, as he always had, only this time his wife was inconsolable. *Family.* Family meant everything to Sophie and now her mother wouldn't be around to see theirs grow.

Two months later she had gone into labour. Eight hours and Sophie had held a new daughter in her arms. Although she was gladdened by the birth of her third child, she couldn't help but cry, the pain of losing her mother more acute than ever before. Once again Robert held his wife. Naming their daughter after Sophie's mother had been his idea.

With a swoop of her hand, Sophie released the ties of her

apron and draped it over the back of a chair. She pulled the door to the kitchen closed and crossed the hallway to the sitting room.

'What's wrong, my strawberry?'

Alexander lay on the sofa, feet up, arms crossed over his chest, an open book balancing across his eyes and brow. He lifted the corner of it and peeked out, eyes squinting, at his mother.

'Reading,' he said before letting the book drop back over his eyes.

Sophie perched on the large, dark green velvet pouffe that jutted against the sofa and squeezed her son's leg. 'You know you can talk to me about it,' she said. 'It might help.'

He sighed deeply and the book slipped and fell to the floor. Its aged spine rested against Sophie's foot. 'My head,' Alexander said quietly. 'I just can't shake it.'

'Still?' Sophie asked, raising a hand to her son's forehead. It was warm, but no warmer than usual. Eyes closed to keep the light away, he simply nodded.

Truth be told, Alexander had had the same headache for days. As it was, he didn't know if it was a side-effect of the drugs or a side-effect of everything else. Aurélie ran into the room screaming and he covered his head with a pillow, biting the velvet so hard that it made his teeth feel fuzzy. He heard Sophie hush his little sister and the screaming subsided to giggles.

'She's chasing me!'

Now Guinevere ran into the sitting room. Alexander bit down on the pillow harder.

The girls were squabbling. Aurélie had taken and hidden something of her sister's, and — although she found it amusing — hadn't anticipated Guinevere's wrathful disapproval. The older girl had chased the younger down the stairs threatening to 'feed her to the swine'. Light-hearted Aurélie had been both thrilled and terrified.

'Guinevere,' her mother reprimanded, 'leave your sister be.'

Guinevere pouted crossly. Sophie stood up and led Aurélie out the room. 'Come now,' she said gently. 'Show me where you've hidden it.' The staircase creaked as they went upstairs.

When Alexander didn't move his legs, Guinevere sat on top of them. He moaned at her to get off. 'Mummy says you don't want to go back to school,' she said, ignoring his protestation. 'Does that mean you're staying here with us?'

Alexander discarded the pillow and shuffled to be more upright. With hopeful eyes, Guinevere looked at him from the other end of the sofa. She had never wanted him to leave and, at such a tender age, had never understood why he had to.

'I don't know what I'm doing, Guinny.'

Guinevere's brow furrowed. 'But Mummy says you told her you're staying,' she responded crossly.

'Well, sometimes we say things we don't mean.'

Alexander pulled his feet from under his sister and turned to sit up more properly.

Absentmindedly, he began twisting a coarse strand of beard hair between his finger and thumb. *To be thirteen years old again.* He sighed. Even as a thirteen year old he had been over serious and sedate. *The lie of innocence.* Alexander hadn't shaved for weeks.

Sophie reentered the room just as Guinevere left, tears forming in the corners of her eyes.

'Just leave her,' Alexander said from the sofa. 'She's got to grow up someday.'

Sophie pursed her lips. 'She admires you very much,' she said.

A pause. 'I don't know why.'

It was not self-pity, but rather genuine despair. Sophie perched on the arm of the sofa and rested her head on top of her son's. His frame softened at her touch. 'You're her brother,' she replied, smiling as she stroked his unshaven cheek. 'It's your job to be admired.'

Alexander held his mother's hand, smoothing his thumb over her wedding band. His parents' love for each other had made him — he was a product of their partnership.

'I know it's difficult,' Sophie soothed. 'The expectations. We've all grown up with them. Your father and I.'

Alexander carefully unravelled himself from Sophie's embrace so as to face her. 'With Grandpa that's easy to imagine, but you—'

He trailed off, waiting for his mother to step in and carry the conversation. Sophie straightened her back and smoothed the creases in her trousers.

'You wonder how I could have had such expectations,'

she smirked playfully. Alexander's eyes dropped to his lap. 'A woman,' she continued, 'and not of the Founders.'

'I didn't mean—'

She hushed him and laughed. 'It's quite alright.'

It had been years since Sophie had spoken about her childhood. Before, when Alexander was younger, it had all been days wasted searching for fox dens and birds nests with her brother, mushroom foraging and secret sunset picnics. Precisely the sorts of enchanting adventures that are lived solely for the purpose of sharing the stories with children once the memories had all but faded away. Such an upbringing was without expectations, he had assumed. Sophie's father, on the few occasions Alexander could recall meeting him, was a kind and quiet man.

'What was it really like?' Alexander asked.

'It's natural for a parent to want things for their children,' Sophie began, her eyes drifting into the distance. 'My brother, he was destined to inherit our homestead the day he was born. That meant I was destined to leave, to one day grow up and find a new home. To carry on the family's genes and make them better.' Her eyes returned to the present and she laughed. With a gentle hand, she tweaked her son's nose as though he were a boy again.

'I suppose it wasn't easy trying to make a new home here,' Alexander pressed.

Sophie shook her head. 'Your grandpa loves this place — loves your father — very much. *He* had expectations. An interloper was not one of them.'

'But Father had to marry someone,' Alexander said, narrowing his eyes.

'Of course,' Sophie chuckled, 'someone of good blood, yes, but better if of the very best of blood. As I said, it's natural for a parent to want things for their children. Sometimes,' she shrugged delicately and smiled, 'we don't always get what we want.'

Alexander ran a hand through his hair and considered. 'He got over it, eventually. Grandpa, I mean.'

'Yes, of course,' Sophie laughed, 'Your father was happy. Even a stubborn man could see that. Ultimately, that's all a parent truly ever wants for their children.'

'That's what you want for me?'

'Of course, my strawberry.'

'Even if I end up walking a different path from the one you had hoped?'

Sophie examined the concern on her son's face. 'As long as you are happy at the end of it, Alex, I'd be greedy to ask for more than that.'

'And Father,' Alexander asked, 'he would be happy just the same?'

She met his gaze then looked away. A noise from outside startled her. Sophie uncrossed her legs and moved to the window, gesturing for Alexander to join her.

Outside, standing on the grass that ran alongside the gravel driveway, Alexander's father and grandfather were in heated discussion. Robert motioned to a length of wood on the ground as Robert Senior shook his walking cane at him. In front of them, a half-collapsed fence begged to be repaired, bits of broken wood scattered throughout the leaf-strewn grass. From the window, it was impossible for Sophie or Alexander to hear what the men were saying, aside from the occasional shout from the older Robert.

'He doesn't want to be like him,' Sophie said, turning from the glass to her son. 'It's something he's resisted his whole life — the bitterness, the arrogance, the heavy-handed way of managing everything — but watching your son become a man makes you question everything, until, all of a sudden, the way your own father treated you doesn't seem so strange anymore.'

On the grass, Robert sighed and picked up the wood, holding it out for his father to inspect.

'Expectations,' Alexander said quietly.

'Yes,' Sophie replied, turning back to the window. 'Expectations.'

They stood in silence for a moment, watching the two generations wrangle over how best to repair a fence. A wind chime hanging by the front door jangled as a breeze pushed through the air.

'He wants you to have this place, Alex,' Sophie said solemnly, eyes still fixed on the drama outside. 'He's always wanted it. It's not something he's ever questioned, it's just how it's supposed to be.'

Alexander didn't say anything.

'He's made so many sacrifices to keep it going. Your grandpa, the same. Things you'll never know.' She paused before continuing softly, 'In their minds, it's reasonable for them to expect the same of you.' Sophie twisted her head and placed a hand over Alexander's cheek. 'You're of the same blood — the very best of blood. Your father wants you to be happy, Alex, of course he does, but he also knows you must take your place and be a part of your family tree. For all our sakes.'

But what if I don't want to be a part of it?

Watching the two men argue on the grass outside, Alexander felt like he was living someone else's life.

Fourteen

'You could always eat my cunt again if that'd encourage more of an interest in the sounds coming from my mouth,' Mary said, her eyes peering provocatively over the rim of her glass.

Alexander hadn't been listening. He had been looking past her — through the centre of her forehead, straight through where her third eye supposedly was — for at least five minutes.

'I'm sorry,' he said, red rising in his cheeks. 'I was miles away.'

Mary took a sip of water, letting her lips linger on the glass for a second too long. 'No matter,' she grinned triumphantly. 'Later, I'm sure.'

They were standing in the hallway, huddled against the wall as everyone bustled around them, carrying plates and glasses and food from the kitchen to the back door. Guinevere had already dropped a bowl of potatoes on the lawn and Robert Senior was on his second glass of Scotch.

'Do you need me to do anything, Sophie?' Mary asked

Alexander's mother as she came out of the kitchen carrying a jug of cordial.

'Oh, I couldn't, dear,' Sophie smiled, side-stepping to avoid a collision with Aurélie as she skipped past her clutching a wad of napkins. 'Besides, I think we're almost done.'

Sophie continued to the back door, being helped out to the table with the jug by Robert who was on his way back inside. Watching them from the hallway, Mary emptied her glass then tugged Alexander's sleeve. 'Come on,' she said, pulling him towards the door.

The back lawn had been transformed. A long wooden table, decorated with candles and vases bursting with the last of the season's blooms, stood on the grass opposite the back door. Two identical stainless steel patio heaters flanked either end, with chairs draped in soft blue blankets filling the space between. Delicate strings of fairy lights trailed up and along the trellis that divided the lawn from the vegetable garden beyond, their yellow bulbs gleaming like glow worms against the fading evening light.

At the table sat Robert Senior, twirling the honey-coloured drink in his glass as he energetically recited an anecdote. Roaring laughter and he paused to take a sip. Besides him, a man wearing a burgundy bowtie adjusted his glasses and flicked a tear from his eye.

'Goodness, Robert,' the man said after catching his breath, 'you are an old fart, aren't you?'

The old man simply shrugged his shoulders and took another sip of whisky.

Alexander quietly took a seat at the other end of the table and helped his mother pour the drinks, arranging the glasses in front of her one by one. Her bracelet, its bright gems shimmering in the candlelight, chinked against the jug as she poured.

'Is elderflower cordial okay for now, Ern?' Sophie asked, tilting the lip of the jug over the glass that Alexander had just moved. 'We're having sparkling wine with dessert.' The man in the bowtie leant forward. 'Perfect, wonderful!' He grinned before sitting back in his chair. Alexander slid the glass down the table.

By the back door, Robert and Mary were talking. Despite pulling Alexander down the corridor, she had ushered him away when his father had come over to talk to her. Alexander observed them from the table. She was wearing her hair loose, its colour a striking contrast against the emerald silk dress that draped her bust and snaked around her waist and down her thighs. The dress cut off just below the knee. Her legs were bare alabaster. Heads bent together, she and Robert were locked in spirited conversation. Smiling, he reached inside his jacket — a brown relic he had no doubt acquired from the other Robert — and pulled out a small wooden box. Mary took it gratefully, nodded her head, then walked over to the table.

'My girl,' Ern beamed, swinging his left arm out in Mary's direction. She took his hand and allowed herself to be pulled onto his knee. 'Or, should I say lady. Look at you.' He studied her face and touched her cheek before saying, 'Isn't she beautiful?'

'Thank you, Daddy,' Mary responded, holding his gaze.

'No, really,' Ern laughed, looking down the table, 'isn't she beautiful? I don't know how I let you keep her from me!'

Sophie and Robert — both now seated at the table — laughed, too. 'We couldn't do without her, could we, my darling?' Robert said, turning to his wife.

'Indispensable,' Sophie said. 'And every day more and more like Francesca.'

Mary inwardly winced at the sound of her mother's name. Her father squeezed her hand but she slid out of his grasp and stood up. 'I know it's my birthday,' she said, attempting a smile, 'but it really needn't all be about me! Let's eat before the food gets cold.'

'A smashing idea,' Robert Senior boomed, slapping the edge of the table. 'You heard her, get the girl some food!'

Sophie and Robert stood and began uncovering the various dishes that carpeted the table. The crinkling sound of aluminium foil merged with Robert Senior's low tone and Ern's guffawing as the pair continued talking. Once uncovered, Alexander took the first dish — a large blue porcelain bowl brimming with cauliflower dripping with creamy cheese sauce — and placed it in front of Mary, who had taken her seat beside him. She asked him for the large silver spoon which lay just out of reach.

'I'll serve yours if you like,' he offered, picking up the spoon. 'How much do you want?'

'Just a spoonful, please,' Mary replied, holding her plate up close to the bowl. When he had spooned the food onto it, she shuffled her chair and moved her lips to his ear. 'This dress is quite close-fitting, after all,' she whispered. She imagined Alexander's mind involuntarily flashing back to when he had watched her get into it only a few hours earlier.

Mary, of course, knew that Alexander was — *what's the word?* — rebounding. She wasn't simple-minded, but neither was she ungrateful enough to look a gift horse in the mouth. *Tammy*, as far as she was concerned, *was a means to an end*. A preparatory step along Alexander's predetermined path that would ultimately bring him to her. *Everyone around the table knows it*, she thought as she caught Sophie glancing at the two of them. Alexander offered her a roasted onion. Mary shook her head and sighed. *Everyone, that is, except perhaps Alex.*

They were always meant to end up in each others' arms. Who was she to question the strange — and what she considered to be unnecessarily painful — quirks in destiny's plan?

Sophie called Guinevere and Aurélie to the table, the girls having been playing a hoop toss game together on the lawn until that point. When they were seated, she uncovered the final dish, which had been warming in the oven until Robert brought it outside only seconds before. 'For you, my marshmallow,' she beamed, nudging the dish in Mary's direction. 'Shanks slow-cooked in a red wine sauce.'

'They look divine,' Mary said with rare soft sincerity, nudging out of her chair to strain over the flame of a nearby candle. She turned her eyes to Alexander's mother. 'Thank you so much for preparing all of this, Sophie.'

Eight cuts of meltingly tender meat, a browned bone

pointing up out of each, sat in a dish of mahogany red sauce. Chunks of onion, carrot and celery swam in the dish alongside the shanks, which, along with the bone marrow that had softened as the meat had slow-cooked, only helped to deepen the flavour of the red wine sauce. One by one, the pieces of meat were spooned from the dish onto appreciative plates.

'I know to always expect the best meals whenever I visit,' Ern said, after swallowing his first bite. 'Thank you, Sophie.'

'Yes, thank you, my darling,' Robert said, touching her hand as he used his fork to pull a slither of meat off the bone.

Everyone issued praise and thanks to the cook as they started eating their food. Knives and forks clattered against porcelain and teeth gnashed against flesh. The meat was succulent and juicy.

'Ah,' Robert said, placing his cutlery down, 'we've forgotten!' He picked up his glass and raised it. Everyone except for little Aurélie, who continued sucking on one of the few potatoes to have survived the journey to the table, followed suit and raised their glasses.

Ern stood up. 'Happy birthday, my love,' he said, glass in the air and looking down the table at his child. Mary raised two fingers to her lips, kissed them and stretched her hand out in her father's direction. He leant across the table and touched her hand. 'May all your dreams come true,' he smiled.

'Happy birthday, Mary!' Everyone around the table exclaimed in unison. Glasses clinked and, looking at their happy faces, Mary couldn't help but feel overwhelmed. All the people she loved — *my family* — sat with her that night. Under the table, she sought out Alexander's knee.

They ate slowly. Conversation was generously shared and liberally lengthened. Barely two bites could be had before they found their lips diverted back to speech. Mary's father, by far, spoke the most. It had been many months since Ern had last visited the homestead and, a widower who lived alone when his daughter was away, he had the capacity to suffer from incredible loneliness. In Mary's absence, his work was his only joy.

'It's admirable, Ern,' Robert said, dabbing the corner of his mouth with a napkin. 'I'm not sure I could manage it.'

'Aye,' the older Robert confirmed as he chewed. 'You must have patience by the barrowload.'

Ern chuckled. 'It can be frustrating, yes,' he said. 'But, how else can we educate the ignorant? If we don't, no one else will.'

'And you see progress, Ern?' Sophie looked up from her plate and asked.

'Why, yes,' he nodded. 'It's slow progress, as you would expect, but progress nonetheless.'

'Tell them about the new society, Daddy,' Mary urged from the other end of the table.

'Yes, of course!' Ern exclaimed. His eyes twinkled as he spoke. 'I couldn't remember if I'd told you.'

Robert shook his head. 'Not that I recall.'

'Well,' Ern continued, pausing to take a drink, 'it all began last year, the start of Lent Term. A group of second year students established a new society. A little peculiar to set one up midway through the year, mind, but they were all inspired, you see, something about a film they had watched over the Christmas vacation. When they came back, they'd all decided to stop eating animals, well, animal derived products in general, I believe.' Ern paused and turned to Robert Senior, who was listening as he ate. 'Milk and cheese, old man,' Ern laughed, nudging Robert Senior with his elbow, who proceeded to swat him away, pretending to be annoyed.

'Vegans, I think they're called,' Robert said, clearing his throat. 'Is that right, Ern?'

'Yes, quite,' Ern replied, gesticulating with both hands. 'They set up the university's first vegan and vegetarian society. A society for students — actually, the head of my faculty joined as well — a society for those who don't consume animals.'

'And tell them what you thought, Daddy,' Mary said drily, her curls jiggling as she shook her head.

Ern erupted into laughter. 'Why, I thought,' he grinned, 'I thought that if they didn't eat animals, then perhaps they'd be interested in how we live!'

The two Roberts started laughing also. Sophie, chucklingy meekly into a napkin, waved her hand out in front of her, pointing across the table at her father-in-law. 'You,' she eventually managed to say to Robert Senior, 'you thought the same thing when—' Sophie paused, her laughter suddenly muted. She looked at her son before continuing. 'Alexander had a friend from university who was a vegetarian,' she explained to Ern. 'Robert, here,' she gestured to the older man, 'had never heard the term before.'

'Oh, it's becoming rather more common than you might think, old man,' Ern said to Robert Senior. 'Popping up all over the place, especially among the youth.' Ern looked down the table at Alexander who, having not said anything for a long time, had almost finished his meal. 'So, it's the same at the other place, then?' Ern asked jovially as he cut himself another piece of shank. His eating was a signal for Alexander to talk about his university.

'Yes,' Alexander began, his voice a little hoarse. 'I suppose it is. I know quite a few vegetarians and vegans. They take it very seriously.'

'That must be strange, dear,' Sophie said, leaning forward in her chair, 'living with people with such strong ideas.'

Alexander shrugged, scraping his fork around his plate to collect the last few remnants of meat. 'Everyone has their beliefs.'

Mary swallowed the carrot she had been chewing, 'But that's precisely the problem, isn't it,' she said, eyes turned to Alexander. 'If everyone believes one thing or another, how can they possibly ever know the right way.'

Ern nodded. 'She's right, you know. That's what makes my job so difficult. Always sneaking around, trying to educate those who are like us — as if I'm the one doing something wrong. I have to be careful how I operate. One wrong word and I'd be in a heap of trouble!'

'At least no one ever suspects a professor of economics, though, Ern,' Robert chuckled.

'Far too stale a profession, I'd say,' Robert Senior barked, turning to his companion and poking him in the chest. 'Better a medical doctor!'

'Well, you would say that, wouldn't you, Father,' Robert eyed him across the table, shaking his head. Robert Senior just snorted and loaded another forkful of food into his mouth. Grinning, Ern straightened his glasses as he rolled his eyes at Robert.

And that was how the rest of the evening went. Sharing stories and laughter, reminiscing and reflecting, catching up on each other's news. Hours floated away like clouds over the Moon, until all they were left with was an empty night sky, starless and blue. It was time to go. Mary blew out the candles and helped Sophie carry the plates inside.

On the driveway, Robert was helping Ern load Mary's bags into the back of his car.

'Here you go, old friend,' Robert said, passing Ern a plastic cooler box. 'Sophie put together a selection for you, to keep you going until next time.' Ern thanked him and placed the box in the car next to the bags. Beside them was a crate of the family's wine, the word Dionysus etched in elegant font on the wood. 'There's quite a nice variety of cheeses in there,' Robert continued. 'A fresh one we've been eating rather frequently. It goes wonderful on toast. And,' Robert patted the pockets of his jacket and pulled out a folded piece of paper, 'Sophie also told me to give you this.' Robert handed the paper to the other man. 'Cooking instructions,' he grinned and Ern laughed.

'I probably need them!'

'You know Sophie takes food very seriously,' Robert smiled.

'Besides, it's a good idea to listen to her. There are a few cuts of mutton in there.' Ern raised an eyebrow. 'We had an unexpected dispatch a few weeks ago,' Robert explained. 'It might be a bit tough, so it's probably best slow-cooked.'

Ern took the paper and smiled. 'Thank you,' he said as he patted Robert on the arm. 'Not just for this,' he waved the piece of paper in his hand, 'but for looking after my baby girl.' Robert wafted his hands as if to stop him. 'No, I mean it, Rob,' Ern continued, his voice deep and serious. 'All these years, you and Sophie, looking after her as you do, for so many months at a time, treating her like your own—'

'Please, Ern,' Robert interrupted. He placed a hand on his friend's shoulder. 'There's no need.'

The two men looked back at the house. Mary and Alexander were standing on the front step talking.

'Look at them, Rob,' Ern said, taking a deep breath. 'We must be old men.' They both laughed and then embraced.

'Take care of yourself,' Robert said, slapping Ern's back as they held each other.

'You, too,' Ern replied, pulling away. 'I'll have to stay longer than a single evening, next time!'

'Without question,' Robert said.

On the doorstep watching their fathers say goodbye, Alexander saw Mary shiver. 'Here,' he said, taking off his jacket and placing it over her shoulders. She looked at him, their faces only inches apart.

'What about you,' she said, teeth chattering. 'You're going to need it.'

'You can give it back to me later.' They both smiled, remembering the last time one of them had said that. Above them, the Moon was bright.

'You won't see me again until Christmas,' Mary said, searching Alexander's eyes for a response.

He touched her chin. 'I know,' he said.

Mary hesitated, then asked, 'Does that bother you?'

Alexander's eyes narrowed and a smile tugged at his lips, 'Do you want it to?'

She let out a short laugh. Touching his cheek and without saying another word, Mary walked down the steps and over to her father. Alexander stayed outside until the car was out of sight.

For the first time in his twenty-one years, he realised he was going to miss her.

ACT II

A Treatise on the Creation of a New Eden

Then God said, 'Let Us make man in Our image, after Our likeness. And let them have dominion over the fish of the sea and over the birds of the heavens and over the livestock and over all the earth and over every creeping thing that creeps on the earth.'
- *Genesis 1:26*

The Bible expresses two qualities for man: image and likeness. It is the purpose of this treatise to propose the identification of a sub-homo: an animal that has the image, but not the likeness of the Creator.

It has long been acknowledged that there is a duality of man, an incessant struggle between barbarism and civilisation. This struggle has strained the fabric of human society for millenia, with the construction of gaols, houses of correction, asylums, workhouses, and so forth a testament to the ancient wrestling for governance over society's noxious elements. Through mechanisms including confinement, surveillance, and novel experimentations, society seeks to correct such degenerate moral habits as alcoholism, insanity, vagrancy, and prostitution. Yet, this indicates a blindness, for barbarism cannot be amended: the inmates of the aforementioned institutions, and indeed others who hold seemingly innocuous positions within the community, are not suffering from a form of degeneration, a change in state from a complex form to a simple one, but rather have their behaviours dictated by a secret repulsion in the blood. It is this biological affliction that distinguishes them as a species different altogether; a sub-homo who was created in the Creator's image, but never in His likeness.

Today, as beneficiaries of the rapid wave of industrial, political, and economic advancement that has swept across Western civilisation, we are also the inheritors of a unique paradox: we are the collective recipients of the dark side of progress, a sort of black death of societal decay whereby the sub-homo species has finally shifted the balance in their favour. A consequence of rapid population increase is a rise in rates of violence, gambling, insanity, prostitution, and pornography. Never before has barbarism, the effect of the sub-homo, been so strongly felt. We, the true image and likeness of God, are as such enslaved to this sub-homo species, the 'creeping thing' which is so accurately described in Biblical texts, and thereby prevented from reaching Eden again. We, in short, do not have dominion over them, as was given to us at Creation, they have dominion over us.

The divinely given resources of this planet are by no means limitless. As custodians of the Earth, it is our duty to stem the tide of swelling poverty, scandalous waste, and moral decay as is naturally engendered by the sub-homo. I therefore propose that the first step on the path to achieving the creation of a New Eden is the formal recognition of the sub-homo species, and subsequent agreement on a methodology of characterisation and identification.

Dr. Richard Alexander Wheatleigh, 1879

Fifteen

The mud wouldn't wash off.

'Look what they did to you, Rosie,' the girl said, pointing at the mirror. An ugly brown stain patterned the front of the wet dress, the fabric sodden from having been run under the tap so many times.

She wanted to cry, but she didn't. Crying didn't achieve anything. In fact, it was crying that had got her and Rosie into this mess to start with. 'I'll make you another one,' she sniffed, rubbing her nose with the back of her hand. She knew she wouldn't be able to, however, not so long as the other girls were watching. With a fingernail, she scratched at the mud. Perhaps this time it would be different.

It never was.

Rosie, meanwhile, didn't say anything. Rosie never said anything. Rosie was a ragdoll.

The doll had been a gift from Cherub's mother. A very long time ago, she had woken to find Rosie lying next to her on her pillow — a scrap of fabric tied around a hairbrush with a piece of tatty green ribbon. Her mother, Nanny had explained to Cherub later that day, had made it for her birthday. Cherub hadn't even realised it had been her birthday. Ever since then, she had kept precious Rosie safe. That was until today, when those girls took her and ruined her dress.

Filly was waiting for her outside the bathroom. 'Let's do something,' she hissed at Cherub, catching her by the elbow as she walked by. The other girl shook her head.

'You always wanna do something,' Cherub said, wriggling away from her. 'That's why they chew on us so much.'

She was right. Filly was hardly the best at making friends.

Thin as a stick and as easily broken, blotchy-skinned Filly was the butt of every joke. Her scratchy hair always smelled of sweat and her legs were so scrawny that they looked like they belonged to a boy half her age. Cherub had only become friends with her because her bed was next to hers. That and how she could read.

'I taught myself,' Filly had whispered to Cherub the evening she had found her curled up in the cupboard in the bathroom, the ceiling light barely illuminating the pages of an old paperback. Filly had told her it was about a girl who fell down a hole and woke up in a different world. 'She had to drink a magic potion to get small enough to leave,' she had explained, as if such a thing made perfect sense. Cherub hadn't known what a potion was and so Filly had explained that to her too. Of course, she could have just been making it all up. There was no way Cherub would have known.

'Don't speak,' Cherub hushed, tucking Rosie under her dress

and walking ahead of her friend. One in front of the other, they hurried to the tree on the far side of the garden. Under its gnarled limbs, the girls sat on a bed of decomposing leaves.

Picking at the dirt beneath her fingernails, Filly broke the silence and sighed. 'Can I speak now?' Cherub ignored her and rolled onto her back, letting the leaves slime all over her white dress. *Now we're the same*, she thought, looking at Rosie, who she was holding above her in her right hand.

Ahead of them, clustered around a soggy picnic bench, were the girls. They were giggling and bubbling with trivial conversation. Jessica, who always wore her hair in two thick plaits down her back and could perfectly mimic the sound of Nanny flatulating, was their self-appointed leader. She had also been the first of them to bleed, and so that naturally made her regnant. The others revolved around her like satellites — her gravity was inescapable. Cherub would have gladly joined Jessica's tribe, but she had been excluded years ago.

'They're only jealous, you know,' Filly said, glancing down at Cherub. 'Their mothers never made them anything.'

Cherub blew a strand of hair off her face. 'Doesn't matter,' she said glumly. 'They still chew on us.'

At the table, the girls shrieked. Two, a short blonde thing and one with bright green eyes, ran away. Jessica had found a toad in the wet grass and was holding it out in front of her by its back legs. The amphibian floundered, croaking and chirping.

'She'll get warts,' Filly muttered, pulling her knees up to

her chest as she watched. 'Then she'll look like a witch as well as act like one.'

The toad was flung into the bushes and the girls cheered. Cackling, Jessica chased the short blonde girl, trying to rub her hands on her face.

After a minute, Cherub pulled herself upright and turned to Filly. 'Do you ever think,' she started slowly, 'about why they left us?'

'Who?'

'Our mothers,' said Cherub.

Filly's eyes were brown and wide. She hesitated and then replied, 'I don't think they wanted to leave us, Cherub.'

The other girl was confused. 'What'd you mean?' She tucked Rosie against her chest.

Filly shrugged, still holding her knees. 'I just don't think they did.'

Cherub nudged her friend. 'Why?'

Filly shrugged again. 'I saw her once,' she eventually said. 'Well, I think I did.' She turned her head away and looked at the ground. The mud squelched between her toes.

Cherub shuffled closer and whispered. 'How'd you know it was her?'

Filly dropped her knees and pointed to her face. 'She had this,' she said, poking the veiny red blemish that bloomed across her cheek. Similarly mottled patches patterned the rest of her face. 'She saw me,' she continued quietly, 'for a second.'

Her companion was captivated and drew closer still.

'What'd she do?' she whispered, their conversation now tip-toeing into contraband.

'Screamed,' Filly said plainly. 'Then I couldn't see her no more.'

Cherub nodded with understanding. Their view of the world was limited.

If it had been within her, Cherub would have pressed Filly more, but the thought never occurred to her. Thin brown hair and a little pudgy around the middle, Cherub knew — in a rough and roundabout sort of way — that she wasn't anything special. She didn't understand the fancy squiggles in Filly's books and she couldn't copy the sound of someone passing wind like Jessica. Her chest was the only flat part of her body and she knew the other girls could hear her crying when they were supposed to be sleeping. Rosie was just a hairbrush, Cherub knew that, deep down, but that simple object was the only thing she had ever had that made her different from the others.

Stretching her legs out in front of her, Filly told Cherub about a new story she had found.

'I thought you knew them all,' Cherub said.

Filly smiled. 'Me too. This one was down the back of the shelves. Must've fallen a long time ago.'

Goldilocks and the Three Bears was its name. The book even had pictures, although someone had ripped out the last two pages. No matter, Filly told Cherub, she had designed her own ending.

'The bears kept her,' Filly explained. 'Then some other girls came and they all lived together in the bears' house. Baby Bear shared his porridge with them and they helped fix the chair Goldilocks broke.'

All the books Filly found were old and defective. Once well-thumbed, no one had touched them in a long time. Only Filly knew how to extract their stories. Well, her and Nanny, but she hadn't told them stories for a long time. *They like the telly box better anyhow,* Cherub thought, imagining the girls gathered around it as they did each evening.

'We could ask Nanny to get more stories,' Cherub suggested, fiddling with Rosie's green ribbon.

Filly shook her head and said, 'She wouldn't.'

Cherub pulled a face. 'She got Rosie.'

'That was ages ago,' the other girl replied. 'You know how she is now.'

Pinks, oranges and purples blossomed across the sky, signalling to the girls that it would soon be time to go inside. Looking like a spectre in her white smock, Nanny fussed and pestered at the door as the girls began to trickle in. When she saw Cherub, she shook her head.

'Look at you,' the white-haired woman tutted, pulling at Cherub's mud-stained dress. 'That was clean on this morning.'

Red-faced, Cherub apologised and said she would change. Hurrying to her bed, she ripped the dress off over her head and stuffed it through the little door in the wall that ate all their dirty clothes. A fresh dress, pristine and white, was waiting for her behind a second door.

Filly was standing by their beds, in her arms the book about the three bears. Sitting together on Cherub's bed, the girls poured over its pages, studying its vibrant illustrations, imagining how the story was supposed to end. Across the other side of the room, Jessica and the others gathered around the television, having mounded blankets and pillows on the floor so as to construct a giant, spongey platform to lounge around on and gossip. Nanny sat in her chair watching on, helping the smaller ones to brush their hair for bed.

An outsider looking in could be mistaken for thinking the girls were having a jolly time. A summer camp or sleepover, days filled with friendship, laughter and television. They would, however, have been mistaken. There was no home to go to at the end of the holiday, for this was their home. Rows of metal-framed beds and identical white smocks, a red-eyed camera in each corner, all on endless repeat, one day indistinguishable from the next, everything always perfectly arranged, perfectly the same, from the moment they were born.

Sixteen

Last night had been exceptionally windy. It had drizzled all day, until the fields were saturated with grey and the trees shivered every shade of brown, from almost white to almost black. By the time the night had rolled in, cloudless and cold and darker than death, the wind had taken up residence in the gaps between branches and inside the damp nooks of the homestead's old stone walls. Trees filled with brown, dead leaves were snatched from the ground and left to rot by the force that had created them. In the morning, a squirrel weaved through their splintered graveyard, scratching the earth, her sylvan home obliterated.

A light rain pattered on the roof of the farm buggy and dribbled down the windscreen. Robert's jacket was buttoned up to his chin. His fingers seemed to creak as he gripped the steering wheel and his nose felt red. Despite the discomfort of the cold, the winter air made everything smell fresh and he savoured its crisp purity.

He had risen before the Sun. The wood pellet boiler that

heated B and C Buildings had failed last winter and Robert was haunted by the fear of it failing again. Against the dark, he had tightened the pipes and seals and checked that the fire was burning. Breakfast had been eaten at his desk in C Building — a leftover sandwich whisked from the fridge, wrapped in a damp piece of kitchen towel.

'I am too blessed to be stressed,' he muttered to himself as he eased his foot off the pedal and turned to avoid a large puddle in the road.

Robert hadn't seen Mary since her birthday and Alexander had returned to university only a couple of days after she left — a decision that had not been made lightly but was inevitable all the same. Robert had said nothing to him that morning as they ate breakfast together at the kitchen table. Sophie had boiled him two eggs, but he hadn't managed to peel the shell of either. After shaking his hand at the front door, he had watched his son climb into his old red car and leave, driving, as he always seemed to be, against the tide. Holding Sophie on the doorstep, Robert had wished Alexander would hurry up and become a confident and capable man, and simultaneously hated how he was no longer his little boy.

As busy as he was on the homestead — Sophie his only aide, his father too antiquated and Frank too unreliable — Robert was counting down the days until Alexander came home for Christmas. Mary had been due to return the previous weekend but had cancelled her train at the last minute. She had sent Robert a text message five minutes after he had arrived at the train station to pick her up. He suspected that something was blossoming between Alexander and Mary, although he was not quite sure if blossoming was the correct word to describe it. Images of rose thorns and beehives filled his head. *It's never so sweet without the sting.* He chuckled and pulled up alongside the house.

Sophie was waiting for him in the sitting room.

'The boiler?' she asked, steam rising from the coffee cup cradled in her hands. Robert peeled off his gloves and sat down on the sofa.

'Fine,' he said, shaking his head. 'Just me.'

She sighed and touched his knee. 'You worry too much.'

Leaning back against the sofa, Robert ran his fingers through his hair. Sophie took a sip from her cup and asked if he had eaten breakfast. He yawned and she told him the girls were upstairs in bed, then went to the kitchen to bring him some coffee. When Sophie returned, cup in hand, Robert was gone and the door to the study ajar.

The room was cocooned in dark oak panelling. Hand-carved linenfold panels edged the bookcase that stretched the width of the far wall and an impressive ribbed ceiling drew the roof down. The lighting was low, the heavy ruched curtains still drawn over the window. In the centre of the room, facing the door, a desk of waxed mahogany stood scattered with papers.

'I was looking through them yesterday evening,' Sophie said, placing the coffee on a coaster on the desk. Her husband looked up from the files and thanked her.

'I brought yours in,' he said, nodding to the end table by the door. She took the cup and perched on the desk beside him.

Still in her nightclothes, she pulled her dressing gown more tightly around herself as she sat.

Robert handed Sophie a piece of paper. 'You don't think this one's too young?'

'Perhaps,' she said as she scanned the page. 'Then again, it might make him more malleable.'

Robert sniffed, the cold still in him. 'Or, it might do the opposite,' he said. 'You can never truly know their temperament until it's too late.'

'It's never too late, dear.' Sophie handed the paper back. 'Especially with a young one. The cost of a miscalculation would not be so great.'

Robert considered and nodded. 'You're right. But we shouldn't do anything until Alex is back — it will be good for him to be a part of this.'

'I agree.'

Robert closed his eyes and massaged his temples. Sophie placed her cup down and laid a hand on his shoulder.

'Have you spoken with your father about it?' she asked.

'He knows it's time, yes,' Robert replied, eyes still shut, 'but he hasn't said all that much. I sense he's waiting for me to make a mistake.'

Sophie's eyes narrowed. 'It's the most difficult task to undertake. Surely, even he's not so cruel?'

When he opened his eyes, the first thing Robert saw was concern. He took his wife's hand and rubbed his thumb across her knuckles.

'I don't like this,' she said. 'This competition between you and him — it's dangerous.'

Robert raised an eyebrow. 'I would hardly call it that. Besides, competition suggests we have both chosen to play the game, and you know I never have.'

Sophie's eyes softened. 'I know, dear,' she said. 'But it's dangerous all the same. You helped him when it was time, it's only fair he returns the favour.'

'Ah, yes,' Robert grinned, 'but that's the issue — he considers having *allowed* me to help him favour enough.' He paused, then changed his tone so as to mimic his father, 'Weren't you paying attention, my boy!'

Readjusting herself on the desk, Sophie laughed and touched her husband's cheek. 'We'll manage,' she soothed. 'Providing you don't make yourself ill with worry, we'll manage.'

'A wrong decision and it will jeopardise the success of everything—'

'I told you,' Sophie interrupted, 'the cost would not be so great. Everything will be alright.'

Robert laughed and tapped the back of her hand. 'Now you're talking to me as if I'm one of them!'

'Well, stress is never a good thing — for us or them,' she giggled and pinched his cheek. Robert pulled her hand to his mouth. Her skin was soft against his lips.

'You've been baking,' he smiled, kissing her hand. 'I can smell the sugar on your fingers.'

Sophie laughed and pulled her hand away. 'Guinevere requested biscuits.'

'I bet she did!'

Robert imagined his daughters asleep upstairs, their breath sweet against their pillows as they chased rabbits and rainbows in their dreams. *I am blessed.* He breathed deeply and felt the stress that had been coursing through his veins dissolve to nothing.

Unfolding her legs and sliding off the desk, Sophie moved to stand next to him. He offered her the chair but she shook her head.

'This one.' She pointed to one of the pieces of paper on the desk. 'This is the one.'

Robert moved it in front of him and pushed the other papers to the side. Sophie's finger traced the top few lines on the page.

'In many ways, he is ideal. And plus—' she leant forward on the desk, 'I've met him.'

Robert stopped reading and turned to face her. 'You have?'

Sophie smiled, her top lip pulled up and revealing her teeth. She nodded.

'How so?' Robert's eyes were quizzical. 'When?'

'He delivers to the shelter,' she explained. 'A few months ago he was taken up as an apprentice by the company who handles the laundry.' As she straightened up, the collar of her dressing gown loosened and exposed the porcelain skin of her décolletage.

'And so you have spoken with him?'

She nodded. 'On occasion. He helps the driver to carry the baskets and bags and whatnot.'

'Why did you not say before?'

She shrugged. 'I wasn't sure,' she said. 'Now, all options considered, I believe he's the correct choice.'

Robert looked again at the paper. 'Clifford,' he said. 'It's a bit old-fashioned, isn't it?'

'He lives with his grandmother,' Sophie said and pointed to a paragraph further down the page. 'Father, deceased. Mother, goodness knows where. I think he's been with the grandmother since he was an infant. If I had to say, she was probably the one who named him.'

Eyes oscillating from one side of the page to the other, Robert nodded. 'And would she pose a problem?'

'A carer comes by the house three times a week. Given the rate of decline, I imagine she'll be in a home before too long.'

'Anybody else?' Robert asked.

Sophie shook her head. 'Not that I can tell.'

Robert bit his lip and turned to thought. *It would be easy. Or at least, easier than most.* After a minute, he pushed the paper away and turned in his chair to face Sophie. 'Well, my darling,' he said as he reached for her hand. 'I — as in all matters — trust your judgement implicitly.'

'Thank you, my dear.'

'And you can no doubt secure a sample?'

'I think,' she said, a strand of hair falling across her eye, 'I can manage that the next time I'm at the shelter.'

Robert raised her hand to his lips. 'Monday, then.' He kissed her. 'And then we'll know soon enough.'

As Sophie nodded, footsteps rattled the ceiling above them. Thunderous movement came down the stairs.

'The girls are up,' Sophie said and they both laughed. 'I'll get started on their breakfast.' Robert dropped her hand and rose from the chair, following her from the study. She turned as she walked and said, 'I can make you something else if you're hungry.'

Robert glanced down at his watch. The hands signalled quarter to eight. 'Thank you, my darling, but no,' he said. 'I've got to put them on to be milked.'

'Perhaps when you get back, then,' she smiled. 'I'll put the biscuits in the oven — we can have those.'

'Warm biscuits and a glass of fresh milk. It's a date,' he grinned and kissed his wife one more time before they parted, she for the kitchen and he for the front door.

Robert could hear the girls talking in the kitchen as he pulled on his boots. His gloves were still damp as he dragged them back over his fingers. Rain had somehow managed to seep inside rendering them redundant. Leaving them tucked over the radiator to dry, he checked his pocket for the key to the farm buggy before opening the door. As Robert pulled the front door closed, the last thing he heard was the sound of Aurélie laughing.

I am blessed

And, in more ways than one, he was.

Seventeen

There was always some tussling. Under pressure from the rear to keep moving, the line had buckled in the middle.

Robert latched the backing gate and moved to the front of the herd. The lead fresher had stopped. Her nostrils were flared and her knees locked. From the other side of the fence, Robert softened his expression and attempted to soothe her. All herds developed a social hierarchy: freshers followed their herd mates, and so, when the more dominant members of the group stopped, the whole system came to a halt. Gently, Robert encouraged her to move. When she did not, he reached for his prod. Slipping its length between the bars of the fence, he contacted the stalled fresher's side. The voltage inspired her to move. A short yelp and her knees loosened. The herd was allowed to move ahead.

They settled into their stalls without fuss. Robert began with the newest and worked his way around to the more experienced members of the group. Before he had entered the parlour, he had, as he always did, turned on the speakers. The third of Vivaldi's *Four Seasons* violin concerti, *Autumn*, played as he rinsed the bucket out for the seventh time.

The solution was warm water and soap. The suds calmed the experienced fresher as Robert drew the cloth across her teats. *Winter* trembled out of the speakers and Robert started to hum.

After she was washed and her milk had let down, he cupped her right breast and squeezed the area around the nipple. Stimulating three full squirts from the teat, he let the creamy liquid dribble to the floor, then moved to the other breast and repeated the process. Any unsavoury residue or puss now cleared from the teat, Robert guided the silicone cups over one breast at a time. After easing the nipples into the middle of the funnel, he switched on the machine and watched as fresh milk flowed.

Master of his universe, he moved to the next, and the next, and the next, until all residents of the parlour, seated in their individual stalls, were being milked by the machines in perfect harmony. Robert took his seat, the stalls curved toward him in a crescent, and rapped his fingers against his knee in time with the music.

They chattered, of course, as their vital force was sucked from their mammary glands by the machines. That and the rhythmic humming of the pumps were the music of milk — the music which Robert conducted from high up, in the centre of them all.

When the first was thoroughly stripped, Robert returned to her and removed the teat cups. Pulling a round tin from a pocket in his white coat, he unscrewed the lid and dabbed a quantity of the ointment contained within onto his finger. It was a herbal salve — a homemade creation of beeswax, sunflower oil, calendula flower extract and aloe vera — which he applied to each nipple. Rubbed into the skin in delicate circular motions, it would help to prevent cracking and keep the teat sterile, forming a barrier to stop anything from getting in and infecting the nipple while it was still loose and open.

'You may go now, Rhiannon,' said Robert. Leaving her stall, the fresher followed the marked path and exited the parlour.

It was important that each fresher was stripped of all her milk. Only then would she produce an optimal yield. Robert returned to his seat and waited for the next to finish.

The milk was collected into stainless steel buckets. As one reached capacity, Robert covered it with a lid and moved it to the fridge that stood against the far wall of the room. Back at the house, the milk would be filtered into glass bottles to be cooled down in the freezer for an hour before being stored in the kitchen fridge. From there some of it would be drunk fresh, the rest being processed into butter, cream, yogurt, and all manner of cheeses, fresh and aged.

Another application of salve and another bucket of milk. This fresher was eager to go, but he did not rush his work. It was imperative that the nipples were cleaned to maintain good teat health.

Only after they had given their quantity were they allowed to see their offspring. On the other side of the parlour door — the door through which Robert permitted them to go after he was finished with them — were their babies. They had been separated all night. As each fresher left, the sound of cooing and happy murmurs coming from the other room grew louder. It was for this reason that Robert attended the more experienced in the herd last: they had developed the composure required to wait.

In all of this, Robert was by no means dispassionate. He ran a smooth operation, humane and mindful, and as pain-free as possible. This, he truly believed. He was a father, and the husband of a mother — he understood the bond between parent and child. These creatures, however, were not the same as him. Although some of them may have felt a naive sort of love, this was a consequence of base biology that was not as fully integrated into their sense of being as his emotions were in him. Even then, he was not entirely convinced that all of them were capable of true maternal emotion — the required strength of feeling fatally undermined by moral defect.

It was, then, of no consequence what he did to them. How he treated them. How they cried for their children in the middle of the night. How happy they were to see them in the morning. How gladly they encouraged their babe to suckle them. Any kindness he showed them was, in a sense, more for his benefit than it was theirs. *The tenants of tranquil living.* They were, after all, base creatures, and any pain that they felt — physical, emotional or otherwise — was superficial. A short shock that was minutely felt and soon forgotten.

Eighteen

The vomit was every shade of wrong.

'What'd you call that?'

Samantha looked from the bowl of the toilet to Evelyn, who was wiping her mouth with a square of toilet roll. She dabbed the corners of her lips and threw it on top of the sick.

'Pregnancy,' Evelyn said. 'I call that pregnancy, Sam.'

She flushed the toilet and the green and yellow flecked vomit spiralled down and away to become somebody else's problem.

Evelyn had been posted through the door a few hours after Samantha. *Of course she was. It's all part of their plan.* Samantha had hugged her and Evelyn had held her back. The other women in the room were all strangers. Evelyn was the only one who had known her name.

Weeks had passed before Jade had materialised. Deposited through the door by Robert, she had been thoroughly unconscious. A woman with sharp green eyes had lifted her from the floor and moved her to a bed.

The woman with the green eyes called herself Mother. No one remembered her real name, or so Evelyn had told Samantha when she had asked her about it. She always spoke in whispers and worshipped the feminine enterprise of child-rearing. Pregnancy was divine; the doctor was doing God's work. A veteran of the forgotten war, she had surrendered years ago.

All of the women in the room were strange. In all manner of bizarre and colourful ways, they had adjusted to their life on the homestead. This was why Evelyn gravitated towards Samantha. *I'm the only one of them who isn't fucking crazy.*

'Let's get you to the sofa,' Samantha said, wrapping her arm around her friend's back and guiding her away from the toilet. Evelyn placed her head on Samantha's shoulder.

The foetuses in their wombs now eleven weeks old, Evelyn had vomited every morning without exception for several weeks. Sometimes the nausea stayed all day. Such days left Evelyn exhausted, her body racked from the constant seizing of her muscles, her stomach sore and dry from having expelled impossible quantities of liquid. The past week, the nausea seemed to be abating, Evelyn's vomit now having the decency to keep to an early morning schedule and show mercy to the rest of the day.

Fortunately, Samantha had been spared morning sickness. Her breasts, on the other hand, kept her up all night. They felt tender and bloated, sometimes agonisingly so, and her ultrasensitive nipples rubbed against the fabric of her smock as she tried to sleep. Even so, and irritatingly, she had come to appreciate the dress Robert had given her: it kept her cool as her core body temperature rose and gave her breasts plenty of room to swell.

'I assume it gets worse than this,' Samantha laughed, trying to be lighthearted. Eyes closed, Evelyn breathed heavily and rested her head against the back of the sofa.

When Samantha thought about it — which, generally speaking, she tended to avoid doing — the thought of giving birth terrified her. One quiet evening, she had asked Evelyn about it. Another time, whilst eating breakfast together, Jade had gifted her a graphic description. Other women in the room had each shared their experiences of the process. As natural as it was supposed to be, Samantha couldn't help but conclude that her body simply wasn't capable of the feats the women described. Vaginal tears and catheters. *Fuck no.* There had to be a way out of this.

Evelyn placed a hand over her ever-so-slightly-protruding abdomen. 'Tell me about what you did before this.' She opened her eyes and looked at Samantha. 'If it's not too painful.'

Samantha shrugged. 'It's a pretty short story.'

Evelyn smiled. 'I doubt it.'

'Really, there's not much to tell. Just hangovers, bad decisions and a lot of wallowing.'

Evelyn shifted to get more comfortable. 'What did you have to wallow about?' she asked.

A thread had come loose on the arm of the sofa and Samantha picked at it with her nail. 'How shit I am,' she said. 'How shit everything is.'

Eyes closed again, Evelyn's eyebrows raised. 'I don't think you're shit,' she said.

Samantha laughed. 'That's awfully nice of you to say, but, considering where we are, I think your judgement's screwed.'

Evelyn laughed too. 'I suppose you're right.'

One of the women in the room, a second trimester brunette called Beth, passed by the sofa. She stopped to ask Evelyn how she was feeling. Samantha picked at the thread some more. Next to her, the two women exchanged brief conversation.

'So, why are you shit?' Evelyn asked Samantha after Beth had walked away.

Samantha turned and laid her head on the back of the sofa next to Evelyn's. 'I was a liability. On my dad. On everyone.' She didn't blink and neither did Evelyn. 'It's like I wasn't even there. Wasn't in reality. Just fuck around now, think about it later.'

'That hardly makes you shit.'

'Try telling that to whoever's in control of all this.' Samantha gestured lazily to the ceiling.

Evelyn's eyes narrowed. 'You can't think you *deserve* this.'

Samantha shrugged. 'Don't you?' Evelyn didn't say anything. 'Even if it's bullshit, sometimes you must wonder if you're being punished for something.'

'I think,' Evelyn began, 'that the people in control of this are just people. Sick, disturbed people, but people nonetheless. Being negligible, especially when you're young, is hardly a mortal sin, Sam. And,' she paused to lick her lips, 'even if it *is*, who are these people to dole out punishment?'

'So you do think you're being punished, then?' Samanath asked.

'Punished suggests we've done something wrong. I've just said you haven't.'

'But what about you?'

Evelyn laughed. 'Why? Are you looking for evidence to suit your theory of divine justice?'

Samantha itched her neck. 'Just answer the question.'

Eveyln paused then said, 'I think I've suffered enough at the hands of others to even begin to think I deserve this.'

'What do you mean?'

Evelyn rolled over. Her long hair crinkled against her smock as her chest rose and fell. Samantha waited for her to speak.

'I was with someone,' Evelyn said, almost too quiet for Samantha to hear. 'We'd only known each other for six months when I moved in. Two weeks,' she breathed deeply, 'two weeks of living together was all it took for him to hit me.' Her voice wobbled. Samantha reached across for her friend's hand.

'Sometimes he would go weeks without doing it,' Evelyn continued. 'It was easy for me to pretend that it — violence — was not who he was. That it was a one-off, a fluke, a bad day at work.'

'But it wasn't,' Samantha said under her breath.

'No,' Evelyn nodded. 'It wasn't.' Samantha watched as a tear rolled down her cheek. A single bead, it caressed her skin and dropped, without sound, off the edge of her jaw and onto her smock. 'The smallest thing would set him off. I don't know what I was thinking, staying with him, but I did. And he was smart — always careful to hit me where it wouldn't be seen. My escape was working at the art gallery. The paintings always seemed so—' Evelyn sniffed and wiped away a tear, 'they were so romantic. I deluded myself into thinking that one day I would be okay, and I'd have that romance for myself. *That* was what I deserved.'

Samantha swallowed the lump that had formed in her throat. Her own eyes had started to leak.

Evelyn took a breath and carried on. 'One day, he beat me so badly there was no hiding it anymore. I had to leave.' She turned to Samantha. 'I tried to manage by myself. But, I had no resources. No one I could fall back on. My parents—' She paused and caught her breath. 'And then I found out I was pregnant.'

Samantha was listening and nodded for Evelyn to continue.

'I couldn't have his baby, Sam,' she said in a whisper. 'I would have got rid of it in a heartbeat. I had done it before. But, this time it was too late. Too late for an abortion. So, I went to a women's shelter. A safe place,' Evelyn paused and then said, 'or so I thought.'

Samantha asked her what she meant.

'That was where they took me,' Evelyn whispered. Her pupils grew large and seemed to cloud over with terror.

Samantha recoiled. 'What the fuck, Evelyn.' She shook her head in disbelief. 'What the fuck are you saying?'

'The woman, the doctor's wife,' Evelyn explained in a low voice. 'She was at the shelter. That's how they brought me here, Sam. I pretty much gave myself to them.'

Samantha was still shaking her head. *What the fuck. What the fuck.*

Evelyn continued. 'When they took his baby out of my body, I was glad — actually *glad* to have what he had done to me taken away.' Evelyn dropped Samantha's hand and instead held her own stomach. 'Of course, that was only to begin with. I howled when I was parted from her.'

'I'm sorry,' said Samantha. It was all she could say. She knew it was a pathetic response.

'That was years ago, but I've never forgotten,' the other woman said. 'Not her, not *him*, not my second child, not any of it. That—' she paused and looked at Samantha. 'That is how I know I don't deserve this.'

Samantha reached across and touched her friend's cheek, wiping a tear away with her finger. 'No, Evelyn, you don't deserve this.'

The other woman breathed. 'I cry now, not so much because of what he did to me, but because of how his actions led me to *them* — led me here.' She closed her eyes and breathed again before continuing. 'Don't ever forget.' Evelyn took Samantha's hand and squeezed it. 'I know it's difficult — this place. This Hell. But you mustn't forget who you were before. Even if you were shit,' she laughed despite the tears. 'You were you, and you still are you. A survivor, not a liability. Don't become like them.' She nudged her head to the side, gesturing to the rest of the room. Across the way, sitting in a chair by the door which opened onto a small enclosed garden, a woman held her swollen stomach, caressing it as she mumbled sweet things to her unborn child. She was about two months away from delivery and glowed with contentment.

'She was never free,' Evelyn said to Samantha. 'A native. Born and raised here — a product of this place.'

The woman was young and her hair was arranged on her head prettily. Two thick, rich, chocolate-coloured plaits crossed over each other in an elaborate coil. By contrast, Samantha's hair was a rancid mess — half blonde, half her natural brown, and matted in at least forty different places. She hadn't brushed it for weeks and no longer gave a fuck about it. The woman with the nice hair was humming.

'How can she be like that?' Samantha asked.

'She doesn't know any different.'

'Ignorance is bliss, I guess,' Samantha muttered.

Evelyn shook her head. 'Ignorance is ignorance. Use what you know, use what you feel, and maybe — one day — we just might be able to get out of here.'

Nineteen

It had all started over a towel.

Nathalie was certain that she had left hers hanging on the back of the bathroom door. Ladybird was equally certain that it was she who had left hers hanging there. Nathalie's was blue. Ladybird's was also blue. Beth's was blue as well, but no one cared what Beth had to say as her role in this was irrelevant.

'How'd you know it's yours?' Ladybird shouted across the room.

Nathalie, fist clenched, held the towel out in front of her and shook it. 'Because I Goddamn know!'

'Probably because of the obvious smell of skank,' said Jade. She stretched her legs and placed her feet up on the coffee table that stood between the two sofas. Sitting next to her, Samantha dropped her head into her hands.

'Fuck you, Jade!' Nathalie shook the towel again.

'Just give it to me,' Ladybird said. She walked over to Nathalie and went to snatch the towel out of her hand. Nathalie pulled it away from her just in time, and the two women's bellies contacted each other. Ladybird screamed, 'Give it to me, you whore!'

The women reached for each other. Clutching her stomach in one hand, Ladybird slapped Nathalie on the arm with her other. The towel was dropped to the floor and Nathalie tore at Ladybird's hair. Clearly, she had not had the foresight to tie it back before approaching the other woman. Ladybird screamed and cursed as Nathalie yanked several strands from her scalp. Ladybird kicked. Nathalie launched a globule of spit into her eye. Beth, seizing the opportunity, scuttled from the other side of the room, crouched down and inspected the towel on the floor. A stray foot nudged her in the bottom and she fell face first onto the carpet. She elbowed the responsible leg and found herself a part of the scuffle.

'So many hormones,' Jade said from the sofa. She reached for her glass of water and took a sip. Samantha's head was still in her hands. Now in the seventeenth week of pregnancy, hers was a pathetic existence.

Someone stirred from the armchair behind them. A green-eyed woman approached the three brawling pregnant women. As more strands of hair were tossed into the air, she raised her hands out in front of her. 'Ladies,' the woman whispered, her voice barely audible.

On the floor, the women stopped. Ladybird released Nathalie's leg and Beth pulled her teeth away from Ladybird's arm.

The green-eyed woman crouched beside them. 'This is not befitting behaviour, is it?' Her words were slow and delivered with care.

'No, Mother,' the three women said in unison.

It was eerie, but of all the things Samantha had seen and experienced over the past few months, the dominance which Mother exerted over these women was far from the strangest. She had flowing grey hair and was surely too old to be able to conceive — or at least, conceive easily — but carried a foetus inside of her the same as all the women in the room. A natural matriarch, perhaps. A damaged lunatic, most certainly.

Mother beckoned for the women to come closer. She held out her arms for an embrace. Beth was the first to move. Abandoning the other women, she collapsed into Mother's arms.

Here we go again.

'Oh, Mother,' Beth cried as she clutched the older woman, 'I'm sorry.'

'It's okay, my child,' the green-eyed woman whispered. 'Hush now and come to Mother.'

Nathalie and Ladybird threw themselves at Mother's feet and oozed remorse.

'My children,' Mother said, touching them both on the head, 'come now, sit up.'

Nathalie and Ladybird sat up. Jade moved to the sofa opposite and strained over the back of it to get a better view.

'Cooperate, do not compete.' Mother paused to kiss Beth on the forehead. 'Receive your celestial mission as friends, not enemies. This time is a blessing.'

Nathalie and Ladybird nodded. Beth laid her head on Mother's swollen stomach.

The green-eyed woman placed a hand over her décolletage.

'Breathe,' she whispered. Her followers breathed as one. 'Receive your sacred mission. Breathe. Receive the child that grows inside you. Breathe.'

A woman, the chocolate-haired native who Samantha had only spoken to twice, stood up from the bed where she had been lying and moved to the circle that had formed on the carpet. Her face looked flushed as she moved to sit beside Ladybird on the floor. Mother leant forward to stroke her forehead.

'Pandora,' Mother said. 'You feel warm. Are you feeling okay?'

The chocolate-haired woman, Pandora, nodded.

'You are the closest of us to deliverance,' Mother continued.

Pandora breathed. 'Yes, Mother.'

'And do you embrace your celestial purpose?'

'Yes, Mother.'

'And are you ready to receive the child that grows inside you?'

'Yes, Mother.'

'And, sweet Pandora,' Mother touched her well-rounded bump, 'are you prepared to give the gift upon deliverance?'

Pandora nodded. 'Yes, Mother. I am ready to give the gift.'

From the sofa, Samantha saw Evelyn, who was on her bed, peer over the pages of the book she was reading and shake her head.

After being brought to the room by Mary all those weeks ago, it hadn't taken Samantha very long to realise she had, essentially, been dumped in an asylum. The room was pleasantly decorated and indeed, Robert hadn't lied, there was a television, but the atmosphere was rotten, and the women held within even further into the process of decomposition. Their minds had turned to mush. Women like Mother, who had been in this place for innumerable years, had invented ways to rationalise their experiences as something meaningful. Simple-minded natives like Pandora, Beth and Ladybird lapped it up like babes on the teat. Others, Nathalie and Jade included, couldn't help but be drawn into the circle of insanity, desperate for something to hold onto.

Their celestial mission.

Strangely, it wasn't difficult for Samantha to see why Mother thought the way she did. Nine months of relaxed convalescence was certainly easier than any amount of time spent with Lee. *I'd take television over being fucked by him any day.* The blessing, so it turned out, was simply to have their bodies returned to them for nine months. After that, they would enter a new cycle of shame. By the time they made it back to the room — back to their sacred mission — they were each a little more fucked in the head.

And so, they sat on the carpet in a circle worshipping the feminine state of pregnancy. Nine months of peace and quiet in exchange for the giving of their gift. Nine months of peace and quiet in exchange for handing over their child to the doctor.

Samantha both pitied them and felt repulsed by them at the same time.

On the carpet, the women were becoming more restless.

'Praise her.' Mother's eyes flashed as she presented Pandora to the others in the huddle. 'Praise your sister and embrace her. Praise her for the gift she is soon to deliver.'

Ladybird started humming and Beth shuffled away from Mother to be closer to Pandora. Their hands were all over the young woman as they caressed her. The hair on top of her head was loosened and allowed to tumble down over her slender shoulders. Samantha could see the young woman was shivering and decided she couldn't stand the insanity any longer. Sighing as she stood, she walked to the circle of pregnant women and clapped her hands.

'Alright, that's enough of this for one night,' she said. 'Bedtime for the celestial children.' She turned to look at Mother. 'Bedtime for the celestial mother, too.'

Mother held her gaze. 'You do not believe, Samantha?'

Believe what? That you're a fucking lunatic?

'I believe,' Samantha said, 'that I like sleep.'

Cross-legged on the floor, Pandora placed a soft hand on Samantha's leg.

'She's right, Mother,' she said. Her teeth were chattering. 'I'm tired and—' Pandora stopped and squeezed her eyes shut. The others in the group turned, concerned.

'Are you okay, Pandora?' Beth asked, touching her arm.

Pandora tried to speak. After swallowing, she nodded. 'Yes, I'm okay.'

Mother reached across and placed a hand on Pandora's forehead. When she removed her palm, it was covered in sweat. The younger woman balled her fists and breathed suddenly.

'The wave, Mother,' Pandora uttered between clenched teeth. 'The wave.'

In a burst of energy, Mother nudged the other women out of the way so that she was in front of Pandora. Samantha stepped to the side and leant against the back of the sofa.

'What is it, my child?' Mother asked, wrapping her fingers around Pandora's fist. Pandora dragged in a lungful of air. Mother touched her stomach. 'Her abdomen,' she said, 'it's hard.'

Samantha watched as Evelyn put down her book and joined the group. She straightened her smock over her growing stomach as she approached. 'How many weeks along is she?' she asked.

Mother shook her head. 'Not enough.'

Pandora relaxed and unclenched her fist. The wave had subsided. Mother encouraged her to stand.

'Let's change position, sweet Pandora.' Mother pulled herself up onto her feet and held her hands down for Pandora to take. The younger woman gripped her wrists and wobbled to her feet. Mother supported her. 'See if this helps, my child.'

Evelyn carefully lifted Pandora's smock and began rubbing the small of her back. Balanced between Mother and Evelyn, she seemed fine for a moment. Then, another wave rolled over her.

'Mother!' Pandora cried. Her knuckles were white as she held onto the green-eyed woman.

Taking her by the arms, Mother and Evelyn helped Pandora

to the sofa. Jade hurried out the way as the other women crowded closer.

'Give her some space,' Evelyn snapped as she helped Pandora onto the cushions. Beth and Ladybird moved to the sofa opposite.

Whenever a wave came, Pandora squeezed her eyes shut. Mother knelt on the floor beside her, her skin pinched red inside Pandora's fist. Her forehead was hot to the touch so Evelyn went to fetch a flannel from the bathroom. When she returned, she placed it on the young woman's skin. Pandora, meanwhile, was remarkably quiet, especially considering the pain she was so obviously experiencing. Samantha wanted to look away, but found she couldn't.

'They must be false contractions,' Mother whispered. 'It's too soon.'

Some of the others nodded their heads in agreement.

Evelyn leant in close to Pandora and said her name. The other woman's eyes fluttered open. Her teeth were still chattering. 'Pandora,' Evelyn repeated, 'we need you to tell us something.' The contracting woman nodded. 'Do you feel as though the baby has dropped?' Pandora didn't say anything so Evelyn repeated her question. When she still didn't answer, Eveyln lifted the woman's smock. With careful hands, she inspected her abdomen.

'It's definitely dropped,' Evelyn whispered.

Mother shook her head. 'It's her first — it doesn't mean she's in labour.'

'Perhaps, but I don't think the baby agrees,' Evelyn replied.

She picked up the flannel and squeezed a few drops of water from it onto Pandora's forehead.

Mother instructed Jade to get the clock off the wall so they could time the contractions. A flurry of movement and she dragged the armchair underneath it so as to stand on it to reach.

'I've got it,' Jade said, placing the clock on the coffee table.

Mother nodded. 'Good. Now, when the next wave comes, remember the time.'

Standing awkwardly to the side, Samantha caught Evelyn by the elbow as she went to refresh Pandora's flannel. 'Should we get the doctor?' she asked.

Evelyn shook her head. 'Not now. He won't be interested yet.'

'But she's early.'

'Exactly,' Evelyn replied. 'It might just be false labour. We'll time the contractions and wait.'

Pandora's contractions came at regular intervals. A low wave at first that peaked and then, after about a minute, ebbed away. Sweat had melded with her hair and she no longer looked so pretty. After almost an hour, the screams were loud and long.

'I think it's time to get the doctor,' Evelyn said to the group. Beth was crying. Nathalie was biting her nails.

Mother stood up and moved to the big metal door that kept them in the room. So late at night, there was no way there was going to be anyone on the other side of it, but she banged her fist against it all the same.

On the sofa, Pandora wailed as another wave engulfed her.

Certain that it was the only use she was going to be in all of this, Samantha joined Mother at the door and started hammering on it.

'Robert!' Samantha screamed. 'We need help in here!'

As Pandora's cries got louder and the contractions closer together, Samantha beat the door even harder. Her back ached to be on her feet, but still she flung a cushion from the sofa at the camera in the corner of the room, hoping to catch someone's attention.

Eventually, after what seemed like far too long, they heard a click on the other side of the door. The electric lock.

He yawned before he spoke.

'Good evening, ladies,' Robert said from the other side of the door. 'If you can help her — gently — to the door, I will see to her.'

Samantha had never been so happy to hear a voice she hated so much.

Twenty

His hand cupping the back of her head, he nudged her back to the wall with his body and began kissing her neck. How she always smelled so good, he didn't know. How he had never noticed her smell before confounded him even more. No human words could describe *that* smell. There was just *something* about it. His trousers were tight. There was no hiding his excitement.

Following the curve of her neck up, he rolled her ear lobe between his lips. 'You can unfasten them, if you like,' he breathed.

She didn't fold.

He let his fingers tangle in her curls. 'You torture me,' he said.

She pressed herself against his groin. 'I know,' she whispered.

His teeth were on her throat now. Ever so gently, he ran his incisors across her exposed skin. His right hand under her clothes, his palm contacting her bare back, his fingertips massaging her body, he felt her shiver.

'Why didn't you come when I asked?'

She shivered again as he trailed his tongue across her throat.

'I didn't realise I was your possession,' she replied, her voice softer than he had ever heard it before.

'Three weeks—' He groaned as she slipped her hand under his waistband. 'That's how long you made me wait.'

She was holding him now.

'Not a word for three weeks.'

'I'm not your plaything, Alex.'

Gripping the back of her neck, he kissed her deeply then pulled away. 'It seems to me as if you are.' He smiled, his eyes fixated on hers. He was the first to blink.

She released him, but he caught her hand as she pulled it out from his trousers. Enmeshing their fingers together, he crouched in front of her, slowly, making sure to hover in front of her most delicate area before moving on. With his left hand he caressed her thigh and lifted her skirt.

'Oh my,' he teased, 'what do we have here? Knee socks? How—' he looked up at her and grinned, 'interesting.'

Dropping her hand, he peeled the socks, one at a time, down her legs and — despite feigning reluctance — with her cooperation, over her feet. They were white and delicate and suited her perfectly. Her skin prickled when he kissed her calf.

This time she folded.

There was no saying otherwise, Mary vivified him in a way that Tammy never had. A living contradiction, she fascinated him. She was soft, *but she isn't*. She was easy, *but she isn't*. Most importantly, she was the same as him. *But she isn't*. A soft, sweet centre wrapped in a hard, beautiful — near untouchable — shell, Mary had been crafted just for him.

If his parents had been surprised when he had pulled up on the driveway with Mary in the passenger seat of his car, they hadn't shown it. Alexander was acutely aware of the awkwardness of having returned home from university with a woman for the second time. That it was a different woman made it worse. That Mary was the different woman redeemed the entire situation.

He had only picked her up from the train station, *of course*. She hadn't joined him in his college room, despite — or perhaps in spite of — his insistence. In the end she had ignored his requests altogether. This miserable, and infinitely less exciting, reality his parents didn't know. Whatever their assumptions were, he wasn't about to correct them. That evening, seated next to each other at the table in the house, he had burned for her. She had passed him the bread basket and poured him a glass of wine. He had imagined her naked, stretched across his bed.

Tonight was the first night he had managed to ensnare her. On every other occasion since they had arrived back, she had been unavailable. Too busy or too torturous. He could hardly tell the difference.

Would his parents notice? Did he even care? At Mary's request it had been many weeks since he had smoked cannabis and he was quietly suffering, suffocating, desperate to escape reality.

He loved it — *no, adored it* — when she orgasmed. She made

a sweet, purring sort of sound that was just so unlike Mary. Or, at least, so unlike the Mary the rest of the world knew. Here, in his arms, she was his and his alone. Shapeless and natural, free of the rules that sought to control them. If he could save them both, he would.

The curtains of his bedroom hadn't been drawn. Moonlight streaked into the room and fused with the orange glow of his bedside lamp. Cast half in shadow, Mary's cheek rested against his chest. Falling from her skin onto his, her curls were girlish and precious and inspired in Alexander an unexpected sense of pride. Trying not to disturb her, he reached to turn off the lamp, but she lifted her chin as he did. He had thought she was asleep.

'What do you think of this?' she asked slowly.

A strand of her hair had caught in the corner of her mouth. Alexander pulled it away. 'Think of what?'

Mary opened her eyes. 'Think of us?'

As drowsy as she was, she couldn't conceal her genuine insecurity. Large and bright, he could so easily get lost in her eyes. *Take a deep drink and never look back.* Alexander placed a finger over her lips and soothed her. Lying in his arms, she looked small and delicate. *Easily broken by careless hands.*

'Don't worry,' he said. 'Sleep if you're tired.'

A sleepy smile and she exposed her teeth to nibble his finger. 'That's not an answer,' she teased after releasing him.

Keeping his arm around her, he shuffled down the bed so his face was in line with hers. He pressed the tip of his nose against hers then kissed her.

'What do you want me to say?' he asked after he pulled away.

'The truth,' she whispered. 'Is this real?'

With only a few months between them, Alexander had known Mary for as long as they could both remember. A woman and a girl living side by side in the same body, she was timeless to him. Admittedly, he had not always seen her that way. Unconscious of her transformation into womanhood, until relatively recently she had been just a girl. The girl with the freckles who stayed with them every summer. The girl who practically moved in with them after her mother died. The girl who had laughed so hard that milk shot out her nose whilst eating breakfast cereal. The girl who used to spray the hosepipe at the children on the other side of the fence. The girl his grandfather once let slip he was one day supposed to run their homestead with.

'Of course it's real,' Alexander replied. 'What else would it be?'

The sigh was either relief or disbelief, he couldn't tell which. 'Why now?' she asked.

Alexander shook his head and rolled onto his back. He drew her close so that her face was once again resting against his chest. 'Sleep, please,' he said.

Her eyelashes tickled his skin. 'Okay, but only because I'm tired.'

Alexander laughed. 'Well, that's the general idea.' An exhale blew over the hairs of his chest. 'Goodnight, Mary.'

'Goodnight, Alex.'

This time he waited until the rhythm of her breathing

altered before reaching for the lamp. In the light of the Moon, he stayed awake and watched the rising and falling of her chest. The quilt had slipped, exposing her breast. He pulled it up and tucked it around her.

What are you? he wondered as he watched her sleep. *Who are you to me?*

Alexander found it immeasurably difficult to be upset with his parents. He loved them both very much and could only think that they had raised him to the best of their abilities. *But how could they expect this? How could they expect her and I?*

It was reckless. A clumsy thing for a child to be aware of, whether it was intentional knowledge or not.

Alexander had been seven years old when he had learnt about the Four Families — the four families who had, in one way or another, shaped his entire existence. His father, Robert, was the head of one of these four families. Another family lived somewhere in Scotland. Another Alexander had met members of throughout his childhood, mostly at events where everyone came together. The fourth family was headed by Ernest Stansfield, and Ern was Mary's father.

The death of Francesca Stansfield had been a shock to everyone. Mary lost her mother and, in a way, her father in one fell swoop. She also lost a brother. Francesca had been pregnant when she had crossed the road that day.

This great tragedy had engendered a second catastrophe. As Ern's only child, the Stansfield line would end with Mary. Remarriage was unthinkable. The Four Families would shrink to three and the name of one of the Founders would be stolen by circumstance. A solution of sorts was agreed upon: Robert's heir, Alexander, would be quietly encouraged to wed Mary. She would be placed within his reach and their children would unite the two families.

It's not her fault. Alexander ran his thumb across her hair. Yet, he had made her suffer. When Robert Senior had accidentally — or so he claimed — revealed to an eleven year old Alexander that the girl he now shared his parents with would one day be his wife, he had made a point of distancing himself from her. No longer did they play together in the woods. *His* books were for *his* own consumption and she could find her own. He remembered with shame how she had cried when he had screamed at her to go back to her own mother.

How could they expect this? Or, a better question, *how has it come to this regardless?*

He wished he had never known. He wished they could have left them alone to be children and figure things out for themselves. But — *as with everything* — they simply couldn't. *We are not a normal family.* Alexander swallowed his frustration and turned his eyes to the Moon.

Sleep was starting to find him when he heard a knock on his door. It was a soft knock and was preceded by an apology. Eyes half closed, Alexander turned on the lamp. The door to his bedroom creaked open. It was his father.

'I'm sorry, Alex,' Robert whispered. He was fully dressed and wearing his white coat.

Alexander squinted and pulled the covers higher over Mary. 'What is it?' he asked.

Robert sighed. 'A springer. Gone into labour early.' He was still holding the door with his right hand and it creaked as it swayed in his grip. 'I need your help.'

'Sure,' Alexander said. 'Just let me get dressed.'

Robert turned to go but stopped before he did. 'Wake her up as well, please.' He nodded at Mary, who was still sleeping against Alexander's chest. 'It will probably be all hands on deck.'

Alexander's cheeks were hot. 'Yeah, sure,' he said. 'We'll meet you down there.'

Robert smiled, then left the room.

How could they expect this? Alexander sucked in a lungful of air. *How could they not?*

Softly, he placed his hand on Mary's cheek and encouraged her to wake. When she opened her eyes, she was pleased to see him.

Twenty-One

The contractions were not going away.

'Mary, the wire—' Robert reached across Pandora's swollen abdomen to where the cord of the foetal heart rate monitor had slipped. Mary caught it and pushed it back into the device. Robert turned to his son. 'Your assessment?'

Alexander shook his head. 'No signs of foetal stress. Uterine contractions clearly present.'

On the bed, Pandora pushed her head back into the pillows and screwed her eyes shut. She was shivering and her mouth was open, her breathing ragged. The waves were getting away from her. Robert placed a careful hand on her face. 'Pandora,' he said, firm but gentle, 'you need to get ahead of your contractions. They're not going away. Baby is coming. It will be easier if you can prepare yourself for them.'

This was Pandora's first delivery. She had been pregnant before, but had miscarried at ten weeks. Robert had suspected her second pregnancy might not run smoothly. At thirty-five weeks, her labour was over a month premature.

Soon after taking over the homestead, some twelve years earlier, Robert had made a point of distancing himself from his father's *laissez-faire* attitude. Springers, previously left to deliver by themselves, were to be separated from the herd and supervised. High-risk deliveries were allocated greater oversight. A particularly profitable year, when the grapes had sweetened on the vines in greater abundance than usual, had enabled Robert to purchase medical equipment that his ancestors could have only dreamed of using. A pioneer of their great experiment, it was Robert's duty to set the example and break new ground. Being more hands-on meant he was better able to make observations and, in turn, innovate. *Learning in motion. Motion in pursuit of betterment.* Of course, Robert Senior had lamented his son's interventionist policies — such was his prerogative — but, ultimately, the old man's time was over and his ideas, so Robert believed, out-moded.

Not so, thinks she. Robert watched as Mary pinched the back of Pandora's hand and inserted an intravenous needle. Mary hadn't spoken to the labouring woman since entering the delivery room. That was her principle. *Why ask for anything when you can simply take?* Robert hoped that his son would balance her disdain and help her to see that, even as they were, simple swine — as Mary considered them to be — served a noble purpose.

Robert signalled for Alexander to join him at the end of the bed. 'Tell me what you see,' he instructed. The younger man moved closer to the woman's open legs. Blood and a foul-smelling glutinous yellow fluid stained the inside of her thighs.

'Vaginal loss is excessive,' he said and turned to his father.

Robert nodded. 'Her cervix is exposed — and looks to have been for a while. This—' with a gloved hand, he wiped the woman's skin with a damp cloth, 'is too much discharge. Her waters haven't broken yet.'

'An infection?'

Robert tossed the soiled cloth into the sink in the corner of the room. 'Let's hope not,' he said.

From the bed, the woman mumbled the doctor's name. 'Dr. Robert—' Pandora paused to catch her breath. 'The wave—'

The electronic CTG machine signalled that another contraction was peaking. As the pain increased, the young woman started moaning. Pulling herself forward, her slender legs spread apart and bent at the knees, she gripped the plastic side rail of the bed. For forty seconds the bed rattled until the wave ebbed away and Pandora sank back against the pillows.

'That's seven minutes since the last,' Alexander stated.

An hour and fifty minutes later, Pandora's waters broke. Alexander heard the pop from the other side of the room.

'She's moving into the next stage,' Robert announced from the end of the bed. Mary handed him a pair of fresh gloves. 'Five centimetres dilated and clear signs of infection,' he said.

There was nothing that could be done to soothe her. Any attempt at getting ahead of her contractions had failed: Pandora was at the mercy of her body. In spite of cool flannels placed on her head and the hydration provided by the intravenous drip, the young woman's temperature continued to rise. As if her body sensed the urgent need to expel the child from her womb, the contractions quickly increased in regularity and strength. Labour was progressing fast and Robert was anxious that the baby be born before Pandora was overwhelmed.

After encouraging Alexander to perform a vaginal examination, Robert was alarmed by his son's announcement that he was feeling 'either fingers or toes.' Fingers would have been fine. Toes would have meant the baby was breached. Fortunately, considering all the other complications with the delivery, Robert stepped in and confirmed that the baby was presenting itself as it should. Pandora, meanwhile, was wailing.

'You should catch a break,' Robert said to his son as the latest contraction ebbed away. 'There'll be more to come.'

Alexander nodded at the young woman on the bed. 'I'm hardly the one who needs a break,' he said.

'It's much the same now until she's fully dilated,' Robert replied. 'I'll need you more then.'

'And you?'

Robert pulled a chair up to the bed and sat down. Smiling, he patted Pandora's hand. 'We'll be fine.'

Mary was arranging a blanket in a plastic baby crib trolley parked by the door. Robert suggested she take a break too.

She wheeled the crib to the end of the bed and handed Robert a fresh flannel for Pandora's forehead. 'Do you want anything?' she asked.

'Coffee would be nice.'

She nodded and walked to the door. Alexander followed. Pandora screamed as he crossed the threshold; her contractions were now only three minutes apart.

It was dark outside and they could hear Pandora's screaming even from over by the Seat. Mary sat on the low stone wall that edged the path to the building and stretched out her legs. In the moonlight, Alexander saw her head droop and wondered if she was about to fall asleep there and then. He moved to sit on the wall next to her.

'What do you think it's like for them?' he asked. Mary lifted her head but said nothing. 'In there,' Alexander continued, 'giving birth like that?'

Mary yawned. 'What do you care?'

He yawned as well, then shrugged. 'It's strange, I guess,' he said. 'It's been a while since I've helped with a delivery.'

'There's nothing strange about it,' Mary said as another scream drenched the night sky. 'Just the way it is.'

Alexander nodded. 'University—' he rubbed his eyes, 'it's different.'

Mary looked at him and searched his face. After a pause, her voice softer than it had been before, she said, 'It must be difficult.'

Despite her tiredness, her eyes were alert and radiated a unique tenderness as she waited for him to reply. 'Yeah,' he said. 'It messes with my head — seeing how other people are.'

Mary turned her face to the building from which they had come. 'Being with Daddy's the same. Staying with him after being here for so long,' she paused and looked at him, 'it messes with my head.'

'Do you prefer it?' Alexander asked.

She considered, then shook her head. 'Not really,' she

explained. 'I love being with him, of course, but here—' she rolled her head back and looked up at the sky, 'it's real. More connected.'

Alexander rolled his head back, too, and followed her gaze. A cloud drifted over the Moon. His limbs felt heavy and he wished they were still in bed.

'It's all so much work,' he said. 'Sometimes, I wonder if it's worth it.'

Mary turned to him. 'Now *that's* strange,' she said, elbowing his arm. 'Saying things like that.'

He laughed and feigned pain from where she had nudged him. 'Well, don't you?' he asked.

Her lips stretched into a smile. 'You're asking me this after I've been pulled from my bed—'

'*My* bed—'

She elbowed him again. 'After I've been pulled from *a* bed in the middle of the night to watch an infected springer push a baby out?' Mary turned her face back to the Moon. 'Ask me again tomorrow when I've had some sleep and eaten my breakfast.'

'Speaking of breakfast, it's already—' he looked down at his watch, 'three thirty in the morning. Want something to eat?'

'If you can eat after seeing all that — *smelling* all that,' she pulled a face and tutted, 'well, you really must be strange!'

Alexander laughed and stood up. He held his hands down to her and said, 'Come on — coffee at least.'

She looked up at him, his elegant frame silhouetted silver in the moonlight, nodded and took his hands. 'Coffee, then.'

Robert was helping Pandora to change position when they reentered the room. Alexander placed his father's coffee on the counter by the sink before offering another arm for the young woman to hold onto. Her fingers dug into his skin as she shuffled about the bed to get on all fours. Robert steadied the woman's legs as Alexander held her arms.

'We're pushing already?' Alexander asked.

Robert nodded. 'Preterm labour is always shorter.'

Mary pushed a handful of pillows under Pandora's body to help support her weight. Dripping with sweat, the labouring woman's face was only inches away from Alexander's as she rolled into yet another contraction.

From the other end of the bed, Robert shouted for her to push. 'Bear down through the wave, Pandora!'

Her face was strained and red, her teeth clenched underneath taut lips, as she pushed with all that she had.

'Now stop! Catch your breath. Take a breath.'

'Burning, burning! Dr. Robert! Burning!'

'Breathe, Pandora.'

Alexander steadied her as she wobbled on the bed. He could taste her short, breathless pants on his face.

'Mary,' Robert instructed, 'counter-pressure, please.'

Staying on the same side of the bed as Alexander, Mary moved to apply pressure to Pandora's lower back. Kneeling on a chair to reach, she used her knuckles to press into the other woman's pain. As the next contraction swelled, Mary glanced across at Alexander and rolled her eyes, before shifting so as to use the heel of her hand to apply maximum pressure.

The screams were endless.

Despite Robert insisting she save her strength for pushing, as the baby's head stretched Pandora's already inflamed skin, there was no stopping her. Half of the time her eyes were closed, the other half they were locked onto Alexander's as he supported the front of her body. He knew he would see them — *popping, agonised circles of blue* — in his dreams for weeks.

'Keep pushing, Pandora,' Robert instructed. 'That's it — you're getting closer.'

Gravity was slowly helping to coax the baby down.

'Please, please, please—' Pandora panted as she tried to catch her breath. Her eyes probed Alexander's as she begged for relief from the pain. He tried to help her by pushing some of her hair off her face, but each time she moved her head, it fell again, plastering itself to her sticky, sweat-smeared skin.

Another contraction. Another push. This time Robert announced that he could see the head emerging. Another contraction. Another push. The head was clear.

'Wait, Pandora,' Robert instructed, 'I need to clear baby's airways.'

She waited, as she was told. When he was done, she pushed, as she was told.

All the while, Alexander watched as Pandora laboured. Her endurance was incredible. If he hadn't seen it with his own eyes, he would never have imagined that this slither of a woman was capable of such an extraordinary feat. No matter how tired she cried she was, how many times she pleaded for the pain to stop, she kept going. Of course, a more detached individual might have shrugged and said that the woman hardly had a choice in the matter: the baby was coming out regardless.

'Baby's almost here, Pandora. Now, push!'

Once the head was clear, it happened quickly. With a pop, the shoulders came free and the baby slithered out of Pandora's vagina and into Robert's arms. She started crying and so did her mother.

Alexander held Pandora's hands as he helped her to lie down on the bed. Tears, no longer of pain, but of absolute joy streamed down her cheeks. The torture was over and the relief was magnificent. After the initial euphoria, her breathing started to soften and her strength receded. She closed her eyes and let her head fall against the pillow. A sudden taut expression and it was clear she was still in pain. Robert waited until the umbilical cord had stopped pulsating before clamping it, so as to allow the placenta to deliver a final transfer of blood and nutrients to the baby. Once mother and child were separated, he carried the newborn over to the crib trolley that Mary had prepared.

She was smaller than she should have been. Patched with blood and waxy, white fluid, her skin was very red and she only had a few hairs on her head. So delicate a life did Robert hold in his arms.

The doctor cradled the baby close to his chest, staining his white coat with blood. 'You'll need some help getting stronger,' he said softly. The infant was no longer crying. 'But, I'll be here for that.' He smiled down at her, then said, 'One day — that is all I ask. One bad day in exchange for all the rest.'

He lowered the baby into the crib and pushed it to Mary, who was standing ready. She wrapped the newborn in the blanket then wheeled her out the room.

On the bed, Pandora, shivering, asked to see her child. Robert shook his head. 'Later,' he said. 'She needs to spend some time in an incubator first.' The young mother protested but Robert was already leaving the room.

Pandora was sobbing now.

'I didn't mean it,' she cried between tear-ladden gasps, 'I didn't— I didn't—' She sucked in a breath of air. 'I've changed my mind.' She realised she was still holding Alexander's hand and turned to him. He searched the door, anxious, looking for either Mary or his father to return. 'I didn't mean it,' the woman sobbed. Her grip weak, she tugged on his hand and cried, 'I don't want to give the gift anymore.'

Twenty-Two

Alexander could feel his heart throbbing in his throat. Onwards, his feet pressed into the earth and propelled his body forward. Cold pricked his cheeks as he cut through the air. He was panting now. *Breathe.* Rude light, expelled from the heavy, winter fatigued Sun, strained his eyes. A rogue branch snagged his sleeve and threatened to knock him off course. *Steady.* He could hear his heart in his head.

After delivery, Pandora's infection had intensified. Robert, eager to advance his son's medical learning and involvement in the daily affairs of the homestead, had assigned her care to him. Three days later, Alexander was straining under the pressure.

She cried all day. Or, at least it seemed that way. Whenever Alexander went to check on the new mother, she would beg him to allow her to see her baby, her body gripped by fever, her skin stained with sweat and tears. He had tried deflection, he had attempted deafness, on one occasion he had even resorted to bargaining. Pandora's daughter, meanwhile, slept in an incubator in a room at the other end of the corridor.

Breathe.

The gate to the bottom vineyard had been left open. Alexander ran through it and alongside the first row of vines. Wizened below the wire trellis, the denuded plants could have been dead. With every step, fog misted from Alexander's mouth, temporarily blinding him. Only a few days before Christmas, spring felt very far away.

That morning, Pandora's milk had come in. She had wanted to feed her baby but the antibiotics she was taking to treat her infection meant she couldn't. Alexander had helped her express milk and had suffered her tears as he washed it down the drain afterwards. Trying to leave the bed to stop him, she had torn her stitches.

At first the newborn had trouble latching onto the rubber teat. Alexander had sat her on his lap, supporting her head with his left hand, mumbling clumsy words of encouragement. She was small and warm and he had been scared of hurting her. Balanced on his knee, she had cooed and then cried after struggling to get a seal on the teat. Alexander had never fed a preterm before. Chin and cheek support, his father eventually showed him, were the key to successful feeding. Now the infant was taking from the bottle eight times a day.

By the fourth row, Alexander needed a rest. He stopped at the headland and leant against a post that marked the outer boundary of the vineyard. Measuring his breathing, he pulled the woollen hat he was wearing from his head and fluffed his hair with his other hand. Cool air rushed across his scalp and down into his skull. Below, his brain needed the rejuvenation.

This was by no means the first time in Alexander's life that he felt a deep sense of confliction. He was, by nature, an overthinker and profound internal conversations in many ways hallmarked his existence. Yet, the combination of his time away from home at university, his fledgling relationship with Mary, and now caring for Pandora and her baby had birthed in him a novel conflict. For the first time, he was not merely contemplating a parallel existence, but living one.

He was a devoted son, cartwheeling between being a shameless mummy's boy and a man duty-bound to follow in his father's deeply-trodden footsteps. He was also a repressed malcontent who increasingly fantasised about mutiny against — or, at the very least, quiet withdrawal from — the world that his father expected him to inherit. He simultaneously wanted to be a part of it, and apart from it. *Duty or defiance.* Some days he leant more strongly towards one than the other. Other days, he worried that he only wanted one because it was what his family wanted, and then only wanted the other for precisely the opposite reason. He was a leaf being blown in two different directions, caught between the crosswinds — neither force of his own origination.

Inwardly, Alexander was a free spirit. Outwardly, he was whatever the person nearest to him supposed he was.

His breathing back to normal, he popped the metal press studs on his coat and pulled a cloth pouch out from an internal pocket. Turning, he balanced it on top of the fence post and unwrapped the tobacco pipe tucked inside. A small cache of cannabis, sealed inside a clear plastic bag, slipped from the pouch onto the wet grass. He crouched to pick it up, wiping it dry on his sleeve. A knock on the fence post made him jump.

'I used to have a pipe like that,' a voice said as Alexander stood up.

Robert Senior withdrew his walking cane from the post and bayoneted it into the earth. The old man exhaled as he transferred his weight onto it. Despite standing both taller and straighter than his grandfather, Alexander felt like a small boy in his presence. Before he had a chance to stutter a response, the old man spoke again. 'Your father know you're using that?'

A brown tweed flat cap pulled low over his brow made it impossible for Alexander to see his grandfather's eyes. He shook his head.

'Good,' replied the older man. 'It would upset his sensibilities.'

Alexander nodded. He turned to put the pipe away but Robert Senior stopped him.

'You're not going to offer me a puff?' he asked.

The bag of cannabis felt hot in Alexander's hands. He looked across at the old man. 'You want to smoke?'

'Well, it's my bloody pipe, isn't it?'

Alexander stiffened. 'It's quite a strong blend of tobacco—'

Robert Senior laughed. 'You think I don't know what grass smells like, lad? I can smell it funking out of the pouch from here. Now light the thing and hand it over.'

Like a good boy, Alexander did as he was told. Loading

a pinch into the bowl of the pipe at a time, he packed the cannabis down with his thumb then wafted a lit match over the top of the pipe. Circling the flame over the surface of the bowl, he drew gently, exhaling the smoke as the cannabis began to smoulder. He stopped to tamp the top of the bowl, then lit a second match, waiting for the sulphur to burn off before wafting again. When the pipe was evenly lit, he passed it to his grandfather. The old man inhaled until he coughed. Watching Robert Senior splutter and choke, one hand clutching the pipe, the other gripping his walking cane, Alexander thought about how he would have to explain all of this to his father when he inevitably had to take him to hospital. When his grandfather stopped coughing, Alexander breathed a sigh of relief.

'Ah,' the old man exhaled, 'that's the ticket.'

He pulled his cane from the grass and shuffled over to the fence. Reclining against a post, he took a few short puffs before offering the pipe to his grandson. Alexander drew heavily. A second, slower draw, then he passed it back to Robert Senior. Leaning against the fence, the two men passed the pipe back and forth, smoking together in silence, the smell of cannabis polluting the winter air.

'So, what are you doing out here?' Alexander asked his grandfather after a few minutes.

The pipe hooked over his bottom lip, Robert Senior exhaled and said, 'Clearing my head.' Alexander nodded and the old man took another draw. After releasing the smoke, he asked, 'You too?'

'Yeah,' Alexander replied. He looked up at the sky and entreated the warmth of the Sun. The star was unyielding and so the cold pinched his cheeks some more. 'How's your knee?' he asked after a pause.

Robert Senior handed him the pipe and shrugged. 'Can't complain now,' he laughed. His cap had slid back, exposing his grey eyes. They were loose and, unusually for the old man, pain free. Alexander felt it too — the easy relief the cannabis provided.

'You're father used to cry like a heifer in heat,' Robert Senior said as he twisted his walking cane against the palm of his hand. 'Screamed the house down when he was a baby. Cry all night, cry all day.' Alexander laughed at the thought. His grandfather nodded and said, 'It's true. He always was a milksop, my boy. Now—' he paused to readjust himself, 'this stuff, a good pinch of grass—' he watched as Alexander exhaled a puff of smoke, 'the only thing that kept me sane.'

Alexander almost choked. 'You smoked cannabis when my father was a baby?'

Robert Senior shrugged then snorted, 'You're smoking it now he's a grown man — what's the difference?'

Alexander snickered and wafted his hand at his grandfather. The old man convulsed as he laughed, an eerie grin twisting the weathered features of his face. A comfortable lull in the conversation and Alexander let his eyes close.

'You grow it yourself?'

Alexander opened his eyes. 'No.'

Robert Senior leant back against the fence. 'Used to grow it back behind E—' He looked at his grandson. 'You know where the hill tucks into itself?'

Alexander nodded.

'There,' the old man said, grinning. 'Whole thicket of plants.'

Alexander laughed and passed him the pipe. 'How much did you smoke?'

The older man shrugged. 'When I was young, a lot—' he exhaled into the air. 'Too much.' A shadow fell over his eyes. Alexander saw it and watched, waiting for his grandfather to say something more. 'Harry,' the old man paused and looked at the sky, 'used to look the other way.'

Harry was Alexander's great-granduncle — the brother of Robert Senior's father. He had died when Alexander was a child and, although the memories were faded, he could still see the liver-spotted, silvery old man in his head. In many ways, Harry had been a father to Robert Senior, a terrible accident on the homestead when he was only three years old having deprived him of a normal family life. Rarely, if ever, did the old man speak of the day the bull got out and killed both his father and grandfather.

Alexander exhaled and watched the cold fog his breath. Inside the hedgerow on the other side of the fence, a bird scurried from one branch to another before flying into the sky.

'Birds always want to fly the nest,' the old man mumbled. Alexander rubbed his nose with the back of his hand and sniffed. His grandfather nudged him. 'You thought about it yet?'

A leaf in the crosswinds.

Robert Senior nudged him again. 'You wouldn't be down here puffing grass if you hadn't.'

'Leaving this place?' Alexander laughed. 'That's treason, right?'

'Doesn't mean you don't think about it.'

'That would make you happy. Prove you right.'

Robert Senior cackled. 'I can read you like a book, lad. Always have. Was the same with your father.' He paused to draw on the pipe. 'You make for shoddier reading, though.'

Alexander couldn't help but laugh. 'What's that supposed to mean?'

Robert Senior closed his eyes, as if remembering. 'Robert always knew who he was. What he wanted,' he said. 'That was the problem.'

Alexander rubbed his nose again. It was getting colder.

'Always had big ideas,' the old man continued. 'Wanting to do this or that. *Change* this or that. Raising him was like one big head butt. Head butting each other every day until—' he opened his eyes and laughed. He touched his knee. 'Well, the young always win. Natural, bloody advantage.'

Alexander took the pipe and inhaled.

'But you,' Robert Senior chuckled and stabbed the ground with his cane. 'You don't know who you are, don't know what you want.' Alexander went to interrupt but his grandfather spoke over him. 'You think too much about stuff.'

'*Stuff* needs thinking about,' Alexander exhaled and said.

His grandfather laughed. 'Spoken like a true intellect.'

'It's better than—' Alexander gesticulated into the open

air, 'bumbling about, heavy-handed, bumping into everything you touch.'

Robert Senior turned to him and laughed some more. 'Oh, I never said you don't do *that*, lad. From what I've heard, you have no problem bumping into things you touch as well as thinking too much.'

Alexander raised an eyebrow.

'Well, your father told me you're finally bumping Mary,' the old man sniggered.

Alexander laughed. 'You're disgusting.'

Robert Senior smirked. 'Like a book, my lad.' Clawing at the earth with his cane, he pulled himself upright, then turned to his grandson and said, 'Now, help me back to the house. I can't feel my toes.'

Dizzy, all Alexander could do was tuck his hand under the old man's arm and heave him across the grass.

Twenty-Three

The switch crackled when she turned it on. Overhead, three strip lights flickered into life, their aged fluorescent lamps buzzing as electricity excited the mercury vapour inside the tubes. Each seemed to glow a different shade of white, the effect being that the refrigerated meat locker looked even more unpleasant than it was.

Mary crossed the room to the back wall. Behind her, Alexander. Behind him, Frank. The latter was wearing an old apron, the colour of which, once presumably white, was indistinguishable and now only definable as soiled, many years of heavy use having spoiled the fabric altogether.

'I'm surprised your mother wants chops,' Mary said, looking at Alexander as she stopped in front of an especially gruesome specimen.

Alexander shrugged. 'I think she's saving the best cuts for New Year's.'

For thirteen days the carcass had been hung. Acephalous and without skin, muscle fibres bulging red, the body had been cut clean in half, split straight down the backbone, exposing its fat flecked ribs to the cool temperature of the room. In the days since slaughter, natural enzymes had broken down much of the connective tissue in the muscle. Controlled decomposition. Improved tenderness was the result.

Mary nodded and turned back to the carcass. Frank, grey-haired and insignificant, stood on the other side of it.

'Well,' Mary sneered at the man, 'are you going to unhook it?'

It was dirty work, but someone had to do it. A dreg of their genetic caste, *who better to perform the task than he.*

The body bloodied his apron as he heaved it from the hook. Bent-backed and hobbling, the man struggled to move it to the door. Neither Mary nor Alexander offered a hand to help.

'Set it down,' Mary said as Frank carried it out of the refrigerated room. Opposite the door, a stainless steel table had been prepared. When he had laid the body down, he stood back, careful to move out of the young woman's way. Mary drew her hair into a bun behind her head, securing it with a single, wooden hair stick, then reached for one of the two black vinyl aprons on a hook next to the door. From the table, she selected a blade, testing its sharpness by making a small incision on the surface of the meat.

Alexander closed the door to the locker before putting on the second apron. He joined Mary at the table whilst Frank waited in the corner of the room. Mary moved the knife over the carcass, counting the ribs.

'Will you be eating with us this year?' Alexander asked the older man.

Frank shook his head. 'Driving to my sister's when we're done,' he said.

Mary looked up from the carcass, said nothing, then returned to counting the ribs.

'Is she keeping well?' Alexander continued.

The other man nodded and shrugged his shoulders at the same time. 'You know how it is,' he said. 'She's never been all that well, and Rick and all that makes this time of year worse.'

Rick was Frank's brother-in-law. He had died on Christmas day two years previous.

At the table, Mary made her first true cut, separating the rib cage from the lower half of the body. Next, she cut away the shoulder and the associated limb and neck fragment.

'These can go back,' she said to Frank. He took the lower half first, Alexander moving to open the door to the meat locker for him. When it was secured on a hook, he returned to the table and grabbed the other chunk.

The flesh was raw and wet. 'That's too flimsy for the hook,' he said to Mary, nodding at the flap of flesh that connected the limb and shoulder. Wordlessly and in one fluid motion, she cleaved the piece in two. Frank grunted and walked to the locker, where he hung the pieces separately.

Drawing the blade of the knife across the rib cage, Mary sliced away a dense layer of fat. The ribs now better exposed, she began partitioning the loin, making cuts perpendicular to the spine so that each portion contained a piece of bone.

'Do you need my help?' Alexander asked, watching as the knife dissected the flesh with ease.

Mary shook her head, then changed her mind and said, 'I left the dish in the front room. Could you get it for me, please?'

'Sure.'

Alexander exited the room, leaving Mary alone with Frank. The older man shuffled closer to the table and nodded at the chops that Mary had started to stack to the right of the remaining carcass. 'Pretty good,' he said. Mary looked up at him. 'Your butchering,' the man explained. 'It's fine work.'

She ignored him and sliced another piece.

Although Mary would never care to admit it, it had been Frank who had taught her the skill. As a girl, he had shown her the importance of a sharp knife and how to define the best cuts. This was before Mary had grown old enough to realise that, of those who had been born better, some had been born better than others. Unlike her, Frank was not of the Founders. Whilst he was by no means a defective, to Mary his was a status that meant very little aside from immunity from the knife. Sophie — Alexander's mother and the woman who had loved her like her own after Francesca Stansfield's death — was the only subordinate Mary cared for. That Frank oozed filth and tobacco made him all the more difficult to tolerate.

Frank continued to watch as she cut another chop. Alexander returned with the dish. One by one, he loaded the cuts of meat into it.

'What's your mother got planned for dessert?' Frank asked Alexander.

Placing another chop in the dish, he smiled and said, 'Crème brûlée. I saw her getting the ramekins out the cupboard this morning.' Alexander paused as Mary nudged another chop in his direction. 'She always likes to have everything ready the day before,' he finished.

Frank nodded and rubbed his hands together. 'Sounds like a treat.'

'And you?' Alexander asked. 'Do you know what you'll be having?'

The other man laughed and said, 'We don't all have a mother as young as yours, Alex. Ma will have her feet up whilst my sister cuts us a slice of dry sponge cake.'

Alexander grinned. 'Sounds like a treat,' he joked.

'Yeah, if that's how you describe a trip to the hospital,' Frank snorted and itched his forearm. 'Last time she baked a cake, it was so dry it got stuck in my throat on the way down.'

The younger man laughed and shook his head. Mary meanwhile had finished and had moved to the sink. The water washed the blood from her hands and sent it swirling away down the plughole. From a pocket somewhere underneath her apron, her phone rang.

'That will be them,' she said, turning to the men. Alexander nodded and covered the meat in the dish. He joined her at the sink to wash his hands.

Frank gestured to the table. 'I'll clean this up,' he said.

Mary nodded and hung her apron up on the hook. 'It will need washing,' she stated.

'That's okay,' Frank said. 'I'll join you when I'm done.'

'Try not to take too long,' Mary replied, already leaving the room.

Alexander quickly dried his hands. 'Thanks, Frank,' he said, grabbing the dish from the table.

'No worries.'

Alexander rushed to catch up with Mary. They had been in E Building, meaning that the drive back to the house was a long one. Trees closed in on all sides. Above, the Moon caressed their naked limbs and threw down just enough light to make the path visible.

Mary's shoulder brushed against Alexander's as the farm buggy bounced over a rock. He turned the wheel and asked, 'Do you think we'll get a white Christmas?'

'Perhaps. It feels cold enough.'

Out of the corner of his eye, he could see the moonlight glistening on her face. Her pale skin looked reflective in the light and made her shine like silver. An unknowingly sensual being, seemingly unattainable, yet completely within his reach.

She's yours. If you want her.

But, being with Mary meant so much more than simply being with Mary. It meant family, it meant expectation, it meant pressure.

Perhaps it would be worth it.

Some days he really did think he was falling for her. But then, other days, he concluded that she was just a convenient way to satisfy the tension he felt between his legs.

The buggy bounced over another rock.

'Is Sophie really making crème brûlée?'

Alexander looked across the buggy at her. 'I think so,' he said.

Mary smiled at him. 'I can't wait.'

As they approached the house, a large white van came into view. It was parked on the gravel driveway next to Alexander's car. He drove the buggy in between the two vehicles then switched off the engine. Next to them, the van was silent and still. The driveway was flooded orange by the lights that edged the steps to the house. As Alexander stood up and out of the driver's seat, the passenger door to the van opened.

'Look who we found at the station!' someone called from inside.

Bespeckled and straightening his corduroys, Ern clambered out of the van and onto the gravel. He smiled when he saw Mary, who rushed around the farm buggy to greet him. He wrapped his arms around her.

'My love,' he said, kissing the top of his child's head. 'I miss you all the more when you've only been gone a short time.'

Nuzzled against him, Mary had made herself small and looked up at him. 'We're together again now, Daddy,' she soothed, before letting him kiss her again, this time on the cheek.

Alexander watched before turning to the van. The cab contained three seats and Sophie had shuffled across from the middle to the door. Her hair was tucked behind her ears and it swung from side to side as she moved.

'Help me down, my strawberry.' She held her hands out in front of her for her son to take. Alexander reached to meet her and guided her, firm yet soft, through the door and down onto the driveway.

From the other side of the van, Robert appeared. 'A stroke of good fortune,' he said as he approached the others. 'We were on our way out anyway when Ern phoned to say he was taking the train.'

The other man nodded. 'Not much point bringing the car when it's just me. The environmental impact is excessive,' he said.

Mary linked arms with her father. 'I'm glad you came.'

Ern looked down at her and smiled slowly.

'Of course you came,' Robert chuckled, leaning to pat his friend on the arm. 'It wouldn't be Christmas without you.'

Ern sniffed. 'Indeed, indeed,' he said with uncharacteristic impassivity.

Robert pulled back before looking to his wife and then again to Ern. At her father's side, Mary nestled closer to him and touched his hand. 'What's that, old friend?' Robert asked. 'You weren't going to come?'

A piece of gravel rolled onto the grass as Ern nudged it with his shoe. 'Think nothing of it, Rob,' he said, summoning a smile. 'Just a touch melancholy as of late.'

The two men looked at each other. For a fraction of a second, Ern's gaze slipped. Momentarily, he met Alexander's eyes, a brief and troubled contact which jolted the latter to drop his eyes to the ground. No one else seemed to notice. Sophie stepped closer to Ern and draped an arm around Mary.

'You're with family now, dear,' she said to the man.

'Yes,' he replied, before widening his mouth into a grin, 'Yes, I am.' He squeezed Mary, kissing her one final time and then let her go, slapping his hands together as he moved closer to Robert. 'So, Rob,' he exclaimed, 'you caught a fish tonight?'

The other man laughed, combing his fingers through his dark hair.

'It was not so much a catch, but a lure,' Sophie said before her husband could speak, a hint of mischief in her eyes.

Ern's left eyebrow raised. 'Oh, really?'

Robert chuckled and took his wife's hand. 'It emasculates me to admit it, but I was little more than a chauffeur on this one, Ern.'

The three of them moved to the back of the van, Alexander and Mary following close behind. Robert placed his hand over the handle. It clicked as he tugged, the doors opening to reveal the cargo area. Light from the outside trickled into the dark interior. Alexander leant over his father's shoulder to get a better view. In the far right corner, crumpled on the plywood floor, was a man. His wrists and ankles had been bound with tape. Neck bent, head halfway balanced between the floor and the side panel of the van, he turned upon hearing the door open. His mouth wasn't covered — there was no need. Here, there was no threat of rescue.

His voice croaked when he spoke. 'What happened?' He sounded surprisingly young, his high-pitched, squealing intonation belying his impressive physical build.

Beyond tilting his head, he didn't move. Clearly, he was groggy. Robert climbed inside the van. The floor creaked as he shuffled just inside the cargo area.

'Clifford,' he said, lowering himself so that he was closer to the man on the floor. 'Everything is alright.'

The young man mumbled and tried to raise his head. Robert lifted a hand.

'No,' he said, 'it's better that you don't do that.'

The bound man leant back against the side of the van. 'Where am I?'

In the darkness, Robert relaxed his hand. 'Somewhere you'll be looked after.' He paused and then said, 'Looked after properly, Clifford. Like you've never been looked after before. I just need you to come with me.'

Outside, Alexander edged closer to the rear bumper, watching as his father moved towards the back of the van. His mother placed a careful hand on his forearm.

'How do you know me?' the bound man asked, once again trying to raise his head. His hair was covering his eyes.

Robert stopped and crouched, rearranging his trousers as he did. 'Come with me and I shall explain.'

Despite his drowsiness, the man on the floor laughed. 'Explain why I'm gagged and bound in the back of your van?'

'We could not have this conversation if you were gagged, Clifford.'

The man considered and again asked, 'Where am I?' He could no longer conceal the fear in his voice.

Robert sighed and stood up, bending his neck so as not to touch the top of the van. 'You have a choice, Clifford. You can cooperate with me, or—' he paused and looked at the man, 'or you can make this difficult for yourself.'

Alexander was already inside the van by the time Clifford had pulled himself up from the floor. Arms still tied together at the wrists, he had planned to loop himself around his captor's neck and drag him to the floor, beat his face, tear at his skin with his teeth if need be. But, before he even got close, Clifford found himself constricted, his legs pinned in place by Alexander's boot, a strong arm tight against his jugular.

'It is such a shame,' Robert said, almost too quiet to hear. Clifford gulped, struggling to catch his breath under Alexander's arm. 'I always hope for cooperation.'

He screamed, of course. He shouted, naturally. But nothing could save him. Like constrictors, they glided over him and bound him tighter. As he was, it wasn't difficult to transport Clifford out of the van. Robert helped to steady the man as Alexander stepped down out the back. Ern and Sophie moved to the side to give the men space. Mary had taken the keys to the farm buggy from Alexander and was repositioning it close to the van's rear doors.

It was when Clifford was out of the van, squinting and bathed in the light from the house, that he saw her.

'You,' he whispered in disbelief.

Sophie held her position and looked at the young man.

Clifford shook his head, his brown eyes wide and fearful. 'No,' he stuttered, 'How can it be you?'

With a sudden burst of strength, the young man reeled away from Robert's grasp and towards Sophie. Alexander gripped him tighter, shoving his arms underneath Clifford's armpits and dragging him back. The man screamed and wailed and tried to pull away.

'How can you stand by and watch this happen?' the man shouted at Sophie. 'You're supposed to be a good person!'

Robert snatched at the man's face and turned it away from his wife. 'You need to calm down, Clifford.'

His cries of resistance only increased as Alexander and Robert pushed him into the farm buggy. 'Stop them!' he shouted at Sophie. 'How can you help all those women and let them do this to me?'

Standing besides Ern, she said and did nothing.

'Stop them!' Clifford cried over and over again, even as Robert climbed into the driver's seat of the buggy and started driving away. 'Please, help me,' he appealed to Sophie, his voice becoming more and more desperate.

'Mrs. Wheatleigh, please, don't let them do this!'

Twenty-Four

Nanny told them that a man with a red suit and a big white beard had done it. 'Came down the chimney,' she had explained, wafting one of her fat arms at the gold and silver plates that had appeared on the table overnight. Cherub had wanted to ask what a chimney was, but the other girls were already swarming over the food and she didn't want to miss out.

Squares of pink and yellow held together with a sweet and sticky orange-coloured jam. A spongy, cream-stuffed brown log, decorated with multi-coloured sprinkles and vanilla swirls. Little men wearing red hats, jelly buttons and chocolate boots. Stars that twinkled with sugar.

'I like these best,' Filly said as she bit off a chocolate-coated gingerbread leg.

Cherub nodded. She liked them too. In fact, she liked them all. Her fingers were already sticky and covered in cake.

'Why'd he give us this?' Cherub eventually asked her friend.

Filly looked up from the plate she was studying. 'Who?' she asked.

'What Nanny said — the man with the beard and the red suit,' Cherub explained between mouthfuls. 'Why'd he give us all this stuff?'

Filly shrugged and toyed with another gingerbread man.

'Remember when we had those little fruits,' Cherub said. 'Do you think that was him, too?'

The other girl shook her head. 'What little fruits?'

'The multi-coloured ones. Apples and pears and little, bitty oranges.' Cherub licked her fingers and said, 'You thought they tasted funny.'

'Oh, I remember.' Filly wrinkled her nose at the memory. 'They were yuck!'

Cherub laughed. She was sitting on the end of her bed, swinging her legs back and forth so that the metal squeaked. Across her lap, tucked in front of her ragdoll Rosie, a plate loaded with sugary delights made her already full tummy grumble for more. Filly moved from her bed to Cherub's and took a square of cake from her plate.

'So, you think that man really brought them, then?' the blotchy-skinned girl asked, offering the first bite to her friend. Cherub took it and shook her head.

'Sounds weird.'

'Yeah,' Filly agreed, also taking a bite. 'Perhaps Nanny did it.'

Cherub shook her head again, then leant closer to Filly and whispered, 'Nanny'd just eat them all herself.' Filly giggled, clapping her hand over her mouth to stop crumbs of cake from falling out. Cherub shared in her laughter, leaning her head on her friend's shoulder, wrapping her arms around her skinny middle.

'You should eat more,' Cherub said when they had finished laughing. 'Here—' she passed the plate to Filly, 'eat mine. I have too much chub.' She poked her own belly and grimaced.

Filly shook her head and nudged the plate back. 'No, I like it when we share,' she said. Cherub pulled a face and so she nudged the plate some more. 'You shouldn't listen to the others,' Filly said, her voice soft.

'They're right though,' Cherub responded. 'I am chubby.'

Filly turned, her brown eyes full of expression. 'I've said before,' she said. 'They're just jealous.'

'Yeah, yeah, I know,' her friend huffed.

Across the room, a girl with two thick plaits was munching on a piece of chocolate cake. She was savouring it, pausing to lick the sprinkles off the top in between bites. Another girl, sitting next to her, wide-eyed and anxious, was waiting for her to finish with the plate. Cherub felt for Rosie on her lap and held her closer to her.

'Make sure you girls share with the little ones,' a voice said from behind them.

Filly and Cherub turned to find Nanny standing over them. She was an ancient woman, or at least the girls thought so. White-haired and plump-bossommed, Nanny had been a part of Cherub and Filly's lives for as long as they could both remember. She nursed their injuries when they fell, helped to wash the parts of themselves they couldn't reach, and — once upon a time — read them bedtime stories and kissed them goodnight. Now, she was simply tired. Old and tired and fast approaching retirement.

'Some of them haven't had anything yet,' the old woman said, nodding to a small, black-haired girl who was clutching the hem of her smock.

Cherub patted her bed, encouraging her to come sit next to her. The girl was sucking her thumb and looked from Nanny to Cherub and then back to Nanny again in search of confirmation. The white-haired woman nodded and so the girl let go of her smock and clambered up onto Cherub's bed. Cherub offered her a star biscuit and the child took it without saying anything.

'You should make Jessica share,' Filly said to the old woman.

Nanny sighed and shook her head. 'You girls know better than most that Jessica's not a very generous soul — even at Christmas.'

Cherub watched the black-haired girl take a second bite of the biscuit. Granules of sugar stuck to the corners of her mouth. When she realised the older girl was watching, she suddenly dropped the biscuit and scurried off the bed and back to Nanny, timid, hiding in the skirt of her smock like a mouse.

'What's Christmas, Nanny?' Cherub asked after the girl had left the bed.

The old woman touched Cherub on the head. She took a moment to consider, then said, 'It's a time to be grateful for what we have, sweet child.'

'Like for the cakes,' Cherub replied.

'Yes,' the old woman looked at the depleted plate on the

bed, 'like for the cakes.' From behind her, the black-haired girl peered out. 'And,' Nanny continued, encouraging the small girl back towards the bed, 'Christmas is also a time for generosity — for sharing.'

Cherub held out the half-eaten biscuit to the girl. Careful and quiet, she took it. It looked huge in her small hands. Filly shifted closer to the other two girls and watched as the younger one ate. After a moment, she turned and looked at Nanny.

'So, is that why the man brought us the cakes?' Filly asked.

Nanny laughed. It was a louder sound than the girls were used to hearing from her and it caught them off guard. Filly glanced at Cherub and, nose-twitching, the black-haired girl stopped chewing. When the old woman regained her composure, she touched each of the children on the head in turn.

'No, inquisitive child,' she said to Filly, 'it wasn't generosity that brought you your sweet treats.' Her voice was peculiar and dark, and betrayed a sombreness that contrasted the usual convivial atmosphere of their shared home. Confused, Filly went to ask another question, but Nanny stopped her. 'Enjoy your cakes, girls,' she said. 'Be grateful for what you have. The man can take as easily as he can give.'

Twenty-Five

Morning had barely arrived when the note was pushed under her door. Hours later, she found it on the carpet, corners folded where it had rubbed against the brass threshold that separated her room from the hallway outside, and carried it to her dressing table. There, still in her pyjamas, she lifted the red seal with a nail file. 'Red box under the tree.' The cursive was elegant and carefully written. Pulling on a pair of thick socks, she tightened the cord of her dressing gown, slid out her bedroom door and snuck down the stairs to the sitting room.

Everyone was still in bed, but he was on the sofa, asleep, glasses crooked and half-falling off his face. In the far corner of the room, beside the fireplace, a blue tinged spruce tree sparkled with lights. Tucking the note into the pocket of her gown, she sat on the pouffe next to the sofa and placed her hand on his face. He stirred as she thumbed his cheek. Caught somewhere between slumber and wakefulness, he smiled.

'Tell me you haven't been here all night,' she whispered.

He pulled himself upright and straightened his glasses. 'I

couldn't sleep,' he whispered back, then, with a sleepy grin, said, 'Too excited.'

Her eyes lit up and she laughed softly. 'Happy Christmas, Daddy.'

'Happy Christmas, my love.'

The box was where he had left it — under the tree, placed just in front of a ceramic reindeer. It was small and covered with red velvet. He watched as she opened it, balancing it on her knee as she untied the gold ribbon which kept the lid closed.

'It was your mother's,' Ern said as Mary inspected her gift.

It was a ring — a rectangular faceted emerald encircled by a halo of champagne-coloured seed pearls. The central stone caught the light as she tilted it between her finger and thumb. The gold of the band was old, dulled, but not tarnished: well-loved and hinting at a history that new things simply didn't have.

'It was my grandmother's before,' Ern continued from the sofa. 'I gave it to your mother when I proposed to her.'

A love story, a symbol of hope and shared dreams, of a lineage that was meant to continue.

'It's beautiful,' the young woman said, looking from the ring to her father. 'But why are you giving it to me?' she asked.

A slight smile. 'It was yours a long time ago. I just had to find the strength to let go of it.' Ern moved forward in his seat. 'And, to let go of you.'

Mary again looked at the ring before slipping it onto one of her fingers. It was a perfect fit.

'Thank you, Daddy.' She reached out her hand and he took it gladly. Raising it to his lips, Ern kissed the finger now decorated with the ring.

'You are very welcome,' he breathed. Then, after a pause said, 'Francesca would be so very proud of you.' Behind the lenses of her father's glasses, Mary could see tears had formed in the corners of his eyes. She squeezed his hand and he smiled, at first melancholy, but then wider and with more exuberance, before starting to laugh.

'You've turned me into a soppy old fool,' he chuckled, removing his glasses.

Smiling, Mary was about to respond when they heard movement out in the hallway. Expectant, they both turned their heads to the sitting room door just in time to see it open.

'Good morning,' a tired-eyed Alexander said as he peered around the door frame, 'and Happy Christmas.'

'Happy Christmas, Alex,' Mary said from the pouffe, still hand in hand with her father. On the sofa next to her, Ern also offered seasonal greetings.

'I thought I heard someone in here,' Alexander said before turning his eyes to Mary, 'and when you weren't in your room I—' he rubbed the side of his neck and smiled. 'Anyway, would you both like some coffee?'

'Tea, please,' Ern replied as he returned his glasses to his nose. Mary responded likewise, then offered to help him in the kitchen.

'If that's no bother,' Alexander said, looking at Ern. 'I don't want to interrupt.'

Reclining back against the sofa, the other man wafted his hand. 'No, not at all,' Ern grinned. 'Just bring me some biscuits with the tea.'

Mary stood up. 'Of course.' She touched her father on the cheek before leaving the room to join Alexander.

On the stove, the kettle started to whistle. Mary draped a tea towel over the handle to lift it then poured the boiling water into the cups. The teabags floated to the surface.

'I thought you offered to make the drinks,' she said, casting a wry glance across the kitchen at Alexander, who was leaning against the old oak sideboard next to the door.

'I offered to make *coffee*,' he said, catching her eye as he looked between her and a book he was holding in his hands. 'You wanted tea.'

'Well, at least I know what I want.'

Alexander closed the book and placed it on the sideboard next to him. Mary moved to the fridge for milk. She took the top off the bottle, poured the creamy liquid into the cups, then returned it to the shelf. Alexander watched her, arms folded across his chest.

'I didn't want to—' he paused when she looked at him. He considered, then said, 'I don't want you to think poorly of me.'

The spoon rattled against the porcelain as she stirred. Unspeaking, she held his gaze, waiting for him to continue.

'I suppose I felt bad. What with your father being in the house.'

Mary's eyes urged for more.

'It— it just felt improper.'

Mary finished with the spoon and placed it in the sink. 'Improper,' she finally said, 'is pushing someone away when they have given you no reason. Improper is—'

'I—'

'Let me finish. Improper is holding your tongue, failing to say anything at all, when someone tells you that—' Mary's voice wobbled. She cleared her throat, then continued, so quiet that Alexander would have had to strain to hear had he not already known what she was about to say. 'When you say nothing when someone tells you that they love you.'

Alexander winced. He would have argued that she made it sound so much worse than it had actually been, but he knew that would have been a lie. He felt terrible and wished he could tell her something to make it better, but 'I don't know what to say,' was the only response he could manage.

Mary sighed. 'It's Christmas, Alex. At least try to show some charity.'

She picked up the tray with the teas and the plate of biscuits and carried it to the door. Wordlessly, he moved to open it for her. As she passed, he caught a whiff of her scent and inwardly cursed himself for being such an imbecile.

She kept her distance from him all morning until it became obvious to all that she must be punishing him for something. The previous evening, after the excitement on the driveway, he had walked her inside the house, ahead of Ern and Sophie, who stayed talking together on the gravel. In the sitting room, Robert Senior had been minding Guinevere and Aurélie, beguiling the younger with fanciful and fantastical stories. As

Alexander had passed by the door with Mary, it being slightly ajar he had caught his grandfather's eye. The old man had paused, winked at him, then returned to his story. Later, when Mary opened up to him, the bitter taste in his mouth had still been there.

'What gift did you get Mary?' Sophie asked him as they arranged plates together in the dining room.

Alexander turned his head, avoiding his mother's questioning eyes as he heard someone open the fallboard to the piano in the sitting room and run their fingers over the keys. 'I haven't given it to her yet,' he said.

This was true — he had bought her a gift. It was upstairs, sitting on top of the quilt on his bed, wrapped in blue tissue paper. He had intended to seek her out, present it to her in private, make her reaction his and his alone, but last night had made things awkward.

'Why not?' Sophie asked, folding a napkin.

Alexander moved around her to place a plate at the far end of the table. 'I'm waiting for the right moment,' he said, quiet and keen to end the conversation.

His mother touched his elbow. 'You cannot wait forever, my strawberry.' She stopped what she was doing and waited for his eyes to lift from the table. When they did, Alexander shook off her gaze and reached for another plate.

At least try to show some charity.

'Do you need help with anything else?' he asked.

Sophie shook her head. 'Not until the food is ready.'

'Okay,' Alexander said, 'just find me then.'

Sophie nodded and watched him leave the room.

Christmas day or not, there was always work to be done. In the hallway, Alexander laced up his boots. The lace on the left shoe had frayed, so he tucked what was left of it behind the tongue before pulling on his coat. He checked his watch and took the keys to one of the farm buggies.

Pandora's baby was already noticeably bigger. Little over a week old, it was starting to become difficult to tell that she had been born preterm. Big-eyed and bonny, the newborn gurgled when she saw him.

He poured the water into the bottle first, being careful to check it was the right temperature before adding the formula. Holding the edge of the rubber teat, he put it into the retaining ring, then screwed it onto the bottle. Once the cap was over the teat, he shook it and the powder dissolved into the water. A drop of the mixture onto the inside of his wrist told him the liquid was safe for the infant to drink. He sat her on his lap and supported her cheek and chin with the same hand he held the bottle. She started to suckle, eager and hungry.

Bottle feeding wasn't ideal. Labour intensive and messy, it was something that the family tried to avoid. In certain circumstances, however, it was the only option. Pandora's milk was laced with antibiotics, and, even if it hadn't been, she was still too weak to meet the demands of a hungry newborn. For now, Alexander had replaced the infant's mother, and it was to him that the child looked to for nourishment, warmth, cleanliness and, strangely, affection.

The newborn gazed up at him whilst she fed, holding his

eyes for a few seconds before turning her attention to something else. So young, her vision was limited to objects that were only a short distance in front of her. Alexander didn't speak to the child as he had done those first few days when he had coaxed her to feed. Instead, he snatched impatient glances at his watch, its face clinking against the plastic of the bottle as it bobbed up and down in the infant's mouth. As the milk drained, she paused, and Alexander drew the bottle away slightly, giving her time to catch her breath. While she rested, he patted her back and switched sides, moving the infant from one knee to the other. Once she was settled again, he allowed her to draw the bottle back in and continue suckling.

When the formula was gone, she needed burping. Alexander lifted the infant to his chest, resting her chin on his shoulder. She hiccuped twice as he arranged her. Cupping his hand, he began patting her tiny back and waited for her to burp. It was important to get the air that she had swallowed whilst feeding out.

Better to be sick on me now than all over herself when I'm gone.

He threw the towel into the sink when the infant was finished. Softly, he returned her to her crib and turned off the light.

Pandora was sleeping when he looked around the door to check on her. Her hair was flat against the pillow and there was a flannel on the floor which must have slipped from her brow. Quiet shoe steps and he picked it up from the tile. He found a fresh one in the cupboard under the sink, dampened it with cold water, and folded it over the woman's forehead. Caught in fever fatigued sleep, her eyelids fluttered and she mumbled something inaudible. If her daughter had grown stronger in the days after delivery, Pandora had grown weaker. Alexander put the window on vent to allow some of the cool Christmas air inside then closed the door to her room. Before climbing back into the farm buggy, he checked the lock on the entrance to the building. He would be back in a few hours.

Twenty-Six

The food was almost ready to be served by the time Alexander returned to the house. Mary was in the kitchen, spooning condiments into small, round glass bowls. The cranberry sauce was homemade and she licked the spoon after emptying the jar.

'I hope you're not going to put that in the bowl.'

She raised an eyebrow, slid the spoon out of her mouth and, with over-exaggerated motion, dropped it into the empty jar.

'What do you want?' she asked as he walked across the room.

'To help you carry these in.' Alexander nodded to the bowls on the worktop next to her. At first suspicious, she relented and stepped to the side. He picked up two bowls of cranberry sauce. She took one of mint and one of mustard and went to follow him through the door.

'You know, I used to really like cranberry sauce,' he said as they placed the bowls on the table in the dining room. Alexander set the second bowl down and turned to Mary. She straightened the mustard and, unblinking, held his gaze. 'But,' he continued, 'one day, I dropped some all over my shirt and everyone teased me about it afterwards, every single time we ate it. And so, because I was stubborn, I decided I wouldn't eat it again. I convinced myself it was so inherently tart that I could never enjoy it. That it wasn't to my taste.'

'If this is an apology, then—'

'But then I tried it again,' he interrupted, 'and realised that it has a hint of sweetness. Subtle. Delicious,' he grinned, and she dropped her eyes, a smile starting to pull at her lips. 'And *then* I realised that, actually, I really do quite like cranberry sauce.' Softening his grin, Alexander took her left hand in both of his. She looked up. 'I got you a gift,' he said gently, guiding her around the other side of the table. 'If you'll accept it.'

Tucked under the table and concealed by the tablecloth, he had placed it on her seat. He pulled out the chair, picked up the present, and gestured for her to sit. She did, and took the blue tissue paper bundle from him with careful hands.

'It's heavy,' she said as Alexander pulled out a second chair. 'What is it?'

He smiled and shrugged. 'Open it.'

Mary peeled the tape off the corners piece by piece, fully immersing herself in the moment, relishing in how, with every cut, with every fold, with every fastening of the paper, he must have been thinking of her. He leant against the back of his chair, trying to appear relaxed and nonchalant despite being anxious to witness her reaction.

To a casual observer, it was a straightforward enough gift. A luxury version of the game Scrabble. A rotating wooden cabinet, complete with built-in storage drawers and a brown leather board, it was an exquisite, expensive, suitably impressive present. Yet, when Mary unwrapped it, she knew she had been right to wait, right to suffer, right to pine and cry and need him so badly in her darkest moments.

We are meant to be.

Alexander's choice of gift was marked by an honesty that said, 'I see you. I know you'. It told her that *he had been listening, he had been there,* all those times she had spoken of her sadness and of that inexorable tide of grief she had borne, oftentimes alone and in silence, since childhood. How she had cried over the loss of her mother. How, as the newness of the injury had dulled in the years afterwards, she had adopted her love of word games as her own.

Mary pulled open one of the drawers, revealing the bag of letter tiles, and thought of how she and Alexander might play the game together, and that, in giving her this gift, he had expressed to her — in actions, if not in words — that *he wants to play the game together.* She closed the drawer and placed a hand on either side of his gift.

'Do you like it?' Alexander asked, leaning towards her, aware that she had not yet said anything.

Mary nodded. She touched the board, running her fingers over the grid where the letter tiles were meant to be placed. 'I do,' she replied, being careful to moderate the emotion in her voice. 'Very much so.'

He smiled and said, 'I'm glad.'

She absorbed the warmth of his expression then said, 'And

now I suppose you expect something from me?' Her tone was both playful and severe.

Alexander laughed and ran his hand across his cheeks and down over his chin. 'Never,' he said, eyes bright. *And yet, always,* Mary thought, remembering the first night he had come to her.

'It's just as well, then,' she said, rising from the chair, 'that I got you something.'

She placed the board game on the table before she left the room to get it. Alexander stayed where he was, wondering what gift she might have chosen for him. He knew her to be sharp-eyed, sharp-witted — *even a little too sharp on occasion* — and serious, the owner of a clever tongue who knew how to hide her soft parts behind an armour of silent contempt and, indeed, cruelty. But, he also knew that it was that sharpness which gave Mary a depth of perception that could only be regarded as empathy. When directed towards the right person, she had a great ability to understand — and thus, if the wrong person, to manipulate — the feelings of others.

When the door to the dining room reopened, it wasn't Mary, but Alexander's father who stood on the threshold. He was wearing the jumper he wore each Christmas, and never any other day of the year: a blue and white knitted nightmare with Christmas trees on the cuffs and a chain of octagram stars across the middle. Robert had once told his son he only wore it because Sophie liked him to, but Alexander suspected that he himself rather enjoyed the cheery comfort of that garish jumper.

'Your mother wants to know if you're done in here,' Robert said, one hand on the doorframe.

Alexander turned in his chair. 'Almost,' he replied. 'We can move out the way if she needs.'

Robert shook his head. 'Finish up,' he said. 'I can see you're in the middle of something.' He noticed the Scrabble board on the table and smiled. 'Your gift?' he asked. Alexander nodded. Robert was about to say something else when Mary came in from the hallway.

'Is Sophie ready, Robert?' the young woman asked as he stepped to one side to allow her into the room.

Robert shook his head. 'Ten minutes or so more.' He looked at his son and said, 'I'll leave you to it. Do come and help your mother when you're done.'

Alexander nodded and watched as his father closed the door behind him. Mary was already back in her seat. Lavishly carved, time-worn and robust in her delicate hands, a wooden box housed her gift to him.

'For you.' She placed it on the table next to him. Alexander took it and opened the lid. 'For whenever you are feeling lost,' she said.

It was an antique nautical compass. Made of brass, a metallic aroma rose into the air as Alexander lifted it from the box. The device's rose, the diagram that displayed the points of the compass, was exquisitely engraved, and laid out the eight cardinal and intercardinal points. Perfectly sized to slip inside a pocket, it had been crafted to help lost sailors find their way home.

Alexander balanced the compass on the palm of his hand. The needle pivoted, oscillating above the rose for a few seconds, before settling into equilibrium. At its centre, helping to hold the needle in place, was a small red stone. Mary pointed to it and explained that it was a ruby. 'And,' she said, placing her hand over his and turning the compass, 'I had it engraved.'

On its back, in the centre of the compass, etched into the brass, were his initials. *A.R.W.*

So I don't forget who I am.

It was a symbolic gift, a heartfelt gesture that came from a place of understanding. Alexander thanked her and asked whether she would like him to keep it safe in the box, or on him, in one of his pockets. She hesitated, before telling him that was for him to decide.

At least try to show some charity.

He slipped the compass into one of his trouser pockets and kissed her on the cheek. Her skin was warm and soft beneath his lips, and beckoned him to stay longer. Christmas dinner, however, was in the kitchen waiting to be served.

A bowl gorged with roast potatoes formed the central dish, and from it spiralled plates of roasted carrots and brussel sprouts, honeyed parsnips, buttered cabbage, sage and onion stuffing, and large, crisp Yorkshire puddings. Jugs of gravy flanked the ends of the table and on each individual plate was a perfectly juicy, perfectly tender chop, seasoned with fresh herbs and peppercorns, first seared, then transferred to the oven to finish cooking. Aromatic, sweet white wine was poured into crystal glasses. For the children, cups of fresh milk, frothing with thick cream. A veritable bounty of homegrown produce. It truly was an occasion to be merry.

'Oh, my dear,' Sophie giggled, clutching Robert's hand on the table, 'you are silly!'

At the other end of the table, Ern was shaking with laughter, trying to put his glass down without spilling his drink. Next to him, Robert Senior was chewing furiously, shaking his head. 'You'll be old one day, too, my boy,' he said, mouth full of meat.

'Indeed, Father,' Robert smiled, 'so you remind us all.' At his side, Sophie giggled some more.

Ern swallowed his laughter and was able to return his glass to the table. 'Rob,' he gestured to his friend, 'such talk makes me wonder, what shall you do once young Alex here is finished with his studies?'

Alexander looked up from his plate and pulled a quizzical face.

Robert laughed. 'On the subject of being old, Ern? Be careful what you are insinuating — you and I were infants together.' The other man cut himself a wedge of potato and chuckled. 'Well,' Robert continued, 'it may not be for a few years yet, but I suppose it is a valid question.' He turned to his son, who was sitting beside him, and, grinning, asked, 'So, what do you think? Shall you displace your old father when you're done with university?'

Robert Senior whooped with laughter and his fork clattered onto his plate. 'The lad couldn't displace an ant, let alone a stubborn bugger like you!' At the old man's side, Ern once again began shaking with laughter.

Sophie shook her head and leant across the table to touch Alexander's hand. 'Let him speak, Robert,' she chastised her father-in-law. The old man continued laughing, retrieved his fork from his plate and impaled a brussel sprout on its tines.

'I have no intention of *displacing* you,' Alexander said to his father. 'Besides, as you say, it will be a few years before I'm finished.'

'A dedicated scholar. Very proper,' Ern nodded and then nudged Robert Senior. 'It's not all brawn, old man.'

The adults at the table considered the hobbling and aged figure of Robert Senior and all — the old man included — erupted into laughter.

'Brawn? You really do need those glasses, don't you?' Robert Senior boomed.

The laughter was ravenous now. Ern crushed a napkin in his fist and swallowed, red-faced, jovial, and trying not to choke on his food.

'Take a drink, Daddy.'

Also laughing, Mary pushed a glass of water into Ern's hand, and, between shuddering chuckles, he just about managed to wash the food down. At the other end of the table, Sophie dabbed her eyes with a tissue and Robert smiled, teeth large and white.

'It's well that Ern is such a jolly soul,' Robert chuckled over the food at his father. 'Others might not take your remarks in equal good spirit.'

'Pish,' the old man responded, cutting himself another chunk of meat. 'I shan't waste the time I have left concerning myself with the feelings of cissies, Robert.'

'Can't change an old habit can you now, old man?' Ern beamed. Robert Senior, chewing, clapped him on the back enthusiastically and smirked. His son, still smiling, simply shook his head.

Changing the subject, Sophie looked to Mary. 'You did a lovely job with these chops, dear.'

The young woman raised a napkin to her mouth and swallowed. 'Thank you.'

'Yes,' Robert agreed, 'a good portion. Generous, but not overwide.'

Ern took his daughter's right hand and raised it up off the table. The snowy pallor of her skin glistened against the gold and green of her mother's ring. 'The hands of a butcher,' Ern teased. Mary wriggled her hand from his grasp and shook her head.

'Shall we benefit from your skill again on New Year's, Mary?' Robert asked.

She looked from him to Sophie, who smiled and nodded her head. 'Certainly,' Mary said. 'Although, I imagine a lot has already been prepared.'

Sophie nodded and addressed her husband. 'Yes, dear,' she explained, 'most simply needs to be defrosted.'

'I don't know how you manage it each year, my darling.'

'Indeed,' Ern said, 'it's always a wonderful occasion. It is a true skill that you have, to arrange it as you do.'

'Thank you, Ern,' Sophie smiled. 'I have plenty of help. And, let's not forget the work that goes into it over the course of the year.' She turned to her right and touched her husband's cheek. Robert matched her smile. 'Hard work. Work that, too often, goes unthanked,' she said, holding his gaze.

'You do work very hard, Rob,' Ern said. 'Harder than I. Harder than most.'

'Thank you, old friend.'

Robert Senior nodded. 'It is true, my boy.' All looked at the old man. 'What?' he laughed, 'Even I am not such an old fart to raise a quarrel there.' He met the younger Robert's eyes. 'You do a good job, son.'

Unsure, Robert smiled strangely. 'Thank you, Father,' he said with genuine tenderness. 'It means a lot.'

'Well,' the old man snorted, 'it's bloody Christmas, isn't it? I'm obligated to say something nice to you, aren't I?'

Laughter and more head shaking. Ern straightened his plate and chuckled, 'Thank goodness for that. For a moment, I thought the wine was making me hear things!'

At the other end of the table Robert smoothed the cuffs of his jumper. 'Thick skin and a healthy breathing technique — that's what you need living in this house.'

The old man snorted for a second time. 'Not to mention a healthy amount of substance abuse.' With a flourish, he held up his glass and drained the last of his wine. 'Isn't that right, lad?' Robert Senior turned his old, devilish eyes to Alexander, who was taking a sip of his own wine. The old man guffawed when the younger man's cheeks turned red. Sophie tutted and once again chastised her father-in-law for picking on her son. At Alexander's side, Mary narrowed her eyes, wondering what secrets the old man knew that she didn't.

Twenty-Seven

'Cannibal.'

It was a rudimentary word. Not an obvious option for success, its impressive breadth did little to detract from a relatively low base value. Strategy was what made it effective. Well positioned on the board — spread across a double letter and two triple words — it was an exceptional play. In short, a winning move.

'One hundred and seventeen, I believe.'

Robert reached for the bag and pulled out seven new letter tiles. Careful not to allow the others a chance to glimpse them, he arranged them on his letter rack before clasping his hands together in front of him, a self-satisfied smile on his face.

'You never said you were so good at this game, Robert,' Mary remarked from the other side of the Scrabble board. At her side, Robert's daughter, Guinevere, pulled a face, disgruntled that her thirteen-year-old wit wasn't great enough to best her father. Robert straightened his back and laughed. Guinevere stuck out her tongue and so Robert did too.

Sophie caught her husband's eye and fiddled with the letter tiles on her rack. 'You should give the children more of a chance, dear,' she said.

'Yes, Father, you should give the children more of a chance,' Alexander teased. After pulling two 'Z's and a 'Q' with no 'U' out the bag early on in the game, he had consistently scored low.

They were arranged about the coffee table in the sitting room, huddled around Alexander's Christmas gift to Mary. Guinevere and Mary shared the pouffe, whilst Alexander sat on the rug, his back against the side of his grandfather's armchair. Robert was on the sofa, next to Ern, who was napping. Sophie had the other sofa, young Aurélie fidgeting between the cushions and her lap.

The golden-haired girl clambered on top of her mother and draped her short arms around her neck. 'What does it mean, Mummy?' she asked.

Sophie wrangled her child into a more comfortable position, moving her pink-socked foot from where it had dug into her thigh. 'My angel,' Sophie said, 'you are heavier than you think.' Aurélie giggled and rolled off her lap back onto the cushions.

'But, what does it mean, Mummy?' the girl asked again. 'Cannibal?'

Sophie arranged herself. 'Well,' she considered, 'it's when someone, an animal or a person, eats their own kind.'

'Eats?' the child responded.

'Yes, when an animal eats an animal that is the same as it.'

Aurélie pulled herself upright and looked at her mother. 'What about the animals outside?' she asked. 'Is that cannibal?'

Sophie giggled and tweaked her daughter's nose. 'No, my angel. That is not the same — they are not the same.'

The girl looked confused.

'Well,' Sophie continued, her voice light and playful, 'how about this—' she leant closer to her daughter, 'if I were to eat you,' she tweaked the child's nose again, 'that would make me a cannibal.'

All of a sudden, she grabbed the little girl and began tickling her, pretending to nibble her little arms and little legs. Aurélie shrieked with laughter, kicking her feet away from her smiling mother. Meanwhile, it was Alexander's turn and he sat eyeing his letter tiles, a pained expression on his face. Bridging off his father's 'C' and onto a double letter square for a score of eleven, 'cable' was the best he could manage.

'And with that, I shall retire,' he said, pulling himself up from the floor. The other players groaned in unison.

'Don't go, Alex. We haven't finished yet,' Robert said from the sofa.

His son laughed. 'I think you mean *you* haven't finished yet. Besides,' he looked at his watch, 'I need to head down to B Building.'

Robert nodded. 'When you check her fluids, her bag might need changing.'

'Sure,' Alexander said and returned his remaining letter tiles to the bag.

'We'll have cake when you're back,' Sophie smiled.

Next to Robert on the sofa, Ern stirred. 'More food, Sophie?' Everyone laughed.

'Not yet, Daddy,' Mary said, shaking her head. 'Later.' He mumbled something, readjusted his head on the pillow, and seemed to fall back asleep. Mary turned to Sophie. 'Your cooking is the highlight of his Christmas.'

'I think it's the highlight of mine, too,' Robert smiled, reaching to touch his wife's hand.

She patted his fingers and looked at Alexander. 'You'd best be quick, my strawberry. I'm not sure these gluttons will wait if you take too long!'

Alexander smiled and said he would be as quick as he could, stopping to tickle his youngest sister under the chin as she dangled over the arm of the sofa, trying to grab him as he went to leave the room. In the hallway, boots, coat and keys, and he was out the door.

Outside, it was already starting to get dark. It was a creeping sort of darkness. Having been dull all day, the impending night seemed little different from the daytime, everything draped in grey, cold and heavy, indifferent to time. He had to be careful on the hill. A layer of frost had coated the ground like icing sugar. The last thing he wanted to do was spin the tyres and have to call his father to tow the buggy out of the bramble asphyxiated verge. The decline negotiated, he increased pressure on the pedal and turned left onto the track that coiled through the trees to where most of the homestead's buildings were located.

It was warm inside the grey cladded building. He hung his

coat in his father's office, exchanging it for the white laboratory coat that they always wore when working. It was their uniform — a clear delineation between who they were up at the house and who they were down here, interacting with the livestock. Standing in front of the mirror that hung over the sink in the bathroom adjacent to the office, Alexander wondered just how different he felt wearing that coat. *A little boy playing dress-up in his father's clothes.* He tugged on the cuffs that didn't quite meet his wrists, flattened a stubborn kink in his hair, turned off the light and left the room.

Pandora was awake when he unlocked the door. Her blue eyes were big when she saw him. He slipped into the room, the door automatically locking as it closed behind him.

'How are you feeling?' Alexander asked as he moved to her bedside. Her intravenous fluid bag was almost empty.

'Hot,' the young woman said. 'Cold, too.' She smiled. It was weak and yet still somehow bright.

Alexander walked to the sink and washed his hands before pulling a new fluid bag out of the fridge that sat under the worktop. It would need time to warm up before being changed. When he turned around, Pandora was trying to pull herself upright. He went to help her.

'Careful,' he said, slipping his arm around her back to move her. She placed her hand on his shoulder and used it to support herself. 'I don't want you tearing your stitches again.' She nodded and allowed him to arrange her on the bed. When she was upright, Alexander walked back to the sink and washed a glass he had left there earlier in the day.

'I imagine you're hungry.'

'Yes,' Pandora replied.

'After you've taken these I'll get you some food.'

He held the glass, now full with water, out to her and placed two blue-coated pills on the blanket that covered her legs. With slight, shaking arms, she took the drink from him and raised it to her lips. He watched as she took the pills, her eyes looking right back at him as she swallowed.

'You're looking better than you did earlier today.'

The woman on the bed didn't say anything.

'You were sleeping,' Alexander explained.

Pandora nodded as if she understood.

In the small room that they used as a kitchen, Alexander spooned three heaps of a special blend of milled oats, nuts and vitamin supplements that they fed the women into a bowl. The electric kettle clicked when it rolled into a boil. He poured the water and stirred. It was watery, so he added an extra spoonful. Back in the room, he placed the food on a tray on the bed in front of Pandora. She took the spoon from him with grateful eyes.

'Can you manage?' he asked.

She nodded.

'I need to feed your baby,' he said, moving back to the door.

Pandora said something that he didn't quite hear. He turned around and asked her to repeat what she had said. The spoon was in the food, abandoned and resting against the plastic edge of the bowl. In front of her, raised above the blanket, the woman's hands were clasped together, her face soft and pleading.

'My baby,' she said to Alexander. 'Please, let me see her.'

Alexander sighed and ran his hand over his stubble. 'We've spoken about this before. You can't feed her. Not whilst you're taking those pills.'

'No,' Pandora shook her head, 'I know. I know I can't feed her. I just want to see her. Please.'

She looked woefully pathetic, weak and feeble, hair unwashed and matted, brow moistened with fever, her smock, sweat drenched and loose, clinging to her body. Alexander thought back to the woman he had watched deliver her first baby only a few days before. *Popping, agonised circles of blue.* Her eyes stared at him with the same intensity that they had done then.

'Please,' Pandora said again.

At least try to show some charity.

'Okay,' Alexander relented. 'But not for long. And no feeding.'

On the bed, the young woman seemed to swell with happiness, her physicality, which had been stolen from her in the days after delivery, returned to her, and, momentarily, made her appear stronger and more able. His teeth digging into his bottom lip, Alexander exited the room, wishing his father had not thought to burden him with this responsibility.

The infant was pleased to see him, as she always was. Alexander meant milk and Pandora's baby adored the stuff. The child's hair was thick and brown, and she already bore a resemblance to her mother. Stuffing a fist into her mouth, she made a smacking sound with her lips. Alexander took a breath, swaddled the baby in a blanket and lifted her from the crib.

Pandora cried when he carried the infant through the door. The sound of her mother's tears must have startled the baby, as she began crying too, her little arms fighting to be free of the blanket. *Of course she's crying*, Alexander chastised himself, *you're tormenting her — tormenting them both.*

The baby's mother held out her arms for her child. Alexander could see her chest heaving beneath her smock, oxygen being syphoned from her lungs to feed her tears. He resisted her sobbing and sat, cradling the child to his chest, a short distance from her on the bed.

'Pandora,' he said, his voice stern, 'you need to calm down if I'm going to let you see her. You're scaring her.'

A short sob and a sudden cessation. She drew the back of her hand across her nose and swallowed. 'Okay,' she whispered. 'I'm sorry.'

Alexander rocked the child and tried to soothe her. Pandora watched on, enchanted, captivated by the breathing, living, tiny version of herself that he held in his arms. She was yet to touch her, yet to smell her, yet to know the warmth of her fresh, new skin. Pandora had dreamt about how it might feel to hold her, of how big and blue and beautiful her baby's eyes might be. As the infant's cries softened, her dreams were about to become reality.

Alexander shuffled along the bed, closer to the young woman. 'You can hold her whilst I mix her formula,' he said, his voice low so as not to disturb the child. As he transferred the little body into her arms, he stopped and looked at Pandora. 'Please don't make me regret this.'

The young woman drew the child to her bosom. Silent tears rolled down her cheeks. 'Thank you,' she whispered to Alexander, and then again, to no one in particular, 'Thank you.'

When he had mixed the formula, he took the baby back from her and started feeding her. Pandora watched, wide-eyed.

'She likes it when you hold her chin,' Alexander said, supporting the baby on his knee. 'Like this.'

Pandora didn't say anything, only watched, beguiled.

A silence enveloped the room. The only sound to be heard was that of the infant sucking on the teat, hungry as ever. Before she could drain the bottle too quickly, Alexander took the milk away and rubbed the child's back. 'You have to burp her,' he explained. 'Otherwise she'll be sick.'

He could tell that Pandora wanted to feed her daughter, if not from her own breast, then as he was, using the bottle. Despite her fragility, she had strained away from the headboard, moving closer to him and the child. When she was close enough that he could smell the stale sweetness of her breath, he adjusted the infant on his lap and offered her to Pandora.

Sitting on the bed, he watched her bottle feed her baby. As he did, Alexander remembered how she had laboured for hours, sweating, screaming in pain. She had been so glad when her child was born, the pain was over, but — more than that — she had brought new life into the world. *Her gift, she said.* It had been magical — until it wasn't. Watching her baby being taken, wheeled out the room away from her, Pandora had said she didn't mean it. *That she didn't want to give the gift anymore.*

Pandora looked up from her child and smiled at Alexander. 'Thank you,' she said again.

He swatted the memory away and smiled back. *Simple swine*, he told himself. *She's probably forgotten all about it.*

With the bottle empty, it was time to take her back. Alexander positioned himself close to the mother and her baby, so that he could slide the child out of Pandora's arms and into his. Gently, he guided her head into the crook of his arm, strands of Pandora's hair tickling the side of his face as he leant in closer to support the baby. She was in his arms now, a trail of milk drooling down her chin. As he pulled away, drawing the child to him, Pandora's face was in front of his. Their noses contacted, just for a second, and then, unexpectedly, she moved forward and kissed him on the lips. It was a simple kiss. Short, sweet, soft. Over before it had started. Pandora pulled away and apologised, and then, eyes solid and wide, thanked him yet again.

Baby in arms, Alexander quickly stood and stepped back from the bed. 'Sure, no problem,' he said. He mumbled something about needing to put the baby back in her crib and hurried out the room.

Just get the baby back in the crib, Alexander. Just get the baby back.

Terrified he was about to drop her, or worse, that, for some reason, his father would decide to come down and check on him, he rushed down the corridor to the room with the cribs.

A flash of his keycard and he deposited the child into the plastic container, before clutching the rail of the incubated crib trolley with both his hands.

Breathe.

He breathed.

That's better.

He had no idea what had just happened or why it had happened.

It's your fault. You should never have let her see the baby.

He breathed again.

Why did she do it? What was she thinking?

There was, of course, one explanation for the kiss and that was that Pandora was too simple-minded to even realise what she was doing.

A feeble-minded, high-grade defective.

Alexander loosened his grip on the trolley and ruffled his hair with his hand, before letting it slide down the side of his face to his chin. He stood there, chin in hand, for a moment, before straightening himself and moving to the door.

Go home, Alex. Your mother's made cake.

He breathed, walked out the room and to his father's office to retrieve his coat. As he arranged the thick collar of his coat around his neck, he brought his hand up to his forehead and sighed.

The IV bag.

He had not yet changed it. Not bothering to swap his coat again, Alexander walked back to Pandora's room. As before, he unlocked the door and slipped inside. She was lying down, her back to him. Silently, he walked to the sink and washed his hands, before picking up the fresh intravenous fluid bag and moving to her bed. She rolled over and watched him as he removed the old, almost empty, bag. He kept his eyes on what he was doing, not saying anything, until the new bag was attached and the old one was in the bin. He washed his hands again and walked to the door.

On the bed, Pandora fidgeted. 'See you in the morning,' she said.

Alexander nodded and said, 'See you in the morning,' before slipping back through the door.

The farm buggy was where he had left it and he climbed inside and started heading back up towards the house. It had started to snow, a light flurry, powdery and delicate.

A white Christmas.

On the driveway, sheltered by the darkness, he could see his family inside the house through the sitting room window. Happy silhouettes, laughing and talking. His mother's head on the left-hand side, bobbing up and down, probably talking as she sat on the sofa, unmoved from where she had been when he left. A shape that could only be his grandfather hobbled in front of the window, seemingly going out through the door into the hallway. And there, standing, long-necked and slender, her silhouette in the centre of the window, Mary.

Alexander pushed his hand inside his pocket and pulled out the compass. The metal was lukewarm, guarded against the cold night air by the warmth of his body. He placed it on the palm of his hand and opened the lid. The ruby caught the light as the needle span, oscillating back and forth, determined to remain indeterminate.

Twenty-Eight

'Are you a religious man, Clifford?'

On the bed, the young man didn't raise his head. Robert stepped out of the shadows of the corner of the room and closer to him.

'You've heard of Eden, no doubt?'

Still the man said nothing. Robert crouched beside the bed, rearranging the fabric of his trousers as he did.

'It was a garden, a perfect garden created by the Lord. Adam and Eve—' Robert paused and looked up at the man on the bed. 'You know of them?'

Clifford was silent.

'Adam and Eve, the first man and woman created by the Lord, lived there, in the garden of Eden, until, one day, they couldn't live there anymore.' Robert's brown eyes hardened. 'Do you know why that was, Clifford?'

The other man raised his head to look at him. 'You're crazy,' he said.

Robert's face softened into a smile. 'It would surprise you

to know the number of times I have been called that,' he said. 'Crazy. Monstrous. Evil, even. But,' the soles of his shoes squeaked as he readjusted his footing on the tile, 'I am rather of the opinion that *you*,' he nodded at the man on the bed, 'are the crazy — indeed, monstrous — one.'

Clifford laughed. 'Yeah, okay, whatever you say, man.'

Robert sighed and stood up. Clifford's eyes followed his movement. Honey-skinned and athletic, the man on the bed was wearing only a thin cotton vest top and a pair of boxer shorts. A vein in his neck rippled as he clenched his jaw.

'Perhaps a different story,' Robert said. He was back in the corner of the room, his silhouette bleeding into the shadows. 'It may be a little too sophisticated for your palette, but I shall tell it to you nonetheless.'

A moment of silence as if he were organising his thoughts. On the other side of the room, Clifford would have leapt up from where he sat and charged the man in the white coat, only his arms were chained to the frame of the bed.

'In Ancient Greece,' Robert began, 'there were many gods and goddesses. Zeus and Poseidon, Athena and Apollo — all very important, all very well-known, even today. Each had a task.' Watching, Clifford strained his eyes, trying to focus on the shadowy figure of his tormentor. 'Some even had multiple tasks,' Robert continued. 'A pantheon of divine beings associated with specific aspects of life. People prayed to these gods, worshipped them, asked them to intervene in their lives, to help make them better. What do you think of that, Clifford?' Robert moved and the dim light of the room illuminated his face for a second. 'Do you think that made them feel powerful, being given so much responsibility?'

In a low voice, Clifford said, 'Yeah, if that's what you think.'

'It is what I think,' Robert replied. 'In fact, there was another who believed in this idea so strongly — that being given such responsibility made him powerful — that he dedicated his life to becoming a god.'

Clifford laughed.

Robert breathed and said, 'You laugh because you do not understand — but he did.' He walked the edge of the room, tracing his finger along the tiled wall. 'Dionysus was his name — or at least the name he chose for himself.'

'Dionysus?' the man on the bed asked.

'Indeed.'

'Like the wine?'

A short laugh. 'Yes, Clifford, like the wine,' Robert smiled. 'Dionysus, the Greek god, was associated with wine and wine-making, but, more than that, he was the god of male fertility and virility. Do you understand what that means?'

'Of course I know what that means,' Clifford spat.

'Well,' Robert continued, 'this man wished to become Dionysus. He wished to take all of the power and responsibility of Dionysus, to *become* all of that power and responsibility, but to exercise it here on Earth—'

'Let me guess,' Clifford interrupted, 'this guy is you, right?'

Robert stopped walking and chuckled. 'No, this man — for all his nobility — was a lunatic.'

'So, he couldn't have been you then?'

'No, Clifford, he couldn't have been me,' Robert said. 'As it was, it was a symbolic act. To become a god — chained, here, on Earth. To become Dionysus — god of winemaking, fertility, virility and, even, quite fittingly, insanity. And so,' Robert looked at the man on the bed, 'he did. Dionysus gave up his life and became a god. Liberated. Powerful.'

Clifford reclined so that his back was touching the wall. 'What's this got to do with anything?'

'Ah, I was hoping you would ask that.' Robert moved closer to him. 'You see, Dionysus lived a long time ago. Never again was there one such as he.' He paused and smiled. 'Until, quite possibly, now.'

Clifford looked down at the chains that bound his wrists to the bed. *A god, chained, here, on Earth.* His skin prickled. Robert was right beside him now, smiling down at him. *I have to get out of here.*

'So, what do you think, Clifford?' Robert asked. 'Would you like to become a god?'

Before the young man had a chance to respond, Robert looked up to the corner of the room and said, 'You can let them in now.' Clifford turned his head to follow the man's gaze. There was a click and then the metal door, which marked the only way in and only way out of the room, opened. Through it, a woman was pushed. And then another. And then another. All three were naked. They held onto each other, wide-eyed and buxom, quivering wordlessly in the corner of the room. The door closed and clicked again.

'A god is all powerful, Clifford. A god,' Robert gestured

to the women, who scampered closer to him at his command, 'can take whatever he pleases.'

Clifford tried to shuffle away as the naked women crowded around the man in the white coat. When he spoke, his voice was low. 'What are you saying?'

Robert smiled at him and said, gentle and with soft eyes, 'I am saying, why reign up in heaven, when there are so many delights to be had here on Earth.'

With one hand, Robert guided the most curvaceous of the three women forward, taking her by the shoulder and nudging her closer to the bed. She had pink, soft lips and they parted like a budding rose as she lowered herself onto the mattress. Tumbling in front of her as she clambered across the bed on all fours, her hair was thick and shiny and eager to be touched. The second woman, whose dark skin looked pearlescent in the meager light of the room, approached from the other side. In the middle, Clifford didn't know where to look. When the third woman, wide-hipped and amorous, blocked any exit he might have wished to make from the bed, his body betrayed him.

Robert took a step back. He smoothed the sleeves of his coat and said, 'I shall leave now and let you consider our conversation.'

Outside, sitting on a chair in the corridor, Mary was half-watching the proceedings in the room via the monitor on the wall in front of her. When she saw Robert approach the door, she pressed a button and then turned her eyes back to the pages of the book she was reading.

'Done?' she asked when Robert appeared through the second door. He nodded and she pressed the button again, making sure both the inner and outer doors to the room were locked.

Robert combed his hair with his fingers before moving a chair from further down the corridor next to hers. 'What are you reading?' he asked as he sat. Without lifting her eyes from the page, Mary tilted the book so he could see the front. 'It looks a bit dark,' he said, nodding at the image of a noose that dominated the cover.

'It's a classic,' Mary replied, still reading. 'You'd find it amusing — it's set on an island and there's a doctor in it.'

Robert stretched his legs and yawned. He sat there for a moment, and then, referring to the monitor on the wall, said, 'There shouldn't be any issues.'

Mary turned in her chair and looked. A mound of flesh, writhing on the bed. 'No, doesn't look like it.' She pressed the button to turn the screen off and returned to her book.

'We'll see how he does with these and keep increasing his supplements. After that, we can think about introducing him to some of the unwilling ones,' Robert said.

Mary hummed and nodded in agreement.

Twenty-Nine

There were seven of them now.

It had been days, weeks — *who knows how long?* — since they had helped Pandora through the metal door of their prison. In the time since, they had heard nothing of her, save for the agonising screams that had floated down the corridor and under their door for hours after Robert had taken her. When it had stopped, Samantha had surprised herself. She realised she wanted to learn something of the young woman's fate. *Was she okay? Was the baby healthy?* The answers to these questions never came, and so she was left wondering what had happened to her, and if she, too, would one day disappear through the door, fate unknown.

Here, time was irrelevant. The hours were measured by the intervals between the meals that were deposited through the hatch in the wall, and the days by the regular appearance of vomit in the two toilets of the women's communal bathroom. Evelyn still threw up, although — mercifully — with declining frequency.

Today, Jade was in the bathroom with them, slouched over a basin, staring at her breasts in the mirror.

'They're getting bigger,' she said, cupping the left one with her hand. 'That's not normal. It's too soon, right?'

Behind her, Evelyn's body shook and ejected a mouthful of vomit into the bowl of the toilet. Samantha was slouched on the floor, back against the door, her hand resting on her stomach. She felt gassy; her belly was bubbling. 'Shut up, Jade,' she moaned. 'No one gives a shit about your boobs.'

At the toilet, Evelyn's hand slipped and a clump of her hair tumbled into the sick.

'Definitely bigger,' Jade said, squeezing her other breast and looking at Samantha on the floor. 'Yours are going to be huge. Milk machines.'

'Fuck off,' Samantha said. It was passive and low effort. Jade shrugged and returned to looking at herself in the mirror.

Still shaking from the sick, Evelyn crawled across the bathroom floor to the other sink. She took a moment, then, hands clasping the rim of the porcelain, dragged herself to her feet, turned on the tap and put her mouth under the water. Grains of sick had got stuck between her teeth, so she rinsed the water back and forth, side to side, around her mouth. On the floor, Samantha could hear the liquid rush against the inside of the other woman's cheeks. Evelyn spat the water out and wiped her mouth.

'You're in your second trimester already,' she said, inclining her head in Jade's direction. 'Of course they're getting bigger.'

Here, time was irrelevant.

Breast still in hand, Jade glanced at Evelyn out the corner of her eye. 'You've got sick in your hair,' she said, pointing. Evelyn looked down, sighed, scooped her hair up, and shoved it under the tap.

Samantha felt the door move behind her. When it didn't open, her body blocking it and keeping it shut, there was a light knock on the wood and a whisper from the other side. 'Can I come in?' it said. Samantha shuffled across the floor on her bottom to allow it to open.

It was the green-eyed woman. When she saw the three of them, she looked at each of them in turn, as if she were seeing something other than what they were, an image of themselves that lay beyond the mortal senses, metaphysical, and, to most, beyond the boundaries of vision. *Our celestial mission.* 'Ladies,' Mother whispered as she moved to one of the toilets. Samantha said nothing and watched her close the door to the cubicle, slowly and with quiet grace. The sound of urine hitting the edge of the bowl and she pulled herself up from the floor.

Samantha moved to Evelyn. 'Are you done?' she asked. The other woman squeezed the water out of her hair and nodded.

Escaping had morphed from a dream to a possibility in the days immediately after Pandora had gone into labour. That Robert could be made to appear — *summoned from the bowels of Hell* — had inspired Samantha. Maybe all hope wasn't lost. Maybe, just maybe, they could use this to their advantage and get out of this place. Of course, inspiration was a long way from an idea, and an idea a long way from an actual, executable plan, but it was inspiration nonetheless. *A possibility. A way to escape and bring down all these fucks.*

Evelyn had been in two minds when she had told her. Ever since she had met Samantha, the younger woman had talked of getting out. It was only natural. She had just arrived. Fresh to this place, her spirit was not yet entirely broken, her body not yet entirely stolen, sacked and pillaged and looted of every usable asset. In her head, there was still hope. Evelyn had told her friend to abandon the idea. She would only upset herself more.

Upset? Samantha wasn't upset. Upset was how children felt when their mothers denied them the last biscuit in the tin. *Upset is chipping a nail after giving that skank from the pub twenty quid for a manicure.* Upset didn't even touch the sides of how Samantha felt. She was fucking furious. The only way to sate her rage was to get out, *and make sure Robert, his pretty little wife and that ginger bitch get what they deserve.*

'Let's just think about it,' Samantha said in a whisper to Evelyn as they sat, as they did for much of the day, on the sofa. 'Maybe we can come up with something.'

Evelyn shook her head. 'I've been here for so long. This will be my third baby here. You think I wouldn't have left already if I could have just jumped Robert at the door?'

Samantha drew her legs up off the floor and crossed them underneath herself. Recently, they had started to cramp during the day. 'That's not what I mean,' she said as she rubbed her thigh. 'I'm not saying I know better than you and you're some sort of idiot for not getting out. I'm saying the opposite — if

I can do this, I need you. Together — that's the only way we stand a chance.'

The other woman sighed. 'Samantha,' she said, 'look at me. Look at *us*. How?'

More and more pregnant with each passing day, hormonal and fatigued, they were hardly the ideal candidates to enact a great escape. Between them, they didn't even possess a pair of shoes.

'But if we don't go,' Samantha hissed, 'then what?' Her blue eyes were wide and Evelyn could see the fear that she carried — locked away and half-starved of oxygen — in her heart. 'You said so yourself, one day we might be able to do it.'

'But not like this. One day, when the circumstance is right.'

Samantha shook her head. 'It'll never be *right*. We have to make it right.' Holding her abdomen, she shuffled closer to Evelyn. 'I know — I know you're scared.' The other woman fidgeted away from her. 'Listen, Evelyn, listen—' Samantha laced her fingers through her friend's and tried to appear strong, but the fear was still visible in her eyes. 'I almost got out. I was that close. I swear I felt the handle move. If I could have just—'

'That's what they want you to think,' the other woman interrupted, her voice strained and feverish. 'It's perverse, what they do, the games that they play. They think they're better than us—'

Samantha squeezed her hand. 'They're just people, Evelyn. You told me that.' She was cooler now, her eyes calmer. 'I can't have a baby here,' she whispered. 'I just can't.'

Evelyn nodded. 'I know. I'm not asking you to. I don't *want* you to. But what choice do you — do we — have?'

'If we think, really think about it, maybe we can think of a way. Outsmart them—' Evelyn went to interrupt but Samantha spoke over her. 'They can't have thought of everything,' she said, and then again, this time slowly, pronouncing each word apart from the next, 'They are just people.'

Evelyn looked at her, mouse-eyed and scared, before sighing. 'Okay,' she said. 'We'll think about it. But, we're not doing anything unless we have a proper plan.'

'I wouldn't want to,' Samantha said, her voice darkening as she remembered how it had felt to have been dragged down the corridor by Mary. 'I don't want to give her the satisfaction of catching me again.'

Find a hole. Make it bigger. Find a hole. Slip right out through it.

'Well, let's think about it then,' Evelyn continued. 'We know they watch us,' she moved her head to one side, tilting it in the direction of the camera that perched high in the corner of the room.

'Jade broke one before,' Samantha said, recalling the day she and Evelyn had found out they were pregnant and that Jade, to her displeasure, wasn't.

Evelyn shook her head. 'Something like that would get their attention. Whatever we do needs to be out of sight. They can't suspect us. And, that makes me think,' she drew her head closer to her companion, 'the others can't know.'

Samantha looked about the room. Jade had found a new source of entertainment and was kneeling in front of the television, feeding a disc into the DVD player. Beth and Ladybird were sitting together on a bed, one playing with the other's hair as they spoke and laughed about stupid things. Nathalie was elsewhere, presumably in the bathroom, and Mother, the green-eyed fruitcake, was cross-legged on the floor by the window, eyes wide open, lips moving fast and silent, meditating or conversing with the angels or whatever it was that she did.

'Agreed,' Samantha said, turning back to her friend. 'Just us.'

'We'll help them if we can,' Evelyn said, 'but they can't be involved.'

Samantha nodded.

'It might take time to think of how to do it,' Evelyn continued, 'so we have to be patient.' She gripped Samantha's hand and, with a passion that Samantha hadn't before seen her demonstrate, said, 'We have to be watchful. We have to be there when they make a mistake. We have to be ready for an opening.'

'They're only people,' Samantha whispered.

On the floor by the window, Mother started to sing.

Thirty

The first guests started to arrive just before six p.m. Luxury vehicles crunching over the gravel, clean shaven men in black bow ties and ladies dripping in diamonds. For those in the know, the Wheatleighs' New Year's party was the social event of the year.

At the back of the house, an infrequently used room had been opened up, its wooden shutters taken down from the windows, its curtains freshly laundered and its large open fireplace lit. Candles adorned the walls and about the room tables draped in red cloth over-spilled with silver trays of sparkling wine and delightful canapés; finger sized slices of bread topped with fresh cheese and cranberries and quails eggs and chive and fragrant mint and cucumber and thinly sliced slithers of cured meat. In the corner, a string quartet played, two violinists, a viola player, and a cellist dressed in black, and the warmth of the fire and the music drew the visitors to the house into exuberant and exciting conversation. The cellist drew their bow over the strings of their instrument and a well-groomed man straightened his bow tie, laughing. At his side, his female companion twinkled as she regaled an equally lavish couple with stories she had waited all year to share.

The sound of laughter and classical music drifted up the stairs of the house. The landing was dimly lit, just a red-shaded lamp on a dark oak console table, so as not to entice guests away from the ground floor. Bare-footed, a pair of heeled shoes in hand, Mary slipped across the carpet and into a bedroom on the right side of the house. Inside, leaning against a chest of drawers, was Alexander. He was wearing a white shirt, a black satin bow tie at his throat and gold cufflinks at his wrists. In his hands was his grandfather's pipe, the bowl stuffed with cannabis. His fingers shook as he tried to light a match.

'For goodness sake, Alex.' Mary closed the door behind her and crossed the room.

She took the matches from him and struck one. The pipe hooked over his lip, he watched as she lit the cannabis for him. When it started to smoulder, she blew out the flame.

'I thought we'd agreed about this,' she said, her eyes searching his. Alexander drew on the pipe to keep it lit. 'No matter,' she continued. 'I'd rather you do it than have to argue about it now.' She wrung her hands together and breathed, her posture straightening as she did. 'Your mother asked me to ask you if you're coming down. Guests are arriving. She wants you to greet them.'

At the mention of guests, Alexander closed his eyes and drew heavily. Smoke seeped out through his nostrils.

Mary sighed and smoothed the front of her dress, a simple,

yet elegant, black silk satin evening gown. 'You know that I don't enjoy this any more than you do,' she said, the back of her throat dry and constricted. 'Parading ourselves in front of all those people as if we have something to prove to them.'

Alexander took the pipe from his mouth and inclined it in her direction. She looked from him to the cannabis and he nudged it towards her again. Meekly, she placed her lips on the mouthpiece and closed her eyes.

'It helps,' he said, holding the pipe for her as she inhaled. She released it and coughed. 'Better?' he asked.

She coughed again and pulled a face. 'No,' she said, trying to be serious, but smiling as he started to laugh. Eyes soft, he took the pipe back for himself. One last draw and he was finished.

'Can't be too stone-faced,' he said, leaving the warm pipe in the sink of his bathroom. Walking back to the chest of drawers, he offered a hand to Mary. 'To the circus?'

She smiled and took his hand. 'To the circus.'

Robert was at the front door, a single red rose tucked into the buttonhole of his jacket, smiling as he welcomed a man with thin grey hair into the house. Beside him, his arm wrapped around her waist, was Sophie, her hair gathered into a small bun at the nape of her neck and held in place by two dazzling hair clips. She beamed, falling closer against her husband as the man with the grey hair said something that made them all laugh. Robert turned when he heard movement on the stairs. His smile widened and he extended his arm, shepherding Alexander and Mary over to them.

'My son, Alexander,' Robert smiled at the man with the grey hair, 'and Ernest's daughter, Mary.'

The older man smiled and introduced himself. 'Gerald Foye,' he said, reaching to shake Alexander's hand. 'I'm sure we've met before. Unfortunately, I'm not always able to attend your mother's excellent parties.' The man, Gerald, smiled at Sophie, after which he turned to Mary and took her hand. 'Very beautiful,' he said, raising her fingers to his lips. She smiled and thanked him, before pulling her fingers back to her side.

'Gerald does a lot of work overseas,' Robert explained. 'He's quite a pioneer.'

The other man laughed. 'Aren't we all, Robert!' Both Robert and Sophie shared in his laughter.

'What sort of work do you do, Mr. Foye?' Alexander asked. 'Research or application?'

'Both,' the grey haired man replied. 'I'm a bit of a dabbler, I'm afraid — and, please, call me Gerald.' His body language was open and charming and invited easy conversation. 'I may be wearing a suit this evening, but such formalities really aren't to my liking. I'm much more of a cotton slacks, sandals and socks sort of man!'

More laughter and Robert suggested that Gerald might like to join the other guests at the back of the house. 'We have wine and plenty to keep your hunger tantalised until dinner is served,' he said, smiling and holding his arm out for the older man to follow. As he and Sophie went to accompany their guest, Robert looked over his shoulder and said, 'Alex, stay here — welcome the next guests.' He gestured with his hand, wafting it to encourage his son to move closer to the door and take his place at the front of the house. Alexander feigned a smile, creasing his eyes and holding his father's gaze until he was sufficiently far enough down the hallway.

He turned around and moved to stand next to the front door. Mary touched his arm and, looking at him, said, 'It's alright. I'm here.'

A small nod and Alexander smiled at her. Even so, he couldn't help but groan. *Let this be over.* He thought of how many old men's handshakes he would have to endure, and how many younger men — eagle-eyed and ambitious — he would have to play politics with that evening.

The next to arrive were a middle-aged man and his wife. He was serious and squeezed the bones of Alexander's hand when he shook it. She was effervescent and laughed too loud each time Alexander said something that was barely humorous. *And I thought I was high*, he said as he laughed with her, his eyes tearing at the corners as the laughter kept coming.

Another man, less serious than the other but with all the charisma of a wart, was persistent in showing Alexander his shoes. 'I made them myself,' he boasted, encouraging the younger man to touch the leather. Alexander ran a finger over the supple skin. 'Very nice,' he lied, smiling, before inviting the man to come inside.

A young man and his sister, who had recently inherited a sizable operation just outside of the capital, regarded Alexander with suspicion as they passed through the front door. They didn't stop to talk, and neither did the old woman who came next, although Alexander suspected her behaviour was more a symptom of her dottiness — the old woman having stopped to converse with a vase of flowers on a sideboard after hobbling past him and Mary — rather than be an indication of conceited rivalry, as it was with the younger guests.

In the back room, the quartet was playing an uptempo piece. The sound of strings swirled down the hallway and around the house.

'Who's that?' Alexander whispered to Mary as they watched yet another guest arrive.

Lifting herself out of the driver's seat of a black sports car, the woman was impossibly tall and wore a red silk jumpsuit. It was pleated at the waist and had a low neckline, so much so that it grazed the edges of her breasts, tempting any onlookers to look harder, daring them to try to catch a peek of something they had no right to see. Her hair was stylish, cropped short, leaving her neck exposed, the deep umber brown tone of her skin rich and sensational as she started to climb the steps up to the front door.

'Her name is Zéphyrine,' Mary replied, speaking straight into his ear. 'She has a homestead somewhere in the south of the country.'

The red silk woman arrived at the door. She stepped inside the house and Alexander and Mary greeted her. 'Good evening,' the woman replied. Her voice was sultry and low. She held out her hand for Alexander to take and, sensing her meaning, he took it, raised it to his lips and kissed it.

'Your father has made you a guard dog, I see,' the woman

named Zéphyrine said. She was taller than Alexander and looked down at him as she spoke. He didn't know how to respond other than to laugh. At his side, Mary smiled at the woman and complimented her on her choice of outfit.

'It is striking, isn't it?' Zéphyrine ran the collar — if such a loose piece of fabric could be called such — between her fingers. 'It certainly keeps their attention. Which,' she paused and leant closer to Mary, as if she were about to share a secret with her, 'is precisely what you want when you play this game, Miss. Stansfield.' She pulled back and smiled at Alexander. 'Your father is in the back, I assume?' Before he had a chance to reply, she was walking away from them. They each stepped to one side of the hallway to give her space, Zéphyrine having parted them without word, her aura stronger than spoken language.

More guests arrived. In the end, it was Ern who saved them, materialising from the back of the house and beckoning for them to follow him.

'Your cousins are here, Alex,' he said, a blue and yellow paisley pocket square tucked into his jacket. 'They came around the back. Your mother's with them now.'

Standing close to the fire, a man with tousled blonde hair held Sophie's hand as they laughed together, an expression of honest exultation on each of their faces. Alexander approached with Mary and the man turned when he saw them.

'Alexander!' He dropped Sophie's hand and immediately moved to embrace the younger man. Holding him close, Alexander shared in his delight as the man chuckled and slapped him on the back.

'You shall squeeze him to death, Luc,' Sophie teased, her hand reaching to touch Alexander's chin as it rested on the other man's shoulder. Alexander smiled at his mother and the man, Luc, released him, only after he had held him out in front of him, a hand on either shoulder, as if admiring him.

'It's been too long, nephew,' Luc beamed at Alexander, 'You have grown too fast! And too handsome!' He laughed, then turned on his heel and called out across the room. 'Sabine, Jack — come and greet Alexander!' A teenage boy, with the same blonde hair as Sophie and Luc, and a young woman, dark-haired and a similar age to Alexander, were over by a window in playful conversation with Guinevere and Aurélie, who were dressed in matching white gowns and silver shoes. They heard their father and, smiling, walked across the room, Alexander's little sisters close behind.

The boy had the same buoyancy as his father and held his cousin with equal warmth. Alexander ruffled Jack's hair as they parted and then gestured to his face. 'You shave now, cousin,' he said, smiling.

Jack laughed and touched his cheeks, as if self-conscious, and then, a sparkle in his eyes, nodded back at Alexander and said, 'And I see you don't!'

Alexander laughed before turning to greet his other cousin. For one reason or another, it had been three years since they had last seen each other and she had hardly changed at all.

'Sabine,' he said, moving to kiss her cheek. She took his

hands in hers with a fondness that could only have been familiarity. As children, they had often played together, Sophie's family having visited on a regular basis, until circumstance, as with all good things, had interrupted life and caused them to drift apart.

'You look well, Alex,' she said, their faces close. 'Happy.' She smiled and held his gaze. Around them, Luc was once more talking with Sophie, animated and loud, and Jack had started a conversation with Mary, who now held a giggling Aurélie in her arms, having picked the girl up to stop her, wild and carefree as she was, from running about the room and into guests. Sabine squeezed her cousin's hands. 'Happier than I remember seeing you before,' she said.

Alexander thanked her. 'You look well, also,' he said.

She smiled and her hair, which was arranged in an elaborate coil, shuffled as she shook her head. 'I mean it. You seem different, somehow.' She smiled at him curiously and then laughed. Leaning closer still, she whispered, 'If I had to guess, I would say it probably has something to do with the company you seem to be keeping.' Sabine tilted her head and looked at Mary, who was starting to struggle to keep Aurélie, wriggling and writhing and blowing raspberries, from wreaking havoc. The young girl was messing with Mary's hair, unfastening a clip that had, until that point, kept her curls neatly drawn around the back of her head and down over one shoulder. Mary laughed at her and pretended to bite her nose.

Alexander grinned as he watched, the drugs still busy in his brain. 'Yeah,' he said to his cousin, running his hand through his hair as he turned back to her, 'I suppose you could say it's something like that.'

He would have liked to have spoken more, to have asked Sabine about his aunt, her mother, and their grandfather, whose decline in health, both physical and mental, in the years after Sophie's mother's death was the reason why their visits had become so few and far between, but before he had a chance, the chinking of glass washed over the room, and with it a quiet, as everyone turned their heads towards the sound's origin.

At the end of the room, a couple of feet above the ground, standing on a platform carpeted in red fabric, was Robert. Behind him, two thick curtains were drawn and oversized gold candelabras marked either end of the stage. He had a glass in hand, and smiled generously as his guests turned to look at him. The string quartet, who had been playing continuously until this point, put down their bows. Robert waited for absolute silence to descend before addressing the gathering.

'Thank you,' he began, his voice loud and clear, 'for making the journey today.' In the crowd below, murmurs were accompanied by approving nods. 'I know that, for many of you, it is difficult to take time away from your work, and so your presence here tonight is greatly appreciated. You are all our treasured guests.' Robert raised his glass and smiled, an action that was mirrored by almost everyone below. Aurélie now with her mother, Mary was back at Alexander's side and she raised a glass before letting Alexander, who was without one, share a sip of her wine.

On the stage, Robert continued. 'It goes without saying that I have my wife, Sophie,' he paused to look at her, which made her blush, the eyes of the room now on her, 'to thank for arranging this evening as marvellously as she does each year.' Robert paused again, and when he continued, spoke in a softer voice that seemed as though it was meant only for her, 'Thank you, my darling.' Taking their cue from Robert, the guests thanked their hostess in unison. By the fire, Sophie giggled and pushed her face against the sleeve of her brother's jacket in an attempt to conceal her bashfulness.

'And, of course,' Robert boomed, recapturing the attention of the crowd, 'what would an evening such as this be without music?' He gestured, a wide, elegant movement of the arm to the string quartet. 'Let us show our appreciation for our musicians tonight, who have played beautifully and with impeccable good taste.' A man close to the front of the stage shouted, 'Hear, hear!' and the rest began to applaud, turning to face the string players, who dipped their heads with grace and gratitude. 'Such good playing,' Robert said over the continuing applause. When it had died down, he brought his hands together in front of him and invited the musicians to leave. 'Return home and enjoy the rest of the year with your families,' he smiled, his brown eyes as gentle as always. The applause returned as they gathered their instruments and left the room. Once they were through the double doors, Ern, who was standing close by, moved to close them, drawing the large brass handles together before standing back to the side.

'Good, good,' Robert smiled from the stage. Those in the

crowd turned back to face him, eyes eager, awaiting his next words. Robert moved to place his glass down on the edge of the stage and walked back to the centre. 'As I said,' he continued slowly, 'it is wonderful that so many of you made the journey tonight. It is,' he held his hand up and drew his eyes over the crowd, 'important that we see each other like this. Come together and share our stories, our experiences, our—' he paused and took a step towards the curtains at the back of the stage. 'Our discoveries.' He placed a soft hand on the thick red cord that kept the curtains drawn. With a tug, the heavy fabric withdrew and, in doing so, revealed a tremendous sight.

Standing beside Robert on the stage, bound in chains between two stone pillars, entirely naked save for a single piece of cloth draped around his hips, was Clifford. Another strip of fabric was over his mouth, and his eyes, terror filled and wide, darted as a wave of gasps came from the gathering. Once they ebbed away, the gasps were replaced by another sound: the sound of praise and of glee and of more applause. Red rose in his buttonhole, Robert stood and absorbed it all, smiling and waiting for the silence to descend again.

Observing his father's exhibition, Alexander noticed how Clifford struggled, his wrists tugging at the manacles that tied him to the pillars. He thought the man looked like a cartoon Samson, short-haired and weak, his strength sapped by the actions of his lover. Alexander laughed loudly and Mary elbowed him in the ribs.

Back on stage, Robert spoke again. 'The sub-homo,' he began, gesturing to the man in chains, 'a term first used by Dr.

Richard Alexander Wheatleigh, my ancestor and one of the four founders of our movement. His was a proposition that would change the course of history.' Robert paused and looked at his audience. 'His was a proposition that has us all gathered here this evening. As you know, he said that we, homo sapiens — discerning, wise, sensible — share our planet with another, another who, although they may look like us, are anything but discerning, anything but wise, anything but sensible.'

At Robert's side, Clifford strained against his bonds, the fabric that gagged his mouth tight against the corners of his mouth.

'Dr. Wheatleigh,' Robert smiled and continued, 'called it 'a secret repulsion in the blood', something inside of these creatures that makes them barbarous, makes them noxious, makes them,' he paused and smiled, 'suitable for only one purpose.' Chuckles from the audience. He waited and then said, 'And whilst there were certain moral habits which Dr. Wheatleigh identified as being the prerogative of the sub-homo, it was the creeping nature of this creature's behaviours — the very essence of their vulgarism — which made them difficult to identify. And so, our ancestors turned to the institutions — the prisons and the asylums — to find examples of the creature that sought to imitate, and, ultimately, displace us, whilst, sadly, knowing that these places only held but a small sample of the wider sub-homo population. The secret repulsion in the blood being just that, secret, and therefore difficult to uncover.'

Robert moved across the stage, walking in front of Clifford to stand on the other side. 'A perfect science,' he said, shaking his head, 'imperfectly applied. But now—' Robert laid a hand on the man's bare shoulder and drew his eyes over the audience. 'Now, I give you a perfect method.' He spoke with bright confidence and exposed his teeth as he smiled. 'A way to identify the secret repulsion in the blood in a manner that our ancestors could have only dreamed.'

The crowd was on tenterhooks. A great mass could have come crashing in through one of the windows and still their eyes would have remained on Robert.

'Genetic identification,' he stated. 'A concept that, as some of you will no doubt know, I have been experimenting with for many years. The identification of the genetic element which separates us from them.' He prodded Clifford's shoulder to emphasise his point. 'And here,' he prodded the man again, 'the manifestation — I give you the first breeding bull to be selected using genetic identification.' Bobbing heads and hushed voices came from the audience. A man at the back strained his neck, as if trying to get a better view. 'He was profiled,' Robert continued, 'in much the same manner as we have done previously, and then, prior to selection, I obtained a sample — saliva on a drinking glass — and had it tested. The genetic element,' Robert beamed as he spoke, 'was present. He, this creature here before you, is the culmination of generations' worth of effort. A perfect science, *perfectly* applied. And now,' Robert clapped his hands together and stepped forward, 'I invite you, my friends, to come forward—' He gestured to his guests. 'Come and observe him, come and find him to be the proof that you need, so that we may continue to advance, continue to advance towards the creation of a new Eden.'

Some people started to applaud, others shuffled through the crowd to get to the front, where Robert took their hands in his and invited them onto the stage, slapping their backs and laughing with them, guiding them over to the man chained between the two pillars. He squirmed as they touched him, trying to get away as they poked and prodded his naked body, commenting on the structure of his legs and the thickness of his torso. He closed his eyes as they lifted his loincloth, screaming into the fabric that gagged his mouth as they nodded approvingly at his scrotal size.

They swelled the stage, all those clean shaven men in black bow ties and ladies dripping in diamonds. They told Robert just how impressed they were with his work, telling him that he was an inspiration, shaking his hand as they thanked him for being a true example of self-sacrifice and dedication. Robert took it all in his stride, graciously accepting their compliments, thanking them again for coming, encouraging them to get a closer look, reminding them to listen for the bell to let them know dinner was ready, smiling as he told them he hoped they would enjoy the feast that was about to be served.

Thirty-One

After his father's speech, Alexander left Mary with Ern whilst he went to his bedroom. He told them he needed to use the bathroom, which was true, but the trip upstairs was necessitated not so much by that, but by the urge to retrieve a personal artefact he had left to cool off in the sink. He slipped the cloth pouch into the inner pocket of his dinner jacket and closed his bedroom door. Later, there would be fireworks.

People were already starting to take their seats at the table when Alexander returned. Names, printed in gold foil on thick cream card, announced where everyone was to be seated for the meal. After a short walk about the table, Alexander found his — the tail of the 'A' elegantly looped in spidery cursive — and glanced at the name cards either side of his place. On the opposite side of the table and some way further down, Mary sat alone, neither place either side of her yet occupied. She didn't see him watching her, her eyes instead focused on something in the distance, her expression plain, as if she were locked away inside herself, thinking.

Years earlier, a teenage Alexander had complained to his mother about her persistent, and what he considered to be irritating, tendency to seat him next to Mary at this annual event. He had hurt Sophie's feelings when he had shouted at her the evening before New Year's Eve. Afterwards, he hadn't sat next to Mary anymore, and neither he nor his mother had ever mentioned the issue again.

Alexander picked up his name card and walked around to the other side of the table. *Gerald Foye*. He looked at the card to the right of Mary and, with two fingers, flicked it away, off somewhere into the middle of the table. Her trance broken, she looked up and, noticing him, smiled as he sat down. He placed his own name card in front of him, in line with hers. 'Please, call me Gerald,' he teased, pulling a funny face as he took her hand in his and kissed it, lingering a little too long over her fingers. This made her laugh and tilt her face in his direction.

Laughter subsided, Mary nodded down the length of the table to where others were looking for their seats. 'Your father spoke well,' she said as Robert entered the room.

Alexander turned a little in his seat, so that his back was to the door and his face closer to hers. 'You think so?' he asked, leaning forward, curious as to what she really thought.

'He's a clever man,' Mary said. 'I admire him very much.'

Alexander nodded. 'I know. But, I wonder if you would have done it differently.' Mary looked at him to determine his meaning. 'All of this,' he said, raising his right hand and gesturing to the room. 'New Year's, the speeches, the theatrics, the—' he paused and grinned, struggling for something to end his list, 'the *music*.'

Mary laughed. 'I rather like your father's taste in music, Alex.' Teasing, he rolled his eyes at her. 'I understand your meaning,' she said, her hand absentmindedly straying onto the tablecloth to straighten his cutlery. 'And yes, I would have done it differently — I would not have bothered at all.'

Alexander shook his head, grinning. 'You see,' he said, leaning forward again and touching her wrist, 'you can't say things like that.'

'Whyever not?'

'Because *I* can't say things like that,' he laughed. 'No New Year's party — that's heretical talk, especially coming from someone of the Founders. You'll be in charge, head of one of the families one day,' he said, his eyes on hers. 'It'll be your job.'

'Oh really, I'll be in charge,' she said with subtle provocation. 'And what will your job be?'

He shrugged and slouched back in his chair. After a moment, he said, all of a sudden dark and serious, 'That's my point.'

Down the other end of the table, most of the guests now seated, Sophie was attending to a problem. Gerald Foye, the man with the thin grey hair, couldn't find his seat and was at a loss as to where to place himself. He took the issue in good cheer, saying there was no need to worry as Sophie apologised and said she would locate his place immediately. Alexander and Mary, and indeed many others at the table, watched on as she searched for the missing seat. Eventually, an empty chair with no name was found, and Sophie guided Gerald to it, touching him on the shoulder and apologising once again before returning to her own seat. She looked down the table and caught Alexander's eye. When she raised her eyebrows at him, he simply shrugged.

The first course was ready to be served. It was brought in on a large silver platter, covered by a domed cloche. Placed in the centre of the table, it was warm, tiny droplets of condensation blanketing the polished metal like morning dew on the petals of a flower, and steam billowed out from under the lid as it was lifted.

On a bed of fresh sage, rosemary and parsley, crispy, glossy and the colour of caramel, a baby. The infant was served whole, five kilograms of delicate meat, fat drooling from its toothless mouth, which was slightly agape to accommodate the placement of a single, roasted crabapple. Eyeless, black olives having been inserted in the place of eyes, it lay curled, on its stomach, as if in peaceful slumber. Little fingers and toes had crisped in the oven and glistened gold. A lack of muscle and an abundance of fat made it a culinary delicacy. Fed solely on its mother's milk before being slaughtered at just seven weeks, the suckling babe was gorged with collagen, which kept it juicy and tender and sweetly perfumed.

The gathering was allowed to admire the animal before it was carved. There was something uniquely gratifying about having an infant cooked and served in its entirety, and the guests were allowed to absorb this primaeval sensation before the knife was drawn along its spine.

An arm was removed first, the knife starting at the top of the shoulder, separating what was one of the richest, most fat abundant areas from the rest of the carcass. The leg of the same side came next, and then the scant meat from the middle of the babe's back. Crispy ears were cut from the head, and the cheeks, an especially tender part of the infant, were sliced away, reserved for plates of the hostess' choosing.

The pluck — the heart, liver, kidneys, lungs and tongue — had been removed from the carcass prior to roasting, and was served now alongside the rest of the body as pâté. Plates of caramelised cauliflower and buttered green beans and crumbly white cheeses were also brought to the table, as well as baskets ladened with warm petits pains.

A showpiece appetiser, it was exceptional fare and the guests were eager to fill their plates. After the spectacle of carving the suckling babe was concluded, two further silver platters arrived at the table and placed an equal distance away from the first. Lids lifted and two more babies, plenty to feed the party. As the animals were carved, the feasting began. Heaps of green beans and baby swelled individual plates, and petit pain was layered with homemade pâté and cheese. Some, in the ecstasy of consumption, abandoned their cutlery, and instead used their hands to push heaps of buttery, fatty flesh into their mouths. For Gerald Foye, by way of apology for the botched seating plan, a cheek, and to Luc's daughter, Sabine, the other.

So moist, so succulent, so satisfying, all the guests could do was eat and give thanks and eat some more.

As they ate, one of the guests dabbed his fat jewelled lips with a napkin. 'It is a shame that such a delicious thing cannot be had more often,' he said, putting down his knife and fork and addressing the table. His plate was still almost full and it was clear he had taken more than he could manage.

At the head of the table, Robert swallowed. 'Indeed,' he smiled. 'But it would not be a delicacy if one ate it every day.'

Another man, close to Robert and older than the first, held out his finger, signalling he wished to speak. He swallowed the piece of suckling babe he was chewing and said, 'That's not what Rupert says. I've heard he serves baby quite regularly.'

Several sighs came from around the table. Everyone knew the name: it was one that needed no further introduction or explanation. Robert Senior looked up from his plate and shook his head. 'Here we go.'

Before anything more could be said, the man who had encouraged Alexander to admire his shoes earlier in the evening interjected. 'It is true, Robert,' he said, holding a wine glass in his hand. 'It's baby every other day up there!'

The younger Robert smiled at such a ludicrous statement. 'Whilst I am sure Rupert has his own way of doing things,' he said, 'I can hardly imagine such consumption to be sustainable.'

Shoe man laughed and, before taking a sip of wine, responded by exclaiming, 'When has Rupert ever cared about sustainability!'

Like Robert, Rupert was head of one of the four founding families. An eccentric libertine who ran a homestead — if his operation could be thought of as such — in Scotland, he was considered to be a controversial figure by those with conservative tastes.

To Robert's displeasure, the conversation was far from exhausted. 'Not so,' another person at the table, this time a woman, said, 'I hear he has one female who gives him quadruplets every time. It's a miracle of science!'

Incredulous laughter and Sophie put down her fork and placed her hand over her husband's.

'Quadruplets? Each time?' Robert asked, his eyes crinkling with amusement. 'I would have to see such a thing to believe it.'

The woman nodded in earnest and encouraged her husband, who was at her side, to say something. Looking from her to Robert, he put down a hunk of bread covered in pâté and shrugged his shoulders. 'What can I say, Robert? You know how theatrical the man can be — at his parties he says it is so, but who is to know the truth of the matter when it comes to him?' Sighing, his wife shot him a disapproving look before returning to her food.

Robert's father laughed and banged his fist on the table. 'You simply cannot eat a newborn every other day,' he barked, bits of meat showing as he opened his mouth. 'Have you,' the old man jabbed his fork in the direction of the woman, who raised her hand to her bosom in a show of shock, 'ever considered that Rupert's just full of shit?'

Giddy, inebriated laughter erupted. In their seats, Alexander and Mary grinned, the former having to put his fork down so as to avoid choking on the infectious gaiety that was sweeping across the table. Alexander had never met Rupert — or at least wasn't old enough to remember meeting him if he had — and the stories he had heard about the man made him seem too maniacal to be real. Audaciously egotistical and, according to some of the stories, a philanderer of shameful proportions, Rupert was also said to be competent and well-connected — two sets of qualities which Robert had raised Alexander to believe were incompatible with one another. That the man was younger than Robert made him even more of a sore point for Alexander's father.

'Come now, Father,' Robert said, chastising the old man, but still smiling. 'It is rude to speak of absent friends in such a way.' It was then that Robert turned in his seat in the direction of the red silk woman, Zéphyrine. She hadn't contributed anything to the conversation and sat silent, back straight in her chair, cutting a piece of meat with her knife and fork. His tone affable, Robert addressed her by name. 'Since we are on the subject, you must tell us,' he said, 'how is Rupert keeping these days?'

The table quietened. Several people looked up from their plates. Zéphyrine continued cutting her food, forcing Robert to wait for a response. When she was done, she placed her cutlery on her plate and, coolly, said, 'I don't know why you would suppose I know anything about the man.' Her eyelashes were long and black. They held each other's gaze until Robert smiled and let her return to her food.

'What was that all about?' Alexander asked Mary after people had returned to their microcosms of conversation about the table.

She drew closer to him and, keeping her voice low, said, 'She's one of Rupert's spies. One of his mistresses. His favourite, quite possibly.'

Alexander smiled in disbelief. 'A spy?'

Mary nodded, nibbling on the end of a green bean. 'It's a game he plays with your father. And, I suspect, he with him. I've heard him mention it before, once or twice.'

Alexander laughed. 'So, right now, my father has a spy of his own at Rupert's New Year's party?

'I wouldn't know,' Mary shrugged, 'but quite possibly.'

Alexander laughed again and imagined his father instructing a legion of spectacle wearing, moustachioed informants. 'Ridiculous,' he grinned, shaking his head and moving his fork over his plate.

Thirty-Two

By the time the second course was served, the conversation had turned to Robert's speech and genetics. Seated in what should have been Alexander's chair, Gerald Foye was describing what he referred to as the hypothesis of the upward anomaly. 'After all,' he said, moving his head to look at others who were seated around the table, 'were we not all born of apes?'

Someone further down the table chortled and, helping themselves to a second heaping of roast potatoes, asked the man where he got such ideas.

Gerald sat back in his chair. 'You would be surprised,' he began, 'by the great number of remarkable things that you observe when out in the field. I am left with no doubt that Robert,' he inclined his head towards the host, who, brown eyes soft, acknowledged his deference and nodded in return, 'is correct in his proposition of their being a genetic element. What interests me, is if one can defy bad genetics. Is it possible for the offspring of the sub-homo to be born *without* their parents' genetic defect?'

'What are you saying, Gerald?' a woman with long, sparkling earrings asked. 'That genetic heritage can be changed?'

The man moved in his seat. 'If so, it would be a rarity,' he explained. 'Just as certain disorders are caused by the mutation of a single gene, could it not also be so that a beneficial mutation may occur? An upward anomaly.'

Two seats down from Mary, Ern put down his glass and joined the conversation. 'I concede, in the past I myself have witnessed some quite extraordinary behaviour from students who came from sub-homo families.' A couple of others nodded and murmured in agreement.

'Anomalies,' Gerald said, looking at Ern, 'that could be identified using Robert's genetic method.'

Opposite him, a man wearing a large-faced gold watch, put down his napkin. 'I am sorry, I must interject,' he said, his watch hitting the table as he lowered his hand. 'We have not observed any evidence of this. Alligators haven't changed their genetics for aeons. What is to say these creatures will ever change theirs?'

Shoe man was chewing and turned his head when his neighbour cleared his throat to speak. 'You are far too liberal in your thinking, Gerald.' It was the young man who hadn't stopped to speak to Alexander at the front door. Dark haired and tight-lipped, he was pompous and sounded like his lungs were full of helium. Alexander, having just emptied his plate for a second time that course, took a sip of wine and grinned. 'I do not believe such a thing is possible,' the young man continued, looking at Gerald with contempt.

Alexander set his glass on the table and laughed. Eyes now on him, he looked about the table and, after a pause, said, 'If we put stock in the reluctance of a few narrow-minded individuals, science would never progress.' At the head of the table, Robert looked at his son, a curious smile on his lips. 'Say Gerald is wrong—' Under pressure to continue, Alexander nodded at the man with the thin grey hair, trying to keep his eyes away from the young man, who was, by now, seething. 'Nothing is lost. But, if he is right and all we do is ridicule him, then our understanding does not evolve.'

Gerald smiled and nodded at the younger man. 'Such is my point,' he said, 'we must ask questions or risk stagnation.'

Alexander matched his smile before reaching for his glass, eager to retreat from the conversation he had inadvertently entered. It was too late. Another at the table, a woman wearing a bold, oriental-style green and gold velvet jacket, was desirous to hear more from Robert's heir. She asked him if he, in the course of his studies at university, had, like Ern, come across anyone who challenged his expectations of the sub-homo. As he considered his response, he hoped that his father might hijack the conversation and relieve him. He didn't and so Alexander floundered, not knowing how to reply. He recast his sentence twice before settling on, 'I don't think so.' The woman looked disappointed. 'I just think we always have more to learn.'

Next to him, Alexander noticed an impish smile forming on Mary's lips. She picked up her napkin and, covering her mouth, pretended to cough.

Back on the other side of the table, Gerald raised a query about the emotional capacity of the sub-homo. Several guests had something to say about that and spoke over each other trying to express their opinion. Gold watch man seemed to snarl when Gerald dared to suggest they had any form of emotional intelligence. The woman in the bold jacket interrupted him and spoke of the grief displayed by a fresher after her infant had died.

'Jiang,' Robert said, addressing the man with the gold watch, 'you cannot seriously believe they have no capacity for emotion whatsoever?'

The other man didn't say anything and pushed a forkful of food, a slither of meat dripping in a red wine jus, into his mouth.

'Gerald here is not suggesting they feel the same complexity of emotion as you or I,' Robert smiled, 'merely that, in their own simple-minded way, they experience some sort of primitive feeling.'

Gold watch man, Jiang, swallowed and looked at Robert. 'It's this sort of thinking that will get you in trouble,' he said, his tone serious. 'You are projecting — confusing their emotions with your own.'

Without thinking, Alexander was speaking again. 'I have seen it,' he said. 'Emotions in these creatures.' Once again, heads turned in his direction.

Alexander was thinking of Pandora. How could he not? For the past eleven days she and her newborn had been at the centre of his existence. *Constant alarms on my phone, milk bottles every three hours, IV bags, blue pills and unceasing tears.* How could he deny that she — the young mother who still cried for her child each time he tended to her — felt emotion? It would take more than the stubborn posturing of a few old men to make him think otherwise.

'I've been attending a heifer,' Alexander continued, trying to keep his voice steady as more people at the table turned to listen. 'She has recently given birth, preterm, and has had to be separated from her infant.' Under the table, he was bouncing his left leg up and down, nervous. 'She cries,' he said, his voice firm. 'All the time she cries.' The way he said it made the whole table fall silent. He dropped his eyes to his plate and said, 'I don't think that's a projection.'

Alexander felt a soft pressure on his knee. Mary offered him a small smile, and he let her expression wash over him before breaking eye contact and taking a drink.

Dessert couldn't come soon enough. For those who still had space in their stomachs, a pyramid of profiteroles, dripping in chocolate sauce and dusted with icing sugar. Mary half nibbled one and then offered her bowl to Alexander, who happily ate two servings, and would have finished a third if one had been offered to him. Most of the guests stayed at the table for coffee, but Alexander excused himself, he and Mary leaving the room to get some fresh air, outside at the back of the house.

They sat down together at the top of the steps that led away from the back door. The night air was cool and a breeze rustled the branches of the winter trees. Alexander gave Mary his jacket and she rested her feet against his.

Her voice was quiet when she spoke. 'What you mentioned in there—' she broke off and, after a pause, said, 'You can speak to me, you know?'

Alexander looked at the lawn. Only a few months earlier they had celebrated Mary's twenty-first birthday on that lawn. In many ways, life had been less confusing then, and, in many other ways, moreso.

'You wouldn't want to hear it,' he muttered. 'And, to be honest,' Alexander continued, 'neither do I.'

Mary breathed heavily and swayed, nudging his shoulder with the side of her face. They sat together in silence for a moment, until Mary bent over and reached for her shoes.

'What are you doing?' Alexander asked, amused.

Her hair tumbled over her face as she fiddled with them. 'My feet are in agony,' she complained, loosening the clasp on the right shoe. One at a time, she took them off. 'Be thankful you were born a man and are not expected to wear heeled shoes,' she laughed, placing the shoes on the step next to her.

Alexander grinned and pointed to her, now bare, feet. 'You'll freeze.'

'Not for a while,' she said and patted her stomach. 'I am stuffed. The heat my body is generating to digest it all is tremendous.'

'Well, if that's the case, can I have my jacket back?'

She laughed as he tried to take it back, his hands tickling her skin as he slipped them under his jacket and across her back and shoulders and arms.

'My,' he teased as she squirmed in his arms, 'you are warm!'

'Alex, please,' she said in between giggles, 'I am very full.'

'Okay, okay.' He laughed and pulled the jacket back over her shoulder, his eyes lingering on her lips. 'But, you might have to share your warmth with me.'

A suggestive glint and she elbowed him. 'Because you ate nothing?'

He laughed and shrugged. With her permission, both now grinning and suspicious of the other's touch, Alexander slipped his hand back under the jacket to reach into the inner pocket. She didn't say anything when he pulled out the pipe and started loading pinches of cannabis into the bowl. The match crackled in the winter air and sent smoke up into the sky. A skunky fog of pine and lemongrass.

'My toes look so very far away,' Mary whispered, eyes focused on her feet as she passed the pipe back to Alexander. He laughed and inhaled. Millions of miles away, a star burnt itself out.

'Do you think they're wondering where we are?'

Slowly, Mary shook her head and wafted her hand. 'They're all drunk.'

Alexander rolled his head back and laughed. 'Outrageous,' he said to the sky. Mary followed his gaze, shaking her head so that her curls loosened and fell down her back. They both jumped when a bang came from the front of the house and a light flashed in the sky. Sparks of ruby red and blazing orange erupted against midnight blue, and fizzes of silver and purple and a magical shade of teal sprinkled across the night.

Turning his eyes from the fireworks, Alexander put his lips

to Mary's ear. 'Happy New Year,' he said, close enough for her to hear over the noise. She turned and smiled, bringing her face in line with his so that they were eye to eye.

He kissed her, at first soft, and then with a hunger, ardent and zealous, parting her lips with his own, his hand on the back of her head. Placing his other hand on the base of her spine, he drew her even closer to him, she half standing, half shuffling along the step, until she was close enough that he could feel her heart pounding inside her chest. He tried to lie her down, his fingers ragging at the silken fabric of her dress. She pulled her lips away, eager for air, and so he moved to her cheeks and her chin and her neck and her chest, decorating her skin with his kisses. In soft, breathless words, she asked for more, more, as much as he could give, and then, suddenly, to stop, stop, to stop right now, 'Alex, stop—' she pushed him away and, before he had a chance to be bewildered, giggled and hushed, 'Quick, someone's coming!'

Taking his hand, she pulled him away from the steps and hurried, barefoot, onto the grass. There, she dropped to her knees and, still leading him, crawled underneath a large, evergreen bush. Leaves tickled the sides of their faces as they held each other, watching the back of the house, trying to suppress their laughter.

Two figures emerged. The first, Alexander immediately recognised as his father. The second, tall and sensual, could have only been the red silk woman Zéphyrine. A firework flashed overhead and revealed their faces in its transitory light.

'—it always has been,' they heard Robert say from the bush.

It was but a fragment of a longer sentence, the booming of exploding pyrotechnics muffling the rest.

Zéphyrine took a step closer. Her hands were out in front of her, gesticulating as she replied. When Robert spoke again, his hands were also raised. Even from a distance, his posture could be seen to stiffen as a tension set in his shoulders. Alexander strained forward in the bush, trying to hear what was being said. Anger was an emotion that he had rarely, if ever, seen his father display. But now, under the cover of darkness, at the back of the house and in heated conversation with one of his guests, Robert looked angry.

'It risks us all,' he said, loud enough to be heard over the fireworks. Zéphyrine was quick to respond, her words causing Robert to turn, sharply, on his heel. He took two paces away from her before returning, running his fingers through his hair and softening his stance.

Mary looked at Alexander and mouthed, 'What?' He shook his head and turned his eyes back to his father and Zéphyrine.

An abatement in the fireworks. 'Give him my best,' they heard Robert say in his normal voice. The woman said nothing. She walked along and around the back of the house, as if to join the rest of the party at the front. Robert stayed where he was, hands at his side and then up again to arrange his hair.

In the bush, Alexander and Mary had returned to laughter. Alexander's drugs still fresh in their systems, the scene they had just witnessed was transformed from enigmatic and conspiratorial to something comical and absurd. Their eyes were back on each other by the time Robert moved. Walking to the back door, he noticed a pair of shoes at the top of the steps. He leant down and picked them up, confused by their desertion, before opening the door and stepping inside, bringing the shoes with him.

ACT III

Pioneering a New Order: The Patrimony of the Homo Sapien

In a previous treatise I proposed the existence and inherent characteristics of a hitherto unclassified species of the homo genus. In this, my second treatise on the sub-homo, it is not only my intention to affirm and expand upon my previous discourse, but to propose a solution to the threat posed by this species, to both civilised society and to the health of our planet, so that we may find ourselves restored to Eden.

In Genesis, this species is referred to as a 'creeping thing': a creature that bears the image but not the likeness of the Creator. We, on the other hand, possess both these divine qualities, and have as such been given the classification homo sapien, meaning wise man. Mirroring this logic, I propose that the sub-homo also be given a classification reflective of its disposition: homo subrependus, meaning creeping man, in recognition of its serpentine nature, a creature who seeks to imitate its superior and, through moral deformity, barbarism, and wastefulness, steal their natural position as custodians of this planet.

The prominent economist and author of over two-hundred

and fifty papers and books, Professor Francis James Stansfield, has spoken of an imminent crisis: rapid population growth in combination with insatiable consumption of seemingly abundant resources will send this country, and others around the world, into a dark era of starvation and destitution. The resources of this planet, although they are treated as such by the homo subrependus, are not limitless, making it the responsibility of the homo sapien, the superior of the two species, to ensure that our planet is not entirely squandered, and is safeguarded for future generations. Efforts have been made to try to manage the barbarism of the homo subrependus, through soft means, such as programmes of education, and through harder methods, including gaols, houses of correction, asylums, and workhouses. As has been made apparent through the warnings of scholars like Professor Stansfield, these methods have failed in their intention: the homo subrependus is still very much a threat to the stability of this planet.

Some would argue that the only way to stop any further progression of, and to begin to undo the damage already caused by, the homo subrependus is to exclude them from society by means of terminating their ability to reproduce, and thus their ability to spread, sabotage, and dilute the purity of the homo sapien. Yet, whilst it is, of course, correct to warn against the dangers of unchecked breeding, it is my belief that the homo subrependus can, and indeed should, serve a purpose.

The resource which experiences the greatest levels of strain during times of excess population is food; it is something that none of us can live without and on which we all depend for daily sustenance. It is here that the homo subrependus can serve a purpose: these otherwise useless creatures can be used to meet much of the nutriment needs of society.

Whilst the concept of consuming the homo subrependus may, at first, seem abhorrent, once one comes to accept that these creatures are not our kin, and are but base animals not all too dissimilar from bovine or swine, or any number of the other species of this planet that we consider fit to eat, then it becomes easy, and indeed sensible, to consider the advantages that would be born from a system of human husbandry. No longer in charge of their own wretched selves, and instead a part of an efficient and sustainable agricultural scheme, the grotesque amount of waste that these feeble-minded creatures cause would cease, their shocking moral habits would be restrained, and their biological affliction would be limited to their own kind, with the interbreeding of homo subrependus and homo sapien prohibited.

Asides from these benefits, in companionship with my own medical research, I have been reassured by the distinguished biologists Drs. Theodore F. D. Helton and George Claridge-Hunt that the nutritional quality of milk from the female homo subrependus is superior to the equivalent from any species of cow, sheep, or goat. Already perfectly tailored for the human body, it can be considered to be a life-affirming nectar, one which suits our digestive system well and can even be consumed without ill-effect by those who regularly experience terrible reactions and inflammations after drinking cows' milk. The meat of the homo subrependus can also be considered to be of a similar, if not better, quality to meat harvested from other animals. As with conventional livestock, programmes of selective breeding and optimal slaughter weights would be employed to produce the best product.

By better managing the population and thus resources of this planet, as rudimentarily outlined by this document, we can not only maintain a high standard of living, defined by sustainability, gallantry, and good taste, but also start to correct the centuries' worth of decay that has been caused by the homo subrependus.

The establishment of any new order necessitates the eradication of the old. In this, we must be absolute. In order to create a New Eden, there can be no compromise or half measures; no accommodation should or ought to be given to these creatures: for too long we have been bound by their foul chains. With this awareness, it must also be stated that the establishment of such a new order, and therefore the complete destruction of the old, will take time. We must not be under any illusion of seeing such a feat achieved within our lifetimes, or even the lifetimes of our children. We must, instead, be pioneers, martyrs of a sort, content to dedicate our life's effort to forging a path for future generations to follow and expand upon. This is the patrimony of the homo sapien.

Dr. Richard Alexander Wheatleigh, 1880

Thirty-Three

Twenty-six seconds. That's how long it had taken for the whole skip to go up in flames. In hindsight, they should have realised that flicking a match into what was essentially one large metal incinerator was a dumb idea. That the skip was filled with tins of paint, industrial solvents and other flammable materials had made it all the more dumb. But they were just kids, and so that made it acceptable.

Her dad had been upset. 'I don't know where it all went wrong,' he had muttered, shaking his head as he had pulled the car into the driveway of their house. She had wanted to shout at him, 'How about the day you shoved your dick into the wrong hole?', but her heart hadn't been in it. She was tired, and her favourite television show was due to start in fifteen minutes.

Six weeks. That's how long it had been before she was allowed to leave the house again. School, of course, was the only exception. He forgot to mention that, as he stood in the kitchen, red-faced and furious at having to have left work early to deal with her, but she figured that it went without saying. And, unlike in the past, that time he had been serious. It really did end up being six weeks. She didn't care. *Fuck him*, she told herself as she reclined on the sofa, television remote in hand. *Fuck them all.* She hadn't even wanted to be there anyway. She didn't like the taste of cigarettes and had only done it because the others told her — led her — to do it. *It's their fault.*

It was during those six weeks that she had met Ryan, *and that's when everything really did turn to shit.* She was fifteen years old and he was seventeen. Her dad half-read the local newspaper every evening and their house had been on Ryan's delivery route. Every evening during the week and just before midday on Saturdays, he pushed a rolled up wad of paper through their front door. By the time the six weeks were out, he was pushing other things into other holes, and so Samantha had found someone else to be led by.

The first time he cheated on her she had tried to kill herself. Of course, she would have never done it, not properly — she just wanted him to feel something. *Wanted them all to feel something.* Her dad. Her aunt. Herself, even. She had fucked it up anyway. *Couldn't even manage to do that right.* After that, she had fallen into a cycle of deplorable behaviour and hopelessness, drinking too much and being punished for it by having her heart broken every other week. With her dad's help she had gone to university, to try to get away from all the bad that she had surrounded herself with, but that had turned out to be an even bigger shitfest. Money in her pocket and no parental oversight, she woke up face down on the side of the road on no less than three occasions. Destined to be a disappointment, she had dropped out and slunk back home.

And look at me now.

Over the past few weeks, Samantha had ballooned. Her seemingly ever-expanding belly made it troublesome to walk, her centre of balance having shifted and the ligaments in her joints relaxed and loose. The back pain and the tiredness she could just about tolerate, but the breathlessness scared her

The doctor assured her that it was normal — her swelling uterus was pushing up against her lungs — but that didn't stop her worrying. She sometimes awoke in the middle of the night, startled and struggling for air. However, with less than two months before her due date, it was the thought of getting the baby out of her body that scared her most of all.

The baby was energetic, kicking and wriggling and twisting and punching all hours of the day. She liked to imagine that it, her child, would come out fighting, and that, as a child of rape, they would be born wrathful and full of rage and hatred. But, what could a baby do? As impossible as it seemed, Samantha knew she had to help herself. *Help my baby.* She hadn't planned to become a mother, but, now she was one, she felt obligated to do something. *To lead and not be led.* For the first time in her life she was bigger than herself.

The Seat. That was what they called it.

It was Evelyn who had first mentioned it to her, a place referred to by the doctor and the redhead when they worked together, she passing him the instruments of his trade, the instruments he then used to examine and belittle the women he had dragged into his care. After her ears had been opened to the word, Samantha had heard them speak of it, too. 'No,' the ginger bitch had said, 'Alex is at the Seat.'

Who the fuck is Alex? What the fuck is the Seat?

It didn't matter. Whatever the Seat was, Samantha knew it was important and as such somehow vital to the success of her and Evelyn's plan to escape.

'I really don't think we can do it without knowing more,' Evelyn said as she rubbed her belly.

On the sofa next to her, Samantha shook her head. 'I just don't get it,' she said, 'All the time you've been here and you hardly know anything about the place.'

'They're very careful, Sam. Careful that you don't see, careful that you don't think.'

Samantha remembered how she felt every time she finished a meal in what she had ironically and inappropriately started to refer to as the Love Shack. Now that they were carrying precious cargo, their food was sedative-free. Robert, it seemed, wasn't overly concerned by the problems pregnant women could cause him.

'There must be something there, at this Seat place, we can use,' Samantha said, eyes far away and thinking.

The women had already spoken about the unlikeliness of being able to escape on foot. Not knowing where to go and limited by their physical conditions, they would need transportation if they were going to stand a chance of getting away. Evelyn remembered seeing a vehicle once, something similar to a golf cart, parked outside one of the buildings. She had been half-conscious, being transported between two of the buildings, strapped into a wheelchair, a baby having been stolen from her body only the day before.

'Perhaps they have keys there,' Samantha continued, turning to her friend. 'Keys to the carts.'

'Perhaps,' Evelyn replied, 'but it's a lot to gamble on.'

Samantha laughed. 'Yeah, because we have so much to lose.'

'You, maybe not,' Evelyn said, quiet and serious, 'but don't forget I have others to think about.'

Her children. The girl and the boy that Robert had taken from her. If they were still able to be saved, Evelyn was willing to do anything she could to get to them. Escaping, getting out, meant she could get help, help that would reunite her with her children. If they tried and failed, they had no idea what the consequences would be. In all the years she had been on the homestead, Evelyn had never heard of anyone escaping. They either didn't bother trying or were quietly disposed of after being caught.

Scratching the side of her neck, Samantha nodded and said, 'Okay, I understand. But, I still think we need to get into this Seat place. There could be keys, a map, a *phone*.'

A phone would be ideal. But they both knew Robert was too smart to leave one of those lying around.

'I agree with you, Sam,' Evelyn shifted and straightened her back, 'but we still need more information. Where even is this place? How do we get into it?'

'You know,' the other woman replied, 'Mary has this key on her—'

'I'm sure she has many keys—'

'No, some sort of special key,' Samantha intonated, stressing the words as she said them. 'She wears it around her neck, on a chain.'

Evelyn pulled a face. 'She does? I've never seen it.'

Samantha shook her head, 'I've *felt* it,' she said, reaching for Evelyn's hand and pulling it to her back. 'Here,' she said, pushing the other woman's fingers against her spine, 'when she dragged me down the corridor.' Evelyn furrowed her brow and went to say something but Samantha continued. 'And,' she said, excited, 'it was showing. Over her clothes. She must usually keep it hidden. Why keep it hidden unless it's important?'

Evelyn considered. It was sunny outside. Light streamed in through the window. Earlier in the day, the door to the fenced garden that the women were allowed to wander around had been opened. Everyone else was outside, relaxing under a tree and enjoying the warmth of spring. Samantha didn't like the outside. They were trapped; the fresh air was an illusion. Better to remain indoors and focus on their incarceration.

'I bet Robert has one, too,' Samantha said. 'A special key.'

'Okay, and how do we get one of these special keys?'

Samantha shrugged. That was the problem. How were two pregnant women supposed to do anything?

'We could steal it from one of them without them noticing.'

Evelyn raised an eyebrow.

'Or, we could make a distraction and get it then.'

'It needs work,' Evelyn said, shaking her head. 'And we're running out of time.'

Samantha placed a hand over her swollen abdomen. 'I told you, I can't have a baby here, Evelyn.'

I want to get out of here, to go home, to see Dad, to tell him I'm sorry.

Evelyn gripped the arm of the sofa and pushed herself up and off the seat. She took a moment to steady herself before arranging her smock. Samantha could see her nipples showing through the light-coloured fabric.

'You're not going to have a baby in here,' Evelyn said, looking down at her friend. 'And neither am I. Not again.' Her hair was behind her back, and she pulled it through her hands to her front and parted it over her shoulders. Her eyes were sharp when she spoke again. 'We'll get the key.'

Samantha smiled.

'Just let me think about it,' Evelyn continued. 'I'll see if I can spot it the next time we see either one of them.'

Samantha breathed heavily, her eyes widening.

'What's wrong?' Evelyn took a step towards her and placed a supportive hand on her shoulder.

On the sofa, Samantha shook her head. 'It's nothing,' she said, a faint smile on her lips. She took a breath again. Underneath her skin — inside of her — her baby was kicking, desperate to be free.

Thirty-Four

It was a depressing sound. With one arm and his eyes still closed, he reached for his phone to turn off the alarm. *Don't go back to sleep*, he told himself as he tapped the screen, before letting his head fall back against the pillow. Here it was warm. He rolled over and pushed his face into the curve of the back of her neck. Here there was no pressure. Under the covers, he felt her hand seek his out. When she found it, she pulled it around herself and tucked her body against his. Her hair tickled his nose. She smelled like sleep.

'I should get up or I won't be able to leave.' His voice was muffled by her hair. She breathed and let go of his hand. He inhaled her scent one last time before pulling away. When he sat up, he drew the covers back over her.

Alexander had returned to university for the final term of the academic year two weeks earlier. It was exam season and he felt woefully unprepared. He had finished writing his dissertation — 6,000 dry words on the subject of prenatal stress — but had neglected much of his reading over the Easter vacation. Now, just before six o'clock on Monday morning, he was at home, having driven back for the weekend late Friday evening. It was a trip he had made the previous Friday also. Exhausted, he just needed to make it through the next few weeks, after which he would receive his bachelor's degree and be able to start clinical training. *And fulfil my destiny.* It was a grim thought.

He put on his socks, one heavy foot at a time. Next to him in the bed, Mary rolled over and drew on his back with her finger.

'It's early,' he yawned. 'Go back to sleep.'

She yawned too, then asked, 'Are you coming back again on Friday?'

Friday. As tired as he was, the end of the week might as well have been next year. He stood up and pulled up his boxer shorts. 'We'll see,' he said, walking to his wardrobe. He picked out something plain, a simple light blue shirt, and put it on. There was an ink stain on the right cuff. He didn't have the energy to change into another.

Alexander came back to the bed and put his hands on the covers, leaning forward, close to where she lay. 'You could always come with me.'

She smiled and, eyes fuzzy with fatigue, swatted him away. 'I've already spent too much of my life at universities,' she said, referring to her father and his work.

Alexander leant closer and brought his face to hers. 'You know I don't mean *that*,' he said, a smile on his lips.

She laughed.

'Come with me,' he grinned. 'Come on.'

'Stop it, Alex.'

'Just say the word.' He rubbed his nose against hers. 'Say the word and we can leave. You know we can.'

Smiling, she rolled onto her back to get away from him.

'Okay,' he said, touching her chin before moving away from the bed and reaching for the linen-covered journal on top of his chest of drawers. 'Friday then, if I'm not too tired.'

Downstairs he found some leftover food in the fridge and packed it into a glass container to eat later in the car. On his way out of the kitchen, he grabbed an apple from the fruit bowl and the flask he had filled with coffee. In the hallway, his father had left his key to the Seat hanging by the front door. It would be back before he would be awake to miss it.

Asides from seeing Mary and his family, there was another reason for Alexander's journeys home. Careful to close the door behind him, he entered the room. A switch to the left turned on the lights. Ahead of him, the screens were all off. He sat down in the chair and swivelled it to face the main desk, the toes of his shoes scuffing the carpet. C Building. Camera five. With a press of a button, he turned on the monitor and shuffled forward.

She was sleeping, the same as the others. A few clicks and the cameras in the room were off.

Alexander locked the Seat and stole over the lawn to the red sandstone building that was C Building. A flash of his key-card and he was inside. Two doors down on the right, a storage room, one of the only rooms in the building not covered by a camera. He got the child first, then woke her and brought her to the room.

'I got you an apple.' He held the fruit out to the chocolate-haired woman.

She took it from him. 'Thank you.'

The third week of March. That was the first time he had removed her from the herd. Pandora had been reunited with the others earlier in the year, having recovered from her infection and been determined by Alexander, as per his father's expectation, to be healthy enough to re-enter the system. After New Year's, he had kept her in B Building under his care for as long as he could, but when the time came for him to return to university, her movement to C Building — the place where they housed the freshers — had been inevitable. Her baby was kept separate from her all night and for much of the day, and she was expected to give milk every morning until her child was weaned and she was dried off. Then, when Robert decided she was ready, she would be sent back to A Building to begin the cycle all over again.

Seated on an old plastic chair, Pandora brought her daughter to her breast and allowed her to suckle. Alexander leant against the wall by the door and watched the young woman feed her child.

Tending to Pandora had awakened the unexpected in him: a sense of purpose. Of course, such had not always been the case. Sleep-deprived and frustrated, he had at first resisted the responsibility. Christmas had been just around the corner and, tired from the task of university, he had longed for little more than the soft comforts of a warm bed and the muted watercolour tones of cannabis. That had soon changed. And so, his actions — once aimless, clumsy, boyish — had become deliberate, so much so that he was now starting to believe that, maybe, somehow, he could make a difference. *That's why I turn the cameras off.* He didn't want anyone — his father, his grandfather — commenting on what he was doing. The moment it became theirs, it would stop being his. Besides, he was always careful to do it when everyone else was asleep. Unless they had reason to check, they would never look.

Pandora's baby, who she had named Petal, played with her mother's hair as she drank. She was much bigger than she had been only a few short weeks ago and when he looked at her, Alexander couldn't help but feel proud at having been a part of her development. Her eyes were big and blue, like her mother's, and her cheeks were chubby and dimpled. Sitting in the chair, Pandora whispered to her as she nursed, and, at one point, the child seemed to react to her name.

'Did you see that?' Alexander asked, stepping away from the door.

Pandora looked up at him. 'What?' she replied.

He nodded at the baby. 'I think she recognised her name.'

She turned her face back to her daughter. Her mouth close to the infant's scalp, she whispered, 'Petal,' and again, 'my Petal.' The second time, the baby turned, her mother's teat still between her lips.

'There,' Alexander said, moving closer.

Pandora looked at him and smiled. 'She knows who she is.' Her eyes widened with delight.

He was sure she didn't understand — didn't even question — why she received preferential treatment over her peers. As they slept, she was given precious minutes with her child, feeding her, clutching her, singing to her. Minutes that the others would never get. They were expected to give the milk that was meant for their babies to Robert. Only then would he reward them with access.

Alexander knew he could never explain to her why. And yet, as feeble-minded as she was, she was perfect.

'She's a gift.' In the chair, Pandora was still looking up at him. 'She's a gift,' she repeated, her face flooded with joy as her baby continued to suckle. With wide, heaven-heavy eyes, she asked Alexander if he would like to hold her.

Smiling, he shook his head. 'Let her finish.'

It was miraculous. In spite of everything, each kindness — however negligible on his part — she multiplied ten-fold. *That's why she kissed me.* She may not have had much to offer him, but what resources she did possess were hers to gift.

A few more minutes and Petal had finished. Pandora held her to her chest and started rubbing her back. The child hiccuped and cooed, her little fists opening and closing as her mother told her how much she loved her and how much of a cherished thing she was. Eventually, she looked up from the child and once again asked Alexander if he would like to hold her. He shook his head.

'I have to go soon.'

She nodded as if she understood and then returned to her baby, lifting her up and making her giggle.

The apple Alexander had brought from the house was on a shelf, where Pandora had placed it after he had given it to her. 'If you want it, you should eat it before I take you back,' he said and inclined his head towards the fruit.

Pandora looked up and nodded. 'Yes,' she said.

He passed it to her, and she adjusted her baby so that she could hold the apple in one hand and Petal in the other.

'Can you manage?' he asked as he watched her struggle.

She nodded, but he could see Petal squirming in her arm.

'Here,' he said, taking the apple back. 'I'll cut it up for you.'

He left her in the storage room whilst he went to the kitchen to get a knife and plate. The door only pulled to, he knew Pandora wouldn't try to leave. She had her baby, *and what more could her simple mind desire?*

He held the plate for her as she ate, a slice at a time. She offered a piece to her daughter, and let her suck on the fruit until juice dribbled down her chin. Pandora grinned, looking up at Alexander to show him her child's sticky face. He matched her smile and nodded. Petal giggled and bounced on her mother's lap. They both looked so innocent. *How do they even exist?*

When only a few slices of the apple remained, Pandora said she was finished.

'You eat the rest,' she said to Alexander, her eyes on her child.

He looked at the plate. Alongside the slices were the soggy

remains of the piece Pandora had offered to Petal. He thanked her and said he would after he had taken her and her daughter back to their respective rooms. Sleepy and full of milk, Petal went back peaceably, as did her mother, who was giddy after having spent time with her child. Alexander instructed her to go back to her bed, telling her that he would see her again next week. She smiled and thanked him as she moved across the room. He put his finger to his lips and nodded, encouraging her to be quiet so as not to wake the others. She did as he said and went back to her bed.

Before he left, he tidied the storage room. The plate with the apple was on the shelf. He picked it up and took it to the kitchen. There, he opened the bin and scraped the remains of the food into it.

By the time Robert woke to milk the freshers, all the cameras in C Building were on, and the key to the Seat was back where he had left it, hanging in the hallway next to the front door. Outside on the driveway, Alexander's little red car was gone.

Thirty-Five

Little men hate, bigger men pity, great men try to understand.

Robert put down his pen and leant across his desk to tilt the monitor. A cloud had drifted, exposing the Sun, and the light coming through the window was causing a glare on the screen. A tweak and it was corrected. The image came back into view. A man, naked from the waist down, sat on a bed as a woman, also mostly naked, watched him from the opposite corner of the room.

'Still no movement,' Robert mumbled to himself and picked up his pen. An old gold-plated fountain pen, he had used it since he was a boy. Decades later, it had a tendency to leak ink over the top of the nib.

There was a knock on the door. He looked up from his work and saw Sophie enter. She was carrying a tray. On it, a plate containing a sandwich and a cup of tea, balanced atop a saucer with two biscuits tucked against the rim. Robert smiled at her as she set it down on the desk next to him.

'Thank you, my darling.'

She squeezed his shoulder and moved back to the door. Before she left, she stopped, as if remembering something, and turned to her husband.

'I forgot to mention,' she said, resting her hand on the door, 'one of the hens must have got out in the night.'

Robert glanced up from the desk.

'I found her under a hydrangea.'

'Alive?'

Sophie's face was sombre.

Robert sighed. 'A fox, no doubt. How terrible.' He turned in his seat. 'Do you need me to clean it up?'

She shook her head. 'I've taken care of it. I got Guinevere to help.'

'I bet she was pleased.'

'It's good she sees these things,' Sophie replied, then dropped her hand to her side and walked back over to the desk. Funereal, she said, 'There were feathers everywhere.'

Robert reached to touch her hand. 'I'm sure it was quite a gruesome sight,' he said softly. 'I shall take a look at the coop when I'm finished here — check there's not a hole in the wire.'

Sophie rested against the edge of the desk, careful not to knock her husband's food. 'Thank you, dear.' She tidied a strand of his hair and he smiled at her before returning to his work, taking a sip from the cup on the tray in between pen strokes.

On the monitor, there was movement. The woman, who had been sitting on the floor, stood up and stretched her legs, and then walked along the edge of the room to the other corner. On the bed, the man stayed seated, but watched as the woman moved.

'Has he done it yet?' Sophie asked, looking at the screen.

Robert raised his head. 'No,' he said, 'he hasn't.'

She sighed. 'Perhaps he wasn't the correct choice afterall.'

The woman was on the floor again, her back to the corner of the room. The man on the bed kept watching. She looked at her feet.

Robert shook his head. 'No, he is the right choice. He just needs to be motivated.'

Leaning back in his chair, he reached for the plate. Sophie had cut the sandwich into triangles, and he selected his first and brought it to his lips. The bread was light and fluffy. 'Since you seem to be staying, my darling,' Robert said after he had swallowed his first bite. 'You might like to help me.' She asked him what he needed. He took another bite. 'When I've finished this,' he said, swallowing, 'I shall go in with him.'

Sophie frowned. 'To talk with him again?'

'No.' Robert reached for another triangle. 'I've given him enough of my words. My patience is wearing thin.'

His wife pressed her lips together.

'After he's done it once,' Robert continued, 'he'll realise there's no shame in it, and then we can move on from all of this.' He gestured to the screen and took another bite.

Still resting against the desk, Sophie adjusted herself. 'I don't know, Robert,' she said and placed her hand on the side of his neck, 'you need to be careful with him. You know how upset he was the last time you—'

'Ah, yes,' Robert said, 'but I think I understand him better now.' He reached for his tea. 'Did you make these?' he asked, nodding at the biscuits. Sophie said she had and he smiled. 'I am very fortunate, thank you.' Pinching it between his forefinger and thumb, he dunked the biscuit into the tea before bringing it up to his lips. The end, buttery and sweet, started to crumble as he lifted it from the cup, so he quickly put it into his mouth whole. When he had swallowed, he spoke again. 'Clifford is not someone who understands any level of reasoning. I see this now.' A crumb had fallen onto his shirt and he brushed it away with his hand. 'Whereas some of the others see sense — even if it's just a modicum — he is,' Robert paused to consider his words before continuing, 'he is much more primal in the way that he thinks.'

Sophie leant forward, listening.

'He deflects,' Robert pointed at the man on the screen. 'Humour — or attempts at it, anyway. Nonchalance. He acts as though he doesn't care, and that there is nothing that I can say or do to make him care, when, in fact,' Robert looked up at his wife, 'there is.'

'What are you saying, dear?'

'I just need you to be ready to let me out when I'm done,' he said and picked up another sandwich.

'Should I get Frank to help?'

Chewing, Robert shook his head. 'There's no need,' he said after he had washed the food down with a drink. 'Besides, I sent him out in the van to get something. He's trying to stop smoking, again, and he's been a bother all morning.' He straightened the cup on its saucer. 'No doubt he will have relieved his addiction by the time he returns.'

'My dear,' Sophie said, raising her eyebrows, 'that's not very supportive of you.'

Robert finished the sandwich before speaking. 'As much as we would all like him to, the man's too old to be changing his habits now. I'd rather he just got on with it and made himself useful again.'

Sophie shook her head. 'Your patience really has worn thin.'

He laughed and then stood up, kissing her on the forehead as he moved to a filing cabinet. The bottom drawer, like the others, was locked, and he opened it with a key before pulling out a lacquered wooden box.

'Oh, Robert,' Sophie said, watching from the desk. 'Must you?'

'I told you, my darling,' he replied, carrying the box over to her, 'the man is primal. I have to speak to him in a language he understands.'

'Well, I think you should at least wait until Frank's back.'

Placing the box on the desk, he shook his head. 'You are all the help I need,' he said. 'You, and this.'

There was a gun inside the box. A revolver with a six shot cylinder, its stainless steel barrel glinted in the sunlight that poured in through the window. Robert lifted the weapon out of its casing and pulled the hammer back to half-cock to release the cylinder. Although there was hardly ever a reason to use such a device, he knew how to if it became necessary.

Sophie wasn't happy, family history having made it clear

just how dangerous a bull could be, but there wasn't much use in trying to dissuade her husband. All she could do was be there for him, as he had asked.

'It won't take long,' Robert said, pulling on his white coat and tucking the gun into the waistband at the back of his trousers. He took the last sandwich from the plate and left the room.

He sat her down outside the door, in front of the monitor and the buttons that controlled the locks. He kissed her and she told him to be careful. He said he would and she pushed the button which unlocked the door to let him in.

Clifford didn't look surprised to see him. He merely inclined his head to the left, let his eyes pass over the man in the white coat, and then looked away. In the corner, the woman was panicked.

Robert moved to the centre of the room. 'You disappoint me,' he said to the man on the bed. Eyes on the floor, he didn't respond. His wrists were no longer in chains, but he knew there was little use in trying to fight his captor. The last time he tried, the man had come prepared. Clifford's leg was still red and painful from where Robert had struck him with the electric prod.

'You had no trouble servicing the others. I do not see why this one should be any different.'

Behind him, the naked woman on the floor let out a sob.

Clifford lifted his head. He looked older than he was. 'You know why it's different,' he said through clenched teeth.

Robert didn't respond. In his hand, he held the remaining

triangle of the sandwich Sophie had made him. Keeping his eyes on the man on the bed, he brought the food to his mouth and took a bite. He ate it as the man watched and the woman on the floor quietly wept. When the sandwich was gone, Robert cleared his throat and said, 'You see, Clifford, if you don't do this, then you are of no use to me.'

He was quick to pull the gun. A hand under his coat and he was holding it, his dominant hand wrapped around the handle and the barrel firmly pointed at the man on the bed. It was crass, to threaten like that, but it was the only way to get him to embrace who he really was.

Clifford's eyes were wide and frozen and the woman's sobbing had increased.

'Do it now and we can end this conversation,' Robert said.

'You're crazy,' was all the man could say. 'Crazy, *really* crazy.'

Robert held the revolver steady. 'Do it now, Clifford.'

'No,' he protested, straightening his back. 'I won't.' The barrel was contacting his forehead now. Clifford's eyes had never been so wide. 'You're bluffing,' he spat at the man in the white coat. 'You won't do it!'

Robert's mouth was straight. 'How confident are you that I won't?'

It was a good question, and, delivered as it was, by a man with unblinking, focused eyes, not one Clifford could really say he knew the answer to. From the bed, he looked at the woman. She was howling, hot tears streaming down her face as she pummelled the floor with her fists. With his thumb, Robert pulled the hammer back. Everyone in the room heard the gun click. Despite having been warmed against Robert's body, the barrel was cold and stung Clifford's skin.

'Do her.'

Slowly, Clifford pulled his head away from the gun and slid off the bed and onto the floor. Robert kept the revolver on him as he moved, crawling across the tiles to where the woman was crying. When he reached her, Clifford looked over his shoulder, as if to check that the man with the gun really was still there. Seeing him, his feet shoulder-width apart and his elbows straight, Clifford dragged in a lungful of air and snorted it out through his nostrils. His cheeks were red as he tightened his jaw. In front of him, the woman curled her body into a ball. The wall held her in place when he grabbed her, the corner of the room, which she had thought a friend, turned traitorous, transforming from a place of safety to one of horror. With rough hands he snatched at her bare legs, forcing them apart so that he could enter her. Screaming, he had her on her back, her balled fists imprisoned against the hard tiles by his. Another lungful of air and he pried her open.

A series of indelicate convulsions and it was done.

His skin bristling with perspiration, Clifford dragged himself away from the woman, she quiet and shaking against the wall. Robert lowered the gun and stepped away.

'That was not so difficult in the end.'

The other said nothing.

Three strides and Robert was at the door. He knocked on it and the electronic lock clicked instantly. Before he left, he turned his head to the man on the floor and smiled. It was a nice smile. 'You will eat well tonight,' he said to him.

On the floor, Clifford's mouth was closed. As the man in the white coat left the room, he couldn't help but turn to look at the woman, crumpled, sobbing on the floor.

Thirty-Six

He had been twenty years old when they found him. A daydreamer, he had always seen his life unfolding in front of him, spanning the distance of time — a single gold thread, tangled in a mess of coarse twine, stretched to the point of breakage, but strong. Meant to withstand. Left outside a supermarket when he was just a few days old, clumsily wrapped in an old threadbare bath towel, he had never known his parents.

At first, it had just been the man. He had found him sleeping rough, something he had been doing on and off for the past seven months. The back door to a supermarket. He was aware of the irony, but it was covered and kept the rain off. Plus, the guy who worked at the bakery, an older man named Gordon, gave him the bread that was too stale to sell on his way home from work every weekday. On the weekends, he shared with the rats.

Violence. That's what the last shelter he had stayed at had accused him of when they threw him out. Very few hostels — as they were more properly called — accepted walk-ins. Most needed a referral from the council. After he was thrown out, he knew he was unlikely to get another. Besides, last time he had been on a waiting list for twelve weeks before he was able to move in. Behind the supermarket, there was no paperwork.

The man was kind and bought him breakfast, taking him to a café further down the highstreet. If he had smelled, which he was certain he did, the man never said anything. He didn't pull his nose or look down on him as others did. Instead, he ate with him, and they talked about inconsequential things like the Christmas decorations that were being put up around the town. Eventually, the man had asked him how he had ended up behind the supermarket. He had shrugged and shovelled a forkful of egg into his mouth. Opposite, the man cradled a coffee, quietly waiting for him to answer. The steam from the mug seemed to wrap itself around his smile. He was older than he was and spoke well, like he was someone who knew a lot about a lot, but he never made him feel small or stupid, he just seemed happy to sit and talk with him. When he didn't answer his question, the man hadn't asked again. Putting his coffee down, he had pointed to a little boy outside the window. Dressed in a green coat and wellington boots, the boy was chasing a ball down the street, his mother fast on his heels, shouting for him to slow down. Smiling, the man told him he had a boy of a similar age. He nodded and ate another forkful of egg. Turning his eyes back to the table, the man asked if he had any brothers or sisters. He shook his head. The man nodded and took a sip from his mug.

Two weeks passed before he saw the man again. Just as

before, he bought him breakfast. The same café and the same toast, baked beans and fried egg. Outside, it was getting colder. After they were finished at the café, the man had offered him his gloves. He slid them off his fingers and pushed them into his hands. They were thick and blue. He tried to give them back, but the man shook his head and said he simply wouldn't allow it, and so he had said thank you, and told him that they were by far the nicest pair of gloves he had ever had. In truth, they were the only ones he had ever had. The man had smiled and nodded all the same.

The next time he saw him, the man was energetic. He greeted him like an old friend, touching him on the arm when he saw him at the supermarket. Strange, but nice. His stomach had grumbled in anticipation of the egg and toast. As they ate, the man told him his father had a job for him. He never explained what the job was, but was clearly happy to be able to offer it to him. Food and a warm place to sleep, the man promised as he cut into the egg, popping the yolk and flooding the plate yellow.

He hadn't known what to say. Winter had arrived and it was freezing. Another man on the streets, who alternated between the alleyway that ran down the side of a pub and a covered bus stop, told him that a body had been found in the park. Part man, part ice cube. He was an old timer, so the man said, and hadn't seen a bed for years. He didn't want to die like that. He was meant to withstand.

Before the man left, he accepted his offer. He had been happy — they had both been happy. He had found a way off the streets and the man had done a good deed. Gripping his shoulder as they walked together, the man asked him if he wanted to leave now. He had been in shock, and could only smile and revel in his good fortune as the man invited him into his car. He could feel the twine slackening. The man, smiling at him across the car, his brown eyes gentle and bright, had even let him put the heater on as they drove away. Thinking of the gold thread, he made sure to look for the supermarket as they passed. He wanted it to be the last time he ever saw it.

Lee was thirty-six now. For sixteen years he had worked for Robert and his father, and it had been a long time since he had seen the supermarket or dreamt of the gold thread.

He had been sitting at the window for hours. In the distance, he could see the trees. Over them, the Sun. Earlier in the day, he had seen the younger woman drive past. She hadn't seen him. The glass was warm now. He placed his hand on the window. The Sun was hitting it directly.

Behind him, the door opened. It was Robert. He had a smile on his face and beckoned him into the adjacent room. He stood up and moved away from the window.

In the other room there was a table. Robert gestured to it, and invited him to sit down. It had been laid for two. Toast, baked beans and fried egg.

'It's been a long time since we've had breakfast together,' Robert said as he pulled out his chair and sat. Lee nodded and took his place opposite. In front of Robert's place, a cup of coffee.

'I hope you don't mind,' he said, indicating to his drink. 'I know you don't drink it.'

Lee shook his head. He didn't mind.

Robert pointed to a jug in the centre of the table. 'I got you some juice instead.' Lee strained in his chair to look. 'Fresh oranges,' Robert said. He nodded to the empty glass in front of Lee's plate. 'Would you like me to pour you some?'

Lee shook his head. He could manage.

They ate together in silence. The only sound was that of their knives and forks contacting the plates. Lee scrapped the beans onto the toast with his knife. The butter had been spread thick, just how he liked it. Eventually, Robert spoke.

'I've always treated you well, haven't I, Lee?'

The other man was chewing and swallowed before speaking. 'I suppose you have,' he said.

'That's good.'

They continued eating. Robert stopped to take a drink. Lee poured himself a glass of juice.

'You know,' Robert said after he put his cup down, 'it really has been a long time, hasn't it?' He was smiling. For the first time, Lee noticed the creases that furred the edges of the man's eyes.

'I guess it has,' he said and drank some of the orange juice.

'We're both older,' Robert continued, cutting himself a square of yolk-sodden toast, 'one of us more so than the other.' He laughed and Lee smiled. 'Only the other day I was thinking about how much we've both changed.'

Lee put down his glass. 'You seem the same to me, Robert.'

The other man looked intrigued, but said nothing. He wiped the square of eggy toast around his plate before bringing it to his mouth. Outside, they heard a bird fly past the window. It was singing sweetly. Both men lifted their heads from their food as it passed by.

Lee was eating too quickly. Robert asked him if he would like another egg. 'More toast, too, perhaps?'

Lee nodded and said he would.

Robert wrapped his fingers around his cup and sat, smiling, at his companion. Lee finished the last of his egg and put his fork down.

'Is the food good?' Robert asked, watching the other man reach for his glass of juice.

Lee nodded and drank.

'I am glad.'

As he spoke, Robert stood up and moved to the metal hatch in the corner of the room. It opened and a plate was pushed through. Toast and another fried egg. He carried it over to the table and placed it in front of the other man. By the time Robert had returned to his seat, the fork was back in Lee's hand and the food was being devoured.

'I find,' Robert said as the other man ate, 'that the older I get, the less I am able to eat.'

Lee said nothing. Robert just smiled and took another sip of coffee.

When the food was gone, Lee placed his hands on the table. His shoulders were wide and they overhung the sides of the chair as he leant back against it.

'Satisfied?' Robert asked from the other side of the table.

Lee nodded, a faint smile on his lips.

'Good,' said Robert. 'Don't forget your drink.'

The other man finished what was left of his juice. Robert leant forward in his seat and refilled his glass from the jug. Lee thanked him and drank some more. Robert returned the jug to the middle of the table.

'Food and a warm place to sleep, that's what I promised you all those years ago,' he said. 'I didn't lie, did I?'

Lee looked at him. 'No, I don't suppose you did.' Something must have caught in his throat as he started coughing. Robert raised his eyebrows. 'I'm okay,' the man said, thumping his chest. He coughed again and so reached for his glass to take a drink.

'Slowly,' Robert said, watching him as he drank. Lee's coughing subsided. 'That's better.'

Lee settled back in his chair, Robert's eyes still on him.

After a minute of silence, Robert said, 'You are remarkable, Lee.' His tone softened as he spoke. 'I knew it the moment I first saw you.'

The other man didn't say anything.

'I knew you would be a good fit for the job.'

Still nothing.

'And, truly, you've made me very proud.'

Lee stayed quiet. He tried to reach for his glass, to take another drink, but found it difficult to raise his hand off the table.

'It really will be sad,' Robert continued, his gaze dropping to the table, 'to carry on without you.'

Lee went to say something, but found his lips were too heavy.

Robert took a deep breath. 'Very sad.' Straightening in his chair, he raised his hand to his mouth and took another breath.

By now, Lee knew there was something wrong. With heavy eyelids, he looked at Robert and silently appealed to him. The other man saw the fear in his eyes. He stood up and moved around the table.

'Lee,' Robert said, crouching beside him, 'it's okay, Lee.'

Slowly, Lee turned his head, his neck resisting his brain's command as it struggled to turn. Robert shushed him and laid a hand on his arm.

'Don't be scared, Lee,' he said, his voice low and soft. 'Everything will be okay.'

But Lee was scared, and his bottom lip quivered as he tried to speak. He felt his shoulders droop and start to slip away from the back of the chair. Robert stood up and wrapped his arms around him, holding his thick torso upright as he fell towards the table.

'It's okay, Lee,' he repeated, gripping the man in his arms. 'Just try to relax. It will be over soon.'

Too heavy to keep holding him, Robert gently lowered the man's head onto the table. As he did, he stroked his hair.

'Sixteen years,' he whispered as he positioned Lee's face, so that his left cheek was against the table. 'I kept you as long as I could.' Robert was eye to eye with the man now. Lee didn't blink. 'But, this day had to come.' Robert touched the man's forehead. 'You've sired so many offspring, Lee,' he continued, 'and the day my father passed the homestead over to me, thirteen years ago, I knew—' he paused, his breath catching in his throat. 'I knew I would be okay, running this place myself. Do you know why, Lee?' The other man was silent on the table. 'Because I had you.' Robert smiled. 'A fine bull.'

He held him until the end, even as his last breath died in his lungs and his heart stopped beating. Face next to his, he watched as the other man's essence expired and faded from his eyes. Finally, Robert placed two fingers on Lee's neck to check for a pulse. *He's really gone.* He sighed and closed his eyes, letting his own head rest on the table beside Lee's.

The spool was empty. The gold thread spent.

Thirty-Seven

She hadn't been there when he woke. Tired, he drifted downstairs to the kitchen and made himself breakfast. He ate it in the sitting room on the sofa and must have fallen back asleep after he had finished. Jolting awake, he noticed the Sun was higher in the sky than it had been before. He ruffled his hair and pulled himself to his feet.

The to-ing and fro-ing between home and university was taking its toll on Alexander. He had been doing it for several weeks and the end was almost in sight. *Thankfully*. He had arrived home late last night and wasn't sure how much longer either he or his car could withstand the moving about. Thick white smoke had started billowing out from the exhaust and that seemed to signal its impending demise. He had driven the same car since he passed his driving test aged seventeen. It was probably time for a change.

Of course, he could have just stayed at university, as he had done every other term since he matriculated. He was, however, becoming more and more disenchanted with the place.

What had originally been his escape had become — or perhaps always had been — just another form of captivity. *Yet more posturing, stubborn old men.* Those he had considered friends, he had distanced himself from, and his studies revealed themselves to be more of a process of box-ticking than of genuine enlightenment. His father had cautioned him not to expect too much before he went three years earlier. It was a place of thinking, for sure, but still one that had been infiltrated and subverted by the other, the sub-homo, *and there is only so much you can get from a place like that.*

So why bother then?

He still needed a medical education and it was unreasonable to expect his father to teach him absolutely everything. Robert was a busy man, and he himself had endured the same struggles that Alexander was currently experiencing. *Or so he says.* In addition to that, it was important to be seen as a part of the system. To worship the same institutions and pieces of paper that they did. To — as Ernest Stansfield had dedicated his whole life to — live in plain sight and dismantle them using their own systems. To take advantage of their inherent failings and find sustenance there. *To live as parasites.* It was a terrible truth, but that was what the other had made them: outcasts in their own world.

And so Alexander remained in the system, and would do until he graduated and became a certified, societal recognised doctor. A product of their system, he would be infallible.

He buzzed at the door to the Seat and she let him in.

'Good morning.'

She turned in her chair and smiled. 'Good morning.' Motioning for him to come in, she asked if he had slept well. He sat down in the chair next to hers and said he had. Knee to knee, she told him he looked tired and he agreed he probably was.

'You don't have to make the journey,' Mary said, her chair swaying side to side as she swivelled it with her feet. 'If it's too tiring.'

He shook his head. 'It's okay.'

Behind her, the monitors were on. Each screen bore an image of a location somewhere on the homestead. Women in all stages of motherhood, from conception to pregnancy to lactation. Children could also be seen on several of the cameras, boys and girls of different ages, playing and laughing, their expressions bright with youth and innocence. On one of the screens, which was connected to an external camera, Alexander saw his father carrying a box of equipment. Heavy mechanical weighing scales and a telescopic height measure bounced up and down in the box as he crossed the screen.

'A busy day,' he said, nodding at the monitor.

'He's burying himself in it,' Mary replied, running a strand of her hair through her fingers. 'He still hasn't got over last week.'

Alexander nodded. 'Grandpa said.'

She let go of her hair and grinned. 'I imagine he was his usual sympathetic self.'

'Yeah, and overflowing with sensitive opinions and advice.'

Mary laughed. 'What did he say?'

'You can imagine,' he said, resting his head against the back of the chair. 'About how it was when he was in charge and how disappointed he is that I'd turned out to be even more of a—' he paused, recalling the impromptu lecture he had been subjected to before leaving the house, 'I think the term he used was mollycoddled buttercup — more of a mollycoddled buttercup than my father.'

'Ouch,' Mary said, still swivelling her chair from side to side. 'And what did you say?'

'Nothing,' he answered, closing his eyes. 'Just told him I hoped his knee hadn't bothered him too much in the night and kissed my mother on the cheek before leaving to come find you.' His face stretched into a smile and she laughed again, her knees contacting his as she spun the chair.

When he opened his eyes Mary was looking at him, as if waiting for him to say something more. He touched her knee and smiled. 'Walk with me?'

She nodded.

As they got up to leave, Alexander took one last look at the monitors. *C Building. Camera five.* Pandora was there. *Where else would she be?* Her back was to the camera and she was fiddling with something that he couldn't quite make out. A fresher with short hair said something from the sofa, which made her turn her head. Now in view of the camera, Alexander thought her face looked soft and happy. Her lips moved quickly as she replied to the other woman. As she spoke, her hand trailed over her stomach, her thoughts elsewhere.

'Are you coming, Alex?'

Mary was by the door, her mouth slightly curved as she watched him.

'Yes,' he said, turning away from the screens and walking to her, 'I'm coming.'

They fell into rhythm with each other as they walked. Pulling him by the hand, Mary led him onto a path that grazed the treeline and curved around the base of a hill, and, should it have been followed to its end, would have led to the vineyards that covered the far side of the homestead. She was the same height as him, if a little shorter, and Alexander examined the movements of her face as she told him about a book on metallism she had just finished reading.

'You don't mind?' she stopped to ask, her cheeks momentarily flushed and a sting of doubt in her eyes — a flash of insecurity that was easy to miss, *unless you're paying close attention.*

He squeezed her hand. 'No, of course not.'

She moved her hands as she spoke. Small, excited motions that grew larger each time he smiled or nodded his head. When he asked a question, she was eager to answer, her voice becoming more animated and her body turning, so that she was walking with her back to the unfolding path, the elegant features of her face just for him. Watching her move, watching her speak, Alexander was quite certain Mary wasn't like this with anyone else.

After a few minutes of walking together, they came to a fence. It was high and made of metal, with thick, green plastic-coated posts butting against the path at regular intervals. On the other side, little girls were running and chasing each other. Underneath a tree, close to the fence, two sat together, talking. Alexander and Mary slowed as they passed.

'Do you think they know?' Alexander asked, rubbing his fingers over the back of Mary's hand as he held it.

She turned her face to the children on the other side of the fence and shook her head. 'How could they?' she said, her voice low and monotone.

Still holding her hand, Alexander moved closer to the fenceline. Underneath the tree, the two girls realised they were being watched and raised their heads to look at him.

'Come on, Alex,' Mary said, staying where she was and tugging his hand.

His face was at the wire now and the girls stood up and edged towards him.

'Alex,' Mary urged, 'it's boring, come on.'

He shook his head. 'Just wait,' he said softly, 'see what they do.'

Her lip quivered as if she wanted to say something else. She didn't, and instead joined him at the fence.

One of the girls had a peculiar red mark on her cheek. As she got closer, they saw the rest of her face was similarly blemished. The other, who approached more cautiously, tucked behind her companion and clutching at the fabric of her smock, had brown hair and plump cheeks. Both sides of the fence were silent as four sets of eyes blinked and darted.

Mary squeezed Alexander's hand and inclined her head at

the shorter and fatter of the two girls. 'Look,' she whispered to him, 'she's holding something.'

In the child's hand was a hairbrush. Half of its teeth were missing and the wooden handle was warped and looked as though, at some point, it had been chewed or sucked on. A dirty shred of fabric was wrapped around it and held in place by a green ribbon.

'What on Earth is that?' Mary said, laughing, her voice suddenly increasing in volume and making the girls jump. The one with the hairbrush tucked herself more thoroughly behind her friend.

At Mary's side, Alexander studied the children. *What are they thinking?* he wondered, curious as to whether or not their mental processes resembled, in any way, his own as a child, or if, limited by their base state as they were, the inner workings of their brains would be entirely unrecognisable to him. Before he had a chance to express any of this, one of the girls let out a yelp and scurried back towards the tree. A stick in her hand, Mary had poked her through the fence. The other girl, the one with the hairbrush, remained, frozen and confused, as Mary went to use the stick again.

'Don't, Mary,' Alexander said, laying a hand on her arm.

She paused what she was doing and looked at him. 'I want to see what she's holding,' she explained and jabbed the stick at the child. It missed her hand, where the hairbrush was, and instead hit her arm. The girl cried out, her face crinkling.

Again, Alexander told Mary to stop. 'They're children,' he

said and tried to pry the stick out of her hands. 'You'll traumatise them.'

Shrugging him off, Mary laughed. 'Traumatise?' She pulled a face. 'Poking them with a stick is hardly going to traumatise them.'

'It might,' Alexander replied.

Stick still in hand, she narrowed her eyes. 'They will have forgotten about it in a couple of minutes. They're simply not capable of it. They're just—' Mary shoved the stick at the girl again, 'swine.'

Fed up of being poked, the girl ran away from the fence.

Alexander shook his head. 'You don't know that,' he said.

Fun over, Mary tossed the stick into a bush. 'What, and you do?' she smirked. 'You're not here cleaning up after them every day.'

'I'm not saying I am,' he shrugged. 'But, I think the way we treat them leaves its mark.'

Mary laughed and wiped her hands together to knock off the bits of bark that had stuck to her palms. When Alexander didn't join in her laughter, she stopped and said, 'You're being serious?'

Alexander was silent.

Mary laughed again. 'There's nothing to leave a mark on, Alex.'

To this Alexander shook his head. 'Not so,' he replied. 'Not from what I've seen. There's more to them than we think.'

'What do you mean, what you've seen?' All of a sudden, she moved closer to him. Smile spiralling and eyes quizzical and bright, her expression reminded him of mischief and of how they once used to share all their ridiculous, juvenile secrets with each other.

'Well,' Alexander said with a smile, 'you know how I've been coming back at the weekends?'

More mischief and Mary laughed. 'Yes, I did notice that.'

'I've been coming back to make some observations,' he continued, 'on one of the sub-homos.'

A smile still on her lips, suspended pink and slightly parted, she didn't say anything, only watched him as he searched her face for a reaction.

'The one from Christmas,' he explained. 'The sub-homo from Christmas that I took care of and...' His words grew slower and her smile slipped away. Eventually, there was nothing left in either case.

'A sub-homo?' Mary asked, voice soft. 'You've been coming back at the weekends for a sub-homo?' A curl of her hair had fallen forward and it caressed her cheek.

'Yes,' he replied. 'Well, no. Not at all. I mean I do, but— That makes it sound—'

'Sound like what?' The curl was still against her cheek. A sudden swipe and she stuffed it behind her ear, her thumb rushing to conceal a tear that had formed in the corner of her eye as she did. 'Sound like you come home for a sub-homo?'

He didn't respond.

'I thought you came home for me.'

Her words seemed to melt, warping at the edges until they collapsed into themselves, small and sliding into an oblivion of crushing, wide-eyed, devastated silence. Alexander was standing right in front of her and she waited for him to say something, to kill her worst fears and happily prove her foolish, but all he gave her was silence.

Say something, Alexander.

Squeezing her lips shut, Mary wrung her hands together, pinching the skin between her thumb and forefinger. She seized a breath and held it in her lungs until her cheeks flushed. Alexander could see the hurt in her eyes. He could feel it. Glassy and wide, they seemed as though they might shatter.

Say something.

He couldn't.

When she finally released the air from her lungs, her cheeks were wet.

'I thought you came home for me,' she said again. Every word was laced with pain. The pain of old scars being ripped open.

Slowing his breathing, Alexander drew his hand over his brow. 'Mary—'

Overhead, the Sun was shining.

'I have work,' Mary said, shaking as she dabbed the corners of her eyes with the sleeve of her dress. 'I—'

He could have said something to make it right, to repair the damage and stop the knife from shredding the wound any further than it already had — *you know the words, just say them* — but he didn't. Instead, he let his hand drop to his side as she hurried away from him.

He waited until she had disappeared from view before he

made his own way back along the path. Looking at the children on the other side of the fence, he laughed to think that, only a few moments before, he had considered the workings of their brains unrecognisable. Now, alone on the path, his head in his hands, he realised he didn't even recognise his own thoughts. *I'm an imbecile.* He didn't even know who or what he was. He only knew he never meant to hurt her.

Thirty-Eight

'What's he doing?'

Filly's eyes widened as she put her finger to her lips. Underneath the tree, Cherub hugged Rosie tighter to her chest and waited for her friend to come back.

After the horrible lady with the stick had left, the man had paced back and forth along the path, his hands on the sides of his face, mumbling to himself under his breath. At first, the girls had been too scared to move. There had been crying, and the last thing that they wanted was for another stick to be launched in their direction.

'Why are they so sad?' Cherub had asked the other girl, as they watched from behind the trunk of the tree.

Filly had just shaken her head. When the lady walked away, she had snuck closer to the fence for a better look.

Adults are always sad, Cherub thought, remembering how upset Nanny had been the previous evening when the girls were eating their dinner. Everyone had been given second helpings and as much bread as they liked. Cherub had eaten too much and her tummy had hurt in the night. *Perhaps they all eat too much.* That would explain why she had heard Nanny crying when everyone was supposed to be sleeping.

The man was gone now. The hem of her smock clumped up inside her fist, Filly hurried back to the tree. Cherub pulled her close. 'Did he see you?' she asked.

'No,' Filly said. 'He just left.'

Cherub nodded, not knowing what more to say. The girls' entertainment was limited and so they took it wherever it could be found. Elsewhere in the garden, the other girls were lining up by the door. Nanny was there, one hand on her hip, guiding them inside.

Cherub saw and nudged her friend. 'It's time for bed already?'

At the front of the queue, one of the girls, Jessica, pushed another into a bush. As she fell her smock caught on a twig and she landed on her bottom. Immediate tears and Jessica's tribe shrieked with laughter.

Filly looked on, her face serious. 'It's not late enough,' she said. Covering her eyes with her hand, she tilted her chin to the sky. The Sun was overhead. Following her gaze, Cherub also looked up. The Sun was very bright.

'Don't look at it directly,' Filly said, reaching to cover her friend's eyes with her hand.

Cherub nodded. It had hurt to look. How that meant it wasn't late enough she didn't understand.

'Come on.' Filly tugged Cherub's elbow. 'Let's see.'

Nanny shook her head when she saw them at the back of

the line. 'Where were you two?' she asked, frowning as she walked over to them. Cherub pointed to the tree at the other end of the garden. Nanny tutted and shook her head again. 'I was calling you. Anyway—' she paused and stepped to one side to allow the line to move forward, 'it's a special day today. You need to come inside.'

Cherub nodded. Next to her, Filly pulled a face. 'But it's not the end of the day.'

Nanny sighed. 'I just said today is special, child. There'll be time to play again afterwards.'

A man, so it turned out, wanted to see them. He was waiting indoors, although the light from the outside made it difficult to see him when Cherub and Filly first walked through the door. Inside it was dark and it took a moment for their eyes to adjust.

'Stand here, girls,' Nanny said, placing her hands on their shoulders and shepherding them to the side of the room with the beds. Other girls were already there. Upon seeing them, Jessica stuck out her tongue. Cherub tucked the fabric of her dress around Rosie and looked away. Opposite, on the other side of the room, were the younger girls. They had been told to sit on the floor, their little legs crossed and their hands in their laps as they waited for their next instruction.

Nanny addressed the man. 'That's all of them,' she said. Dressed in a white coat, he was standing close to the wall and had not yet said anything. He looked up now, his eyes lifting from the journal he was writing in.

'Thank you,' he said and nodded at the white-haired woman. Nanny retreated to the far corner of the room.

The man put the lid on his pen and tucked it into the pocket of his coat. When he turned to the girls by the beds, he was smiling. 'Today,' he began, casting his brown eyes over the girls' faces, 'is your graduation day.' Cherub turned to Filly. Her face was expressionless. 'So, what does that mean?' the man asked. Shuffling and a couple of girls leant forward to see him better. 'It means,' he continued, 'that I will expect the very best of behaviour from you all.' His voice was firm, yet gentle. 'You will follow me to another room and there we will conduct the ceremony.'

With a smile he nodded at the children, who, as if informed by some occult means, immediately stepped away from the beds and formed a line in front of him. Filly tugged the fabric of Cherub's smock, pulling her into the queue in front of her.

The door to the room opened and on the other side were two women.

'It's her!' Cherub hissed, turning, wild eyed, to her friend. Just outside the door was the lady who had poked them with the stick. She had her arms folded over her chest and didn't seem to notice the girls as they passed in front of her. At her side was an older lady with shoulder-length blonde hair.

Filly squeezed her lips together and nudged Cherub to keep her moving forward. The line was getting away from them and something told her now wasn't a good time to stand out.

They had never been to this room before. In fact, the girls, as far as their young minds could remember, had never really been anywhere, save for the distance between their beds, the bathroom and the garden outside. It was a big room — or at least bigger than they were used to — with a cold floor and, despite it still being daytime, curtains drawn over all the windows. Cherub and Filly were at the back of the line and the lady with the blonde hair ushered them into the room before closing the doors behind them. The man was ahead, near the front of the line, stick lady at his side.

'Girls,' the man said, smiling as he straightened the sleeves of his coat. 'I will call you each forward, one at a time. As I mentioned in the other room, I expect good behaviour. So remember, low voices and stay in line. We don't want anyone getting upset.'

Cherub strained her neck to look for Jessica. She was further ahead in the line, fiddling with her hair of the girl in front of her. *No one gets upset.* Clearly the man didn't know Jessica.

A girl called Willow was at the front of the queue. When he called her forward, gesturing to her with his hand, the man asked for her name. After she had mumbled it to him, her fists tightly gripping the sides of her dress, stick lady rummaged through a pile of papers that were stacked on a table next to them, retrieving one to give to the man. Behind her, Cherub felt Filly lean forward to peer over her shoulder. Willow looked frightened. She had a round face and a habit of biting her fingernails. She was biting them now. The man didn't say anything as he looked at the paper.

'Okay,' he said, looking up at the girl after a period of silence, 'please step onto the scales for me, Willow.' He pointed to the thing on the floor next to the table. Willow did as he said and he looked at the scales as she stood, quiet, waiting for him to tell her what to do next.

'Can you see?' Filly whispered into Cherub's ear.

She shook her head. 'Not good,' she said, standing on her tiptoes to see over the shoulder of the girl in front. Next to them, the lady with the blonde hair moved along the line, watching the girls as she walked, presumably to make sure they were behaving.

The man asked Willow to do some other things. He had a long pole with numbers written on it and asked the girl to stand next to it before writing something down on the paper that stick lady had given to him. He also wrapped a length of what looked like some sort of ribbon around various parts of her body, nodding his head and mumbling to himself, before once again returning to the paper with his pen. After a few minutes, it seemed as though he was finished. Willow stood still at his side, her fingers in her mouth.

'Willow,' the man said, making sure to look at her, 'well done.' Despite the eye contact, his voice was unemotional. The child didn't say anything. The man pointed to the far right corner of the room. 'You may go wait there until we're finished.' She did as he said and scurried as far into the corner of the room as she could. Stick lady walked with her for part of the way, before returning to the man's side.

And that was how it went. The man called the next girl forward and, once stick lady had given him a piece of paper, measured, analysed and recorded. Some girls were told to go stand with Willow. Others were instructed to wait opposite, in the far left corner of the room. Before too long, the whole event turned into a game of 'whose team would you rather be on?', and once Jessica was called forward and assigned, everyone prayed that it would be the left. When the girl who followed her was told to stand on the right side, Jessica and the others on the left started whooping with laughter. The girl, it so happened, was the one who Jessica had pushed into the bush less than an hour before.

There was tittering in the line and the lady with the blonde hair put her finger to her lips and encouraged the girls to be quiet. 'Come now, children,' she whispered, smiling underneath her finger. The way she said it was nice and so the girls listened.

Cherub turned around to look at Filly. She put her face close to her friend's and whispered, 'Left or right?'

Filly considered and nodded to the girls on the right. 'Anywhere that's away from her,' she said. Cherub agreed. It would be nice not to get chewed on by Jessica for a change.

Cherub and Filly were the last two girls in the line. When the man nodded at her, calling her forward with his hand, Cherub wished she had been last, so she could have watched Filly go first. *Filly is smart. Filly always knows how to do it best.* If she could have seen Filly do it and get told to stand on the right, she could have copied.

The man crouched in front of her so that they were the same height. So close, his face was big. 'What's your name?' His eyes seemed to search hers as he waited for her to reply.

'Cherub.' She said it too quietly and worried he would ask her to say it again. He didn't, and instead thanked her before standing up and turning to stick lady.

'Cherub,' he said to her and she handed him one of the two remaining pieces of paper. As she passed it to him, Cherub saw her glance down at Rosie, who she was still clutching in her hands. The lady's eyelashes fluttered and she threw her gaze to the floor. Cherub, too, looked away.

When he was ready, the man directed Cherub onto the scales. She watched as the red needle swung back and forth, until it settled on a number. The man nodded and scribbled something down on the paper. 'Here now, Cherub,' he said, manoeuvring her to the pole with the numbers on it. She stood next to it and he helped her to straighten her back with his hand. 'Thank you. That's very good,' he said when she was still. Once again he wrote something down on the paper. Next came the ribbon with numbers on it: around her waist, across her chest, underneath her chin, up and down the lengths of her legs. His face was close to hers as he worked and Cherub could hear him quietly humming. When he was done, he returned to the paper. His dark brown eyes ran the length of the page, his lips straight.

Waiting for the man to finish, Cherub looked over her shoulder at Filly. She was alone in the line now, the blonde-haired lady standing next to her. She tried to smile at her friend, but the attempt was feeble. In her hands, Rosie felt warm.

'I'm almost done,' the man said, looking up from the paper.

He smiled at her before turning his eyes back to the page. A minute more and he handed it back to stick lady. 'The right, please, Cherub,' the man said, extending his arm in the direction he wanted her to go.

A breath of relief. *No Jessica!* Cherub squeezed Rosie as she hurried to join Willow and the other girls in the right corner of the room. When she turned around, she looked at Filly and waved. Her friend nodded, before stepping forward to give her name to the man.

The man instructed Filly to do the same things he had asked the other girls. Each time she completed a task or did as he asked, he thanked her, before noting something down on the piece of paper. After tucking the ribbon into the pocket of his coat for the final time, he turned his eyes to the words on the page. From where she was standing, Filly craned her neck and read over his arm.

'Ro-sa-cea,' the girl mumbled, stretching the syllables over her tongue as she said the word for the first time. 'What does that mean?'

The man stopped reading and looked up. His eyes were wide. 'What was that?' he asked.

Filly shook her head. 'Nothing,' she said.

Without breaking eye contact with the girl, the man put the piece of paper down on the table. 'What did you say?'

Filly was frozen and didn't respond.

The man moved closer to her. 'On the paper,' he said, his words slow and soft, 'the word,' he paused and contorted his features, bemused, 'did you read it?' He was smiling.

Again, Filly was unresponsive. The man kept his eyes on her, his lips parted and his teeth showing. When it became clear the girl wasn't going to say anything, he withdrew. Straightening his posture, he rested his chin on his hands, which he clasped, fingers enmeshed, in front of himself. Silence. 'Okay,' the man finally said to Filly. 'Please stand with the girls on the left.'

On the other side of the room, Cherub's heart skipped a beat. *No.* She squeezed Rosie. *Filly.* She watched as her friend shuffled over to Jessica and the other girls. Her heels dragged on the floor as she walked. In her mind, Cherub willed Filly to look across at her. She didn't. Neck bent, shoulders slumped, she slipped behind the huddle of girls and out of sight.

The man and stick lady walked over to the girls on the right. Cherub stepped back, bumping into Willow as she tried to conceal herself deeper in the group. Another girl caught her elbow as she tripped over her foot.

'Girls,' the man said, addressing Cherub and her new companions. 'You've all done so very well.' His eyes softened as he smiled. At his side, stick lady's face was cold. 'Today you have graduated.' The words were expressed with a lightness that could have only meant good things. Once again, Cherub tried to look for her friend, but her view was blocked by another girl's head. 'I would like you to follow me again,' the man said. He opened his arms and gestured to the space in front of him. The girls bustled to form a line. When they were suitably arranged, the man nodded at stick lady, who positioned herself at the back of the girls. Keeping in step with the man, they followed him, in single file, out of the room. As they left,

Cherub turned her head. *Filly.* She still couldn't see her. The blonde-haired lady was standing with the other girls, talking to them. Someone bumped into the back of her so she had to keep moving.

That day, Cherub saw more of the world than she had ever seen before. Rooms she had never been to and corridors she hadn't known existed. With every step, she kept Rosie close to her chest. Ahead of her, the man guided them through a door that led to the outside.

'Please keep together, girls,' he said as he propped open the door and encouraged them through it. They did as he said, remaining in single file as the Sun kissed their skin. Cherub shielded her eyes with her hand and looked at the sky. The Sun was lower now.

There was a dip in the land and in it sat a wooden building. Sheltered by the trees, it looked lonely and Cherub wondered if Filly was coming here too.

'Watch your footing, girls,' the man called from the front. A branch had fallen over the path. One by one, they stepped around it and followed the man to a door at the back of the building. He opened it and waved for the girls to enter.

If Cherub had ever been inside an elevator — which she hadn't — she would have considered herself to have been entering just that: a small enclosed space with plain metal walls. Overhead there was a dim strip light, and several round holes had been cut into the walls like portholes. The metal box room appeared to be suspended in a shaft, with the space outside the holes in the wall dark and hollow. There was enough room inside to stand up, but the man told the girls to sit down as they entered

Cherub sat on the floor next to Willow and arranged Rosie in her lap. There were about a dozen girls and when the last one was ushered inside, the man smiled and closed the door, he and stick lady on the outside.

Almost immediately, the metal box room started to move. A couple of the girls let out a yelp of fright, the unexpected and unfamiliar downward motion of the space having startled them. Above, the light continued to shine. Cherub caught Willow's eye, and the other girl offered her a reassuring smile. Then, all too quickly, the smile faded.

Mouth opening in panic, Willow reached, desperately, her hands out in front of her, as if trying to steady herself.

Cherub wanted to ask the girl if she was alright, but then, she felt it too. *Air*. In her chest, her heart felt funny and, in her mouth, her tongue detected a strange taste. Using her hands, she pushed herself up off the floor and pulled herself to one of the holes in the wall. *Air*. All around her, the other girls were also panicking. One with frizzy black hair was shouting as she reached for another of the holes, her fingers prying at the metal. Willow was screaming now, her face twisted in a fit of terror.

Slumped against the wall, Cherub threw her hands to her neck — *air* — and massaged the soft skin of her throat, gasping in deep breathless gulps as she struggled to find oxygen. Her legs were heavy and cold, and the left started to tremble, until the convulsions spread up into her torso and she found she could no longer stand. Sagging down onto the floor, a frantic hand fought for Rosie, who she had dropped when trying to stand. Ferociously, her mouth opened and closed, pink lips munching the air, hungry for oxygen. Face now pressed against the metal, her eyes began to glaze as unconsciousness swept across her body. Next to her, also on the floor, was Willow, her jaw open and her tongue out. All around, the sound of agonal respiration choked the room.

In total, the girls suffered for thirty seconds. Carbon dioxide flooded the chamber quickly, with the maximum concentration being reached in a matter of seconds. Heavier than air, the lower the metal box room descended, the faster the gas entered their little bodies.

They panicked, of course, but their distress was momentary — Robert made sure of that. Besides, the strong emotions the children exhibited — the screaming, the terror, the gasping for oxygen — were largely reflex movements and not signs of true distress. Their consciousness — if it had ever truly been there to begin with — was imparied by the carbon dioxide and was therefore not a welfare concern. A few arrhythmic beats of the heart and it was over.

After they fell unconscious, the girls were kept in the chamber for a further two and a half minutes. It was imperative they did not recover when the box ascended back into normal air. From there they would be removed and stuck and bled and butchered, the girls' hair scalded from their carcasses with hot water.

Frank thought it was strange when he lifted the child with

the thin brown hair out the room. In her hand, her fingers cold and rigid, was an old hairbrush. It was tatty and had a scrap of fabric tied around the middle, held in place by a length of green ribbon. A quick shake and it loosened and fell from the hand. With his boot, Frank kicked it away and continued his work.

Thirty-Nine

Despite the blood it was only a superficial wound.

'How did you manage this?'

Samantha shrugged her shoulders and leant her head back against the examination couch.

'You really should be more careful — especially in your condition.' Robert glanced up at her as he inspected her arm.

A jagged laceration about four inches long marked the skin above Samantha's left elbow. It stung and was painful to touch. *It'd been even more painful to do it*, Samantha thought, recalling how her hand had shook before she had slashed her own flesh with the sharper half of the DVD she had broken in two. Imagining Mary — *her pretty neck shredded and spurting* — had made the task easier. Blood dripped onto the black vinyl upholstery of the examination couch.

Robert shuffled on the stool and sat more upright. 'It doesn't need stitches,' he said, 'but I will need to clean and dress it.'

Samantha said nothing and turned her eyes to the ceiling.

The first aid kit was kept inside a locked drawer. Robert stood up and retrieved it, carrying the green plastic box over to the couch and setting it down next to Samantha's legs. She shuffled over to accommodate it.

Robert put on a pair of gloves and opened the box. 'How are you feeling otherwise?' he asked.

'Fine.'

He ripped open a sachet that contained a saline cleansing wipe. 'I imagine baby is very active.'

Samantha continued looking at the ceiling.

'It won't be long now,' he said and moved Samantha's arm so that it was better positioned for him to treat. 'This may hurt a little.' Robert started to dab the wound, holding her wrist with his other hand so that she didn't move away. Samantha winced, but made no sound.

'It's quite a sizable lesion,' Robert said, pausing to dispose of the wipe, 'I will need to wrap a bandage around the whole of the upper arm.' He opened a second wipe and continued cleaning the wound. Samantha bit her lip and moved her other arm over her swollen abdomen. Underneath her skin, she could feel her baby moving.

As Robert finished with the second cleansing wipe, an electronic ringing sound came from the other side of the room. Without saying anything, he threw the wipe, along with his gloves, into the stainless steel dish he was using for the waste and walked to the tall chest of office drawers that stood against the opposite wall. Unlocking the top drawer with a key attached to his belt, he pulled out a flip-style mobile phone. It was silver and had a ugly stub aerial at the top.

'Yes,' he said, answering the phone. He waited for the person on the other end to finish speaking before replying, 'Okay, I'm coming.'

A push of the button and he closed the phone, before returning it to the drawer. He locked it and crossed the room back to Samantha.

'I apologise for leaving in the middle of this,' he said as he pulled on his white coat, which he had taken off and draped over the stool, 'but it seems as though one of your friends needs me.'

Samantha would have sneered and made a comment about the relevancy of the word 'friends' when describing the women who were, in essence, her cellmates. Yet, in this instance she let it pass. Besides, the woman who required Robert's attention was indeed a friend. Samantha had told Evelyn to wait at least ten minutes after she left the room before pretending to have terrible, scream-the-place-down-it-hurts-so-much contractions.

Fuck you, Samantha spat inside her head as she watched Robert leave the room. After he closed the door, she heard the lock fasten.

Seated on the examination couch as she was, her back was to the door and the red-eyed camera that lurked on the wall above it. Twisting her body slightly, she reached for the first aid kit which Robert had left open on the couch next to her legs. The box was filled with paper sachets and medical supplies in clear plastic wrappers. *Gel impregnated burn dressing. Non woven triangular bandage. Hypoallergenic washproof plaster.* Samantha strained her eyes and rifled through the box some more, careful to keep her body still so as not to attract any attention from the camera. *Sterile eye pad. 70% isopropyl alcohol swabs.* She stopped. *Isopropyl alcohol.* She wrapped her fingers around three of the paper sachets and pulled them out of the box. Ever mindful of the camera, she used her left arm to shuffle the fabric of her smock. Just underneath her baby bump, she had tied a length of fabric around her body like a belt. Every night that week, whilst pretending to sleep, Samantha had torn away at her bedsheet. Then, yesterday, in the corner of the bathroom that wasn't covered by the camera, she had fashioned the furtively acquired cotton in a makeshift pouch. Into it, she slipped the alcohol swabs.

That done, she arranged the fabric of her smock and pulled herself upright. Her baby was heavy and constantly sought to restrict her movements. Two weeks until her due date, she and Evelyn were long past the point of having an easy attempt at escape. *It's now or never.* Pregnant or not, they were leaving tomorrow.

The tiles were cold against her bare feet and it took her a moment to get her balance after standing up. Samantha tucked her hair behind her ears and walked to the desk. It was hard to believe she had once done this before, all those months earlier, when things had been so different. She rubbed her stomach and opened the top drawer of the desk. *Oh Robert.* Samantha smiled and reached inside. *Only human after all.* She pulled out the chocolate bar — the same sort as the one she had taken last time — and took it over to the stool. Sitting on it in the centre of the room, she looked up at the camera as she bit into the aerated dark chocolate. She wondered if anyone was watching and took another bite.

It didn't take her long to finish it. It had been many months since Samantha had tasted chocolate — Robert's previous bar in fact being her last — and she had hoped she would have been able to savour the moment more. *But this is not why I'm here.* When the food was gone, she smoothed the foil wrapper between her fingers. She folded it into four and took it with her to the examination couch. When she was lying back down, she once again shuffled her smock and hid the wrapper inside the pouch, next to the alcohol wipes. *Fuck you*, she spat again, thinking of the man in the white coat and all that he had done to her. Massaging her abdomen, the blood from her arm stained her smock. She didn't care.

It was another fifteen minutes before he returned. His face was as calm as ever when he unlocked the door and entered the room. Samantha kept her eyes on the ceiling, listening to the sound of water as he washed his hands in the bathroom. When he sat down on the stool, wheeling it across the floor with his feet, he apologised.

'A false alarm,' he said, smiling and pulling on a fresh pair of gloves. Samantha presented her arm to him, which was still weeping blood, and he dabbed it with a wipe. After he had cleaned it, he wrapped a bandage around her arm, taking care to eschew the safety pins provided in the kit for tape.

'Wouldn't want me loose with one of them, would you?' Samantha said as he cut the tape.

Robert looked up at her, his expression plain.

Samantha shook her head and laughed. 'A life without freedom, right?'

Robert pulled on the bandage to make sure it was secure. 'I'm done,' he said and stood up.

Samantha declined his offer of help as she pulled herself up off the examination couch. Wrapping her arm around her stomach, she walked to the door and waited for him to open it. When it was unlocked, she, without saying anything, moved past him and down the corridor to the room she had been confined to for the past several months. The electronic locks clicked and she was inside. Before going through the second door into the room, she turned to look at him through the window. Gentle brown eyes and one of the nicest smiles she had ever seen.

Evil takes many forms.

Samantha pushed open the second door and entered the room. Evelyn was waiting for her on the sofa. Approaching from the side, Samantha placed her hand on her friend's shoulder and squeezed. 'I'm back,' she said and sat down beside her.

Evelyn looked at her and nodded. 'How's your arm?'

Samantha touched the bandage and shrugged. 'Alright,' she said. 'Chocolate helped with the pain.' A smile spread over her face and was matched by her companion.

'No doubt,' Evelyn replied, chuckling.

'And you?'

Evelyn glanced over her shoulder. The other women were over by the beds talking. 'Scared a few of them,' she said, her nose twitching as she spoke, 'Jade was supportive though.'

Samantha followed her gaze and saw Jade — her curly brown hair framing her face like a halo — in animated discussion with one of the other women.

'She was very concerned,' Evelyn continued, turning back to face Samantha, 'fussing me, checking I was okay—' she reached across the sofa and pushed something into Samantha's hand, 'I'm surprised Mary could even see me on the camera to know to call Robert.'

It was a battery, taken from the television remote control. Samantha slipped it into the pouch with the other items, making sure to keep it away from the foil.

'Are they planning on watching anything tonight?' Samantha asked.

Evelyn shook her head. 'I suggested we have a girly evening and share stories with each other,' she smiled and then said, 'to help settle my anxiety.'

Samantha laughed. 'Great,' she said, and then, after a pause, 'and are you anxious?'

The other woman pinched the bridge of her nose. 'There'd be something wrong, surely, if I wasn't?'

'Fair enough.'

Evelyn dropped her hands to the sofa. 'You?'

Samantha considered and then shrugged. 'Not sure if I can tell the difference anymore,' she said. 'Every day I'm here I feel more and more anxious.'

Evelyn nodded and reached across to her friend. 'Tomorrow.'

'Yes,' Samantha nodded, 'tomorrow.'

Underneath her smock, tucked into the pouch she had made from a bedsheet, Samantha could feel the alcohol swabs and the foil and the battery. *Tomorrow.* She breathed deeply. *Tomorrow we burn this fucking place to the ground.*

Forty

'Make happy (6)'. It was a choice between 'please' and 'excite', the 'e' being in the correct place for either answer. She considered the former, but decided to wait until she had completed more of the puzzle in the hope that it would reveal itself. For now 'avoid (4)' was easier. *Shun*. Mary wrote the four letters in the appropriate boxes then placed the pencil on the desk.

It was Saturday morning and she had been in the Seat for hours. The Sun had risen just before five a.m. and she had watched it radiate across the sky from the window of her bedroom. When it was light enough to make the journey, she had — leaving her mobile phone, turned off, in the drawer beside her bed — poured herself a cup of tea, grabbed a blanket, a book and yesterday's newspaper, and drove down the hill in one of the farm buggies. In the Seat, the chairs were comfy and — most important of all — the door locked. Here, unlike up at the house, she wouldn't be disturbed.

Out of habit, Mary glanced at the cameras every so often.

It was impossible to watch them all the time — and unlikely that there was ever anything of particular interest happening anyway — but they had been installed for a reason. Asides from security, they provided an insight into the habits of the sub-homo, an addition that Robert had made in the years after he had taken over the homestead from his father. What he saw in them, Mary did not understand. As far as she was concerned, swine were entirely undeserving animals. That they were allowed to live when her mother had been taken from her and her father all those years before only served to buttress her contempt.

She jumped when the alarm went off. Insistent and shrill, it crackled the speakers on the monitor. Spooked by the sound, her first instinct was to disable the device. The button pressed, she searched for the source of the disturbance. It had been triggered in B Building. She rolled the mouse over the cameras and enlarged camera four. *What's this?* Smoke in the corner of the screen and all the women standing over by the door. One of them, a scraggly blonde springer not far from delivery, was banging on the metal, shouting up at the camera. Mary sighed and stood up. She would go find out what was wrong and call Robert from the intercom in B Building if necessary.

In the room, Samantha had been hitting the door without pause since the fire began to spread. The cut on her arm was bleeding again and had stained the bandage red. She grimaced. Her legs ached. At her side, Evelyn clung to her elbow, her back to the door as she watched the flames climb higher. A dirty grey plume hung over the far side of the room and red-orange blades licked the curtains that framed the windows. There was sweat on her brow as the temperature increased. 'Are you sure they'll come?' she said, turning to Samantha. Next to them, two of the other women were howling.

'Of course they will,' Samantha replied, still banging on the door. 'We're far too precious to them to let us die — yet.'

Sparks reflected in the glassy surface of Evelyn's eyes. She hoped her friend was right: it was too late to turn back now.

Starting the fire had been surprisingly simple. After Samantha's visit to the doctor, she had ripped the foil from the chocolate bar into strips, nicking the centre of each so that they were thinner in the middle than at the ends. Holding the positive and negative terminals of the battery to the foil had created a weak circuit. Not built to withstand the transfer of energy, the foil had burnt out in the centre. The alcohol swabs and a generous amount of paper torn from the books in the room had done the rest. Three strips of foil shaped into three flammable bridges. The curtains stank as they burnt.

'There's something peaceful about it.'

Unlike the others, Jade was sitting down staring at the flames. She had moved the chair to a safe distance, but was still much closer to the fire than the rest of the women. Her feet were rocking against the floor and her fingers lightly tapping the top of her baby bump, as if she were being directed by a tune unheard by the rest of the room.

'Come away, Jade,' Evelyn shouted from the door. 'You'll breathe in the smoke.'

The other woman turned her head and looked over her

shoulder. Her expression was dark. 'If this is our only way out—'

'Don't,' Evelyn interrupted. 'Come away.'

She stayed where she was. Samantha banged on the door harder.

When it opened, it was Mary. Samantha saw her flinch as the heat from the room hit her face. Her eyes were big and she immediately started coughing.

'What happened?' she asked, her eyes moving from the women at the door to the fire that was devouring the far side of the room. Consuming, raging, hungry, it was so bright that it hurt her eyes to look at it. Mary was standing in the doorway and Samantha pushed up against her.

'Get us out of here,' Samantha snapped, pulling the other woman's hand off the door. Mary didn't fight and let her pass. Some of the other women followed, scurrying out into the corridor to catch their breath.

Evelyn caught Mary's arm as she turned to follow Samantha and the others. 'What about her?' she said, gesturing to Jade. She was still seated by the fire.

'Christ,' Mary muttered. She shook off Evelyn's hand and moved across the room to Jade. 'Come on,' she said. 'Get up.' She kicked the leg of the chair and Jade turned to face her. Posture passive, arms crossed over her abdomen, her eyes were watering. Mary cursed and grabbed the woman, wrapping her arms around her torso and dragging her off the chair. At her side, Evelyn hovered and tried to help, guiding Jade's legs towards the door and away from the flames. Her skin was hot to the touch and she started screaming as they got close to the door.

'Just let me burn!'

Jade dug her fingernails into Mary's skin and wrangled in her arms. Evelyn told her to stop but it only made her worse. Hysterical and wild, the back of Jade's head knocked into Mary's chin as she wriggled and fought to be free. Tensing her muscles, Mary shoved her through the door and onto the floor. Outside in the corridor, Samantha saw Mary slump as she caught her breath, the smoke from the room eroding her strength as she pushed Jade back from the doorway.

'Move away,' Mary said, nudging the desperate woman with her foot. Behind her, Evelyn was still waiting to get out of the room. 'Move away,' Mary repeated, kicking the woman a little harder. 'I need to get help.'

Samantha saw Mary's eyes shift to the other side of the corridor. On the wall, fastened by a bracket next to an old computer monitor, was a black box. Samantha had seen one similar in Robert's office. It was an intercom. Before the red-headed woman had a chance to react, Samantha turned to Evelyn and shouted, 'Now!'

As fast as she was able, the other woman wrapped her hands around Mary's neck and pushed her head forward. Samantha was at the door and with all her strength she gripped it and thrust it towards Mary. Her head slammed against the metal. Evelyn immediately recoiled and even Samantha was taken back by just how loud the bang was. With no one to hold her, Mary collapsed against the door and onto the floor.

Still on the ground, Jade scurried away from the crumpled woman. 'Shit.' Her eyes flashed up at Samantha. 'What was that?'

Steadying herself, Samantha stepped around Mary. 'You can thank us later,' she said and extended her hand to Jade. She gripped it and scrambled to her feet.

Crouching down, one hand on her stomach, Evelyn touched the side of Mary's face. 'She's definitely out,' she said, looking from the woman to Samantha.

'Good.' Samantha also crouched and began pulling on the cardigan Mary was wearing. 'Get the keys,' she instructed her friend, who was likewise rummaging through the pockets and layers of the unconscious woman. Above, Jade and the other women watched. By now, the room was filled with fire and the smoke was starting to trail out into the corridor.

'Did she call for help?' one of the women asked. Her eyes reflected her fear.

Samantha laughed. 'We don't want their help. We can help ourselves.'

The woman didn't say anything. Her bottom lip quivered and she turned to the woman next to her, who was sobbing in silence.

'I've got it,' Evelyn said as she pulled her hand out from underneath Mary's top. She was holding a brass key on a chain.

Samantha smiled. 'And this must be the other.' She offered a rectangular plastic keycard to her companion, who inspected it and nodded. 'Let's go.' An inhale and Samantha leant on the door and pulled herself to her feet.

Her friend stayed crouched. 'Wait,' she said, 'what about her?' Evelyn tilted her head at Mary. Her eyes were closed and her head on its side, her freckled cheek kissing the floor tiles. Blood had seeped out from a cut on her hairline and its thin red lines tattooed the side of her face like a spiderweb.

'Leave her,' Samantha said and gestured to the flames that continued to creep towards the door. 'They're made for each other.' A phlegmy hack and she spat on the unconscious woman.

Standing next to Samantha, Jade nodded. 'Come on, Evelyn,' she said, reaching out her hand to the woman she had known and suffered with for years, 'it's only what she deserves.'

Dark-eyed and weary, Evelyn looked one last time at the woman on the floor before taking Jade's hand. Together, they hurried away from the room and down the corridor towards the door that led to the outside. The other women followed, as did Samantha, tapping Mary's keycard in a frantic heartbeat motion against the palm of her hand. They all smiled when they heard the electronic lock release. For once, they had been the ones to make the door open and the ones to choose whether or not they walked through it. Outside, the air was sweet and, looking back at the building as they moved away, gave no clues as to the insatiable horror that raged within.

Forty-One

For Alexander, paralysis was a familiar sensation. It was a condition of his own creation — the regular debilitation he suffered as a result of bloated thought processes and the burden of expectation. He was crippled by over-thinking and that was why he smoked cannabis. When he was high he was free. The pressure evaporated and everything that he had thought mattered, didn't.

He was sick of it.

He wanted her to know that he was, at least, trying — *trying to be better* — and that was why he had come home.

Reclining on his bed, sketching in the journal that was resting against his knee, he didn't know if she would have cared if he came back or not. Perhaps she would have been happier if he had stayed at university. *Perhaps she would have been happier if I'd stayed away from the start.* But he hadn't, and she wasn't. And, despite all of his over-thinking and backtracking, not to mention his miserable resistance to reality, he knew he was happier with her than without her.

Leaving the house the previous weekend, he had wanted to tell her. Early Sunday morning, the day after he had let her down, *let her down yet again*, he had gone to her bedroom to say goodbye. She had pretended to be asleep, but he had felt her muscles tense when he kissed her on the head. She hadn't said anything and so he hadn't either. Frustrated by his inability to act, he had skidded his tyres on the gravel when he drove away.

It wasn't like the last time. *Like Tammy*. He felt strange imagining her so many months later, as though even the thought of her was wrong. Then, he had not acted because he had not wanted to. Fatigued, he had allowed — and indeed unconsciously willed — their relationship to end. Now it was the reverse: he had not acted precisely because he had wanted to. *It was a matter of principle.* Mary had always been his, and that was the problem. He had never wanted to want what they had planned for him. *But they were right.* If it were not his life, it would have been laughable: he had fallen for her regardless. But, it was his life, and so it just hurt.

Extending his arm to his bedside table, he reached to turn the volume down on the music he was playing. He could hear something loud in the background, a shrill beeping sound coming from downstairs. Closing his journal, he switched the music off.

Walking down the stairs, he saw his mother and father in the hallway. They were in frantic discussion, Sophie's hands on Robert's back as he opened the coat cupboard and began discarding the contents. Coats, shoes and umbrellas were tossed onto the rug. Alexander stood on the bottom step of the stairs and watched. The beeping was louder than it had been upstairs. There was a shuffle behind him and he turned. Hurrying up the corridor from the back of the house was his grandfather. Walking cane in hand, his rapid movements looked ridiculous.

'What's happening?' Alexander asked, raising his voice over the sound of the beeping. Hearing her son, Sophie turned to look at him. Her face was lined and weighted with concern.

'My strawberry,' she came to him and placed her hands on his arm, 'when did you last see Mary?'

Alexander noticed his grandfather was watching him. 'Why?' he asked.

'Just answer your mother, lad,' Robert Senior barked, prodding the air in front of Alexander with his cane.

'I haven't,' Alexander replied and stepped down off the last step into the hallway. 'Not since last weekend.'

Robert was now inside of the cupboard, still pulling things out onto the floor. 'How did we end up with so much stuff in here?' he shouted over the beeping and threw out another coat. 'Can someone please turn that dreadful thing off?'

Sophie disappeared into the sitting room. After a minute, the beeping stopped and Alexander heard the door to the study close. When his mother returned, he reached for her wrist and put his face in front of hers. 'What's wrong?' Her eyes darted as she looked past him to his father. Still holding her, Alexander moved to block her view and asked, 'Where's Mary?'

Robert Senior approached from the side. His face was old

and serious. 'They've got out, Alexander.' He never called him by his name. 'There's a fire and they ran loose.'

Alexander shook his head. 'What are you saying?' He looked at his mother. Then, with urgent credulity, asked, 'Why are you still here?' He pushed past Sophie and his grandfather and reached for his shoes, which were now buried under the pile his father had created.

'Alex—' Robert pulled himself out of the cupboard. He had a long aluminium case in each hand. 'Wait.'

Alexander continued pulling on his shoes and moved to the door. In his hand was his phone, ringing out for Mary's with no answer.

Robert put the cases on the floor and reached for his son. 'Alex,' he said again. 'Just wait a second.' There were lines on his forehead and his eyes were round and expressive. 'The livestock are out, Alex.'

'Precisely—'

'No,' Robert shook his head, 'they're *all* out. The locks,' he breathed and shook his head again, 'they all failed or someone opened—'

Alexander shook off his father's hand. 'Let me go,' he said.

Surreal and terrible, the taste of bile and the feeling of falling, the reality Alexander had so bitterly resisted was being snatched away from him.

It was his grandfather who stopped him. Before he reached the door, Robert Senior grabbed him by the chin, squashing his stubbled cheeks between his wrinkled fingers, and pulled his head down to face him. 'Listen to your father, lad.' He shook Alexander's face. 'You need to arm yourself.' The old man let go and Alexander stumbled back away from him. In the corner of the room, Sophie was holding herself, her face overwhelmed with fear.

Robert was kneeling on the floor over the cases. They had combination locks and he twisted the dials to release the lids. Inside, arranged on black foam interiors, were four long-barrelled guns. Robert picked up a round-bodied black-barrelled shotgun and pushed it into his son's hands.

'I don't know how to use this,' Alexander said, shaking his head and trying to pass it back.

Robert held his gaze. 'Point and shoot,' he said, his voice severe. 'Do not hesitate and watch for the recoil.' He stood up and walked over to his wife. 'The same goes for you,' he said, putting another shotgun in her hands. Sophie drew in a breath and went to say something, but Robert interrupted. 'You do not hesitate, my darling,' he placed his hand over hers, 'not even for a second. If they come to the house, you shoot to kill. Do you understand?'

Sophie nodded her head.

'Any losses that happen today can be replaced,' Robert continued, 'but you and the girls cannot.'

Sophie nodded again, her body trembling as she held the gun. Robert kissed her forehead before walking back to the gun cases. He picked up the remaining two firearms — both black hunting rifles — and handed one to Robert Senior.

'Father,' he said.

Robert Senior nodded. 'Son.'

'Keep them safe,' Robert said and then turned to move to the front door. Alexander was standing there waiting for him. 'Come on, Alex,' Robert said, gently touching his son's arm as he opened the door.

Alexander sat next to his father in the farm buggy as they sped down the hill. Driving with one hand, Robert showed his son how to load cartridges into the shotgun and how to disable the safety catch. 'Handle it with care,' he said, eyes darting between Alexander and the road. 'A loaded weapon is a dangerous thing.'

As they got closer to the Seat and the habitation buildings, Alexander once again pulled out his phone and rang Mary. There was still no answer.

They smelt the fire before they saw it. The air was choked with fumes, acrid and heavy, and as they approached B Building their vision was consumed by thick grey plumes of desolation. All the moisture had been sucked from the building, the air, the ground and was being chased into the sky by the heat of the inferno, the breeze carrying dirty clumps of ash, drifting through the air like malignant snowflakes. The skeleton of the building was exposed as segments of vinyl cladding slid down the structure and onto the ground, still alight and roaring as the fire devoured and spread. Alexander had never seen such a sight.

On the ground there were people, adults and children, some running, some panicked, but most huddled together, crying and holding onto each other. Frank was there, a rifle in hand, and he rushed forward to greet the farm buggy as

Robert braked and stopped. Grey-haired and stuttering, Frank clutched the frame of the buggy as he spoke. 'I can't find her, Robert,' he said, breathless.

Alexander leapt from the buggy. The radiant heat from the fire was staggering and made his skin prickle even from a distance.

'Have you checked the Seat?' Robert asked Frank as he hurried to the group of people. Turning to them, he put his finger to his lips and encouraged them to calm.

'First place I checked,' Frank replied, gesturing to the building behind them. 'Door was wide open but no sign.'

All three men turned their faces in the direction of B Building.

'She can't be—' Alexander bit his lip to stop himself.

'No,' Robert reached and squeezed his son's arm, 'you're right — she can't be.' Pulling his hand back, Robert drew his fingers over his mouth and breathed. 'But we must check all the same.' He stepped forward and passed his rifle to Frank. 'Hold this for me,' he said and carried on walking towards the fire.

Frank shook his head. 'You can't be serious, Robert.' He followed the man towards the building. 'You can't go in there.'

Alexander was following too and grabbed his father's arm. 'No, you can't,' he said, his blinking rapid from the heat of the fire. 'Let me.'

Robert turned and held his son by the shoulders. 'No,' he said. 'Never.' He looked Alexander in the eye. 'I cannot lose you. If she's in there, I will get her.' Alexander shook his head, his breathing shallow and rapid. Robert swallowed. 'I love her, too,' he said, his voice breaking, 'and I promised her father that I would look after her. So, please,' he released his son and turned back towards the building, 'stay here.'

The door to B Building was already open. Smoke was billowing out and Alexander watched as his father took a lungful of air before rushing through it. Waiting for him to return, he felt as though the sky was crumbling. *None of this is real.* All he could think of was Mary and how he would never see her again.

The fire as furious as it was, Robert wasn't inside for very long. When he came back out, stumbling through the door, his face black and covered in soot, he was alone. Alexander ran to his father, steadying him and pulling him away from the building.

'I couldn't—' Robert coughed, bending over and thumping his chest. 'I couldn't see anything. Just smoke and fire.'

Hollow, howling emptiness.

'Let me—'

'No.' Robert gripped his son.

A sudden, raging movement and Alexander pushed him off. 'I have to!'

Robert was on him now, his arms tight around his body and his hands, fisted together, burrowing against his son's chest as he pulled him towards him. Struggling in his father's arms, Alexander twisted his shoulders and tried to shake him off his back. Robert held strong, clamping his chin against Alexander's shoulder and dragging him to the ground. 'Son,'

Robert said, his words heavy and soft and twisted with pain, 'no, please, no.'

'Let me go!'

Hot, angry tears and more struggling. Robert wrapped his legs around him and pushed his head to the grass. His hand on his neck, he thumbed the place where Alexander's hair became fuzzy and faded to bare skin. 'Please, Alex, please,' he cried, holding him as tightly as he could without hurting him. Ahead of them, Frank had returned and was dragging a thick hose over the grass. Through blurry vision, Alexander saw it pass in front of him.

She can't be.

Alexander breathed.

I would know.

Inside his chest, his heart was racing. He could hear it throbbing in his ears.

Is this knowing?

Blood in his veins and a beat in his heart.

It would feel different.

He saw Frank turn the nozzle and start spraying the building with water. Robert was still holding him to the ground and Alexander could feel him shaking.

I would know. We are the same. I would know.

Unceasing, the fire raged. It seemed to delight in the water, making it evaporate before it got anywhere near. The smell dominated the air, suffocating and scarring Alexander's lungs.

She can't be.

Dangerously beautiful ribbons of death — roaring, raging, laughing — the flames burned on.

Forty-Two

After unlocking the door and running outside, Samanatha, Evelyn, Jade and the other women headed in the direction of the building with the farm buggy parked alongside it.

'This must be it,' Evelyn said, hurrying along the path and up to the door. In her hand was the key she had taken from Mary. There were two locks: a main manual lock and a secondary electronic lock. The brass key plus the plastic keycard gave them access to the building.

Samantha held the door open for the other women. 'Quickly,' she said, glancing over her shoulder. *How long before Robert comes?* There was no way to know and so they had to act fast.

The building was a single room. Evelyn stood by the entrance as Jade stepped past her. 'Holy shit.' Down one end was a desk, which stretched the width of the space and backed onto a wall filled with monitors.

Everyone inside, Samantha closed the door and joined Jade at the desk.

'Look at them all,' Jade said, her fingers on one of the screens. Samantha's eyes moved over the monitors. There were many, and on each many people. *Prisoners.*

Jade shook her head and stepped back. 'Fuck.'

Evelyn was with them now. 'Help me find the keys,' she said, breathless, her hands on the desk as she shuffled papers and pens. Samantha nodded and began to help. There was a tatty-spined book, its gold font title, *On the Origins of Money*, debossed into the cover. Next to it, a newspaper had been left open on the puzzle section. She lifted it, hoping to find something underneath.

'What are we looking for?' Jade asked.

Samantha turned her head. 'Keys to the cart.'

Jade laughed and started opening drawers on the desk. At the other end of the room, the other women stood together not saying anything. There were four of them, their pregnancies less progressed than those of their companions. *Natives.* Samantha sighed when she looked at them. They were helpless, quivering, tragic things.

'There's so many more than I had thought,' Evelyn whispered, her eyes lingering on the monitors as she searched.

Samantha gulped. 'Yeah. Me too.'

One of the screens showed a group of children. Girls in white dresses — miniature versions of the cotton smock Samantha had worn since first arriving. They were playing together. *Laughing.* A chill raked Samantha's spine. *If you didn't know, what would this look like? Would it seem normal?* The thought was terrifying.

'This one,' Jade said and pointed to a different monitor. Evelyn turned to face the screen and made a mournful sound. A room filled with little plastic cribs.

'Babies.' Samantha touched her stomach and felt sick.

Evelyn stepped away from the desk and straightened her back. 'I can't,' she said. 'I can't leave without them.'

Samantha sighed and moved to her side. 'We said—' The words disintegrated. Evelyn's expression was painful.

'I know,' she said, a finger moving to catch a tear. 'But, how can I?'

She was talking about her children: the girl and the boy who Robert had stolen from her. After many long and distressing conversations, she and Samantha had decided it would be better to leave without them and return later with help. Now, confronted with the cameras, Evelyn's strength was failing.

Samantha shook her head. 'How would we even find them?'

'We could try.'

'We don't have time.'

Evelyn turned back to the cameras, her eyes scrutinising the little faces on the screens. Meanwhile, Jade was rummaging through the last drawer of the desk. A smile and she pulled out her hand.

'Catch,' she said and tossed something at Samantha. She caught it. Opening her hand she saw a key.

'The cart,' Samantha murmured, blue eyes big and mouth mirroring the other woman's smiling expression.

Jade nodded and, rubbing the small of her back as she walked, went to the door. 'Let's get out of here.'

Evelyn was still at the monitors. She turned to Samantha, shaking her head, 'Please,' she said, 'I have to.'

'Now's not the time, Evelyn.' Samantha's tone was harsh as she wrapped her fingers around the other woman's wrist and pulled her away from the desk.

'Please, Sam—'

Samantha was about to interrupt, but they were both cut off by the alarm. A shrill ringing noise blurted out of the speakers. Her baby kicking inside of her, Samantha flew to the desk and grabbed the computer mouse. 'Shit, shit.' In B Building, the fire was spreading and triggering more alarms.

'Turn it off,' Jade snapped from the other side of the room.

A flurry of motion. 'I can't!'

'We need to go!' Jade pressed the button next to the door to open it and stepped outside. Samantha abandoned the desk and rushed to follow.

'Wait!'

Samantha looked back at Evelyn. Her arms were extended out in front of her and she was crying. Jade was able to walk away, but this was Evelyn — *sweet, damaged, unadjusted Evelyn.* Samantha's eyes rushed over the woman and onto the wall behind her. *So many screens, so many people.* It was then that she noticed it: a simple panel littered with labelled switches. Clutching her stomach, she rushed back across the room to it.

'You fuck,' Samantha muttered under her breath as she read the labels on the switches. *A - bull pen 1, B - breeders pen 1, B - breeders pen 2, C - freshers pen 1*, and so on. 'You fuck!' She was laughing hysterically now, her fingers greedy as they raced over the switches. 'You fuck, fuck, fuck!'

By the time she was finished, a second alarm was sounding. This one was louder than the first, so much so that both Evelyn and Samantha had to cover their ears with their hands. Every single electronic lock on the homestead had just been opened and the computer was not happy. Samantha, on the other hand, was gleeful and, even heavily pregnant, would have skipped from the building had it not been for one thing.

'I don't believe it.'

External. Camera six. If her eyes could have pierced the screen and come hurtling out through the camera on the other end, as sharp as knives and just as hungry for blood, they would have.

Samantha clenched her jaw. 'That fucking bitch.'

Mary had just walked out the entrance to B Building.

Forty-Three

She had woken to the sound of her own choking. It had been a full sixty-seconds before she realised where she was. Trying to sit up had been painful. She couldn't recall what had happened — *just a pregnant swine who wouldn't move* — but she assumed she had been knocked unconscious. A hand to her head and it came back covered in blood.

Keeping low to the ground, Mary had crawled under the smoke to the door. It was so hot inside the building that the metal had been impossible to touch. Aside from that, it was closed and therefore locked. A quick search of her pockets and she realised her keycard was missing. The key to the Seat, which she wore on a chain around her neck, was likewise gone. She was trapped inside a burning building.

It did, of course, cross Mary's mind that she might very well die. With no obvious way out and lungs full of smoke, her chances were hardly brilliant. But, giving up meant resigning control of her destiny to the actions of a few sub-homos, and Mary was far too important for that.

Without her keycard, her options were limited. Most of the rooms in the building were inaccessible and any way in or out — windows included — were locked. Wrapping her cardigan around her hand to guard against the metal, she had pushed on the door to the outside, hoping that the heat had somehow warped the locks. It hadn't. All the while, smoke continued to suffocate the corridor and flames crept ever closer. Even when pressing her face to the tile, to suck in the meagre amount of air that filtered under the door from the outside, it was difficult to breathe.

A few minutes more and the urge to embrace hopelessness was irresistible. She didn't want to die — *there's so much I want to do, want to say* — and it stung her heart to imagine her father learning that his only child had perished. *And Alex.* Squeezing her eyes shut against the heat, tears had trickled down her cheeks and Mary had wondered if her mother would be waiting for her in heaven.

It was then that she had heard the click and the door had opened.

Nostrils flaring and streaked with soot, she stumbled out into the sunlight. Oxygen had never tasted so good. Her first instinct was to speak — to call for help — but she found she couldn't. Her throat was parched and her vocal cords swollen. Staggering and panting for air, she tumbled onto the path, her knees grazing the ground. There, she encouraged herself to breathe, focusing on the rhythm of her inhalations and exhalations, until she found she could stand again.

It was impossible to know who saw the other first — him or her.

How did you get out?

He was standing about ten paces away from her, nothing on his feet and his body exposed to the full light of the Sun, naked, save for a pair of loose fitting white shorts. Eyes fixed on each other, Mary straightened her back. Something about her movement must have amused him, as he laughed and took a step towards her.

'You're one of them,' he said, an abhorrent grin on his face. He took another step forward. Mirroring him, Mary took a step back and then leapt to the side. In the corner of her vision, a fast moving object approached. It just about missed her. She felt the disturbance in the air as the farm buggy — the same one she had driven down to the Seat earlier that morning — shot past at full speed. Inside were the women who had escaped from B Building. Hands on the grass, she pushed herself up, just in time to see the buggy round the corner away from the Seat and towards the hill that led up to the house.

A vicious scream and she twisted her head.

Stupid swine.

One had stayed behind and she was coming over to her now. Belly full of baby, the blue-eyed heifer had hate in her eyes. 'How did you survive?' Samantha screamed at her as she approached. 'You deserve to die!' Mary braced herself, preparing to strike the woman with her forearm, but before Samantha got close enough, she was forced to move. Thumping on the ground and she turned her head to see the bull charging her. A cackle of laughter from Samantha and Mary began to run.

Clifford shouted at her as he followed, but Mary couldn't hear anything over the sound of her own heart inside her head. Ragged, congested breathing and she made it to the treeline. She was still holding her cardigan and threw it on the ground as she grappled for a tree trunk ahead of her. Fingers fumbled and she pulled herself around it and onwards, heartbeat in her mouth.

Where are you Robert?

In the distance she could hear the alarms going off.

They must be coming.

Behind her, Clifford was laughing. She moderated her speed too late and slipped on the hill. Losing her footing, she tumbled on the loose leaves and branches. Her mouth tasted of mud and blood and she dragged herself up, fingernails in the dirt.

'You made me this!'

He was at the bottom of the hill too.

'You want me to be this!'

Mary hurried behind a tree trunk, holding her chest and trying to suppress her panting.

Robert. She panted and squeezed her chest more. *Alex.*

He must have heard her breathing and ran at the tree she was hiding behind. The tips of his fingers grazed her skin and she screamed out of fright. Her throat was dry and it was a hoarse sound. Pain and tears pricked her eyes, the ground hard under her feet as she ran further into the trees. Clifford was still laughing as he chased her.

The deeper into the woods she ran, the darker it got.

Circle back. She slipped between two tree trunks. *Circle back to the Seat.*

Mary knew she had to find help, but that meant heading back up the hill. Not yet recovered from the fire, her legs felt heavy and impossible. More panting and her chest hurt.

Lose him. A bush, but not big enough to hide in. Clifford's eyes were on her. She sucked in a breath of air. Damp leaves under her palms and she scrambled back up the hill.

Behind her, 'I wonder if he'll feed me.' His voice was louder. *Closer.* 'Feed me like he did after I did it to the others.'

Through the trees she could see the smoke from the fire. B Building was being rapidly consumed. Gnarled wood and moss, knuckles white and she pulled herself forward. She could hear Clifford breathing.

Keep going.

'He said I can take whatever I please.'

They must be there by now.

The woman was waiting for her at the top of the hill. Mind poisoned by revenge, she lifted a small piece of broken branch from the forest floor and threw it.

'You can't escape what's coming to you,' Samantha shouted and threw another piece of wood. 'What you did to me and everyone else!'

The branch caught Mary on the shoulder, but was not heavy enough to slow her down. Agonised footsteps and she left the laughter behind. Her eyes hurt and she could barely see through the tears. Running back towards the treeline, rays of sunlight punctured the canopy and lit the way.

Come on.

Then, she was flying. Her legs were taken out from underneath her and she was momentarily airborne. His arms wrapped around her waist, they rolled together on the leaves, screaming and cursing and spitting fire.

Hoarse and angry, Mary bucked and raged. 'Get off me you animal!'

It only seemed to incense him. Clifford thrust his face against her neck and tasted her skin. 'So sweet,' he said and kissed her again.

Wrapping her legs around his body, Mary pulled herself up and headbutted him in the face. It must have hurt her more than it did him as, after being taken aback for a second, he grinned and grabbed her wrists, forcing them into the leaves. Red faced, he shook her and laughed. Underneath him, Mary continued to buck. She pressed her shoulders into the earth and twisted her body, using all her strength to throw him off. Clifford's hands still clamped around her wrists, they rolled across the ground until he was back on top of her.

He released her and moved his right hand to her waist, tugging at the hem of her skirt, where the top of her tights were held in place. 'I'm going to enjoy my meal,' he said slowly, bringing his face down to hers. Her left hand now free, she punched him in the chest, beating on his bare skin as he tore at her clothes. Clifford just laughed, until she brought her elbow up to his skull and smashed the soft skin of his temple. Blinking his eyes, he stared at her. Then, in a frenzy, he gripped her shoulders and shook her body, thumping her head against the ground, his fingernails tearing into her skin.

Mary screwed her eyes together and screamed as loud as she could. Her throat burnt as though the fire had returned and she was once more trapped by its flames. The shaking and the pressure of Clifford's hands on her body made her feel sick, and so she embraced the motion and threw back, exciting every muscle in her body and attacking him with equal fury. To silence her, he tore his hands from her shoulders and onto her neck. Without restraint, he choked her, smothering the flow of oxygen to her already suffering lungs. She saw how his eyes bulged as he increased his grip and could see the fear in her own eyes reflecting back at her in his.

Hands and legs pummeling his body, she fought as her lungs ignited.

Against her stomach, she could feel his hardness grow as he squeezed and pushed down on her throat. Laughing, he let go. The air rushed back into her lungs and she was choking. Unresisted, he put his hands under her skirt and pulled down her tights. When they were around her knees, he returned for her underwear. In a fit of coughing, Mary tried to sit and pull herself away from him, but he pushed her back to the ground, holding her there easily, his hand on her chest.

This is it.

For the second time that day, Mary thought she was about to die.

Forty-Four

His father had moved away and was with the livestock. They were scared and looked to him for reassurance. Some had run and would have to be rounded up. Frank was losing the battle against the fire. Sitting on the grass, Alexander turned the shotgun over in his hands. *A single shot would stop the pain.* Perhaps it was melodramatic, but in that moment that was how he felt.

His head in his hands and his father was calling him. The freshers had gone wild. They were trying to get away. Alexander watched himself move to help. He thought one ran towards him. Gunshots. Screams. 'Aim for the legs!' His father wanted to save as much as possible. They weren't a real threat — just trying to get to their babies. *But meat is meat and slaughter is slaughter.* He thought he saw Pandora, but he didn't know. *They all look the same.* Panic. The trigger felt light and the flames were louder than his thoughts. Fear. All he could see was fire. A hand on his shoulder and a pair of brown eyes. 'Sit down, son.' Alexander saw his head shake. Now the shotgun felt heavy. Fire and the smell of burning.

Robert led him back to the grass by the Seat. 'Just wait here,' he said, touching his shoulder and trying to smile. Alexander didn't say anything. He stayed where his father put him, leaning against the wall of the building. Even that made him think of her. He closed his eyes and breathed. If he focused, he could hear her. *A ghost in the breeze.* When he opened his eyes, the sound was still there. *Screaming.* His brain was fractured straight down the middle and he realised he was insane. But then, a second realisation — the screaming was not an hallucination.

Shotgun in hand, he ran.

It came from the trees behind B Building. Electrified, he followed the sound. It stopped when he arrived at the treeline.

'Mary!'

A lump formed in his throat when he saw her cardigan on the ground. Without stopping, he rushed into the woods. No sound to follow and high on adrenaline, he shot through the trees. Leaves and wood and sunlight; a blur of colours and sensations, sounds and scents. He saw a flash of movement up ahead and followed it.

It would have been a lie to say it was an out of body experience. It was not. Every twitch of muscle, every motion of his body was conscious. Time did not slow and space did not bend. It just happened. Stumbling through the leaves, Alexander wrapped his arm around the man's neck and dragged him backwards. A boot to his chest and he kicked him to the ground. The aggression in the man's eyes only made it easier: the barbarity of the sub-homo was unveiled, their cloak of civility dissipated, and along with it any uncertainty that Alexander had nurtured about his place in the world was exposed for what it was. *Futile.* The lie of innocence. Fully corporeal and cognizant, he raised the shotgun to Clifford's head and pulled the trigger. At such close range, one shot and there was nothing left.

Watching from behind a tree, Samantha stopped when it happened. The sharp sound of the gun seemed to shake the ground and it took a moment for her to recover. Close to her, the young man stood where he was, his whole torso moving as he breathed in and out. He was covered in blood, the body at his feet. His head was turned in her direction and, looking at him, she recognised his eyes. Brown and — even in that moment — gentle.

Clutching her stomach, Samantha stared at Robert's son, not knowing what to do. Neither said anything or made a motion to move. Then, on the ground behind him, there was movement. The shotgun was taken from his hands and, three steps forward, the butt was brought down on Samantha's head. As she fell to the ground, she heard more shots being fired in the distance.

Mary staggered away from the unconscious heifer and sank back to the floor. She pushed the gun away and exhaled, her face streaked with tears. Stepping away from Clifford, Alexander crouched beside her. Leaves and bits of broken twigs clung to the curls of her hair. Her top was ripped, flesh showing through the tears, and her tights were tangled around her ankles. Careful, he reached to pull her underwear up. The waistband was twisted from where it had been dragged down her thigh. She jumped when he touched her, her hand snatching his, eyes awash with fear.

'It's only me,' he whispered, bringing his other hand up to her face and touching her cheek. She let go of him and allowed him to help her. Looking at her, he saw the redness on her neck where Clifford had left his mark.

'Did he—' Alexander searched her eyes.

Mary shook her head.

He thumbed the side of her face and breathed. 'I'm so sorry.'

Her shoulders relaxed and she shook her head, a small smile on her lips. 'Alex—' Her voice was so quiet and full of pain that it hurt him to hear it.

'Please, don't speak,' he said, still stroking her face. There was a cut on her forehead and he saw how the dirt from the ground had melded with the blood. He reached for her hand. Her skin was soft and he squeezed her fingers. Beyond the trees, there were more gunshots. Mary's eyes flashed in the direction of the chaos. Alexander turned her face back to his.

'It's okay,' he whispered, 'they'll be alright for a few more minutes.'

Her expression was heavy with concern.

'I need to say this to you now.' Shuffling on the ground, Alexander arranged himself so that he was no longer crouching and was instead sitting on the leaves next to her. He held his face, considering his words. 'I haven't been very good at explaining how I feel.' He paused and she watched him, waiting. 'I've abused the trust you placed in me.'

She went to protest but he stopped her.

'It's alright,' he said, squeezing her hand, 'it needs to be said.' She relaxed and so he continued. 'I haven't always been here for you,' he caught his breath and touched her chin, looking at the red marks on her neck, 'I don't mean like this, protecting you—'

Another moment to catch his breath.

'I mean here for *you*. Here for your heart.' At that, he moved his hand and placed it over her chest. A quiet laugh and her eyes were brimming with tears. 'I've hurt you,' he continued, his voice low, 'and I'm sorry.' Softly, he held her gaze. 'What I'm trying to say is this—' he took both her hands and brought them to his lips to kiss them, 'Mary, I come back for you. I will *always* come back for you. Because I love you. I'm so sorry it took the thought of losing you—' he turned his head to where Clifford lay on the ground, 'of almost actually losing you to say it.' They were both crying now. Smiling through his tears, Alexander laughed and said, 'If you still want me, I'm yours.'

A slow movement and she brought her face to his so that their foreheads were touching. He let go of her hands and moved to hold her, his right hand on the back of her head and his left across her shoulders.

Her lips close to his face, her voice was quiet. 'Thank you,' she said. He nodded and held her close.

He would have carried her if she would have let him. Instead, he helped her to knock bits of tree off her clothes and out of her hair. Her clothes were torn — there was no hiding that — but he did his best to straighten them. Looping his arm around her body, they walked together towards the treeline. Robert was over by the Seat. Seeing Alexander and Mary, his composure collapsed and he ran to them.

'Thank God—' He immediately pulled Mary into his arms. 'Thank God you're safe.' He must have held her too tightly as she made a noise. He released her and stepped back. As unflappable as he usually was, even Robert was affected by the sight of her. He exhaled and held himself when he saw the redness of her neck and the blood on her face.

'How did this happen?' he whispered, his hands hovering over the injuries on her skin. 'This should never have happened. I would never have been able to forgive myself—' Mary reached out to stop him. Robert sighed and embraced her again, this time slower and with more care. 'I'm so very happy you're safe.' He kissed her forehead and then let go of her, taking her hands and passing them to Alexander. When their eyes met, Robert held his son's gaze.

Alexander shook his head. 'It's okay,' he said to his father. 'I took care of it.'

Robert nodded and squeezed his hands into fists. A moment to breathe and he was calm. Alexander had taken care of it. His son had taken care of it.

Over by B Building, Frank had dropped the hose and he hurried to meet them. Tears welled in his old eyes as he approached.

'You scared us,' he said to Mary, wringing his hands together and moving from one foot to the other. 'All I could see was you as a little baby and—' His wrinkled mouth cracked and he swallowed a sob. More shuffling and he reached to hold her. Allowing it, Mary rested her head on his shoulder and sighed. Looking ahead, she could see the burning remains of B Building. Beyond, there were bodies on the grass.

'You should take her up to the house,' Robert said to Alexander. 'And check on your mother.'

Alexander nodded. 'And here?'

Robert turned towards the buildings. 'Most are under control,' he said calmly. 'The rest aren't going anywhere. We'll get them later.'

'There's a springer in the woods,' Alexander said, nodding in the direction of where he and Mary had emerged. 'I'll bring her out before she wakes up.'

Robert nodded.

Frank had released Mary and was now at Robert's side. 'Not sure we can do much about that.' He jerked his thumb in the direction of the fire. Little had been achieved with the hose.

'Such a shame,' Robert sighed, looking at it and shaking his head. There was no way to save the building and the fire seemed unquenchable. 'So much work.'

It was then that Mary caught Alexander by the wrist. He turned to look at her and she smiled, opening her palm to the sky. A few spots of rain hit her skin. Seconds later, a cloud burst and the spots transformed into a downpour. Cold thuds of rain descended and pummelled the earth. Water now streaming down their faces, Alexander and Robert looked at each other and started laughing. The latter raised his hand over his head and, smiling, shouted. 'Well, you know what they say — when it rains, it pours!'

Forty-Five

Samantha's head throbbed — not a little, but a lot — like a jackhammer had been pounding at her skull for the past twelve hours.

She was caught in the space between, flittering in and out of consciousness, the world simultaneously hazy and tactile, bewildering and cold, the ground underneath her lumpy and wet. Someone had covered her with a blanket. She ran the hem through her fingers, her eyes half closed. In the air, toast was burning and she wondered if they had made any for her.

It surprised her to remember she was carrying a child. Hand slipping beneath the blanket, she held her stomach. Her baby was moving and she sighed. Her clothes had stuck to her and she realised she was shivering. Samantha pulled the blanket more tightly around herself.

Damp eyelashes lifted and she could see smoke. Ahead, the ground was smouldering. Figures passed in front of the wreckage, half obscured by sooty vapours. Skeletal pieces of wood and metal stained black; bleak desolation that was more fantasy than real. Her back hurt and her ankles were swollen.

There was something on her wrist and she didn't know what it was. Her eyes were closed now — her head pounding — and so she reached to touch it with her other hand. Cold and hard and all the way around. Blue eyes scouted and she saw a chain appear out from under the blanket and away to a lamp post. *They've handcuffed me to it.*

They.

Her heart folded into itself. *What have I done?* She clutched her stomach and was crushed by the realisation. *I screwed it up.*

It took her a moment to figure out what they were. The wet heaps on the grass. *Bodies.* Acid stung the back of her throat. *What have I done?* One of the figures — *him* — had moved and was now standing amongst them. She saw him crouch down beside one of the corpses. The arm was slender and hung onto the bundle even in death. He tugged. When it didn't loosen, he peeled back the fingers, cold and stiff, one by one. The arm dropped back to the ground. Robert stood up and brought the bundle to his chest. When it started crying, Samantha did too. *What have I done?* Her chest heaved. Through her tears, she realised she recognised the pretty, chocolate-coloured hair. *Pandora. Please. Please don't be my fault.* The body on the ground didn't move.

Samantha squeezed her eyes shut and sobbed.

What have I done?

If she could have taken it back — extinguished the flames with her tears — she would have done. Alone in the mud, two weeks away from delivery, the scent of death heavy on the air, Samanatha thought she had no more sorrow left in her. Then she saw the farm buggy and the pain was so great that she feared — and hoped — she might die.

It was parked on the road at the bottom of the hill. The seats were empty, but the rear bed was full.

How did this happen?

It was a nightmare from which she couldn't wake. Great, immersive waves of anguish passed through her body as Evelyn's dead eyes stared back into hers. Bodies of other women — *the natives* — were there too.

What have I done?

They were too simple-minded to realise what they had been doing. *They only left because of me, because of what I did.* Samantha remembered starting the fire and the confidence she had felt. *That was it, the moment I would change things.* In trying to save herself, she had condemned the others. *They were scared.* The worst part about it was how she wasn't even sure which was better: to live in that place or to die trying to leave. All she knew was it hadn't been her choice to make. *Not for them.* In her mind she could see Robert, standing over her as she lay slumped on the tiles of B Building. He had shaken his head when she had called him a monster.

No, Samantha — you are.

In starting the fire and forcing those women to their deaths, she was no better than him.

Surely it is better to live a life without consequence?

She should have been the one to pay the price for her

actions. *Not them. Not sweet, damaged, unadjusted Evelyn.* But they had both known the risk. Hugging herself to soothe the pain, Samantha at least hoped her friend had found her children before she was murdered.

The woman with the blonde hair was the first to notice her. The cuffs of her blouse had been rolled up and her shoes were speckled with mud. Seeing that Samantha was awake, she came over and placed a hand to her forehead.

'Everything is alright, dear,' Sophie said, crouching as she arranged Samantha's hair. 'It's been quite a day, hasn't it?' She smiled and straightened the blanket. Samantha just continued to cry.

Sophie's eyes flickered between her face and her stomach. Softly, she took up Samantha's hand — the one bound by the chain — and squeezed her fingers. 'Come now, dear,' she hushed. 'Try not to upset baby.'

Samantha wanted to say something but couldn't. She wanted the woman to hold her and tell her everything would be okay — it being all too easy to forget that she, the soft-spoken woman who smelled of flowers and biscuits, played a part in her suffering.

Sophie continued to soothe her as she cried. Eventually the tears started to soften, the exhaustion of sorrow simply too much to sustain. Samantha hiccuped and Sophie chuckled.

'That's better,' she said and patted Samantha's hand. 'Try not to cry. We'll move you inside soon.'

She turned and looked over her shoulder. Most of the others who had escaped after Samantha opened the locks were back inside. In the distance, a group of young boys were loitering close to the red sandstone building. There were about a dozen of them and they spoke quietly, appearing strangely subdued for their age. The woman watched as Robert approached them and ushered them to move.

'Once you're in,' Sophie continued, turning back to face Samantha, 'I'll bring you something nice to eat, okay?'

Samantha nodded. A final squeeze of her hand and Sophie stood up and walked away, heading in the direction of her husband. Robert smiled when he saw her, his lips moving fast as he told her something which made them both laugh. They led the boys away and disappeared out of view.

'Please, let's go to the house now.'

Samantha turned her head. The door to the Seat had opened. Robert's son stepped through it and waited. In one hand he was holding a blanket, his other he held out for his companion to take. Samantha's skull hurt when Mary stepped outside. Watching, she saw her take Alexander's hand and move towards him. It was obvious from the way she moved that she was having trouble walking. She had her right arm wrapped around her torso and there was still blood on her forehead.

Mary leant close to Alexander's ear and whispered something. Samantha narrowed her eyes to see what she was saying but his hair concealed her lips.

He laughed and turned to look at her. 'Okay,' he said and put his arm around her.

The path passed by Samantha and she cast her eyes to the

ground as they approached. She heard a voice call before they got too close. A man with wrinkled skin emerged from the red sandstone building and waved his hand.

'Alex,' the man repeated. 'Ern's on the phone.'

Samantha turned and looked up. The pair had stopped and he said something before releasing her and stepping away. 'I'll be quick,' he called back to her as he sprinted towards the other man. Mary's eyes followed him all the way to the door. As soon as he went inside, her posture slackened and her grip on her torso increased, as if she had been concealing the full extent of her pain. Samantha saw Mary's mouth quiver as she reached for the lamp post to steady herself.

Until that point, it didn't seem as though Mary had noticed Samantha sitting on the ground. If she had, she hadn't shown it. But now, Mary looked down at her. She adjusted her stance. Red hair loose and tangled, it shrouded her face as she dipped her head and caught her breath. When she straightened herself, her face was no longer pained. Still holding onto the lamp post for support, her expression plain, Mary lowered herself to the ground.

Samantha's eyes hurt from all of the crying, salt having formed a crust on her skin, but she tried not to blink as the other woman looked at her. Mary didn't say anything at first. Her eyes crept over Samantha's face and then down to her torso and abdomen.

Mary pulled herself forward. Her lips were close to Samantha's face, so much so that she could feel her breath on her skin.

When she spoke, her voice was quiet and hoarse. 'I'm sorry,' Mary said. Samantha didn't move. She heard Mary swallow as she searched for more saliva to lubricate her damaged vocal cords. Lightly, she cleared her throat and continued, 'I hope I didn't hurt your baby.'

Mary wobbled forward but caught herself. Samantha's breathing was shallow.

'You understand,' Mary paused and swallowed, 'that I had to do it. Knock you out.'

Although she couldn't see her, their faces being too close together, Samantha nodded, her heart loud in her chest.

'You see,' Mary continued, whispering, 'you can't escape what's coming to you.' Samantha winced to hear her own words thrown back at her. 'And neither can your baby.'

Mary pulled away now and Samantha was horrified by the impassive expression on her face. A moment to catch her breath and then Mary said, perfectly calm, 'I'm going to eat your baby.'

The two women stared at each. The silence was broken by the sound of approaching footsteps. Samantha, numbed and aghast, looked up to see Alexander standing over them. His eyes were awash with concern, and he reached down to help Mary up.

'Are you okay?' he asked, searching her face. She nodded, smiled and squeezed his arm. 'No more distractions,' he said, 'I'm taking you to the house.'

Unresisting, Mary nodded again and let him support her.

Without looking down, they moved around Samantha and along the path.

'I spoke to your father,' Samantha heard Alexander say as they walked away, 'he'll be here as soon as the causeway's clear.'

Causeway.

Just as it had taken a moment of crisis for Alexander to embrace his place in the world, crisis had engendered a similar epiphany for Samantha also. Cold and wet in the mud, her arms draped around her unborn child, Samantha realised there never had been any hope; she had been doomed from the start.

The first breath she had taken on the Wheatleigh family's tidal island homestead had been fatal. Indeed, it could be argued that the very first breath she had ever taken, some twenty-three years earlier, had amounted to the same thing: the first in a series of breaths that would ultimately bring her to where she was now. A tiny cog in a machine of death and suffering.

Mary didn't hate her — not really. Watching her walk away now, Samantha knew that the red-headed woman had already pushed what she had said to her to the back of her mind, her thoughts racing onwards to other things. Samantha — and by extension her baby — was just a thing that she could take. Mary, the same as Robert and Sophie and Alexander and everyone else who perpetuated this cycle of horror, did it because they could. That was just the way it was — the way the world was meant to be arranged — with little thought ever being given to the suffering on the other side. That was the prerogative of the blessed.

APPENDIX

Closer to Eden: A Homestead for the New Millenium

Mapping the human genome is one of the greatest feats of exploration that mankind has ever attempted. Initiated on 1st October 1990, the aim of the Human Genome Project (HGP) is demystification of the occult: namely, nature's complete genetic blueprint for the human being. In determining the exact order of the base pairs that comprise human deoxyribonucleic acid (DNA), it is hoped scientific research and clinical care can progress to new frontiers. In this, however, there is a fatal flaw: the assumption that there is but a single genetic blueprint for the human being. There are, in fact, two: a genetic blueprint for the homo sapien, and another for its imposter, the homo subrependus.

In certain circles, it has long been acknowledged that there currently exist not one, but two, species of human being. Until recently, the identification of the lesser of these two species, the homo subrependus, had been fraught with difficulties. Whilst the recognition of certain abhorrent and barbarous characteristics has allowed for some measure of illumination, the true biological nature of the homo subrependus has been hidden from us. In this way, the results of the HGP, and the future research it will facilitate, present us with a novel opportunity: to obtain a cellular understanding of the homo subrependus and the species-specific genetic differences that separate us from them.

Although the HGP is currently unfinished, it has been estimated that the human genome contains some 30,000 individual genes. Already there have been attempts at genetic association studies which aim to pinpoint the specific genetic component associated with the homo subrependus (Wheatleigh et al., 1994; Helton et al., 1995; Fisher and Reid, 1997). The importance of this work cannot be understated. Once the genetic blueprint of the homo subrependus is determined, it will only be a matter of time before mass identification is possible. For the first time in our history, we approach a resolution whereby the 'secret repulsion of the blood', so described by Dr. Richard Alexander Wheatleigh as early as 1879, will be secret no longer. The homo subrependus shall be unmasked.

The implications of such an unmasking will be profound. With the biological basis of the homo subrependus in hand, efforts can be made to expand, and indeed perfect, our current system of managing the species. It is not a fantasy to imagine how the simple testing of biological samples, such as saliva and blood, will revolutionise our movement in the near future, exposing hitherto hidden homo subrependi within a matter of hours, or even minutes, after testing.

Encouraged by the findings of early genotype-phenotype studies, it has been hypothesised that the genetic element will be found in the genes responsible for prion protein production

(Wheatleigh, 1996). As it has been observed that the homo subrependus suffers from cognitive disorders and neurodegenerative diseases caused by misfolded forms of these prion proteins at a statistically significant higher rate than the homo sapien (Wheatleigh and Helton, 1997), it is thought that a variant may exist within these genes that causes the expression of these malformed proteins to occur throughout the nervous system and many other tissues, including the brain, of the homo subrependus. Such an exclusive genetic variant responsible for abnormal, pathogenic agents, particularly in regards to inherited cognitive processes, could offer an explanation as to the differences between the homo subrependus and the homo sapien in regards to degeneration and primitive behaviours. If this is found to be accurate, preliminary statistical modelling has suggested that anywhere between 84.6 and 98.3 percent of the population may possess the genetic element of the homo subrependus (Stansfield, 1998).

Although it has long been suspected that the homo sapien is vastly outnumbered by its imposter species, such a dramatic imbalance between the two populations would necessitate the development of a new model of management. Methods which we currently perceive to be modern would quickly transform into something quaint and out-moded when considered with regard to the wider populace. The new millenium will therefore be defined by this struggle: the struggle to develop a new form of homestead, one which can accommodate the needs of both the abundant numbers of homo subrependi who pollute this planet, and us, their superior, the homo sapien, the true successor to Adam, as we continue towards our creation of a New Eden.

> *Robert Adam Wheatleigh MBBS, MSc, DRCOG, PhD*
> *& Ernest Philip Stansfield BS, MSc, PhD, 1999*

CPSIA information can be obtained
at www.ICGtesting.com
Printed in the USA
LVHW101311111122
732865LV00004B/65